THE GHOST FABLER

P. J. Anderson

Nine Lives Original Books

First published in the United States as 'The Three Signs of the Serpent' in 2019
This revised and retitled edition is published in Nine Lives Original Books 2021

ISBN: 978-1-8383410-2-2

Nine Lives Original Books
The Storey Building,
Meeting House Lane,
Lancaster, United Kingdom,
LA1 1TH.

Acknowledgements

The author would like to thank the editor for the thoroughness of her work and her enthusiasm for the project. He would also like to thank Sorcha and Veritas for reading and commenting on several draft chapters.

CONTENTS

CHAPTER ONE

When I was a little girl in Ireland I was brought up among storytellers. My grandfather was a fount of knowledge on every kind of story that could be imagined, from the mythical and traditional to ones he made up on the spot. They were all good and the ones I liked best were the ghost stories. He was a great actor of a man and could bring everything to life as if it were right there in the room, with the family gathered round the fire and a ghost lurking outside by the window, peering in.

So here I am in England, on 'the other island', another green land of hills and history, dreaming my life away and thinking of him. He was a bear of a man in build. He had a smile that hugged every soul that was blessed enough to see it and a laugh that could rattle the shelves – and now he's dead. I'm twenty-seven and for twenty-four of those years he was the rock that I could turn to whenever I was hurt or lost, or just in need of a bit of wisdom that I couldn't find in my own head. I was in so many different pieces when I heard he'd gone that a wind could have scattered me like sand in a desert and my heart felt as if it had been burnt dry and died with him.

But then, at the point where all the light in the universe seemed to have been swallowed by a black hole, something or someone intervened. It was as if a lone light bulb flicked on in the back of my mind and random words fell out of nowhere, gently pushing and shoving together until they had managed to change nonsense into sense. They told me that I was the new family guardian of the words and the teller of tales – it felt so obvious. I had the gift as he had had the gift and he hadn't so much died as retired after a job well done. Now it was mine and I shouldn't be sad but grateful to him for showing me the ropes. He would still be with me in everything he'd told and taught me. I'd only to think what he would have said on a matter to have the second opinion or the affirmation that I thought I'd lost, but hadn't. I realised that he would live on in my mind and those of all the others he'd loved and helped in his gorgeous gift of a life, and that something of him would be passed down in every generation which followed, just as bits and pieces of the personalities of his ancestors had been passed down to him in the memories and wisdom of his parents and grandparents. It was a long line of continuous history and I was the latest part of it, about to make my own mark on the world.

Which brings me to here, now, in a rented cottage in the north of Yorkshire, a tutor or modern-day 'governess' for the small children of an American industrialist who had relocated to the dales in deference to his English wife, buying a mansion the size of a planet. He is in America as much as he is here, looking after his business empire and at first I saw little of him. His wife is a marginally warmer soul than he is, businesslike but polite and treats me not quite as an equal, but as someone she respects and trusts with her precious ones. I look after her treasures for four hours every weekday and teach them all the things they'll need to help them get off to a flying start when they go to school. That includes loads of the old reading and storytelling and that goes down so well it's unbelievable, particularly with the little girl, Emily. When I first met her I could see in her an echo of myself, a child of the four winds, with a song in her heart and a smile in her eyes. Things have changed more than a little since, as will become apparent later.

The cottage comes with the job, not free, but at a greatly reduced rent. It sits in the grounds and was built originally as the head gardener's abode, an eighteenth-century stone and timber sentry-house in which he could stand guard over all of the nursery trees and plants as they grew from seeds to saplings or sweet-scented flowers. It's had many occupants over the years and one had left his opinion of it on the internet, a not very cheery read that I discovered when googling for details about the estate before my arrival. He said, "It has an atmosphere all of its own, a sense of contemplative brooding, a feeling that death, darkness and sorrow have all cast their shadow here at different times and have left something of their mark within the fabric of the stones." His gloomy description didn't bother me, having encountered similar places back home, with tragic pasts allegedly hanging in the air within them. Ironically, despite my love of telling ghost stories, I didn't actually believe in ghosts at the time I moved in, so dark rumours about the cottage's past were more of historical interest than concern or fear. But when I invited the children to look inside, Emily found it a troubling and forbidding little house and was not at all anxious to linger. I tried explaining that there was nothing to worry about and that I hadn't been bothered by anything of a strange nature or dark disposition while I had been living there, but she was adamant she didn't like it.

Initially, outside of those four hours with the little ones, the time was my own. When the weather smiled, I split it evenly between walks in the grounds and reading and writing the drafts of new tales, or recalling and recording those that my granddad had told me. It was on returning from one of those walks some months ago that I was surprised to find my landlord and employer, Sebastian Engel, sitting at my writing desk in the little parlour. He is a muscular man, the size of a house upwards and outwards and my delicate little swivel-chair looked to be in imminent danger of collapse. He was reading a story which I had finished and printed off recently and looked up at me with eyes that seemed to scan me in a new light. His voice had a deep, resonant burr and all of the quiet authority of the American east coast elite. He said,

"You'd left the door open, so I assumed you wouldn't mind if I came in. I hear you've been talking with my children about ghost stories, I hope you haven't been frightening them. You have a couple here indeed. I took the liberty of reading them while I was waiting for you to come back."

I'd been deep in thought when I'd left and had forgotten to lock up the cottage for that plain and simple reason, but thought it prudent to refrain from expressing my feelings of unease at the idea that he might just wander in and read whatever I happened to have lying around. I said,

"I've told the children I write ghost stories among other things, but I wouldn't dream of telling them a serious one at their tender age. The only ghosts they meet in the stories I tell them are gentle and farcical. My job is to make them happy, not frightened."

"Indeed," he replied, "my view entirely. The kind of tales you've written here would terrify them. But, that said, you're in the right place to write them. This cottage has a history – do you know anything about it?"

"Other than that it was originally built as the head gardener's cottage and some of its past tenants have felt it to be a dark and haunted place, no," I replied.

He leaned right back in the chair, causing it to creak and protest alarmingly, and said,

"Well, I got my people to read up on the past of the Hall and all the land and buildings that come with it before I committed to buying it. This whole estate was in the hands of the Earls of Hedderdale from the eighteenth century until the 1950s, when the tenth earl had to sell it to pay off his enormous gambling debts. His predecessor, the ninth earl, was a dark character with fascist sympathies and a preoccupation with trying to raise the dead. He started off in a relatively modest way. Having read all of M.R. James's tales as if they were gospel, he organised a series of social evenings in this little cottage, based on James's practice of inviting his fellow dons round at Christmas for drinks and ghost stories. The evenings were very successful, it appears, with a dozen or so specially invited guests trooping out here before dinner and being entertained by two or three James imitators of varying levels of talent. It was all very atmospheric, according to the accounts of the time, with candlelight, mulled wine and the crackling warmth of a log fire. You can imagine it just looking around the room – the fireplace is still here, a dozen people would fit in snugly and candlelight would give everyone the original eighteenth-century feel of the place: all very cosy. Then the good Earl flipped over the edge and started holding séances and all kinds of jiggery-pokery. Having believed that on two occasions he'd managed to successfully raise the spirits of previous earls, both of whom were diabolical characters, he got a little overambitious and decided to go the whole hog and try and raise the devil himself."

He paused for dramatic effect. Guessing correctly that I was expected to ask what happened next, I obliged. He said,

"Nobody really knows – it was as if he had become the lead character in a previously undiscovered story by his favourite author, the good Mr. James. He'd locked himself in the cottage so that he wouldn't be disturbed while he fooled around doing his summoning ritual, yet his body was found outside it with all of the doors and windows still locked. He was face down in the grass and when the Hall staff turned him over, his corpse was so scorched it looked as if he'd been cooked. The police spent a year trying to figure out what had happened, believing it to be an ingenious murder dressed up to look like something diabolical and supernatural. They never got to the bottom of things and in the end more or less gave up. But numerous people have said they've sensed something evil as soon as they've set foot in this place. I never have, which is why I offered it to you as part of the deal that goes with the job – and you never have, or otherwise you wouldn't still be living here. So I'm inclined to the view that in the Earl's case the diabolical angle is a red herring and he was a victim of a classic perfect crime."

"Your daughter won't come in here," I said, "she came in once and ran straight out, whimpering, saying that there was something scary inside."

He looked startled and said,

"Emily said that? Was that after you'd been talking to her about ghosts?"

"No, of course not, I've explained how careful I am when I talk to them or tell them stories."

He nodded and stared at the floor. He said,

"My wife has told me that Emily has twice said she's seen someone in the undergrowth near the cottage when she's been driven past in the car, someone who frightens her deeply. She got the gardener to check both times, but he didn't find anyone. The child has a very overactive imagination, I'm afraid."

I said,

"Maybe there is someone, someone who only she can see for all

5

we know."

He said,

"If I see nothing and you're the same, then there is nothing. If there were anything truly devilish here, then we'd certainly know about it, although in my experience the diabolical comes in a rather more urbane and civilised form than the myths and stories suggest."

I wondered what he meant by his implication about the diabolical being 'in his experience', but thought it best not to ask. He continued,

"No, this bogeyman idea's got into her head from somewhere and she'll just have to be kept away from the cottage until she grows out of it. But that aside, the history of this place has potential and I always love potential. When I got the report on the estate's history, the M.R. James thing caught my eye. I read all of his stories – nice little potboilers – and it's given me an idea."

He fixed me with a gaze that was as good as glued to my eyeballs. He said,

"And that's where you come in. I know you come from a storytelling family in Ireland. We found that from the background checks we did on you before giving you the job with the children. Those ghost stories of yours which I read while I was waiting for you to come back to the cottage – very good if I might say so, very impressive. If you're that fine and experienced a storyteller and want a useful bit of extra dough, you can help out with a little social event we've got organised tomorrow night. My wife has some of her academic colleagues from the university coming over. She's been trying to think of something to cap the evening with, something to send them home with the feeling they've had an experience that was a little bit different. You could do a M.R. James-style session in here for her esteemed guests, just like the Earl used to do – log fire, candles, mulled wine. I'll have a few armchairs brought over from the house and we'll troop your little audience over before they have dinner. Those tales I read earlier will do fine. We'll make the event an hour long if we can. Interested?"

"You haven't heard me do a reading," I replied, "I might indeed come from a storytelling family, but they could all have lived in dread of me opening my mouth and groaned, 'Oh no, another terrible tale, when will she ever stop punishing us for our sins?' Don't you want to audition me first to make sure that I'm not a disaster, tripping over my own words or reciting the things in a monotonous tone like a dirge, or a best man's speech where the best man turns out to be the worst at delivering his lines?"

He came the nearest I'd yet seen to smiling, but didn't quite make it the whole face-cracking way. He said,

"You've got the gift of the gab times ten and all the eloquence bestowed by your native Blarney Stone – one of the reasons I hired you for the children was your way with words. I want them to be masters of the language they speak. I already auditioned you when I interviewed you for the job."

He raised his considerable bulk from my chair and headed towards the door. As he stepped outside, he shouted over his shoulder,

"I'll send some of the staff over to lay out the parlour tomorrow afternoon. I'll have the armchairs sent over beforehand. You'll need to be ready to go for 6.30 – don't be late. If it goes well, you'll be paid a professional writer's fee."

And that's how it all began, some many months ago, the interweaving of my fate with that of Sebastian Engel. As I stood at the window, watching him stride back towards the hall, I had little idea of what was to come. But from that day onwards my life and my stories started to merge, and given the terrifying shapes and shadows which inhabit my tales, that has not been good news.

CHAPTER TWO

It was a strange light in the sky, as if the clouds had been pierced by arrows forged from sunbeams, searing down, deep into the helpless heart of the earth below. It gave an eerie and ethereal feel to the little procession bringing the armchairs and other accessories over to the cottage, ready for the excitement of the evening to come. I stood outside and watched as everything was laid out according to a plan that Engel had drawn up himself. Before my eyes the modestly sized parlour was transformed into a tiny theatre, where I would be centre stage for one night only. I shuddered a little, partially because of the damp cold of the low, slow mist that hovered still over the ground outside and partially because of the fear of a failure of mammoth proportions. What if my stories and the storyteller didn't please the audience, one that may well have hoped for something other than an eccentric young Irishwoman reciting two of her tall tales?

When it was all done and the various Hall staff had departed, I wondered whether to fortify myself with a glass of red wine to relax the old nerves and save me from dying a death through sheer panic. I'd told tales many times before at family and local gatherings back home, but that was entirely different. The people there were familiar with me, my granddad and the kind of things that together we did with our aural magic, our little bundles of words set free, like birds, to soar and dive within their dreams and take them to the places where the angels dance and the silent sing. The people who would be shoehorning themselves into my little room were the sceptical and scholarly chums of my employer's posh wife. They might well be underwhelmed with the likes of me and my tales of ghostly ghouls, having expected instead a more intellectually challenging feast to be laid out before them as their first course before dinner. But then wiser counsel prevailed as I considered that a drink or two might over-relax my mind and make it more likely I would fluff my lines, or overact an episode or two which already teetered too close to exaggerated panic without any need of alcoholic assistance.

I rehearsed my little act one final time and then, ten minutes before the appointed hour, went and stood in the doorway to see if I could spot any evidence of the expected crowd. The low-hanging moon seemed to touch the top of the Hall's tallest chimney and the edifice itself resembled a towering cliff, pregnant with menace of a primeval and ill-defined nature. A thin mist still haunted the grounds and the whole spectacle seemed more than gothic enough without me adding to the general aura with my spectral tales. At length a row of lights emerged from the Hall and advanced in processional form across the pathway and the lawns towards my very humble lair. My heart began to race and every insecurity that could be imagined took elfin form and began to dance mockingly around me, calling into question all my claims to competence or dignity. As my granddad had said many times in the nicest and most innocent of ways, I am a 'pretty little thing', but while that could make some of the audience naturally well-disposed towards me, it might just as easily lead others to regard me and all of my works as shallow before I even opened my mouth. Equally, I'd been asked to recreate an act that a high and mighty English scholar had perfected to a tee for precisely this kind of audience, yet I was only a governess, not the Master of a Cambridge college. What on earth would these donnish characters think of such a poor substitute, why on earth had Engel even begun to believe that I could pull this off? It was in this state of gathering panic that I told myself the only way to survive this strange pitting of all my vulnerabilities against the scholarly and sceptical scrutiny of the audience was to use my native Irish wit to the full. I would be larger than life – no, larger than two lives to be on the safe side. I'd bluff and brazen it out to such an extent that people would at least credit me with having the guts to have a go at an impossible task.

My thoughts were interrupted by the little procession trooping in, with Engel himself at its head. He was carrying an antique brass oil lantern, as were the three Hall staff who had helped guide the guests towards their unlikely destination. I felt completely surplus to requirements as he and his wife directed everyone to their seats while the staff hurried round the cramped parlour, lighting the candles and stoking up the fire until it roared and crackled like the mouth of Hades. I retreated back into the furthest corner of the now very crowded room and surveyed the assembled company of the potentially highly critical and disgruntled. They were very much as I had feared. From fierce-looking twenty-something dons on the rise through to middle-aged, ruthless and self-satisfied looking professors and heads, they all looked likely to view me as the lowest life form on the planet, thrown in front of them like meat to the lions. If there had been a door behind me, I would have slipped quietly through it and hidden in the bushes for the night.

Mrs. Engel, as I had been instructed always to refer to her, presented a different persona to the one I encountered on a day-to-day basis when reporting back on the children's progress. Gone was the approachable if formal woman who very obviously trusted in my competence. In her place stood her academic alter ego, surveying me sceptically and anxiously, obviously worried that her permanently bullish husband's hare-brained idea was about to go spectacularly wrong. I had a horrible fear that she might be right and that she would never forgive me for embarrassing her in front of her colleagues. Engel, however, looked to be as superconfident as always and completely untroubled by the possibility of my going down like a bucket of dead ferrets. As one of the maids squeezed round the room distributing a tray full of glasses of mulled wine, he beckoned to me to come over to him. He said,

"You'll have told yourself ten times over that there's no way you can keep a roomful of guys like this entertained with what you think they'll see as feeble little stories. I'm telling you that you're wrong – the stories I read had real power and you have real power.

Take it to them, tell it like you mean it – if you see faces that want you to fail regard them as a challenge, not a threat. Read every line like it's really happening, act the conversations as if the people speaking are in the room – have a ball. I know you can do it, beneath all the doubts and the fear of fluffing your lines, you know you can do it. Come out fighting, hurl the story at them until they surrender – you won't embarrass me and you won't embarrass yourself. This is your chance to shine, so make it and take it."

Then, without any prior warning, he turned round to the loudly chatting little gathering and said,

"Ladies and gentlemen, it is a pleasure to welcome you all to our historic home. Fiona, my wife, will be the hostess for all other parts of this evening, but she asked me if I would look after this little event and I'm delighted to do so. It's always seemed to me that among the greatest masters of the English language and the telling of stories are the Irish and it is my great pleasure to introduce a new talent this evening, Christine O'Donnell, who has something very special to share with us all. Going back a little in history, during the 1920s and early '30s this cottage was the venue for ghost-story evenings in the tradition of those once run by the great M.R. James. Christine herself is an emerging master of the spectral tale and we've asked her to read two of her newest pieces for you tonight in circumstances similar to those from all those years ago. She tells me that the idea for her first tale came after she hired a car for a weekend to explore this strange and mysterious county of Yorkshire which she's moved to. The moors, she said, almost wrote the story themselves. So, to set the mood for its telling, the candles have all been lit, the log fire is crackling and spitting and you are all fortified by a glass of mulled wine. One of my staff will turn the lights out and the candles alone will illuminate the room. In the dark shadows, remember, you can never be sure just what is lurking behind you."

Engel then headed off for the supersized chair that had been squeezed into the room to accommodate his considerable bulk and left me alone and trembling at the head of the little gathering, no more than a couple of feet away from the shadowy faces in the front row. While he had been speaking, a little podium had been brought from the back of the room and placed in front of me, and to my relief it had a light for me to read my script. I shuffled the pages nervously for a second or two and then decided that I had to take a flying leap off the cliff edge and swoop down onto the audience with my story, figuratively speaking, that is. With my eyes lit up like beacons by the reflected glare from the podium light, I launched into the tale with a loud and lyrical vigour that surprised me even more than the audience, some of whom visibly jumped,

"Hello everyone, I've made one noticeable change to the approach of M.R. James, who wrote his stories for male audiences with male leading characters. In my case, I've decided to rebalance things a little for a new century and the leads will be women. I may be Irish, but my tales tonight are both set in England and indeed the first, *The Men of the Moors*, is set not too many miles from this very spot. So let me begin.

Leading up onto the moors from the village of Hawes there is a long and lonely road that, after sunset, is like a ghost road. One clear, cold night a year or two ago, on that same high, deserted road, a figure in black hurried towards a distant light. The quarter moon gave only the faintest illumination and the lone traveller was at most a shadow in its fleeting glow. This spectre in the night was Emily Callaghan, a young schoolteacher from the village below. The two degrees cold of the slight breeze bit into her lightly clothed body and made her shudder and shiver as she battled on towards the light, her dress-shoe heels clack-clattering against the tarmac. She kept telling herself that everything would be all right, that all of the painful cold and the frustration at not being able to get to the dinner party at her cousin's house, ten miles away, would soon be forgotten as she sat in the warmth of what she hoped would be a friendly farm kitchen. There, safe and cosseted from the ice-breeze, she could wait in comfort for the breakdown service to arrive and rescue her stricken vehicle. She couldn't believe her own disorganisation when she'd found that she'd forgotten to charge her phone and it was as dead to the world as the car. The road was so rarely used at night that if she wanted to ring for help, she would have to hunt for the nearest house.

As she got nearer, however, the light changed from a beacon of hope to a source of concern. It didn't seem to be coming from a house at all. At first it had appeared to have the steady glow of an electric bulb seen through an open window, but now, as she got nearer, it had somehow changed and seemed increasingly to flicker like a bonfire. She began to feel the early stages of panic setting in. She was already very cold, though not yet dangerously so, and miles away from the nearest town or village. If all she found when she got to her immediate destination was an unattended bonfire, her options would be greatly limited. She could either plough on, hoping eventually to find a house or a passing car, and risk the onset of hypothermia if the temperature dropped drastically in the early hours, or remain by the fire and hope that it stayed burning until dawn. She could better see where she was by first light and would have more chance of someone coming along the road.

There was no way back, that at least was clear. Behind her lay eight miles of unbroken darkness, with neither sight nor sign of civilisation other than the road. The car would be no refuge because she had been naïve enough to set off without the precaution of a blanket in case of a breakdown, and she had no clothes with her other than the ones she was wearing. The only sensible course of action was to plough on and see what she found at the site of the bonfire. She carried on striding and shivering towards it, her footsteps quickening the nearer it became.

She reached finally a point in the road where the fire was no longer in front of her, but ninety degrees and about two hundred yards to her left. Silhouetted against its now fierce brilliance was a bedraggled stone wall that seemed to be not less than three feet high at any point she could see. On the other side of it the field would not be easy to navigate. It would be sodden from the heavy rain of the previous three days and liberally sprinkled with sheep dung. She decided to investigate whether anybody was tending the fire and called out into the darkness. There was no reply, just the sound of the flames crackling and spitting into the night. She decided to press on in search of a farmhouse. It couldn't be much further to the point where, she knew, the moor would finally start to drop back down into the valley that led to the nearest village, four or five wearying miles further on – or was it more than that? She couldn't be certain. She'd taken the route two or three times before, but always in the car and even then the journey had seemed to take forever.

As she was thinking these things through, she sensed something or someone nearby and turning back towards the fire was startled to see two shapes silhouetted against it on the other side of the wall.

She said a nervous hello, but there was no reaction. The outlines were male, thickset and unmoving. She felt more uncomfortable than menaced, as if she was being warned off the land by her silent watchers. She smiled desperately at them, but they didn't say a word. There was clearly little point asking if she could borrow a phone: best to move on until she found friendlier folk. She turned to walk off and felt her heart kick like a baby. There, right in front of her, was a large, swarthy, bearded man with piercing blue eyes that seemed to drill right through to the back of her brain. He was carrying an oil lantern which looked old enough to have belonged to his great-grandfather and held it up to her face so that he could look at her. She tried to speak but could only gasp with a mixture of fright and shock. He examined her curiously, from the neat, short cut of her tinted blonde hair to the bright, shining black leather of her best shoes. He said,

"Who are you, where are you from?"

She said,

"I live in Hawes. My car's run out of diesel and I need to borrow a phone to ring for help."

He looked at her as if she were a visitor from Mars speaking a language that was as unintelligible as it was alien. He said,

"You don't talk like you're from these parts and a woman who wears her hair like a man begs questions. What brings you here?"

Startled by this blunt directness, she said, "I was on my way to a dinner party. It's too late to go now. I just want to get some more fuel so I can go home."

He looked over towards the others behind the wall. She could just make out their faces in the lantern light, a middle-aged man in labouring clothes made of rough cloth and a teenage boy similarly dressed. Both had dirty red neckerchiefs. They looked more curious than threatening, as if they hadn't seen such a strange sight as a woman out on her own at this time of night before.

"She looks cold," the middle-aged man said.

"That's what I was thinking," the man with the lantern said. Then, returning his gaze to her, he said,

"You'd better come and warm yourself by the fire for a bit. It's not a night to be wandering about without a coat."

She was about to make an excuse and hurry off when the discomfort that the evening's chill had been causing her suddenly multiplied threefold and her whole body started shaking.

"You see, we're right," the man with the lantern said, "you're not wrapped up properly for the night. You'd better come with us and keep warm."

She was now starting to feel seriously worried, but her fears were suddenly calmed by the sound of children's shouting and laughter.

"Are those your children?" she asked.

"They're Jeremiah's," he replied, nodding towards the middle-aged man. "They're innocent things, but they could do with a woman's eye being kept on them."

"Is their mother not well?" she asked through teeth that were now chattering so fiercely they hurt.

"Their mother's dead," he said in a matter-of-fact way. "Come with me, you can sit by the fire and keep an eye on the little ones while we find you something warm to put over your shoulders."

"I'm afraid the wall's too high for me," she replied.

"There's a gate," he said, pointing the lantern towards an open farm gate, "come, follow me."

All of her instincts told her not to, but her body was becoming dangerously cold and she was left with little option. Quite how the temperature could plummet so quickly she couldn't fathom, particularly as there now seemed to be enough cloud in the sky to regularly block the moon's light. She followed him cautiously, staying a good three yards behind to give herself the option of trying to run off if things turned out to be not quite what they seemed. She could still hear the children, laughing and screaming as they chased each other back and to around the fire. That was a good sign. Axe murderers didn't normally slaughter the innocent in front of their own small offspring and rapists would hardly invite their victims to 'meet the family'…

As she'd feared, the field was sodden and muddy and worse, and her shoes and feet were soon soaking. She began to feel warmer as they drew closer to the fire and her spirits rose a little when she smelt the sweet aroma of vegetable broth. She might at least get something decent to eat on this disaster of an evening. She loved vegetable soup and even began to imagine what delights might be in it. Then, as she reached the fire, her mind switched back to cautious mode. She could still smell the soup, but there was no sign of any vessel in which it might be cooking. She could hear the children, but there was no sign of them either. The man with the lantern had stopped a couple of feet away from the huge, fiercely burning pile of old branches and was warming his hands in front of it. She said,

"Where are the children? I can't see them."

He turned and looked at her curiously, as if wondering whether she had a problem with her eyesight or was slightly mad. He said,

"They're here, all around. Can't you see them?"

She looked everywhere that she could see within the fire's bright glow and shook her head.

"You'll find them soon enough," he replied, "just give them time, they'll come to you."

Quite what she should make of this answer she had no idea. The man and the boy, who had been watching her from behind the wall, joined him and they all stood warming themselves in front of the fire. The more she looked at them the more strange they seemed. They were out of time in every sense – in the way they spoke, the way they dressed and their seeming unfamiliarity with anything she said that seemed vaguely modern. She began to wonder if they were all members of some kind of fundamentalist religious sect, one that forbade most contact with the world around other than that which was necessary for the purpose of securing the food and materials basic to survival. She said,

"Have you always worked on this farm?"

"This is our home," the man with the lantern replied. "We've always been here, we always will be."

There was something about the way he said 'always' that struck her. It seemed almost as if he was using the word in a way which removed the normal relationship to time that it had and placed it more in the context of eternity. Perhaps she was reading too much into things, she thought, but the more she looked at them the more they seemed to be relics from a long-past era. She said,

"I don't suppose by any chance you have a phone that I could borrow to ring for help with my car?"

She doubted very much that they had and suspected strongly that they might not even know what such a thing was. The question was as much a means of teasing out more about them as it was a request for help. At first, there was no reply from any of them or any sign that they'd heard what she'd asked. It was as if she hadn't spoken at all. Then Jeremiah said,

"Are you sure you're from round here, miss? Your accent is so strong that there are words none of us can make out. That's not usual. We have no trouble at all understanding what most people from round here say. It's only you we can't."

As he spoke, she heard the brief laughter of a child and felt a small figure brush against her as it ran past, but she could see no-one. The discrepancy between what she could hear and feel and what she could see was troubling. It made her wonder if the chill that had suddenly come upon her was a symptom of a fever causing delusions. She shuddered and began to worry that if this wasn't the case and the unseen presences were real, then they might not necessarily be friendly. If she could physically feel them, then they could, if they wished, push her into the fire and no-one would be the wiser. All that would be found of her would be her heart – she remembered reading how that was the one bit of Joan of Arc that had survived the flames. She stepped back from the fierceness of the blaze for the sake of self-preservation. The trio turned to face her. Jeremiah said, in a flat monotone,

"Don't you trust us then? Do you think we'd push you into the fire?"

"No, no, of course not," she said. "It was just too hot for me, I need to cool off a bit, I've gone from one extreme to the other."

The man with the lantern turned away and looked deep into the heart of the conflagration. She followed his gaze and was startled to see someone looking back at her. It was a woman and her eyes were melting into their sockets. As they did so, the last remnants of their failing gaze burnt deep into the heart of her soul, because the eyes and the face were her own. She looked back at her visible companions and they were watching her intently. She backed a little further away, panic now welling up inside her. She was stopped by a child's hands pushing hard into the small of her back. She then heard the sound of another child skipping, round and round, so close that she could feel the draught from its body blowing through the fine hairs on the back of her hands. It hummed and sang a tune that she'd never heard before and which sounded very old. She looked back into the flames and the face had vanished. She looked down at the firelit ground and was alarmed to see a circle being carved into the damp, muddy earth at her feet. She tried quickly to step out of it, but tiny hands grabbed her leg and pushed it back to where it had been. She was unable to complete even a single step beyond the line that appeared now to be being drawn as the foundation of an invisible prison wall. She heard a child's voice, like a faint whisper in the wind. It seemed to say,

"Stay in the ring, Emily, the ring is safe."

She couldn't see the owner of the voice, but what she could see alarmed her. The men and the boy were beginning slowly to walk towards her. What had been panic before now became sheer terror. She made a sudden lunge and broke quickly free of the unseen tiny hands that again tried to grab her. She ran as fast as the mud allowed towards the gate and had almost reached it when strong, large hands seized both of her flailing arms and stopped her. She screamed and her cry was echoed by a chorus of little screams from the unseen children in the field, as if maybe they hadn't been intending to harm her and were now frightened by the sight of someone who was. Maybe she would have been safe in the ring, who knows, but it was too late now. She was pulled backwards, additional hands grabbing her hair so harshly that it felt in danger of being ripped out of her head. She tried to see her assailants, but could spot no-one other than the out-of-time trio who were standing a little away from the fire, watching her.

"Who are you, what are you, why are you doing this to me?" she screamed at them.

"We're doing nothing to you, miss," Jeremiah said, "those who are are not with us. They've got into your head and you must seize it back from them."

"What do you mean?" she asked, just before being yanked backwards so roughly that she lost her balance and fell onto the cold, damp mud. She was hauled upright again and dragged like a rag doll on the back of her heels, the heat of the fire becoming nearer and nearer.

"It's all in your head," Jeremiah replied. "Change your thoughts to something that will counter the evil and it will stop. It's the only way. It's what we always do."

Before she could even attempt to reply, she found herself at the fire's edge, the heat so unbearable that it felt as if it were consuming her flesh already. She screamed in terror, but simultaneously did as Jeremiah had advised and tried to focus her mind on the hands that gripped her, imagining and willing them to release her. She concentrated also on the thought of heavy, drenching rain, a downpour so violent and sudden that it would extinguish the flames. As she did so, the fierce grip that had held her prisoner let go and she fell to the ground. She lay there stunned for a full minute, her eyes staring wildly at the flames above, while the sweat poured off her face as a result of the intense heat that she'd only narrowly avoided being flung into. She could feel rain also, initially a few droplets, then soon a deluge that bounced off the mud on which she lay. It spattered her face with even more grime than it had accumulated already as a result of her being unceremoniously dropped to the ground. She dragged herself up and staggered back several yards from the fire. Only the man with the lantern was still visible. He stood watching her impassively, as if the near-death experience she'd just had was as unreal as Jeremiah had suggested. He seemed to be unaware of the drenching rain that had reduced her best black party dress to a skin-tight wraparound. She said,

"What's going on, how could I just think of something other than the thing that had seized me and suddenly be free, how could the rain come as soon as I thought of it? It doesn't make sense."

"Oh, it all makes sense," he replied, "it's just that you need to find what the sense is. I can't tell you, you need to find out for yourself."

As soon as he'd finished speaking, the fire went out and the rain stopped. She looked desperately for the light of his lantern, but that had gone too. She floundered around in the mud for a minute or two, reaching out, trying to find and touch any of the men and boy she'd seen and the children she hadn't, but there was nothing. She heard briefly a child's laughter in the far distance, then everything was silence.

She stood cold, motionless and shellshocked for a few moments and then was roused from her stupor by a disembodied voice – low, poisonous and seemingly direct in her ear. It said,

"Oh, E-mily, E-mily, in the shadow of Gethsemane. Today was your lucky day, but your luck will run out – when we next come calling, there may be no-one to save your skin. Bye-bye, sweet lullaby, one in the eye, no-one to sigh, no-one to cry – and a pack of lies about how you'll die!"

She said,

"What? Who are you, what do you want?"

There was no reply, just the sound of indecipherable whispering retreating into the background and then fading to nothing. Before she could say or do anything else, she noticed a light on the horizon. She strained her eyes to try and make out what it was and realised quickly that it was moving. Her heart raced. It was a vehicle and it was coming towards her. She hurried across the sodden mud of the field, her shoes half-sticking in the quagmire with every step. This time no hands reached out to stop her. She just managed to make it out onto the road as the vehicle spun round the bend towards her. She stood waving her hands frantically in the blinding glare of the headlights. The driver slammed on his brakes and stopped about five feet from her. He got out and peered at the mud-spattered figure in front of him for a few seconds, then said,

"What on earth's happened to you, lass?"

A huge tide of relief swept over her. It was an elderly farmer, probably on his way to make some final checks that all of his gates were as secure as they could be against night-time rustlers. She knew instantly that there was little point in trying to explain the full detail of what she'd just been through. He'd think she was demented or on something and might even call the police for help rather than giving her a lift himself. The half-truth of the situation seemed much more credible and easy to deal with. She said,

"I ran out of diesel and found that my phone was dead, so tried to make it across the tops to see if I could find a farmhouse to ask for assistance. You're the first living soul that I've seen."

The irony of this last statement struck her instantly.

"Is that your car then, back there?" he asked.

"The little black one, half on the verge, yes."

"Well, if it's diesel, I can give you some of mine, enough to get you to the next filling station. I always carry some spare in case of problems on the moors. Hop in and I'll take you back to your car. It's lucky for you I've been to see my brother tonight, I don't normally come this way unless I've been into Hawes for something."

She climbed up into the passenger seat of the Land Rover and he gave her a blanket that he kept in the vehicle in case of accidents or breakdowns to put round her shoulders. She was so exhausted that she almost fell asleep while the vehicle turned round and went back along the road to where her troubles had all begun. She felt that she now had only one foot in reality and the other heavens knows where. She couldn't even begin to get to grips with everything that had happened in the field. She said cautiously,

"That field, where you found me, has anything strange or bad ever happened there?"

The farmer, who was watching the narrow road intently as he drove along, said,

"Why do you ask? Everywhere people have lived and worked has had something bad happen at some time or other and that field will be no exception. Did you think you saw something while you were wandering about there?"

"I'm not sure," she said, evasively.

"You wouldn't be the first," he replied as her car came into sight, "all the farmers whose families have been around here long enough will tell you there are places they'd rather not be at night. That used to be Stan Duckworth's land, but he's been dead too long to ask anything about it. His son owns it now, but he took himself off to live in London years ago. Shame really, other people's sheep graze it because there's so many holes in the walls they can wander in and out at will. At least it's feeding somebody's animals."

"Is there anybody called Jeremiah lives nearby?" she asked, as he pulled into the side of the road by her car.

"Jeremiah, now that's an old one," he said. "It used to be a favoured farm labourer's name if you look back through the parish records. One of my cousins who emigrated to America years ago spent hours researching them, courtesy of the vicar, when he came over for a holiday once. Americans do those kinds of things. I remember him saying how names go in and out of fashion and that there'd been ten boys christened Jeremiah between 1700 and the early 1800s roundabouts and then not a one after."

He unbolted the fuel can from the back of the Land Rover and motioned to her to remove the filler cap from her vehicle.

"No," he said, "if you're looking for any Jeremiahs round here, I've never heard of one that's among the living and I know most folk roundabouts. I think your best chance of finding one is in the graveyard."

She shuddered from head to toe for the umpteenth time that evening. He said,

"That shudder wasn't the cold, was it? Not with that thick blanket over you. I won't ask what happened, or what you think happened, because you'd prefer not to tell me and I wouldn't know what to say or do anyway. I keep life simple – looking after the farm, the sheep and keeping a roof over my head. Whatever you think may have happened tonight, forget it. There's no understanding some things and you'd be better off getting home and getting a good night's rest. I've put enough diesel in there to get you a good thirty miles, I'd think. Hold on to the blanket to keep you warm and drop it off at the farm when you're next passing. It's the one with the red door nearest the road two miles further on from where I picked you up. It's called Whittle's Farm -there's a sign on the gate."

"How much do I owe you for the fuel?" she asked.

"Nothing," he replied. "But don't ever come out on these hills without checking your tank again. If I have to rescue you another time, I'll charge you triple." He smiled and gave her a brief wave as he got back in the vehicle and drove off. She was left with the dark and the silence and a nightmare still fresh in her mind. The thought occurred to her that either something or someone had been playing with her mind, as had been suggested to her in the field, or that same mind had gone seriously awry and into delusional overdrive all by itself. The second option was much more worrying than the first. If forces unknown had indeed been playing tricks inside her head, then her ethereal friends had at least shown her how to deal effectively with them. If her own mind had suddenly started writing its own horror stories, with her as lead actress, then worries about potential brain tumours or heavens knows what would come into play. This second possibility truly frightened her. Then, in the distance, she heard the sound of a lone child weeping. A feeling of pure terror shot through her bones and she didn't stop to think or worry whether the sound was genuine or the result of her being in some way delusional. She just wanted to get away, to escape from the darkness and the cold that was eating into her bones as she stood. She got back in the car and, after turning it round in an open gateway, drove off back the way that she had come as fast as she could.

On the exact spot where she'd been standing was a dark shadow, watching her disappear from its world and back into her own. It let out a loud, echoing cry that turned somehow into laughter of the cruellest kind. Then all was silence."

I stood in anxious anticipation for a moment or two. I'd given the story every bit of me that I had to give in the telling, with dramatic gestures and terrified looks that matched those of the haunted heroine – and a vocal delivery that was loud enough for an audience the size of a field. It had been so full of my heart and soul and energy that I felt as drained as if I'd run a marathon with lead weights glued to my shoes. I was afraid that the startled looks which had been the reaction of some to my efforts were more a reflection of appalled disbelief at the rantings of the mad Irishwoman in front of them than anything else – and that my child, the defenceless little story that I'd made to sing and dance in front of them all, was the object of their silent ridicule rather than affection. But then a loud, thumping clap started at the side of the room where Sebastian Engel's bulk was mercilessly squashing his chair. It proved to be the start of a vigorous contagion of applause that spread rapidly all around the audience, save for a sour-faced woman at the back who appeared to be locked into her iPad. It went on for a good two minutes, causing me to take a couple of bows that mixed the graceful and desperately grateful in equal measure. The lights came on and Engel bustled his way to the front to make an announcement. He said,

"Thank you to our resident storyteller for a tale that was even more creepy in its telling than when I first read the excellent original on that true and trusted multimedia technology which still has its place in the digital age – paper. There will now be a break of ten minutes or so and I've taken the liberty of having some starters sent over for people to dip into prior to our return to the Hall after the second and final tale of the night. Enjoy!"

I grabbed a drink from a passing tray given that, in my role as humble artisan storyteller, no-one had thought of providing one for me. As only alcohol was available, I decided to go against my earlier instincts and try a glass, now that the first tale had been delivered without disaster and I could relax a bit. Engel was busy personally supervising the distribution of the food, which gave me the opportunity to retreat to one of the two unoccupied corners of the room and begin a quick, final check of the script for my next story. There being no available chairs I slid gracefully down the wall until my btm made contact with the floor. In between sips of a wine that was ten times above my pay grade, I began to read and make decisions about how best to dramatise various bits of the tale. I was so lost in my little world that the expensive Italian shoes which appeared in front of me at first escaped attention. Then, their presence having been registered, I looked up and recognised the power jacket and skirt of Engel's other half. The earlier look of doubt concerning my ability to deliver had been replaced by something else that was at first difficult to decipher. She said,

"My, my, you are a constant source of surprise, Miss O'Donnell. That was really very good. My husband was very impressed. Knowing him, he'll want to use your talents in all types of functions where he wants things to be a little bit different – be careful he doesn't ask too much of you."

She smiled the smile of the highbrow English when they're sending a threat disguised as a cuddly bunny. Quite what she meant I wasn't sure, but she'd as good as written her message on my forehead using her very expensive lipstick.

Out of the corner of my eye I noticed that various of the academics occasionally looked across at me and some were obviously talking about me, or my performance, or both, but generally the little throng was engaged in networking or exchanging the gossip of their trade. Most were finishing their starters and Engel gestured to me that I should head back to the podium, ready to begin the second of my eerie little tales. I discovered that I'd got pins and needles in my left leg and wobbled back to the podium in the fashion of my Uncle Padraig, a man with an abiding love of one drink too many. I stood, ready and waiting, and noted to my relief that the looks from the audience were now benign and even anticipatory, except for the sour-faced woman at the back who clearly regarded me as unworthy of her interest or intellect. The lights suddenly went down and 'the big man' steamrollered his way across the little room, ready to introduce act two. My heart began to race and my stomach to knot. I'd bluffed my way through part one of the evening with flying colours. Part two could easily be the bit where the wheels came off. With that happy thought sitting in my mind, Engel began his little address.

CHAPTER THREE

Sebastian Engel was the ultimate test of the little podium's strength, as it creaked and groaned while he leant forward on it during his introduction to my final tale of the night. He said,

"The accounts of the storytelling evenings in this room nearly a hundred years ago all refer to two stories being told on each occasion, so we are following in that tradition tonight. Christine's final tale is one that will put you on your guard the next time you include a bit of heritage in your vacation itinerary. I've cheated in so far as I've read it in advance and I can assure you that, with the added bonus of our resident storyteller's dramatic delivery, it will make an excellent precursor to dinner. Ladies and gentlemen, Miss O'Donnell presents!"

Gripped suddenly by another attack of nerves, I had a momentary fantasy in which I wondered what might happen if instead of 'presenting', Miss O'Donnell faked a seizure, escaping in the back of an ambulance and hopscotching it back to Ireland, never to be seen in these parts again. Getting a grip on myself, I decided to do exactly as I did with the first tale. I'd imagine the podium to be a cliff from which I'd jump and soar down over the audience, sailing on a cloud of my own blarney in the hope that it would bring me down once more to a gentle landing in their good favour. Heavens knows, looking at the assembled little throng, there were several I wouldn't want to get on the wrong side of and as for the sour-faced woman at the back, I suspected her right side was several times fiercer than the wrong sides of everyone else. With my heart trembling in my cupped hands, I said,

"Ladies and gentlemen, the second tale set in England, *The Wrath of the Devil*, could perhaps more accurately be described as an English tale made in Ireland. I wrote most of it before I came here to work and it results from a visit to relatives over the border in Lancashire. While I was there, I took to wandering around the ruins of the old abbey that sits a few stone's-throws from a witches' hill and it was that which inspired me to write this little tale when I returned home. Who knows, perhaps what I am about to tell you really happened – and what I thought were my own imaginings was really my subconscious picking up on the echoes of a past event. In which case, the darkness I am about to describe is still there, in the shadows, waiting to terrorise its next innocent victim.

We begin in an old stone house in Whalley, a small village pierced at its heart by the brown, deep water of the River Calder. Sitting by the front window, lost in thought, was a young woman author, Mary Andrews. She had the face of a scholar and a thirst for success. She had rented the house for a few months while she worked on her second novel, which she had decided to set in the surrounding countryside. It was a ghost story, you'll be surprised to hear, and Mary's problem was that one of the ghosts she had woven into the plot was being very uncooperative. No matter how much she wrote and rewrote him, he just couldn't succeed in frightening her and her worry was that her readers would be even less terrified still. She couldn't quite put her finger on what was going wrong and was feeling quite frustrated and despondent.

Prior to that, things had seemed to be going so well. She had written a large and terrifying part for the devil into the plot and reading that made her shiver and tremble so much her earrings rattled, even though 'the devil' in her view was very clearly a fantastical, fictional creature and no more. That part of the book had really taken off on the day she moved in and it is worth recounting the circumstances accompanying that creative burst.

As she brought the last of her bags into the house, she noticed a

Latin inscription carved into a stone above the fireplace. Mrs. Wainscot, the landlord's agent who had dropped in to show her how everything worked, nodded knowingly when she asked her about it.

"That stone is far older than this house," she said. "Originally, according to the owner, it was in a locked room within the abbey, but ended up being plundered like many other bits and bobs of the buildings. Somehow it ended up here. Tradition has it that if you are ever in desperate need of something and prayers and all else have failed, then the reciting of those words three times will often as not see it granted. It's all mumbo-jumbo of course, but you could try it for fun. It has to be something which you want so much that you would take the risk of the spirits."

"The risk of the spirits – what on earth is that?" asked Mary.

The matronly woman laughed, giving the firm impression that it was something to be taken lightly in the extreme. She said.

"Oh, more silly mumbo-jumbo. The legends say that if you ask for help by repeating the inscription, then you are invoking whatever spirits are near at hand – you may be lucky and get the help of the good, but equally you risk accidentally summoning evil – and then who knows what might happen."

"That all sounds very superstitious considering the stone had been part of the abbey, a place where superstition was supposed to be frowned on," Mary said.

"Well, so the story goes, it wasn't written by anyone holy, but someone dark who had conned his way into the abbey and left his mark. But it's all hooey, if you ask me. I've recited it three times and nothing happened, just as I suspect it has never happened in the past. But it's a fun story, nevertheless, if you like that kind of thing."

There was something with which Mary wanted all the help she could get, however, and that was for her book to win the coveted Hamlet Prize for ghost stories. The winner would benefit from a £20,000 payout and would usually expect a considerable boost to publicity and sales as a result. When the agent had gone, she had one drink too many to 'warm' her new house. In that loose state of mind, she went to look at the inscription again and, on the spur of the moment, without any great belief that to do so would bring her success, failure or any form of benefit or harm, recited it the prescribed three times. When she'd finished she turned away, smiling to herself at her own drink-driven frivolity and decided to spend an hour or so continuing her writing of the book. She had walked no more than two paces, however, when a sudden rush of cold air blew through the room. Simultaneously, she heard a loud cry from a child upstairs, followed by an anguished howl that sounded like a terrifying warning. She stopped dead in her tracks. The mini-breeze had ceased, but the room still felt decidedly cold. No windows were open and she was puzzled as to what might have caused the sudden temperature change. Gingerly, she went up the ancient polished wooden staircase to investigate the source of the child's cry and howl, which were a mystery in themselves. The house was supposed to be empty apart from her. She checked each of the three creaky floored bedrooms, but found nothing untoward. In the third, she found that a lead-laced window had been left open, presumably to air the room. Looking out, she saw a small group of children playing thirty yards or so down the road and concluded that the noise must have been from them. The open window had allowed the cry, howl, whatever they were to sound as if they were within the house, so she shut it to make sure that she didn't get any more unwanted surprises.

When she returned downstairs and seated herself at the little table that she had made into a home for her computer, she was amazed at how inspiration came to her. She was working on the part of the book in which she had decided 'the devil' should play a key role. His character and actions now came to her fully formed and ready simply to be typed into the script as an already complete block of text. Within the space of three hours she had written just over four thousand words, a record in terms of all of her previous writing. More chunks of text centred on the devilish character were queuing up in her mind, almost as if they were on a computer screen in her brain for her to read and copy down, and it seemed in a strange way that the book was literally starting to write itself.

This was not how she wanted things to be, however, because she had planned the plot in detail before starting and the new material was beginning to pull it significantly off course. For the story to work in the way she had originally intended she needed an additional phantom figure as a counterpoint. But she found that the highly promising ideas she had devised for this abruptly ran out of steam as soon as she had written the section on the fabled prince of darkness. The situation had remained the same since, to the point where she was despairing of finding a way round the problem. Originally, the additional spectre was supposed to be even more terrifying than the devil himself, but she was beginning to doubt that even a particularly nervous sheep would feel threatened by its current manifestation. The Hamlet Prize seemed to be retreating back to Elsinore.

Now, on the afternoon when she was sitting alone and frustrated at the window, she decided that the best way to refresh her wilting creative powers would be to go for a walk. She would wander down to the grounds of the medieval Cistercian abbey, which lay hidden on the riverbank behind the village centre, the original source of the stone over the fireplace. It would provide suitably atmospheric surroundings for her to imagine her problem character in new and eerier ways.

She pulled on a woollen sweater and a beige jacket that matched the autumn in both its colour and its warming thickness and left the house to contemplate by itself the neatly stacked printout of the book with the problem spook that was too kind to terrify its readers.

She walked first down the quiet road that led ultimately to the abbey's imposing gatehouse, a cool cavern of perfectly fashioned stone where she could hide in the shadows and admire the skill of the builders who had worked on it so many hundreds of years ago. As she walked under its tall arch, a pair of eyes greeted her - small, feline and nervous, a black cat that looked like it was in hiding from one of the fabled, wrongly accused Lancashire witches. She cooed at it reassuringly and, once she had gained its confidence, bent down to stroke its luxuriant coat. It basked in her attention for a little while before suddenly arching its back and pulling away deep into the shadows. It started hissing vigorously, all of the time fastening its gaze unflinchingly on something behind her. She turned round to see what it might be. As she did so, she caught a fleeting glimpse of a dark shadow that seemed to melt into the side of the gatehouse arch before she could properly focus on it. She walked back out into the sunlight, but could see nothing. There was, however, a strong smell of something she couldn't define, something vile but not recognisable. The cat suddenly howled and bolted out of the gatehouse, disappearing through a hedge as if the devil was on its tail. Mary felt every hair on her body stand on end, but still could see nothing. She backed away from the ancient structure. On the one hand, she was annoyed with herself for being afraid of something that may simply be the result of the cat having spotted far down the road a dog that had once bitten it - an unremarkable, everyday case of prey noticing predator, unseen by her because she wasn't looking for it. On the other, instinct was telling her to go away, that there was something present that was not good and that its intentions towards those who lingered in its company were malign. She decided to compromise with herself, to walk away towards the main abbey site, but not flee like the cat, to take her time and not be intimidated by a shadow.

As the gatehouse receded into the distance and none of the unknown darkness within it seemed to be following her, she began gradually to feel safe again and to look forward to the sanctuary of the abbey grounds. The thought that once they had been consecrated land and, despite all the faults of humanity, many of the monks who had lived and worked there must have been genuinely good people made her feel secure, that this would be a place in which evil, if that was what she was sensing and fearing, could lay no hands on her. While she made her living from writing stories about ghosts, she had not previously believed that such things or even 'the devil' existed. She had seen them simply as useful and frightening devices in the kinds of tales she wanted to tell. To have actually encountered something of a possibly spectral nature was more than a little unnerving. While still determined to try and rescue the floundering ghostly character in her book, she decided that she would leave that for later and distract herself with other things while she visited the abbey. It was possible to have too much in the way of spooks and ghouls in a single afternoon.

She paid her fee at the lodge, strode calmly across the cobbled courtyard, past the Anglican retreat house and various outbuildings and into the serene beauty of the abbey gardens.

She wandered for a good hour among the mixture of grey, moss green and smoke-blackened stone that made up the ruined walls, arches, windows and doorways of the much-plundered buildings. Way back in her schooldays, her history teacher had been skilful in engaging the children's interest by helping them imagine themselves into the past. She still enjoyed doing this and imagined herself now to be a guest in Tudor times when the abbey church would have had its tower, its roof and all the glass of its windows, and the monks and lay brothers would have been busy praying, chanting or working at their various tasks. She could hear within her fertile imagination the clatter of the hooves of King Henry's men's horses as they galloped into the courtyard. They were here to seize the abbot after the Pilgrimage of Grace and carry him off to his execution. She could sense his fear, smell it even, as if he were still here, at the moment of his arrest, certain of his inevitable doom but unable to do anything to escape it. She could see the King's men hammering on the door of his chamber and dragging him out as if he were a thief or a murderous convict – binding his wrists tightly with thick rope and then hauling him onto a horse with no saddle, cursing and joking at his expense, spitting into his face. Helpless and humiliated, he was paraded through the village and the countryside which previously had bowed its head to his power and now saw him stripped of all authority, with the once-mighty Church able to do nothing to help him. She could feel also the monks' sudden realisation that, in an instant, their position in England had changed – no longer was an abbey an inviolate or powerful place and no longer was their future solely in the hands of Rome. The King had stamped his authority all over the order and those within it, and there was no way of knowing if such a demonstration of his power and anger would lead to further action against the Church and they, its vulnerable servants. She pondered for a moment on the sheer terror that must have gripped the abbot as his last moments arrived and the noose was closed around his neck.

Her thoughts then wandered from contemplation of the abbot's unhappy fate to the long and brutal record of torture and execution in a country that, ironically, so prided itself on its 'civilised' history. That had been one of the things which had struck her most during her fascination with history at school. She stood looking across the geometric stone patterns that laced their way through the neatly trimmed grass, marking the outline of the once-massive walls of the abbey church and thought to herself,

"So much evil, how can it ever be erased? That's the problem, that's why I sensed that stuff back at the gatehouse, it's all in the ground, wherever it's happened, the evil of the past has seeped into the fabric of everything."

She thought of a programme she'd seen on the Lancashire witches' trial about the hanging of a mother on the false evidence of her vindictive child, of the fact that so many unfortunate men throughout England had been hanged simply for stealing sheep. That human life could be rated less than that of a four-legged ruminant astonished and baffled her. She said quietly to herself,

"So much evil, so much sheer bloody evil."

As she did so, she heard the sound of a child crying behind her. It sounded familiar, something half-remembered from long in her past. She turned round expectantly, but there was nothing to see. She walked on, still deep in thought, but was distracted again by the same sound, this time appearing to come from bushes on a raised walk to the far side of the nave. It seemed for a brief second that she glimpsed a small figure, no more than a shadow in human form and then was shaken when it appeared to call her name. Something in the tone of its voice made it sound like a warning, as if it were about to say, "Look out, behind you," or some such. She started to walk towards it, but as she did so the child's voice faded rapidly to little more than a whisper and then was gone, as if it had been carried off, a prisoner of the wind. She stood staring bemusedly at the place where she thought she had seen something, but the only visible presence was the bushes and the only movement that of their branches in the breeze. She shrugged her shoulders and decided that it all must have been a freak trick of the wind. There was a primary school playground just beyond the abbey walls and a child's voice must have echoed from there, carried on unusually strong gusts so that it sounded loud and near for the brief moments of its duration. It must have been the same kind of effect as before, when the voices of children playing outside had sounded as if they were in the house. She smiled resignedly and concluded that she was so much on edge after her weird experience at the gatehouse that she was prone to imagining all kinds of strange things when the explanations for them were in reality very mundane. Still, the haunting nature of the imagined child's voice and the episode at the gatehouse might be just the ingredients she needed to work into her novel. How wonderful, she mused, in coming here I've begun to solve a problem that looked to be beyond resolution earlier. Her thoughts were interrupted by a sonorous male voice.

"You said so much evil, but what is evil?"

She turned and was startled to see a refined-looking, middle-aged man dressed in the robes of a monk. He said,

"I'm sorry if I seem rude in asking, but I couldn't help overhearing what you said earlier."

He smiled and she smiled back. She assumed that he must be a cleric from the retreat house, the old mansion built out of the abbey's own stone and joined onto the very ruin from which its material had been plundered. She said,

"All of the killing, the suffering that has happened here and in so many other places and over so many centuries, that's what I meant."

"But is that evil itself, or simply its consequence?" the monk asked.

She was a little startled to be engaged in an intellectual discussion by a clerical stranger who had appeared out of nowhere, but his warm smile and apparently genuine interest made her feel obliged to reply, out of politeness if nothing else.

"You're talking about the devil, or the idea of the devil?" she asked. "I know it's central to your religion, but I'm not sure I believe in all of that stuff. A poisonous man-beast with cloven hooves, a tail and a pitchfork has always seemed to me to belong more in fairy tales than in reality."

She thought it would be too complex to add that she was quite happy to use such a figure where necessary in her ghost stories, given its long-established role in adding an extra layer of terror to fictional accounts of the irrational or unknown.

"Quite rightly so," the monk replied. "In the idea of Lucifer in its oldest form we think only of a fallen angel, one whose overweening pride caused him to challenge his own creator and suffer the inevitable consequence of being cast out into darkness. We have little idea of what he looked like, other than the very scant picture of angels that we get from the Bible. But no, I'm not necessarily thinking of him."

"You think evil has other forms?" she asked.

"There are many possibilities," he replied, "it depends ultimately on what you think the evidence tells us. It could be that rather than Lucifer being the cause of all evil he is simply the most spectacular volunteer to fall in its cause, that is certainly one interpretation which can be taken from the Bible. That doesn't mean he and others like him can't be tempters and themselves the causes of much of the evil which has brutalised men's hearts, but equally it does mean he can simply be one more *servant* of evil."

"So if you think that's the case, then what is evil?" she said.

"That's what I asked, so now we've both put to each other exactly the same question," he said, beaming with a smile that made her laugh, despite the gravity and unpleasantness of the subject.

"Do you think it's some kind of elemental force, something that preceded everything that was created, like God himself?" she asked.

"Ah, so you don't believe in the devil, but you do believe in God," the monk replied, "then we are on the same ground figuratively as well as literally. D'you know, I've thought and debated about these things for many years and I think I'm still only a small part of the way towards a definitive answer. I think evil on its highest plane is best thought of not as a devil, a bad angel, or anything of an individualised nature, but more as a great darkness. It is something of many non-human minds, diverse in their means and methods, but all united in one devotion to hatred that seeps constantly into human thoughts and refashions them in fragments of its own collective image. I do believe that it can manifest its darkest self to mere mortals as an 'individual' in a suitably terrifying form when that best suits its purposes, however – and there are reports of it occasionally doing this in the shape of the man-beast resembling the mythical figure of Lucifer. But this creature is best thought of as a mere servant and representative of the greater collective darkness. Occasionally known as Orthorimon, it only makes an appearance in the most extreme of circumstances when all other means of achieving the will of evil have failed. Normally, the darkness is as invisible as the air we breathe. Come, walk with me."

He led her to the foundations of where the rear wall of the abbey church once stood and then turned to face back towards the altar stone. He said,

"The mind, like the soul, is a powerful thing, use it to imagine what all of this must have been like when it was intact – the huge

35

stone tower, the walls that rose to the sky like sheer rock faces, the majestic windows that looked as if they had been borrowed from a heavenly palace and the roof that sealed the weather out and said, 'I am the roof that makes everything beneath me truly a house, God's house'."

As the words left his lips, they seemed to have a magical power and her always fertile imagination was able to see exactly the picture that he drew. When he finished speaking, it seemed as if the building had indeed been resurrected in all of its glory around them, a little hazy in form perhaps, as if a mist had got in through an open door and blurred the sharpness of its lines, but real nonetheless.

"But was it God's house?" he asked. "Look at the majesty of it all. It's easy on the one hand to think this awesome beauty was created all because the abbey church was a building shaped and fashioned to reflect and honour the glory of the Almighty. There were many who lived and worked in and around it who doubtless thought of it only in those terms. For them it was everything it was supposed to be. But what of the others, the monks and even abbots who fell prey to the temptation to see it rather as a symbol of the power and authority of the Church over the ordinary people and their temporal princes? What they had in mind was not a Church that was the *body of Christ*, but rather one composed of and run for the benefit primarily of *their own bodies*. I'm thinking of the monks who came to see the Church as an instrument that could be used to give themselves power over others purely for their own benefit. They were the ones who gave Henry the excuse to accuse the monasteries of corruption and the abuse and misuse of their own power. What followed was what evil, this great all-pervading darkness, always causes in the end, the collapse of everything good and the need to rebuild from scratch."

As he said these last words, in her mind's eye she saw the tower implode and crash to the ground, followed by each of the walls and the shattering glass of the huge, beautiful windows. She could hear nothing, but see everything – until the dust blocked it all from view. It was as if she were looking at the 9/11 of Tudor times.

"Of course, in reality, it all took a little longer," he said, "the abbey church itself wasn't finally pulled to the ground until the eighteenth century. But you get the point."

"Not quite," she said, as some of the dust cleared and she tried to discover where he was now standing. "I can see that this disastrous end to the abbey was the fault of some of those who betrayed the principles of their order and the God they claimed to act for – as well as being Henry and his cronies' fault – but I don't see how much further it gets us towards understanding the nature of evil."

"You'll come to see in time," the monk said. "Evil, that great darkness hiding under the brim of everything, is extremely clever and resourceful and sometimes comes directly to speak kindly with you in a trusted human form, and then it says, 'I did enjoy that conversation. We'll continue it when we next meet perhaps, if you are still in the land of the living, so to speak.' And then it's gone. Or is it?"

He smiled, only this time there was no warmth in his expression. He said,

"Watch out, my dear, something lethal is coming your way – for now it is only fantastical, but when you came to this village you summoned the darkness. Unless you do what it wants, death will be your shroud the next time you hear the ghost child cry."

She said,

"What darkness, what do you mean I should do what it wants?"

"The darkness that was waiting for you in the gatehouse, the darkness that gave you, word by word, all the pages about 'the devil' for your book. You must forget about writing anything of your own in the rest of the novel – every page will be put into your mind and all you have to do is write it down. Do anything different and death will be the consequence."

He pointed towards the sky and, looking up, she was just in time to see a skull-shaped lump of stone plummeting towards her as the last of the walls crumbled and collapsed. What she had thought was a trick of her imagination now seemed to have all too solid a form. There was no time to get out of the way and after the impact had sent a blinding flash of light and pain searing across her brain, her consciousness ceased.

The small group of people gathered round her body parted when the paramedics arrived. The canon temporarily in charge of the retreat house had given her the last rites and explained to the medical team that there had been no sign of life for the fifteen minutes he had been in attendance.

"By no sign of life, do you mean that you've checked for a pulse as well as her breathing?" the paramedic in charge asked.

"Just her breathing," the elderly canon said, "but the poor woman is stone-cold. That traditionally has been regarded as a sign of decease, I believe."

The second paramedic said,

"It's her thick clothes that are hiding the breathing – it's very shallow and her pulse is slow. There doesn't seem to be any sign of physical injury. But you're right, she's dangerously cold, far more than I'd expect even with the most extreme case of shock. And the ground around her is the same, it's as if she's lying on a slab of marble. We need to move her to a warmer place."

The lead paramedic hurried over with a stretcher trolley and, after quickly wrapping Mary in a thick blanket, they lifted her up onto it. As they were about to take her away, she suddenly stirred. Her eyes opened and she gasped, as if new life had been breathed into her lungs. She dragged herself up into a sitting position, pulled off the blanket, lowered her feet onto the sodden grass and slowly stood up. The little crowd of onlookers was spellbound by what seemed almost like a resurrection. She surveyed them all with apparent curiosity and then slowly turned a full three hundred and sixty degrees, examining the ground around her for the stones that her mind's eye had seen collapsing as the abbey church imploded. She was looking in particular for the skull-shaped stone that she'd seen hit her before losing consciousness. It all seemed so real in her memory that she was finding it difficult to distinguish fact from fiction, but, very clearly, there was no recently collapsed masonry in sight and everything was as it had been when she'd first entered the ruins an hour or so ago. She looked worried and confused and was noticeably shivering. Spotting the canon's clerical collar, her eyes lit up and she said,

"Did you see him, the monk?"

"What monk?" the canon replied cautiously, not sure if he was dealing with a woman who was entirely in control of her faculties.

"A monk in black robes, a middle-aged man, distinguished looking, I was talking to him the moment before I lost consciousness."

The canon looked across at the lead paramedic, raising his eyebrows, and then back at Mary. He said,

38

"I think you must be in shock, my dear, I saw you shortly before you fell and there was no-one within a hundred yards of you and there was certainly no sign of a monk. You were entirely on your own."

She saw in the faces of the little group the same doubts as in his. As she did so, she suddenly felt the temperature around her drop to below freezing and her shivering became a violent shaking, her expression changing rapidly from puzzlement to sheer terror. The junior paramedic grabbed the blanket from the stretcher and hurried over to wrap it round her shoulders again. As she did so, the same vicious, freezing cold that had gripped Mary hit her like a fist as soon as she got within two feet of the patient. Her face portrayed perfectly her own amazement at the temperature plunge and within seconds she too was starting to shake violently. She tried to take hold of Mary's arm to lead her back towards the stretcher, but the cold was eating through to her bones and she had to step away. Once she had pulled back a yard or so, the temperature around her returned to normal and her shivering began to subside. Her colleague and the other onlookers were both startled and puzzled by what was happening. The canon's face alone showed signs of a rapid realisation of what might be going on. As it did so, the clock of the parish church across the way chimed the hour and Mary's tremors ceased. Now totally confused, she glanced furtively at the little assembly with the look of a hunted animal and then sank exhaustedly to the ground. The canon said quietly to the lead paramedic,

"This may sound strange and fanciful, but what this young lady has told us does now ring a bell in my memory. According to a local history book in the retreat house library, there was a monk who took his own life here at exactly this time, in this month, during Henry's reign. He was known as the Black Monk, the abbot's betrayer and author of the inscription on a storeroom wall that was said to be capable of summoning demons. I'll check, but I wouldn't be surprised if it was this very date. It may be no coincidence that the chiming of the hour and the cessation of the young lady's tremors coincided. Had they not ceased, I would have commanded that they did and that the spirit responsible get off and stay off what is still sacred soil."

She eyed him darkly and said,

"Thank you for that, reverend, it's a fascinating story and it'll do very nicely for Halloween, but I think we're looking at more of a medical condition here."

Turning to the little group of onlookers, she said,

"If everyone could stand back, we'll deal with this situation from now on and get the patient to hospital as quickly as we can."

As Mary sat drained and disoriented on the ground, one clear thought ran through her mind like an arrow and it was not one that gave her any comfort. It seemed that something in her brain wasn't firing properly. Whatever it might be was causing emotions, fears and visions that were both terrifying and entirely imaginary, and if she didn't get treatment, she was going to descend into a nightmare world of mental chaos and delusion. Ghosts she could cope with, madness she couldn't.

But there was another view among the onlookers. As she was being helped to the ambulance, the canon shook his head and said to one of the volunteers from the abbey ticket office, "They may think I'm an old fool, but it's nothing physical or mental that's wrong with that young woman. Something that's not even half-dreamt of in their philosophy has just done its level best to frighten the living daylights out of her. They won't find that in the medical textbooks."

Overhearing him, the lead paramedic raised her eyebrows to her colleague and muttered "Nutter" under her breath.

Mary Andrews returned to her house the following morning after being kept in hospital overnight for observation. Nothing had been found in terms of a physical condition to explain her collapse and her extreme loss of body temperature and the medics had signed her off as fit to go home.

What happened thereafter was puzzling and disturbing. Her neighbours in the adjoining house heard a lot of hammering in the middle of the day. Subsequently it was found that she had chiselled away all of the inscription on the stone over the fireplace, the alleged handiwork of the Black Monk, making it completely illegible. Shortly afterwards, a child howled in an unearthly and terrifying fashion from somewhere deep within her house. The neighbours said later that the sound of its voice cut deep into their bones and seemed almost like a harbinger of death. A violent commotion was then heard which appeared to move rapidly from the downstairs to the upper storey. The neighbours ran to the front of her house to see what was going on and could hear everything very clearly through the open bedroom window. Mary was heard shouting that she would not be 'the servant of evil' and would write her books the way she wanted to. Someone or something unknown replied in what appeared to be a foreign language. The voice was low and menacing and the words were followed by what sounded like a face being slapped violently several times and then a long and piercing scream. A fierce struggle was heard, with furniture crashing all over the place. Then, to her neighbours' horror, Mary suddenly came flying out of the window, landing heavily, head first, on the flags below. It was not clear to any of the witnesses whether she had jumped of her own volition or been thrown out.

Whatever the detail of her exit, there was no disputing the outcome. She was pronounced dead at the scene by the ambulance crew which arrived five minutes later.

The police checked the windows and exits at the front and rear of the house and all were firmly locked, other than the window she had fallen from. The doors were found to have their keys in the inside of their locks, meaning that nobody could have slipped out through the back door and locked it from the outside. When the patrol crew broke in through the front door, they found the house in a state of considerable disarray, as if there had indeed been a violent struggle, but there was no trace of anyone. When forensics checked for fingerprints, they found evidence of hands other than Mary's on her clothing and on the banister rail going up the staircase. But the traces left were a complete puzzle in so far as they did not resemble any known fingerprint design, but rather were as much animal as human. Mary's face and arms also had deep scratches that were more akin to those caused by claws than fingernails. Some with wilder imaginations theorised that some form of animal kept as an exotic pet must have escaped and got into her house, chasing and attacking her, causing her to scream and try and escape by jumping out of the window. Appealing as it was to some, that explanation did little to throw light on the conversation which the neighbours had heard. Mutterings of 'the coming of Orthorimon' were heard among those few within the village with knowledge of such dark matters.

In the face of the confusing and inconclusive evidence, the

coroner returned an open verdict and the police closed the case six months later, having despaired of ever being able to find out what really happened on that final, fateful day of Mary's life. The house has remained empty ever since, with potential renters or buyers being put off by the freezing air that greets all who enter and which is impervious to all forms of heating. Mary, however, from having once written stories about ghosts is now one herself, having been sighted several times in or near the abbey grounds at night, her hands firmly gripping a book as if to say to the darkness around her, "This is mine, not yours, you failed to get it and you have no place here."

Appropriately, her publisher commissioned a 'ghost writer' of its own. She finished the book in accordance with the detailed plan of the story that was found on Mary's computer. The overblown section on the devil character was greatly reduced and the character she had intended as a counterpoint was strengthened and given the full role she had planned for it. The finished book wasn't quite as good as it would have been had her stylistic imprint been on every page and didn't win the Hamlet Prize. But it was good enough for its readers, sold widely and most importantly, it was as she had intended, not as the darkness had demanded. The ghost of the Black Monk has never been seen since and the child that howled is silent.

The house where Mary died broods alone – cold, damp and falling to rot."

I left a pause for dramatic effect and then said,

"And that, ladies and gentlemen, is the end."

I held my breath and, to my relief, a round of applause much louder even than the last burst out, with one professor of mature years shouting, "Bravo!" Engel was positively beaming. Having offered his congratulations, he commanded that the lights be switched on again and his wife's guests escorted back to the Hall for their grand dinner. As they trooped out, only the sour-faced woman with the iPad addiction looked dissatisfied. She complained to Engel about the ill-mannered man who had kept prodding her in the back when she was trying to complete her correspondence. Engel looked at me and I at him, both with the same puzzlement in our eyes. He said,

"Are you sure you weren't imagining it? I only ask because the seat behind you was a spare in case Professor Hibbet managed to make it in time, which he didn't. I kept looking round to see how the audience was enjoying the story and at no point was that seat occupied."

She said,

"Well, I've never believed in ghosts and I don't enjoy ghost stories and when I see a solid human being sitting behind me with an impertinent look on his face, I know that I'm not imagining things."

"What did he look like?" Engel asked.

The description she gave fitted that of someone with whom we were both familiar. He went over to the fireplace and lifted a photograph of the Hall off its hook above the mantelpiece. It was taken in the 1930s and showed the then Earl with all of his family and servants. She pointed at the grand gentleman and said emphatically,

"That's him!"

Engel looked at me again and then at her and said,

"Well, you may not believe in ghosts, but they seem to believe in you. The man you've identified died on the lawn outside this cottage before the second world war."

She looked incredulous and then said,

"Oh, really, I ask you, what a cheap stunt. Fancy dress, was it? If you think I'm going to swallow that load of nonsense, you've got another think coming!"

She stalked off towards the Hall in high dudgeon. Watching her, Engel said,

"Well, work that one out. The lady who doesn't believe in ghosts is now making up her own ghost stories, just to annoy us perhaps – or perhaps the ghost was making her part of its story, who knows."

He turned back towards me and said,

"You did very well, my dear, and you will be rewarded handsomely. We'll talk about that later this week. I think you'd find the company of some of my wife's academic friends as trying as I do, so rather than invite you over for dinner, I've arranged for dinner to be brought to you. It should be here in five minutes or so, silver service, champagne and all. Enjoy!"

With that, lantern in hand, he disappeared into the dark to join the others. As I watched him go, I wondered whether I would be eating alone, or sharing my feast with the sour-faced woman's ghostly persecutor.

CHAPTER FOUR

"I'm not going there!" Emily cried.

For a four-year-old she was a very cautious child. Sometimes her refusals to do things were because she worried that they presented some kind of physical danger. At others her reasons were more mysterious. This was one of her more mysterious moments. I said,

"What's the matter, Emily? It's a lovely spot for a picnic."

William, the slightly younger child, was looking at her with a look of deep seriousness. She whispered something into his ear and he nodded and stood his ground with her. I caught them up and said,

"So what's the matter with this fine spot? The tree's a friendly giant and only kind little elves live in its branches."

The children whispered to each other again and not for the first time I began to feel like Henry James's famous governess with her older but equally sensitive charges. I said,

"Come on, unless I hear a good reason, this is where we're going to sit. It's the best place in the whole of the garden and only children who want to make the kind tree sad would refuse the pleasure of his company."

"He already has company," Emily said quietly.

"Really?" I said. "The invisible man and his invisible granny, both wearing their invisible hats – is that who you can see?"

Emily wasn't amused. She gripped William's hand as firmly as she could to hold him to the spot, although he showed no inclination to move from it. She whispered something to him again. I said,

"It's rude to whisper, Emily. If there's something that's worrying you, then you should share your secret with me and the tree."

"But then I'd have to share it with him," she said.

"And who is he?" I asked.

"The man with the glass in his hand, watching us. The man sitting with his back to the tree trunk."

This was the fullest detail she'd ever given of one of her imaginary sightings. I said,

"What does he look like, this man?"

Emily gave me a puzzled look, obviously finding it odd that I couldn't see him. She said,

"He's like the man in the photographs daddy has. He always is, he's always somewhere in the garden, or outside your house. He never smiles at me. I don't like him."

I said,

"What if I go and sit where he's sitting to show you there's no-one really there?"

She said,

"He's laughing at you. He's moving away from the tree and sitting somewhere else. He's laughing at you."

I said,

"Well, if he's moved away from the tree we can go and sit there instead. I don't mind somebody laughing at me, they can laugh all they want and I shall ignore them. If he laughs at you, then you should laugh back at him. He'll soon get tired of the game and go away."

She suddenly screamed. I crouched down and took her hand. I said,

"Mary, mother and all the saints, what is it, child?"

"The man," she said, "he was very angry, he was coming over and looked as if he would hit you."

46

"Dearest, darling little Emily, there's nothing to fear, I can't be hit by an invisible man. Where is he now, this strange creature?"

"He's gone away. He turned and walked away when I screamed."

"Well then," I said, "if he's gone away we're the king and queens of the castle. It's our spot now and there's no reason why we shouldn't sit down under the tree and have our picnic."

The children whispered to each other again and then went and sat down where 'the invisible man' had been. I couldn't be sure whether their overactive little imaginations were dreaming up a nightmare from a photograph that had frightened them, or whether there really was something that they could see and I couldn't. I laid the picnic rug down and placed on it all the food and drinks that the cook had made for them, but they only nibbled at things, as if anxious the bogeyman might return. I tried cheering them up, but it was as if a little cloud sat over them and blocked out the sun and anything that might make them smile. When we got back to the Hall later in the afternoon, I told their mother what had happened. She nodded and said,

"Well, I'm glad you haven't been telling them any of your ghost stories. They seem to be quite capable of making up their own. It's probably best just to humour them for now. It's one of those childish things that they'll grow out of. I wish my husband had never shown them those wretched old photographs."

When I got back to the cottage, I took down the portrait of the notorious Earl and his grand family from above the fireplace, photographed him, downloaded the result into my computer and blew his face up as far as it would go. I was looking at the man Emily claimed to be seeing – and the man the sour-faced woman claimed had prodded her. If I were to search for something that fitted the description 'cold and calculating', then his eyes would be it. They weren't so much looking at the camera as possessing it, a natural tendency perhaps for someone brought up in a life of privilege, but his gaze seemed to go considerably beyond that. His mouth was fixed in what might be best described as a sneer waiting to happen. It didn't look as if it had been the author of many kind words, or indeed of any words of love that were more than means to rather less tender ends. The single word that best summed up the face that was staring at me was 'cruel' and I could easily see how it might frighten a child. I still doubted that Emily had really seen the ghost of this unpleasant-looking man, but I could readily believe that once she had seen the face it would stick in her mind. The disturbance it might cause could easily push an overactive childish imagination into overdrive and trick it into believing it could see those callous eyes in all kinds of situations.

My thoughts were disrupted by a knock at the door, followed almost immediately by Engel entering with his usual assumption that his status as my employer gave him the right of automatic access to the cottage at all times. He stared at the photograph for a few moments, then said,

"I see you're looking at the man of the moment, at least as far as Emily's concerned. I've locked all of the old photographs of the Lord of Misrule in my study in the hope that if she stops seeing them, his face will go out of her mind and she'll cease believing she's seeing the bogeyman all over the estate. I'd recommend that you hide that photograph as well – put a pretty picture of Ireland in its place, or a calendar, anything."

"With pleasure," I said, "that's a face I want in a box with a lock on it, not on a wall."

Switching subjects completely, he said,

"I've arranged for my lawyer to come over to see you at this time tomorrow. He's bringing a contract that I think you'll find remarkably generous."

"Contract for what?" I asked, mystified.

"For your new role as my on-demand storyteller," he said. "That little event a couple of nights ago gave me an idea. Want to hear it – well, of course you do. I'm in the habit of hiring the most exclusive of dinner venues and hosting small gatherings of all sorts of people – those I want to persuade to buy into some of the high-value things I sell, those I want to court in order to improve the public face of my organisation, those I want to entertain to get myself more noticed by the society journos, and others besides. Your little act can be part of some of those events, a key ingredient of the entertainment that complements perfectly the serious business of the day. The idea of acquiring a reputation for something as unusual and sophisticated as resurrecting the kind of ghost story evening that the good Mr. James hosted appeals to me. Those academic guys couldn't stop talking about it during the dinner afterwards. If a bunch of acid tongued, self-obsessed careerists like them can be bowled over by your act, then so can loads of other people I need to impress in a way that's several steps ahead of the norm. I want your theatricals to help 'oil the wheels' of the evenings of which they are part and create an 'appreciative and receptive' atmosphere for the business that follows at dinner. I'm going to pay you to continue writing stories like the ones you told the professors and to do the kind of extraordinary performance you laid on for them. Your act will form a small but crucial part of the package that I put in place for those events. I'm hoping that you will say yes."

"But what about the children?" I asked.

"Well, that's not what I expected to be your first reaction," he replied, "but we come from different worlds, so maybe I shouldn't be surprised. I'll tell you what, seeing as you thought of them before you even thought of the money, I'm going to add another five thousand a year to the contract. You're really something, Miss O'Donnell – and the answer to your question is that when you're away on a storytelling gig, I'll hire an agency substitute. The answer to the question you haven't asked is that I'll pay you more money than you're ever likely to get should you manage to get your stories published. So you needn't worry about battling your way through agents and publishers and all that stuff – I'll provide the audience and I'll pay you a salary for entertaining them. So maybe I should ask you again, what d'you think?"

What I thought was wow, but I couldn't quite believe that all these people Engel supposed would be desperate to hear my stories really would be. A little voice at the back of my mind said, "This sounds too good to be true. How long before he finds it's not the great idea he thinks and the contract falls through, will I still have my old job at the end of it?" I said,

"How long is the contract for?"

"A year initially," he replied.

So it's more of a trial than a long-term venture, I thought. He said,

"That's a hundred and fifty thousand dollars in your bank account for a year's work and we'll review the project at the end of twelve months to see if it stands up as a more long-term venture."

I tried to look unfazed by the amount of money he'd just

mentioned, but given that it would last me several years in terms of my modest lifestyle, my financial queries ended on the spot, as he well knew they would. He said,

"I'll take the stunned look on your face as a confirmation of your interest. After you've signed on the dotted line with my lawyer tomorrow, I'll give you a draft schedule that we need to work to for the next couple of months. I'll see myself out."

As you saw yourself in, I thought. I'd come over to England for the 'governess's' job because I like kids, the setting looked idyllic and I'd have enough time for my writing. The pay was OK but not incredible, but in my order of priorities it was good enough to lead the type of life I was looking for. Now I was suddenly confronted with an income that was in a completely different league and I wasn't entirely sure what to make of it. He was a demanding man, used to getting his own way on pretty well everything and I had an underlying worry that he would start to boss me around and maybe even dictate some of my storylines to a degree which I would find uncomfortable. The money might be good, but he was a corporate man who did things in a corporate way and I wasn't in the slightest bit corporate in inclination or behaviour. I was beginning to feel as if I was subtly but surely being sucked into his organisation and that was not what I had come to England for.

The lawyer arrived at the appointed time the following day, a slick-suited City of London-type with a briefcase that probably cost half the worth of all my possessions. He was very much under the impression that all he need do was stick the contract under my nose, give me a pen to sign it and that would be it, a quick in-out job in macho corporate speak. I disappointed him considerably by saying that I would need to read the entire document before I so much as thought about putting my name to it. I duly sat down to go through it in forensic detail to see just what it was I'd be signing up to. Most of what I read corresponded with what I'd been told already, right up until the clause which stipulated that a small number of stories would need to be written to plotlines dictated by Engel or 'his nominees'. On the surface, the requirement might be seen as a quite innocent desire to see some of his own ideas for stories given life at the hands of the woman he was paying to produce the tales for his various events. I couldn't really quarrel with that. But my instincts were telling me to beware of any loss of control over material that was going out under my name. I couldn't quite put my finger on why precisely I felt so uneasy and I told the lawyer I would need further clarification on that point. He looked irritated, but phoned Engel, who apparently was in mid-flight back to the US for a meeting. He got up and went outside to discuss the matter out of my hearing, which was not a good sign. He returned a few minutes later looking impatient and said,

"Mr. Engel says he'd just like a few of his own ideas thrown into the mix, no more than that. Most of what you do will be entirely up to you. It's not a point he's prepared to move on – it's take it or leave it. If you want the job, just sign at the bottom and then he can start the ball rolling."

I nodded and went back to pretending to read the document, irritating him even more. He was clearly anxious to be off to his next high-earning appointment and hadn't anticipated the ponder-time that non-corporate me might require. In reality I was considering whether this was an arrangement I wanted to sign up to, despite the money, or whether I would be wiser declining to sign: the take-it-or-leave-it reply was not a promising harbinger of a future working relationship and was giving me serious pause for thought. I was fairly certain that a refusal would cause me to be thrown out on my ear and to have to look for somewhere else to live and work. An acceptance would be a step into the unknown – I had no idea what these various audiences might be like, what weird or corny ideas Engel might want injected into my stories, or what life on the road as a performing monkey in his entourage might entail. I might well absolutely loathe it and wish that I'd had the courage to turn him down.

In the end, as he knew would be the case, the money swung it. The medium-term security it would give me meant that I would be foolish to turn the contract down, no matter how unpleasant some of the obligations going with it might turn out to be. There was no indication that he had any unwanted sexual interest in me, in fact most of the time he talked to me as if I were asexual. So, what the hell, it was only a year and if it went pear-shaped, then I could bail out at the end of it. I signed on the dotted line. The lawyer gave me a look that said "at last" while routinely thanking me for my time and shot off so quickly his heels nearly caught fire.

I decided to take a walk to get the stress of the decision out of my system. I headed out across the park as the low, autumnal sun nestled above the trees where I had taken the children for yesterday's ill-fated picnic. I decided to have another look at the venerable oak tree at the centre of all the problems and to see if there was anything odd or unusual about it, or the area around it, that might help explain why Emily had been so determined to choose it for the site of her imaginary ghost. The tree itself certainly looked magical, but in a benign rather than a dark sense. Thinking back to when I was a child, I could have much more easily imagined it populated by fairies and elves than a mocking and ill-tempered ghost. Still, Emily was Emily and her mind clearly worked in a different way to mine.

I turned away and started to walk back to the cottage when I spotted Emily herself four or five hundred yards away, watching me. I called to her, but she didn't respond. Worried that she was out on her own, I looked around to see if her mother or one of the Hall staff was near, but could see no-one. When I looked back at where the child had been standing, no-one was there any more. That was puzzling, given that the spot from which she'd been watching me was well clear of all of the trees and bushes, with no cover for anyone to hide. She seemed to have literally vanished into thin air. The thought occurred to me that from that distance I couldn't be absolutely certain that it had been Emily – I'd seen a girl who looked to be of her age, but she had been too far away for me to make out her face. In theory, nobody other than the family or staff should be inside the grounds. Engel had a thing about security and the Hall and gardens were constantly monitored by CCTV.

I began to wonder whether, like Emily yesterday, I had imagined what I'd seen. I'd been thinking about her and the way her mind worked and then suddenly I thought I saw her. Making one last scan of the surrounding area and seeing no-one, I shrugged my shoulders in bafflement and resumed my trek back to the cottage. I'd gone no more than a couple of paces when I heard a laugh, a cruel, male, mocking laugh. It came from the direction of the oak tree and I turned round, half expecting to see now the dark vision that Emily had described, but there was no-one visible. As with the little girl who one minute was there and the next wasn't, I wondered whether I had imagined also the voice.

When I got back to the cottage, another thought occurred to me and it was one that normally I would have reserved purely for my fictional ghost stories. Could it be that, as well as me playing with ghostly characters within those tales, there were unseen presences around the estate now playing with my mind and those of the children?

CHAPTER FIVE

Things quietened down in the days immediately following the strange events in the grounds and the children seemed to go back to normal. I saw and heard nothing from Engel for over a week after the contract signing and I guessed that he was probably annoyed by my queries and my having gone through the clauses line-by-line with the proverbial fine-toothed comb. The impatient lawyer man would no doubt have reported back on the irritatingly long time he had to wait to get the document signed, and billed for his time accordingly.

Then, out of the blue, my landline rang and I found one of the great man's corporate flunkeys on other end of the phone. He told me to switch on the television on my wall and press the E button on the remote.

"What does E stand for?" I asked naively.

"It's the Engel Corporate channel," he replied. "Every bit of the accommodation on the estate is connected on secure, personalised video links. Mr. Engel wants to speak to you."

The line went dead and I muttered something to myself about Big Brother coming to town. I did as instructed and there was the man himself. It was clear that he could see me through a camera above the flat screen. I made a mental note to tape over the tiny lens after my leader's address and never to walk about in the lounge in my knickers or less. He said, with his usual slightly stuffed-shirt formality,

"Good afternoon, Miss O'Donnell, I'm in Chicago until Friday, so I'm going to give you a video briefing about your first gig as my contracted storyteller. It's a baptism by fire for you, so don't mess it up. I've just made a considerable donation to three colleges at Cambridge University and I expect them to do me one or two things in return. As part of my little charm offensive, I'm hosting a couple of social events for the college Masters and various other dignitaries. You're part of the programme – I think M.R. James used to be Master of one of the colleges in question, although I need to check up on it to be sure. I'm hosting a little James memorial ghost story evening, followed by dinner. It's a week on Friday and I want you to think up a couple of brand-new, extra-special tales that fit the bill. Work an academic or two into the characters as the good Mr. James often did. I'll send a car to take you to Cambridge on the day. I'll see you there."

The screen went blank. So, I thought, no challenge there then. All I had to do was write two show-stopping stories that would amuse and entertain a room full of intellectual giants at disturbingly short notice. Not only that, it sounded like some of them were from James's old college and the quality of his tales as compared with mine would be constantly at the back of their minds. My survival trick would be to act my full Irish self and tell the things with the larger-than-life gusto that I used in front of the last bunch of academics he'd thrown me to. It would be a desperate leap into the enemy ranks with all guns blazing, do or die, with the fervent hope that the 'do' bit worked and the 'die' waited until another day.

I spent every afternoon working on the stories after having delivered the children back to the Hall and they soon began to eat up all of my evenings as well. Bits seemed to work well and then, when I added other bits, the tales seemed to collapse in the middle, like the soggy sponge cakes my mother used to specialise in. I worked and reworked the things with an ever-growing sense of desperation until, on the Thursday night before the big day, I had finished both stories to the extent that they ever could be finished.

I had decided to abandon my normal 'once upon a time' approach. Instead I would hit them with a more 'in your face' presentation by using the present instead of the past tense. The dramatic impact of putting the horror into 'the now' might just distract Engel's new-found chums with plums in their mouths from the gap between the intellectual power behind my tales and that within their heads. Then again it might not. Whether or not I would manage to survive would be subject to the law of wait and see.

As soon as I'd delivered the children back to the Hall on the dreaded Friday, a shiny black limo large enough for ten Christine O'Donnells drew up and the friendly driver came with me to the cottage to pick up my suitcase. We were at my hotel in Cambridge in less than four hours. I had amused the driver by rehearsing and re-rehearsing my performance all along the motorway, to the point where he would be able to recite the tales to himself for the rest of the evening.

I had no sooner flopped down on the bed than there was a knock on my door and a sharp-suited flunkey announced that he'd been sent to whisk me off to the venue and the great man had said I wasn't to be late on any account. I had no time to check whether my constant ravelling and unravelling of my hair, as I ran through my little rehearsals on the way down, had left me looking like the mad woman in the attic. I was left to comb my unruly mane as best I could as I was whizzed through the traffic by a man who clearly thought that the accelerator was the brake in his overpowered and no doubt overpriced muscle wagon. When we arrived at the college where I was to be ritually sacrificed, he rushed me through the corridors as though an avalanche, a tidal wave and a tornado combined were following us.

I was finally deposited in a large and rather grand room that looked as though it had seen four hundred years of human foibles and frailties, give a day or two. There was a podium at the front and several rows of chairs arranged around it to try and give a feeling of intimacy in a room that was otherwise too large for the purpose. On the far side there was a long, oak table with wine bottles and glasses set out ready for some serious glugging. The thought occurred to me that if the academics went at that lot with sufficient gusto, they might be in a happy enough mood to tolerate anything I threw at them. A couple of white-coated waiters arrived with a trolley and a mountain of snacks which they proceeded to transfer to the table. As soon as they left, I hared over with the intention of grabbing a sandwich and a pastry as comfort food, but no sooner had my hand hovered over a cake than the great man's voice boomed out behind me, causing me to jump guiltily, like a thief caught in the sweet shop. He said,

"Miss O'Donnell, glad that you're here. I'd leave the vino until after if I were you, alcohol can relieve the nerves but take the edge off a performance, so I'd stick to the fruit juice for now."

"I was aiming for the cakes, not the booze," I replied. "I was working on the assumption that without anything to eat a glass of wine might make me fall over, whereas a cake and a sandwich would do the opposite. I'm famished, to be frank."

"Please, be my guest," he replied. "I haven't checked in with you about the progress with your stories because I know you'll do a great job. People like you I leave to get on with things. You're going to tell me you've got a couple of gemstones to shine and sparkle in the eyes of our distinguished little audience tonight, I assume?"

Managing to bite a chunk out of a cheese and onion sandwich which was so refined in its dressings that it wore a bow tie and tails, I said,

"Well, with a fair wind behind me and a glass or two of the holy grape water down the hatch on the part of the audience, I'm hoping my little tales will pass muster."

"You're too modest, I'm sure," he replied. "Just put on the kind of performance that you did last time and everything will be fine. I presume you included an academic or two in the plots, like I asked?"

"I did, I did indeed," I said, managing a second desperate bite in the process. "What are the academics who'll be here tonight like? Am I being thrown to the lions or is there a human being or two visible in the ranks?"

"It's the usual mix of saints and sinners and those in between. There's a bully or two, but they usually cancel each other out," a voice said. Its owner, a handsome, distinguished-looking man in his early sixties appeared in the doorway. He said to Engel,

"Am I too early? I know that's a strange question to ask in my own college, but for tonight this room is yours and I'm your guest."

"No, not at all," Engel replied. "I've just been checking with the storyteller that we're all ready to go and everyone else should be here within the next quarter of an hour or so. Miss O'Donnell, this is Sir Ian Towner, he's the Master of the college that's been kind enough to lend us this room."

"Ah, so this young woman is our entertainer for tonight," the masterly personage said, while making a beeline for the vino. He had scooped up a glass and descended on me before I'd had time to battle my way through an overlarge piece of toffee cake. I'd shovelled in twice as much as was wise in case I wouldn't get the chance to eat all of it before people demanding conversation of a reasonably intelligible nature started to fill the space around the table. He gave me a searching look while I tried to avoid silently choking and said,

"So, do you find us academics an intimidating bunch, Miss O'Donnell?"

"Only when I get roasted over the spit or challenged about my Irish mischief with the finer rules of the English language," I replied, trying to think of a witty and intelligent reply, but doubting that I had found one possessed of either attribute. Too much of my attention had been devoted to trying to speak without spitting cake crumbs all over the great man's Savile Row suit.

"Well, I wouldn't worry too much about tonight's little gathering," he replied. "We're all getting on in years and many of us are not in brilliant health, so if you think your ghosts and ghouls are not going down well, you can always comfort yourself with the thought that several of us will ourselves be ghosts before a single grey hair graces your head. The Almighty has a litany of means at his disposal to remind one of mortality and he has distributed them liberally among Mr. Engel's distinguished guests. Ah, Professor Alcock has arrived, you must excuse me while I pick his brains about something before I forget."

I grimaced politely while trying to get my head around the curious dark humour of his little homily. The thought occurred to me that if they were all like him, I might do better to ignore Engel's advice and knock back as many glasses of vino as I could manage before stumbling onto the little stage on which the podium stood. Instead I crept off to an alcove with an armchair about eight yards away from the table and hid in it until I was summoned to place my head on the block.

As the various academics arrived, all professors I would imagine, I saw what the Master had meant, with several looking the worse for wear and far beyond the first flush of youth. There were half a dozen women, but most were men. I wondered what on earth it was that had brought them here tonight to be entertained, or otherwise, by someone they'd never heard of before and probably never would again. Money, I thought, must be the root of it all. Engel had given them some and wisdom dictated that they humour him by attending his little soiree. Presumably it was part of his means of 'charming' and getting to know them before making fully known what he expected in return for his cash. I would have thought my role in the greater scheme of things to be entirely barmy and devoid of logic, had it not been for the M.R. James connection with Cambridge and the lip service which tonight's little performance paid to that. But again, the thought of my humble tales, my children in ragged clothes, being compared with Mr. James's refined public-school counterparts, with their confident use of Latin and their scholarship worn lightly, made me cringe and weaken at the knees.

Finally, all the sand ran out of my hourglass and Engel called the little gathering to order. By my reckoning most were on their second glass of wine and that at least was a promising sign. It was a warm room and that, plus a reasonable intake of vino, might well combine to make some more convivial while sending others gently to sleep. In fact, if my luck was really in, they might all go to sleep and I could quietly creep back to my hotel room, leaving them dreaming contentedly in their chairs. My comforting fantasy was interrupted by the reality of Engel's introduction, most particularly by the mention of my name. He had got to the point where he was extolling my supposed virtues and talents and then said,

"Ladies and gentlemen, may I present our storyteller for this evening, Miss Christine O'Donnell."

By now on my feet, my script hugged desperately to my breast, I attempted a dignified walk to the scaffold, but as it drew near I felt gripped by fear, not so much of flying as of going flying. In trying hard to avoid tripping as I stepped onto the little stage, I still managed to misjudge the step and, in grabbing the lectern to prevent further disaster, dropped my script all over the floor.

Scrabbling everything up, I rose back to my full five feet six and looked the amused or simply baffled audience square in the eyes and said,

"As a little commercial break before I started, I thought I'd just do a quick re-enactment of an old Buster Keaton routine - the one where the incompetent woman gets everything wrong and drops stuff all over the floor, but still marries the hero anyway, who is even more incompetent than she is, bless him. I do love the old movies the best. Now, that little job having been done, I'll get on with the serious stuff."

I tried a twinkle of the eye and got one back and a chorus of appreciative chuckles from half a dozen or so of the obviously human members of the little audience. That at least was a promising start, there was clearly a healthy minority who weren't in a mood to lynch me, at least not quite yet. I switched to my serious face as a signal of my intention to perform and in the course of things transport the imaginations of all those who remained awake and interested to a realm of fear – although for some the fear may simply be that I might ramble on too long and delay their cherished dinner. I thought, "This is it, woman, you're faced with intellects that are so big not even a half of one would fit inside your head, but everyone likes a good story, so pretend you've got one and they might believe you. Off you go and don't fall off the bloody stage again!" I said,

"I'd like to tell you a little tale called *The Spirits of the Rocks*. It's the story of a geology professor of some distinction. She's invited to join an expedition to an area near the Jack Hills in Australia. It will be drilling further than ever before into the earth's crust. It's the chance of a lifetime. The driller is a minerals multinational which, while pursuing its own commercial gains, promotes its public image by offering leading academic geologists some of the rock samples that are unearthed during the process. Professor Spode, the don in question, is cock-a-hoop when the first of the sample cores allocated to her is brought up and laid out for inspection. Before her eyes are what she suspects will be among the most ancient rocks ever to be raised to the surface of the earth – and younger ones that should date from the time when humans are now thought to have first appeared. She dreams that night of all the secrets they might reveal when they arrive back in her lab for testing.

She has been back in Cambridge less than a week when her share of the samples arrives a month earlier than predicted. There are far more than she had anticipated, causing a loud whoop of delight normally not expected from a demure academic lady in her mid-thirties. This causes smiles and giggles among her team. They are fond of her kindness and humour, qualities that most had found quite lacking in the previous high-flying professor they'd worked for. The sample cores from the drilling are slotted into special contamination-free metal canisters, then labelled ready for testing.

And there they sit for a week as she and the team clear their existing backlog of work so that they can begin their testing of the first batch of the samples. On the night before the much-anticipated analysis is to begin the professor decides to stay late so that she can ensure that everything is in place ready for the first raft of tests the following morning. She works until long after dark, when she is the last person remaining in the building and she is surrounded by her favourite thing, complete silence.

Finally, being satisfied that all is as it should be, she goes into the room where the cores are stored to label sequentially the cylinders from which the first test material is to be taken. The geological sample storeroom uses energy-saving technology to control its lighting, so that only the ten feet around wherever she is standing is illuminated. As soon as she moves away from any spot the lighting goes out, causing most of the long, drab green room to be in darkness.

She has just finished the labelling when she hears something. At first it is sotto voce. She's not sure whether the sound came from inside the building or whether it was simply a muffled cry that penetrated the silence from outside, which would explain its indistinctness. Her mind returns to the task in hand and she turns to pick up her electronic notebook. Then she hears the noise again, only this time it is much louder and most definitely appears to come from within the room. She feels unsettled and unnerved, because what she is now hearing is the sound of a voice – one that is full of pain, fear, loneliness and confusion. It is neither male nor female, but seems to be a blending of both. The professor inches her way carefully towards the point in the room where it seems to be coming from. The shadows in the relevant section of the cylinder stacks are deep, but vanish when her approach causes the movement-sensitive lighting to click on, bathing the area in the calm rationality of a fluorescent glare. She peers into the stacks, unsure of what she might see. There is nothing unusual, only the long, carefully shelved steel cylinders, with small, toughened-glass windows to enable the samples to be externally inspected – all very cold, clinical and precise – "just what I'm not being in reacting in this way," she thinks.

Then it happens again, but this time the voice is so loud it seems to be all around her, as if she is at its epicentre. It appears to be coming from within the long cylinder shelved horizontally at floor level near her feet. It no longer seems to be the harmonising of a male and female voice into one, but a chorus of many voices. The extra volume reveals more of the nuances within the deep, desperate, passionate and bewildered outpourings in a guttural language which she has never heard before and is unable to decipher. They keep rising and falling for a full two minutes, before gradually fading away to silence.

The professor stands rooted to the spot, terrified and uncomprehending, a great mind for once out of its depth. The air around her grows noticeably colder and she has the feeling that she is being watched. She peers fearfully into the semi-darkness within the room and is startled to see shadowy figures at the far end. She thinks at first that she must be hallucinating, closes her eyes for ten seconds and then opens them again, but the figures are still there. Their form is indistinct and they seem to lack permanence around the edges, almost as if they are composed of some kind of dark mist. She watches them fearfully for a full minute, until it seems that eyes are beginning to form in the heads of the creatures – sharp, piercing, white slits, all focussed on her. At this point she has had enough and runs out of the room, half looking over her shoulder in the expectation that she will be followed. She sweeps up her shoulder bag as she hurries past her desk, hurls the lab door open so violently that it bangs against the wall, avoids the lift and clatters down the four flights of stairs to the basement, then hurtles out of the building. Her car is only two minutes away, but it seems to take ten times longer than that to reach it. She breathlessly squelches across the rain sodden college green, out of the main gate, across the road – narrowly avoiding a collision with a cyclist she didn't see coming – and into the car park. She's so nervous she drops her key and scrabbles around on the dark, wet tarmac before finding it and finally managing to get into her car. As she starts the engine, she looks desperately around to make sure that she has not been followed and then drives off, her hands visibly shaking as she holds onto the wheel for dear life.

She spends half the night wondering what on earth she's going to do the next morning, when she'll have to re-enter the sample storeroom with her colleagues and supervise the opening of the first cylinder. Will the frightening figures still be there, will she be the only one who can sense, see and hear them, or will they scare the living daylights out of her staff as well? Should she tell anyone what she has seen and heard, or will they simply think that she is mad, maybe even begin to lose confidence in her as their professor and team leader? Ethically, whether or not she tells them, should she make it a rule that no-one enters the storeroom alone? If so, she will need to dream up a credible procedural rationale for such a move and she will need to give that some thought when she gets into work.

But most of all there is a feeling of deep discomfort that she, who has always prided herself as being a scientist and a rationalist, someone who treats all beliefs that cannot be backed up by hard evidence as ridiculous or worse, has suddenly been hurled head first into a pit of self-doubt. She has been confronted by something ethereal that is unknown and perhaps unknowable. Her traumatic experience in the lab has in one evening turned her precise, logical and ordered little world completely upside down.

The next morning is not as bad as she feared. She gets into the lab a little later than her usual 8 a.m. All of the ten researchers working under her supervision are already at their desks, or preparing for the various tests that need to be done by setting up the equipment on the lab benches at the far end of the room. The lab itself has large windows and is bathed in daylight. It looks warm, welcoming, scientifically rational and superstition-free. She begins to feel that her late-night experience ten hours ago was simply the product of overtiredness and a hyperactive imagination. The general excitement all around her at the prospect of opening the first of the sample cylinders is infectious. She remembers how much she has looked forward to this day, her first opportunity to begin analysing what she believes may prove to be the oldest rock samples ever found within the earth's crust.

She gathers the team together for a general briefing. She then takes four of her colleagues into the sample storeroom to manoeuvre the first of the cylinders out of the stack and onto a long trolley, which can be used to wheel it into the lab, ready for opening. Despite all of her efforts to reassure herself, she can feel her heart beating much faster than normal as she leads the little party into the room. Despite this, the dominant, rational part of her mind is convinced that all will be well – that the dark shadows of the windowless room will hide nothing but themselves and the ghostly figures which she thought she saw the previous night will have been devoured whole by their creator, her imagination.

She does indeed see nothing unusual and neither do any of her colleagues. But what she sees and what she senses are two different things. She is alarmed to find that, if anything, the feeling of being watched is even stronger than the night before. It is even more terrifying by virtue of the fact that she cannot see who or what is causing it. Two of her colleagues remark on how much colder than normal the room feels. One, a serious-looking woman with even more serious-looking hair, says what three of the others are thinking and that is that the place doesn't feel right, there's something spooky about it. A young man with precise-looking eyes mumbles his agreement. The professor's own fear is multiplied several times by these remarks, given that their authors are hard-headed scientific rationalists and are not usually sympathetic to anything that might to the slightest degree hint at the 'supernatural'. She ensures that the cylinder is removed from the room with as much speed as possible. She says, with false jauntiness,

"Well, if the room is causing people to feel uneasy, perhaps it would be sensible for no-one to enter it unaccompanied. It will be just the lack of windows and lack of fresh air that is making it feel a little odd, perhaps. But I don't want anybody to feel too frightened to enter it when it's necessary to do so for our work."

The rest of the day passes without incident and the first of the tests gets underway. Nobody has further cause to go into the storeroom. It is left in darkness, with all who had entered it earlier giving its glowering door suspicious glances from time to time, as if wondering whether something spooky from within might decide to come into the lab and join them. Just at the point where everyone is about to call it a day and go home, the professor gets a phone call from a colleague at Harvard who was also at the drilling. He wants to know if she has been sent, by accident, a particular sample that should have been his. She agrees to go and take a look. By the time he has delayed her for another five minutes with various bits of news about a controversial professor they both know, everyone else has gone home. She realises that, if she looks now, she will have to go into the room alone and at first contemplates putting it off until after the weekend, when everyone will be back in. But he is a bit of a bullying, persistent man whose cooperation she needs on another project. So, against all her wisdom and judgment, she agrees to take a look and ring him back as soon as she's finished checking. He has told her that the sample in question is distinguished from all the others by a strange patterning of streaked iron which resembles Cyrillic script. She thinks she remembers it and roughly where it is stacked. She hopes that she can confirm very quickly if it is there and flee the room before her ethereal companions of the previous night decide to scare the living daylights out of her again.

She hurries in, head down, and moves rapidly along the stacks, checking the inspection windows of the most likely cylinders for the specified sample. She gets to the end and to her surprise not only is it indeed there, but it's the same one that she'd heard the strange voices coming from. The thought occurs to her that it would be good to see the back of it, so yes, the bullying man from Harvard can have it straight away and good luck to him. Perhaps when it's gone the room might return to normal. She turns to leave and her heart nearly stops with shock. The figures that she saw the previous night are right behind her, with their piercing eyes and vaporous bodies, huddled in a semicircle, staring straight at her. For a moment she's so frozen with fear that she's unable to move or say anything. Then the same paradoxically terrifying yet pitiful cries that she heard the night before erupt again. She moves so fast she crashes into the side of the cylinder stacks before hurtling out of the room, out of the lab and out into the darkness of the night.

By the time she gets home the professor is a quivering wreck. There is something in her lab storeroom that is so terrifying it threatens to make her job impossible – and yet, the dominant, rational side of her mind tells her that such things cannot exist. She has a real, deep and worrying suspicion that somehow her imagination has got out of control and declared independence, inventing things of pure fantasy with such delicate skill that she is frightened out of her wits when they enter her consciousness. There is the slight consolation that those colleagues who last went into the room with her seemed to find it spooky as well. But that could be as much to do with the low lighting and shadows and the common awareness that its great stack of samples dates from before and shortly after intelligent life began on the planet. That in itself is a fact capable of creating an aura of the ancient and the long dead without any help from ghosts in the commonly understood meaning of the word. Her one comfort is that it is now the weekend. She can arrange for the Harvard man's cylinder to be collected by a specialist courier on Monday and hope that when it goes the ghost chorus, real or imagined, goes with it. She feels a little guilty at such a prospect, but then he was so insistent she could hardly refuse his request. If she warns him that he may acquire some unwanted ethereal guests as well, he'll simply think she's lost her marbles – a suspicion that she already harbours herself. So if he wants it he must have it and take things as he finds them.

In between she has a wedding to attend on Sunday afternoon. She feels in two minds whether to go. She worries that her real or imagined vaporous friends might somehow follow her and cause her to make a fool of herself while she is at the reception or, even worse, during the wedding service. The wedding is in Dublin and she has already booked her flight. The bride, Dana, is her best friend from her schooldays. It is Dana's second marriage after the tragic death of her first husband and both she and her mother had been insistent that they wanted the professor to be there with all the other friends they'd grown up with. It might have something to do with her exalted academic position and her showing the world what a talented 'backstreet' girl from Dublin could do when given half a chance, or it might simply be because she was one of Dana's oldest chums. Whatever, she'd accepted their invitation and, despite her doubts and fears, decides that she must honour her promise and go.

The flight to Ireland is delayed by three hours and she arrives at the church just as the bride has finished her parade down the aisle. She hates being late for anything and feels both rattled and embarrassed by fate's casual sabotaging of all her well-laid plans to get there in good time. When she gets to the reception afterwards, she feels completely exhausted and ends up a little inebriated as a result of the strain of everything. She is on edge throughout, the result of an irrational fear that something even more weird than the visitations from the storeroom ghouls might happen at any moment. She has no idea why or how such thoughts have come into her head. She feels angry and frustrated with herself for allowing them in. Her galloping anxieties are interrupted by a question.

"Would you like a piece of our wedding cake, Mary?"

She looks up and there is Dan the man, Dana's beloved. She smiles and accepts the proffered gift. She doesn't feel like eating any of it, but the last thing she wants to do is be ungrateful to someone who has been so kind and courteous to her from the moment she arrived at the reception. Dana is a senior nurse and he is a doctor, and Mary doesn't doubt that it was his bedside manner which had won her affections. Before he moves on to the next guest with his tray full of heavenly delight, he tells her not to forget that her handbag is still in the hotel's conservatory, where she first sat down after arriving. She thanks him and hurries into what is truly a palace of glass, where she is relieved to find the accidentally abandoned object safe and intact on the floor, next to where she had been sitting. She is the only person in the conservatory. She flops down onto a comfortable armchair, throws her head back exhaustedly and looks up through the clear glass roof. She sees above her the vast universe of dominant darkness, with the stars and galaxies mere pinpricks within its unimaginable enormity. She considers, like many before her, the extraordinary nature of what she is looking at – the infinite expanse of space, opened up every cloudless night when the sun goes down, as if a giant set of blinds has been hauled back to reveal the endless sea of matter and nothingness on which the earth rolls and tilts in its ever-repeated voyage round the sun. As with so many others in the history of the planet, she is awed by the humbling realisation of its, and therefore her own, insignificance. She is very literally brought back down to earth by a woman's voice, which says,

"You can see, can't you?"

She turns round to find a little old lady in a grey suit, almost bent double with curvature of the spine.

"See what?" she asks.

"The dead," the old lady replies. "You don't remember me, do you?"

Mary searches her questioner's eighty-year-old kind and wrinkled face for clues, but can't find any.

"I lived just round the corner from you when you were growing up – the lady who picked you up once when you crashed your little bike into a lamp post and called a taxi so that you could be taken to hospital with your mother."

"Mrs. McMahon – I'm so sorry, I didn't recognise you, I didn't know you were here. It's such a long time since I left home and went off to college, work and everything. Of course, I remember, that's why you asked me if I see the dead – my mum said you were a spiritualist."

"Did she really? No, I'm nothing like that, dear, never have been. I don't go in for any mumbo-jumbo, or have any strange ideas about 'energies' and 'ectoplasm'. It's plain and simple, from a very early age I saw what appeared to be the dead and that's that. I didn't ask for such a gift, if that's what it is, and I could never stop them from popping up when they wanted to. Your mother was one of the few people I confided in and then I learnt to keep it to myself. People thought I was fanciful, or an attention-seeker if I told them what I could see. You start to think you're going a little mad after a while. That's how I realised you were the same when I saw you earlier tonight – I recognised the same literally haunted look in your face that I used to see in the mirror when I got up in the morning."

"Oh, I see. I didn't realise it was that obvious," the professor replies. "They only started recently and I've no idea why. The hauntings, I mean, if that's what they are. I've had two disturbing visions within a short time of each other and I'm living in constant dread of a third."

"Oh, it will come," the old lady says, "but it's not to be feared in the way you think. These are not devils or demons, or any form of ghoul, or any of that stuff, but something much simpler and more straightforward in their desires. These are souls from the beginning of the human story and they in turn want you to tell something of their story."

"Me? I'm a geologist, not a storyteller," the professor replies.

"You're a noted sceptic about all things spiritual, an eminent scientist and are blessed with an imagination and an inner generosity the size of a planet," the old lady replies, smiling. "That's why they've chosen you to appear to. You're the perfect person to tell their story in a way that will be listened to. Nobody would listen if a fanciful person told their tale, but you are so respected a sceptic that ears which would normally be closed will open to your words."

"But they don't seem interested in telling me anything in a language I can understand," the professor protests. "They're very good at loud, confused and desperate cries that scare the living daylights out of me, but there's nothing in their little performances which I'd count as telling me their story."

"There, those cries have told you part of it already," the old lady says. "They're telling you what it felt like to be the first to have life before the existence of languages, science, religion, economics – all knowledge, in fact. They're telling you how terrifying, strange, baffling and completely without precedent it all was. They want you to imagine yourself into their minds at that time – trying to work out what this night sky above us was all about, battling with diseases they didn't have the faintest clue about, finding that some things they ate were fine while some, like yew berries, were lethal. They want you to imagine very literally what it was like for them at year zero – with no doctors, scientists, nobody other than themselves to defend their families against wild beasts and murderers, having to work out from scratch how to protect themselves from ferocious storms and freezing winters. Can you imagine just how terrifying all of that was, when the sun went down on a cloudless night and they looked up and saw that they were cast adrift on a huge rock with what looked very much like infinity stretching out above them – and no tangible, immediately visible presence of a creator to explain their existence, or where they were going, how long they might survive and what if anything would happen to them after death? That's what those cries were all about. They want you to understand the fear and pain they went through, to really think it through and record it in a manner that they couldn't at the time for the simple reason that reading, writing and all means of documenting things hadn't been invented. They want someone to do a proper, thorough job of it in a way that hasn't been done before, someone with the humanity and empathy to appreciate fully how they felt and to convey that in their account of their beginnings and the beginnings of all humanity."

"And how do you know all this, Mrs. McMahon?" the professor asks sceptically. "What is it that you think I've seen and heard?"

"What you have seen, my dear, are souls who, for reasons unknown, were stirred by the raising of rock samples from their own time and their own homeland – and who came with them into your laboratory. They have chosen you for the job I have described and they are unlikely to go away until you honour them by accepting it. That's the only way they can be laid to rest. As for how I know all of this, that's another story for another occasion. But whatever happens next and whatever you decide to do about it, you mustn't think that you're mad. You're not. You're like me and I'm still sane, and so will you be. Now, I'm afraid it's time for me to go. I've already overstayed my time here, so I'll have to love you and leave you. Remember what I've said and hold on to it. Be strong."

With that, the old lady is gone. Emotionally exhausted and still deeply sceptical about what she's heard, the professor sinks back into the plush, mock velvet armchair. She is baffled as to how the good Mrs. McMahon could have got hold of the details of her experiences with her ethereal friends in the lab storeroom. She becomes aware of someone watching her from inside the large function room beyond. It is the good Doctor Dan. He smiles and comes through into the otherwise empty space of the ornate conservatory.

He says, "You don't talk to yourself, I couldn't imagine an eminent scientist doing that. So you must have been talking to somebody else. Might I enquire who?"

"That's a strange thing to say," the professor replies, beginning to wonder whether she should revise her previously favourable opinion of her friend's new husband, "it sounds as though you saw me having a conversation with thin air."

"May I ask who he or she was?" Dan asks.

The professor laughs uncertainly and says, "I think you must be trying to pull my leg, the poor old soul hardly looks like a man."

"It was an elderly woman?" he asks.

"Why, yes, of course, you don't see many elderly men wearing a grey skirt, at least not around here."

He smiles and takes a sip from his wine glass. He says,

"Am I right in assuming that the lady in question was Mrs. McMahon?"

"Yes, do you know her?"

He takes another sip of wine and sits down opposite her. He says,

"Well, I don't think this is going to be very helpful, but I knew Mrs. McMahon for a very special reason. I was her doctor."

Mary's face drops as she anticipates what might follow. She says,

"Oh. You say that in the past tense."

"Yes," he replies. "That's because the last place that I treated her was here, in this room."

"And …?"

"And there was very little I could do," he replies. "She'd had a severe heart attack and passed away before the ambulance could get here. It was very peaceful, she was completely unconscious when she died."

"Oh," the professor says, her heart sinking through the thick pile of the floral carpet and the floorboards beneath.

"Medics are no strangers to people seeing and feeling inexplicable things after death and you're not alone in having seen her here. She's known as a friendly ghost to the staff and she has a reputation for appearing to people in some kind of distress. Had you heard about her before?"

"Yes, but not in that sense," the professor replies. "I'd known her as a child, she was a nice old lady who lived round the corner. I had no idea that she was dead, in fact I hadn't seen her for years. I didn't recognise her at first. When did she die?"

"Four years ago," Dan replies.

"Have you seen her – since her death I mean?"

"No," he replies, "but there was a very curious atmosphere in here after she'd died – warm, very human, as if there was a benign presence above and around me. I could see her corpse, but it felt as if she was still alive in the room. There was an overpowering sweet scent that filled the air and a feeling of deep calm."

"So you really don't think I'm off my trolley?" she asks.

"No more than I am," he replies. "Quite why she chose to appear tonight is a bit of a puzzle, but life is full of puzzling and mysterious things. Did she give you any clues?"

"Oh, it was all a bit strange, really very odd in fact, I need to think about it," she says guardedly. "But what you've just told me gives it a bit more in terms of credibility."

She thinks for a few moments and then gets up. She says,

"I must go. This stuff is crazy enough for me to have to cope with without burdening my best friend's new husband with it. You should go to her and enjoy your wedding night. I need to get my skates on or I'll miss my flight back."

Ten minutes later, after having said goodbye to the bride, her old childhood friends and those few other people she knows at the reception she slips quietly away to the airport.

She doesn't get back to her cottage in a lonely country lane until after midnight. She's relieved to see her familiar art deco front door reflecting the glow of the security light as she arrives home. She pays the taxi man and he drives off into the night. As she opens the cottage door, something brushes past her, so quickly that she feels the cold air which it displaces race across her cheek. Frightened and shocked, she turns to see what it was, but there is nothing visible. Simultaneously, a sharp gust of wind blows the leaves at her feet so violently that they swirl up into the air and whirl and swoop around her before dropping back to the ground. It rattles the chimes over the door and causes the gate at the side of her cottage to creak and clatter for a full minute. Seeing and hearing all this, she tells herself to be rational and calm down. What she thought was something rushing past her might just have been the same wind and nothing more. She switches the lights on and goes in.

The professor is still exhausted by the disconcerting experience of finding that she'd had a conversation with a woman who was long dead. She goes to bed early and rapidly descends into the deepest of sleeps. She remains oblivious to all the sounds of the rural night outside until precisely four in the morning, when she is awakened by the slow ringing of a church bell. It continues for a good five minutes which seem much longer and she begins to think that it will never stop. It is loud, deep and rich and sounds very much as if it is being rung for a funeral. Resigned to her much-needed sleep being disrupted, she curls up into a foetal position, subconsciously seeking the protection of the womb from the threat of the unknown, and tries to work out where on earth the sound might be coming from. There is no church nearby, although there are the foundations of a medieval rural chapel in a field a few hundred yards down the road. She's no idea if that had possessed a bell when it had been in use. Then she remembers a story that the elderly man who used to run the post office in the nearest village once had told her. He'd described exactly what she was hearing now and said that if she should ever hear the bell tolling it would be in memory of those who had had no Christian funeral, someone who had died, maybe even centuries before and not been buried in consecrated ground. It wandered in and out of time and history, and occasionally could be heard in the dark, small hours, when the air was still and all the birds asleep and quiet. He'd said it was the chapel bell and she'd smiled politely, while mentally dismissing it as no more than local lore, and yet, here she is, hearing it now.

Then the ringing stops. The silence in her room is complete and intimidating, as if it is a steel door that might suddenly burst open and let through something truly terrifying. She decides to reach out and put her bedside lamp on for comfort and to see if she can sleep with that shielding her from the dark and all of its unknowns for the rest of the night. Her arm freezes almost as soon as she starts to move it. From out of the darkness within her room a child's ear-piercing, desperate cry lacerates the silence.

"Aaaaaaaaaaaaaaaaaaaaaaaaaaaaaaaaaaaaaaaaaaaaaaaaaaaaaaaaaaa aaaaa!"

It seems to come from the foot of her bed. She gasps, her chest seizing up tightly and a nerve in the small of her back temporarily and painfully compressing as a result of the sudden tension that the combination of shock and fear has created. She waits for something to happen, for more cries, some kind of action, an appearance, but there is nothing, only the silence. Unable to stand it any longer, she makes a sudden lunge for the light switch and hits it. Hauling herself back against the bedhead, her knees drawn protectively up against her chin, she visually searches the small, curvy walled cottage bedroom, with its low ceiling and few hiding places, but sees nothing unusual. She slips gingerly out of the bed. Keeping her back to the wall, ready, if necessary, to make a run for the door and flee down the staircase, she eases her way gradually around the room until she can see what lies immediately beyond the foot of the bed and its old-fashioned raised board. Again, there is nothing. She kneels down and looks under the bed, and again there is nothing to see. Somewhere nearby a bird twitters briefly in the middle of a dream and then falls silent again.

It is a cold night, but she can feel herself sweating with fear. She waits a few moments then decides that if anything or anybody has been in her room, it has now gone. She starts to walk back towards the bed.

"Aaaaaaaaaaaaaaaaaaaaaaaaaaaaaaaaaaaaaaaaaaaaaaaaaaaaaaaaaaa aaaaa!"

The voice this time comes from directly behind her. She jumps so far out of her skin that she nearly loses her balance. She lets out a strangled shriek and runs for the door, but it appears to be jammed. She turns round to see who or what was calling to her. Again, nothing is there. She sinks to her knees and starts to weep. She is so frightened she can hardly move. She fears that at any moment something will appear with a child's voice and the head of the devil, but the only thing that she can see is her reflection in her wardrobe mirror. She climbs gingerly back into the bed, pulls the sheets up over her head and retreats back into the foetal position. Within minutes, without her even realising it is happening, sheer exhaustion causes her to slip back into a deep sleep.

Whatever it was that had been calling her makes no move and no sound. Its cry had been one of fear, confusion and utter despair all wrapped into one. It was the cry of someone lost in the night from a time when the cause of darkness and everything else was unknown, with an ever-present potential to provoke terror. When the sun rises shortly before eight, the room fills with light and the shadows that have been standing unnoticed beside her bed fade and vanish. In the garden below, a sudden gust of wind hurls the leaves up into the air before flinging them like a pack of cards onto the lawn.

She gets up a few minutes later, cursing the fact that she has overslept. She looks out of the window and is transfixed by what she sees. The leaves have been arranged in the shape of a child, with its arms outstretched, as if it is pleading with her. A deep sigh rises up from the ground and fills the garden. Then, as it fades, the breeze blows the leaves back into normal, random patterns of no significance, as if nothing has happened. The breeze in turn becomes a fierce gale that rattles her windows and gate with the force of a titan, as if reminding her of the power of nature to harass and frighten anything mortal and vulnerable.

She turns from the window and picks up and examines closely the small sample of ancient rock that she had brought home in her handbag the previous week. She had put it to one side for her own use at the time when the cores were being inserted into the storage cylinders. She finds it difficult to accept, but admits of the possibility that, as with the other storeroom samples, presences as ancient as the rock itself have travelled with it from the drilling site. Perhaps, as Mrs. McMahon had said, they are pleading for her to do something that will lay them to rest – to communicate, on their behalf, a message to modern humanity. Perhaps what their unearthly cries and utterances were most about was just as the old lady had suggested – the desperate wish to convey, through sound, the deep and often distressing impact of the creation of intelligent life on earth on the first race or tribe of humans who experienced it. For they had had to work out how to stay alive without any historical knowledge or understanding of the natural dangers of the planet on which they found themselves, or of the mechanics of the universe beyond it – or of death, disease and all the other threats that they faced. For them, every day must have been a terrifying, new learning curve. That they might wish to communicate all of that through her is startling and difficult for her to believe. But her succession of ethereal encounters, and Mrs. McMahon's strange knowledge of those behind them, combine to persuade her to try and deliver what seems to be being demanded in the hope that, by so doing, she can return her life to normal. The only thing she can think of that might do that job, to enable the experiences of these pioneers finally fully to be recounted, is for her to use her deep scientific knowledge *to imagine* and tell their story as the old lady suggested. Her starting point is to try and rationally but empathetically decode the messages at the heart of the cries, the precise details and nuances of which are burnt into her famously accurate memory.

She phones the lab and tells her assistant that she will be

working at home today. She goes downstairs, and prepares for the profound via the mundane. She makes herself a cup of tea and then sits at her computer desk. She would never have thought of herself as possessed of the kind of creative skills that would enable her to imagine her way into the minds of people thousands and thousands of years ago, at the very beginning of the human story. But everything Mrs. McMahon said comes back to her and she realises that the old lady gave her a template of how to see in her mind's eye *and tell* the story of those first humans. She is surprised at how easily the words now come to mind, at how readily the cries she has heard start to make sense, as if powers unseen are communicating directly with her imagination. She begins to write.

At that moment her fear leaves her and the wind vanishes. All is stillness and silence. The only shadows that she can see now are those cast by the trees in her garden as they are lit up, branch by branch, by the early morning sun. The only sound in her house is the tap, tap of the keyboard. Word by word, she tells the story of those first people whose often frightening experience of grappling with a world in which everything was an unknown had never been fully and adequately evoked. They are the souls for whom the chapel bell rang, she realises. Now that she is giving them a voice they, in turn, fall silent – and leave her to tell their story in peace.

And that, ladies and gentlemen, is the end of the tale," I said, my throat telling me simultaneously that it was desperately in need of lubrication. I sensed, to my surprise, that the collective high-grade brainpower within the room had been genuinely startled and fritted by various parts of my story. Indeed, I'd noticed that my two vigorous renderings of the child's cries had caused half of the little assembly to jump. To my relief my suspicions were confirmed when, after a short pause, there was an outbreak of hearty clapping that clearly went several degrees beyond customary politeness. A beaming Engel joined me on the little stage and announced that there would be a fifteen-minute interval for refreshments and then the second and final tale would follow, at the end of which dinner would be served.

I was simply relieved that I was not being served up on the menu as the main course. I had survived. Now all I had to do was generate enough interest in my second tale of the evening to leave Engel feeling that his hiring of me was money well spent. Given that the audience's minds would be equally focussed on the dinner to follow, that would be more of a challenge than at first it might seem.

I needn't have worried in terms of the dons' reaction. The grand climax to my second performance, in which a ruthless and fiercely ambitious academic met a grizzly end at the hands of a demonic soul catcher, caused astonished gasps and a horrified cry of "Good Lord!"

As the little gathering milled around afterwards, waiting for word that dinner was ready to be served, the Master briefly dropped anchor by me before moving rapidly on to more significant ports. A smile flickered across his lips, so fleetingly that had I blinked I might easily have missed it. He said,

"Well, my dear, that was a piece of clever tuning of subjects to audience. Tipping your hat to the great M.R. went down well with those who've read him and the dramatic impact of your delivery had several of my colleagues quite riveted. If only their own lectures were as compelling. You must excuse me, I need to have a word with the good Mr. Engel about the dinner arrangements, but good luck with your future career. It's been a most entertaining evening."

He then glided away across the waters towards Engel. Two or three of the other dons were kind enough to say how much they had enjoyed my little tales as I liberated a glass of orange juice from the long table. I thanked them profusely. I felt more than a little awkward, not knowing whether I was invited to the dinner as well, or was expected to exit quietly via the tradesman's entrance and order my own food back at the hotel. I was about to find out.

When Engel had finished talking with the Master, he summoned me into his presence and gave me an unexpected, if politely delivered, dressing-down, saying,

"I know it went down well with the audience, but that second story wasn't quite what the doctor ordered, Miss O'Donnell. It was fine until the end and it is the end that's the problem. You see, it's a matter of how my team are tuning our after-performance conversations into the tales themselves: if you finish on a note suggesting that being out for one's own ends – and being ruthless in their pursuit – is all bad, then you're somewhat clashing with the entrepreneurial thrust of the conversations we're trying to have at dinner, if you see what I mean. Having a 'soul catcher' despatch the competitively minded character and send her plummeting into hell is even more what we're not looking for. We're not out to in any way discourage people from contemplating deals that promise maximum benefit to the ruthless – in many schools of thought they represent good business practice. By all means give us tales that frighten the living daylights out of the audience, that's fine and suits our needs, but make sure you keep the messages morally neutral. We expect them to complement, not collide with, the business that follows. I signed you up to tell excellent ghost stories, not morality tales. I'll give you the schedule for the next few events tomorrow – please ensure that you keep in mind what I've just said when you write the next stories. I'll contain the damage tonight – at least the guys enjoyed your performance. You'll find I've booked you a table back at your hotel."

With that he was gone, glad-handing his way around the people he most wanted to buttonhole and impress, and then, like the Pied Piper, leading everyone bar me off to dinner. The whole experience was a little baffling and my role within it one of great curiosity. To be told that I'd rocked a boat I didn't even know I was sailing on seemed more than a little unfair. I'd no problem with writing 'neutral' endings as long as they fitted the stories I was attaching them to without doing any damage. But I found it hard to understand how anyone might have taken my whimsical little tale seriously in the first place – and even harder to grasp how it was supposed to 'tune' with the conversations that Engel would have over the dinner which followed. Feeling more than a little downhearted by his reaction, my most fervent wish was to get back to the cottage, my little writing chair and the children. Whatever the grand plans, hidden plots and powerful schemes which were to be discussed around that donnish dinner table, those modest ambitions were the ones keeping me focussed on what I was really all about.

CHAPTER SIX

When I got back to the cottage, the schedule of storytelling events for the next six months was already waiting for me. Engel had ordered that a paper copy should be run off and express-couriered over, presumably to ensure that I wouldn't miss it in my email inbox. I flung it onto my desk, sullenly. Being in a somewhat skittish mood, I then spun round three times on the tip of my toes, with one leg thrust out at a right angle behind me and one hand grasping the air above my head. I recited at breakneck speed an old incantation from a magician's tale which my granddad used to tell, the gist of which was that all my cares should be disguised as gold coins and stolen by dishonest fairies. My efforts were a little too frantic and I hurtled into an undignified heap on the small sofa by the window. To no great surprise, but my considerable disappointment, Engel's demanding list remained intact and un-stolen on top of my desk. Stretching out one foot, I wiggled the paper half over the edge of the desk and then, by stretching out the other foot, gripped it firmly enough to lift and deliver onto the sofa. My energy for silliness then being exhausted, I became reconciled to my fate and read the worrisome thing.

The various venues and audiences meant little to me at that

stage, but Engel had pencilled in what types of stories would be 'best tuned' to each. More to the point, he had also inserted a list of 'acceptable' and 'unacceptable' types of endings that I was to use 'for guidance' – a clear statement of his intention henceforth to subordinate my freedom as a storyteller to the strange requirements of whatever kinds of business deals he was promoting on each occasion. How on earth my odd little tales could in any way 'tune' to, or even vaguely complement, such deals I couldn't begin to fathom. Clearly, he thought there was some mysterious, crucial linkage that I couldn't see. Having my creative freedom restricted in this way was precisely what I'd tried to avoid when signing the contract and I felt now that I had been more than a little misled. I wasn't proud of the fact that the money was still so powerful a bribe that I didn't yet feel like resigning and throwing it all away, but I didn't feel at ease with the degree of his interference. With a heart as heavy as rocks in a sack, I decided I would have to write and deliver the tales within the prescribed guidelines and schedule – and try and hold on to my sanity in the process. If I could, I would think of ways of subtly wangling my way around the restrictions without his having grounds for sacking me.

I liked writing stories – no, I loved writing the things, but it was all in the context of an audience who shared the love, the kinds of gatherings of family and friends that I had performed for in Ireland, not the assemblies of the great and the good that Engel paraded me before. And while there were definite limits as to the kinds of themes I could cover when kith and kin were in the audience, they weren't anywhere near as numerous or onerous as those now prescribed for me. As the fairies had failed to steal all such cares and worries, I distracted myself by redirecting my thoughts to what I was going to be teaching the children on Monday morning and the various activities I could engage them with, weather permitting. My time with them would be the perfect antidote to the slightly surreal prospect of my continuing role as a tycoon's touring teller of tales.

When I went over to the Hall to pick up Emily and William on Monday morning, I hoped they would be pleased to see me after my two-day absence from their lives. What I found were two anxious little people who seemed to view me as someone who would be taking them somewhere they didn't want to go. I took them into the nursery as normal for the morning's lessons and games, and after a while they seemed to forget their concerns and become absorbed in the gently edited history I was immersing them in. Lunch went well and I largely left them to chatter to each other while they ate. Then it was time for the afternoon's expedition. All of their anxiety returned like a giant cloud hovering over their heads almost as soon as I told them what was involved. The activity was no problem – they both looked enthusiastic when I said I would be taking them somewhere where they could test their skills at brass rubbing. The problem seemed to be where I was taking them, the church which sat snugly within the grounds of the estate and which used to double up as the Hall's chapel. Quite why this was so I couldn't fathom, but was determined not to give way to childish imagination, in their own interests as much as anything else. If things continued as they were, the little darlings would be in danger of becoming afraid of their own shadows.

Our little party progressed down the long path to the church in a decidedly nervous fashion. I tried to cheer them up by encouraging them to join in some nursery rhymes that I was reciting along the way. They managed a few words with no great enthusiasm, but then started to stumble and miss things out. Their concentration was clearly somewhere else and there was little I could do to harness it until their anxieties were eased. As we got near to the church, they both suddenly stopped, their eyes fixed on something in the middle distance. I followed their gaze and realised that they were staring at a monstrously large marble tomb in the graveyard. I didn't have to go over and look to know it was that of the cold-eyed Earl whom Emily was convinced she could see all over the estate. She must have found out it was his while on a previous visit to the church and now it had become one more of an increasing number of no-go areas for them. I didn't ask whether she thought she could actually see the dreadful Earl in the vicinity of his tomb, or whether her fearful stare was simply in anticipation that he might suddenly appear. I said,

"Come on, children, a church is a holy space where wicked things have no place and whatever you think you can see out here will not be able to follow you inside. Come on, let's go in."

They whispered briefly to each other and then, without warning, hurtled down the drive and through the church door before I could even react. If I had been taking part in a sheepdog trial, I would have won first prize for having herded my flock into the pen in one swift move. I hurried after them and found the two little darlings standing with their backs to the wall on the opposite side of the nave. Their eyes were glued to me as I entered. It was as if they believed I'd been knocked unconscious by the invisible Earl so that he could take my place and my face and drag them off into the dark lands beneath the crypt. I smiled reassuringly and beckoned them over to a side aisle where two excellent nineteenth-century brass plaques were waiting for their attention. Deciding that I was really me, if that doesn't sound too complicated, they did as invited.

"Now," I said brightly, "this is where the fun starts. I'll show you how to begin and then you can both make your own rubbings. Once you've finished these, we can move on to some very ornate ones by the altar – you'll be amazed at the copies that you'll have to take home with you. You can hang them in your bedroom as decorations, if you like."

As I'd hoped, they became thoroughly engrossed in the task I'd set them and once they'd finished their first rubbings, they were both impatient for more. As I walked them down the aisle towards the next very beautiful plaques, they suddenly stopped as one and stared at the large stained-glass window on their right. I followed their gaze and was startled to see a shadow behind it, its head motionless as if it was staring in, watching them. I said,

"That will be the gardener doing some weeding in the churchyard, children. You carry on down to the plaques and I'll just go outside and have a word with him."

I walked as fast as I could without inducing a sense of panic in the little watchers who followed my progress anxiously. I was outside quickly enough to make it difficult for anyone who had been looking in through the window to vanish completely. Nevertheless, there was no-one visible anywhere in the churchyard or beyond. I hurried round to the other side of the church, to check there and looked behind the largest gravestones, but again drew a blank. Seeing anything through a stained-glass window is not easy, but the window in question was dominated by bright, angelic yellows and gold, and I was as sure as the children that I'd seen a human form pressed against it. Puzzled, I decided that a white lie would be better for the little ones than the truth, so I would tell them it was indeed the gardener who was outside, a cheerful and friendly soul who had sent them both his very best wishes. When I got back into the church, however, I was in for a shock. A middle-aged woman, dressed as if she'd stepped out of the past, was crouched down with them, giving advice on how best to capture the full richness of the plaques' ornate designs. I hurried down the aisle to find out who she was, having never seen her on the estate before. She fixed me with a critical gaze as I approached and said,

"Oh, hello, the children seemed to have been abandoned, so I thought I would keep an eye on them until someone came back."

"They've not been abandoned," I said, "there appeared to be someone looking into the church and I went outside to see who it was, given that it was worrying them. Was it you?"

"Me? No, I've been inside all the time. I keep the church clean and tidy, so that anyone from the Hall can come down and visit it whenever they want. You just didn't see me. Now that you're back, I'll leave you to it."

She smiled, a dour gesture that was devoid of any genuine warmth, and then walked past me down the aisle. The children were watching me closely, as if I were a stranger in their midst, and I wondered what she had been saying to them. I turned round to question her further and was startled to see no sign of her. She hadn't left the building because the church door creaked so loudly I would have been sure to have heard her – and the pews all had open backs, so there was nowhere for her to hide, yet she appeared to have performed a conjuring trick and vanished into thin air. I said out loud,

"Where on earth has she gone?"

"She's over there," Emily said, eyeing me as if I were lacking a marble or two.

"Where?" I asked, unable to see anyone at all.

"Beneath the tower, polishing things," Emily replied.

"Really?" I said. "Can you see her, William?"

"Yes, she's waving to me," he replied in a matter-of-fact fashion.

It was difficult to know what was real and what was imagined, and I was beginning to feel as if I had mutated into a character in one of my own ghost stories. I decided that the best strategy was to carry on as if there was no-one there and I persuaded them to return to their brass rubbings. Once these were completed, I announced that it was time to go back to the Hall. They neatly rolled up their paper copies of the plaques and then marched in front of me down the aisle. They waved at the invisible woman at the back of the church and I noticed Emily looking at me to see if I would wave too. I pretended not to have noticed her gaze and we proceeded out into the hazy afternoon sunshine. This time there was no anxiety in their step and I had a curious sense that something had changed while I had been outside looking for the individual who had been staring in. They didn't look back towards the marble tomb or show any sign of watching out for frightening figures such as the dubious Earl. They whispered to each other frequently and so quietly that their every word was out of my earshot. I said,

"You two were very afraid of someone or something when we arrived, but now everything seems to have changed and you seem perfectly at ease. What's happened to bring about this change?"

Emily scrutinised me as she walked on, as if trying to work out whether someone so obviously out of the loop would understand what she had to reveal. She said,

"The lady told us that we have nothing to fear, the Earl likes us. He doesn't like you, but as long as we do what he asks, we're welcome to live and play on his estate."

To say I was startled by her reply would be a serious understatement. I said,

"Who is this woman, what exactly did she say to you?"

"She said we're not to tell you," Emily said and with that the conversation was over. I tried probing further, but they went back to whispering between themselves, one or other of them frequently looking up at me as if I was someone who was out of the picture, a mere servant of their father to whom they had to pay lip service at his insistence. I felt both worried and uncomfortable as we walked on. I tried to grapple with the question as to how the woman I had seen so briefly had managed to have such a commanding effect on the children in my short absence and then to vanish into thin air. It was as if she had somehow stretched time and crammed a day's worth of indoctrination into a few minutes and by that conjuring trick had changed their attitude towards the Earl and completely undermined my authority.

When we got back to the Hall, it was time to hand them over to their mother. It turned out that she wouldn't be back until later, so the housekeeper, a firm but gentle soul, took charge of them. I determined that I'd better let Engel know about the strange events at the church – and the fact that the children seemed to be in the grip of a bizarre spell cast by someone with the capacity to melt into the flagstones. I didn't relish the prospect of trying to persuade him of such an unlikely scenario. I asked one of the staff if he was at home and if he would see me on an urgent matter. She returned after five minutes to say that he would be back in a quarter of an hour and I was to wait in his study. She took me down a long red-carpeted corridor and into his lair, a large, Georgian-themed room with an ornate marble fireplace and a huge, stately oak desk. There were a couple of gilt-framed works by genuine old masters on the red satin walls and a collection of photographs on a beautiful rosewood table which adorned the space between two picture windows that looked out on an Italian garden. I went over to examine the photos and was startled to find that they were of the Hall and its staff in the time of the bonkers Earl, despite Engel having told me that he'd carefully removed all such items from view to protect the children. It made me feel distinctly uneasy to look into the controlling, ruthless eyes of the long-deceased would-be Satanist. I switched my gaze instead to the many Hall staff who were standing around him in a photograph that was so well-preserved it looked as if it had been taken yesterday. I was even more startled suddenly to find myself staring into the equally controlling eyes of the woman I'd seen briefly in the church and who had then vanished as if in a proverbial puff of smoke. From her elevated positioning in the throng, I presumed her to be the senior housekeeper. There was an air about her, a hint of something I couldn't quite put my finger on, that suggested she was also something more - his mistress maybe, or even a co-conspirator in his unsuccessful sorcery. She was wearing the same clothes which I'd seen her in previously and the effect of encountering her again in a photograph that would have long outlived her was to throw my mind into a state of total confusion. Had I imagined seeing her in the flesh in a fit of random, out-of-control creativity, had my mind dredged her image up from a photograph I had seen before and forgotten, had the children's fantasies somehow cross-infected my brain, how on earth could anything like this be possible? It made me even more concerned for the little ones. What if I wasn't imagining things and if all I and the children had seen was real – if the spirits of the Earl and the vanishing woman were still around and actively intending to use William and Emily for some dark part of their continuing plan? If that was the case, then the children had to be removed from the estate and all possibility of their influence as soon as possible.

The more I wrestled with these conundrums the more I began to doubt that I could have simply dreamt up the encounter with the formidable woman in the church. Unlikely as it seemed, I appeared to be in the middle of something seriously weird that I couldn't explain and something which might pose a real danger to my small charges. Disagreeable as the prospect might be, I would have to do what I'd first intended and battle with what would no doubt be Engel's incredulity, to make him aware of what had been happening.

As I was thinking all of this, the door suddenly burst open and he swept into the room with his personal assistant in train. He didn't at first acknowledge my presence, sitting down at his desk with his back to me and signing a flurry of documents that his PA put in front of him, stopping only to query a paragraph or two in the papers which he was processing. When he'd finished, he fired a series of instructions at her about things that needed to be done within the next hour and then finally turned to face me. He said,

"Well, Miss O'Donnell, what is it that's so important that you need my instant attention?"

"It's the children," I said, "and in a way it's related to all of this, these photographs. I thought you said that you'd hidden all of the photos of the Earl, so that Emily and William wouldn't see them and begin to imagine all kinds of things which might frighten them."

"I did indeed," he replied, "some I locked away and the rest I put in here, on that table. The children aren't allowed in here and there's no danger that they will encounter them. Is that your sole concern?"

"No," I replied. "Something happened today that is hard to explain, probably impossible to understand, in fact. But it's so serious I think it's vital that the children should leave the estate and go somewhere where they are safe, beyond the influence of two of the people in these photographs."

"Forgive me," he replied, "but it sounds like your night job has started to leak into your day job. Am I right in thinking that you believe there's a real-life ghost story at work here, that the Earl and A.N. Other are trying to exert some kind of malign influence on my children?"

"It goes a little beyond that," I said. "Before, I'd always assumed that their various sightings of the poisonous Earl were childish fantasies, generated by the frightening effect of his eyes in the old photographs which they'd seen. But today something remarkable and deeply worrying happened."

"Go on," he said.

"While we were in the church doing some brass rubbings, my attention was distracted by what appeared to be an intruder in the churchyard. In the short time I was investigating that clever little red herring, a woman with eyes as equally commanding as the Earl's had appeared from nowhere and brought the children psychologically under her control at the expense of my own authority. How she did it I don't know and almost as quickly as she'd appeared, she vanished. When I looked at the photographs on your desk, I recognised her immediately, looking exactly the same as when I saw her today, yet if she were alive now she would be over a hundred years old. When I asked Emily what it was that the woman had told her, she said that she had promised that the Earl would make them welcome on his estates, providing that they did what he wished – and that he regarded me as unwelcome. When I asked them to tell me more, they refused and simply talked between themselves for the rest of the walk back to the Hall."

"You saw a woman who disappeared as if she'd never existed and yet once upon a time, if you'll pardon the expression, she did, but so long ago it's most likely that she's dead and buried. Did the children continue to see her when she vanished from your sight?"

"Yes," I replied. "They were puzzled that I couldn't see her."
He said,
"Well, to be frank, Miss O'Donnell, this very much sounds like one of your stories writing itself in front of your eyes. Let's see what the Engel juniors have to say for themselves."

He phoned the head housekeeper and asked her to shepherd the children into the drawing room. He took me down the corridor with him and we arrived to find the two little ones already seated and waiting, their faces devoid of all the anxieties that I had frequently witnessed in previous weeks. Engel said,

"Now then, Emily, you are the senior sibling here, so I'm going to ask you first. What did you do this afternoon?"

I noticed that she appeared to be looking up at someone I couldn't see for guidance. I presumed it was the real or imagined spirit of the phantom Earl. After a brief delay, she looked back at her father and said,

"William and I went to the church with Miss O'Donnell and made some brass rubbings."

Engel said,

"And did you see anyone else while you were there?"

Again, it was striking how Emily seemed to be looking up at someone before replying. After another brief pause, she said,

"No. We were alone the whole time. Miss O'Donnell was the only person with us."

I found it difficult not to intervene, but Engel was not a man to interrupt while addressing his own family. He said,

"Did you not see another lady in the church?"

Again, Emily looked upwards and then said,

"No, Miss O'Donnell told us about a lady who used to go to the church long, long ago and it was really interesting. She's very good at telling stories and we could almost see the lady as if she was really there in the church with us. But she wasn't."

Engel said,

"I see, and what happened after that?"

Emily said,

"We came back to the house with Miss O'Donnell."

"And you saw or heard no-one else along the way?" Engel asked.

"No, it was just the three of us, we didn't see anyone else," Emily replied.

Engel said,

"And what do you remember, William? Is there anything that Emily has forgotten, do you think?"

William said,

"I saw what Emily saw."

I was tempted to ask if he meant what she actually saw before changing her story, but decided that any such question would only lock them further into their fictional cover story. Engel looked at me as if considering giving me the opportunity to ask them some questions of my own, but then suddenly decided to bring the proceedings to a close. He instructed the housekeeper to take the children back to where they'd been playing and then paced up and down for minute or two in silence, an intense look on his face. Finally, he said,

"OK, so we have two different stories and yes, I did notice that Emily seemed to be checking with someone we couldn't see or hear, real or imagined, before deciding what to reply. If what you told me is all completely accurate, then she has both lied and called you a liar, which is not good. My problem is that all three of you have overactive imaginations and I have to ask myself if your creative brain went into overdrive this afternoon, causing you to see someone who wasn't there, an escapee from a story that you have yet to write. I would hope that isn't true, but you must admit that it's a possibility, even if it seems a remote one. But, equally, I've caught Emily lying on several occasions and I found her performance just now a little contrived, shall we say. Did you, in fact, tell them a story about this vanishing lady as she claimed?"

"No," I replied emphatically. "The events that I remember from this afternoon were exactly as I have described them to you."

"OK," he replied, "so here's what the situation is. I don't doubt that you believe that everything you've told me is true, bizarre though it is. Because it's bizarre and because the children don't agree with your version of events, I have a zero-minus chance of persuading my wife to relocate Emily and William to safer ground, as you put it, simply on the basis of what you say. I'm aware that Emily has frequently claimed to have seen someone whose description fits the Earl in and around the estate and my wife is aware of that also. That is a situation which we have been monitoring in terms of the extent to which it frightens her and the degree to which these various sightings are simply in her mind. All I can do is add today's episode – and the two separate versions of it that have been presented to me – to the monitoring list. I will keep a close eye on the children when I'm around and have the time, and I'll ask Mrs. Engel to do the same. You will obviously do that because it's part of your responsibilities during your teaching hours, but given that Emily is quite a wilful young lady and has just challenged your authority big time, you will also need to think of ways of reasserting your leadership and letting them know who is the real boss, in both the nursery and the classroom."

He gave me a look that seemed more like a reprimand than anything else. I felt humiliated and frustrated at the outcome of my failed attempt to act in the children's best interests, but at the same time recognised that what he had said was the only practical response to the situation, given its deep strangeness and the impossibility of proving anything that I had alleged. He said,

"In the meantime, don't forget that you've got another storytelling evening next week. Perhaps this little episode will stimulate your creative energies even more than normal and give everyone an experience they'll never forget. And speaking of forgetting, please don't forget what I said about acceptable endings."

As I walked back to the cottage, I ruminated on the irony of the situation that I was now in. Here I was, a writer of ghost stories, finding myself turned into a character in someone else's ghost story, being manipulated either by a small child's imagination or, improbable though it may seem, the estate's resident ghosts, who were in turn manipulating the child. I found it difficult to believe that I might have actually seen a ghost, given that all such things strange and spirit-like had lived previously within the comfort zone of my mind as fictional and fantastical only. But on the other hand, all the evidence which I had available suggested that the figure in question could only have appeared as a youngish woman if she was indeed some kind of a phantom. None of this made very comfortable food for thought.

That wasn't the only uncomfortable outcome of a truly bizarre day. My role as a teacher, governess, call it what you like, had now become enormously complicated. It would be difficult for me to deal with the children's supposed new relationship with the estate's real or imaginary ghosts given Emily's preparedness to lie and in turn imply that I was either a fantasist or a liar. What previously had seemed to be a highly enjoyable job with apparently well-behaved children had suddenly become a complex nightmare, one in which I had to contest my authority over them with characters who were either imagined or dead. As I wandered on through the twilight gloom, it was hard to avoid the conclusion that the governess part of my job was something which now looked likely to have an extremely short shelf life. Given the money that Engel was paying me for the storytelling role, I didn't really need the relatively small salary which I received for educating his children, but it was a job that until today I had enjoyed enough to want to retain. The possibility of its loss now was a cause of genuine sadness. That in turn led me to wonder whether I would really want to stay should it go. The storytelling job also was becoming something other than I had hoped and I had the strong suspicion that Engel's interference would not stop at my being required to produce 'acceptable endings'. Sooner or later there would be another imposition on my freedom as a storyteller, followed by another and another. In my mood of despondency, I began to wonder seriously whether it might be best to consider leaving both jobs and starting again, somewhere new and less clouded with complications. The loss of income should I let go of the storytelling post would be huge, but the psychological gains in terms of me becoming a much happier, less stressed person were at the very least worth considering.

When I returned to the Hall the following day for the children's morning lessons and activities, my worst fears were confirmed. Emily had become a little madam and sat watching me with eyes full of a mockery and a contempt that were far beyond her tender years. I had the uneasy feeling that I was looking not just at her but at something which was now operating through her when it so chose. I said the usual good mornings to them both. William acted as if he hadn't heard me speak and, to my surprise, Emily asked me what was good about it. I said,

"Why, every morning is good, Emily – it's good to be alive for one thing and here we all are enjoying the gift of another day."

"How do you know it isn't better to be dead?" she asked, a knowing gleam in her eyes.

I chose my words carefully. I said,

"Well, it depends whether the dead have been good, I think. If they've led a life that has been of benefit to those around them and they've left the world a happier place, then they might well be in heaven and for them that would certainly be something to enjoy."

"Enjoy? I enjoy ice cream," Emily replied, "some people enjoy not being good, why shouldn't they be happier dead than alive as well?"

Words once spoken by my grandmother back in Ireland came to mind and I refashioned them for the children's ears. I said,

"Well, if they end up spending eternity with the devil as a result of being bad, they might wish they were still alive. They would then have had the chance to make up for their badness and end up in a happier place with better company when they died."

"What's wrong with the devil's company?" Emily asked. That drew me up sharp. This wasn't a small child I was speaking to, no matter how much my rational mind told me that such a conclusion was ridiculous. I felt more than a little frightened by just what it was that I might be talking to, but that fear helped concentrate my mind. I decided to call the bluff of whoever, or whatever, it was. I said,

"If I want to speak to the Earl, I'll ask him directly. If I want to speak to Emily, I will speak only to her. Now, let me speak to her and be gone with you."

There was a tense pause during which Emily said nothing. Her eyes seemed to go blank and it was as if her body was temporarily without a resident personality. I said,

"Emily, are you there? Are you back with us?"

The child started as if I had shouted at her and looked at me in surprise. It was theoretically possible she might have been acting and I had to take that into account, but the skills involved were so far beyond normal expectations for her tender years it seemed highly unlikely. William, who had been watching and listening closely throughout, looked both frightened and confused. She said,

"Yes, I'm here, Miss O'Donnell, what are we going to be doing today?"

An enormous sense of relief came over me. The child that I had first encountered when taking up my post appeared to be back, for now at least. I felt that while I had lost round one for the minds of the children yesterday, I had won round two today. At the same time, I had an uncomfortable suspicion that what I had witnessed might be no more than a tactical retreat. The Earl, if it was indeed him who had been responsible for the acidic conversation of a few minutes earlier (and not the less likely possibility of a child prodigy acting her little socks off), had clearly gone too far over the top and presumably had recognised this. If her parents heard Emily speak in such a manner – and concluded that it was improbable she was acting – then they would be highly likely to move her away from the estate and its malign influences. That was clearly the opposite of what the Earl wished at the moment. The danger was that he was now thinking of more subtle means to achieve whatever it was he wanted from the children. I would have to stay constantly on alert, therefore, ready to counter his next move as soon as he made it.

But as I pondered all of this, its utterly bizarre nature made me wonder again whether Emily herself was the extraordinary force here, a child with intelligence, imagination and cunning far beyond her years who was running rings around me with an act which was so sophisticated that even I was coming to believe it. She was undoubtedly very bright and the more I thought about it the less I could completely rule out that possibility. I had become trapped within a strange dual world – one where I had to assume the worst, in the form of something diabolical working through her, while at the same time feeling uncomfortable with the almost medieval nature of this diagnosis and considering the possibility of an explanation that was rooted more mundanely within the psychology of an exceptional child.

I set the children a series of tasks to do that would develop further their ability to paint and to understand the importance of colour and texture, and they became completely absorbed in their efforts. After their lunch, I took them on a walk through the prettiest parts of the estate to enable them to connect what I had been teaching them in class with what they could see all around them. Things seemed to be going fine until we got close to the banks of the sedate river that rambled through the grounds. I was pointing out the various ways in which the water reflected the light when I became aware that their attention was elsewhere. I followed their gaze to the old, stone packhorse bridge thirty yards away downstream. There was no-one visible on or near it, yet it was clear they were certain that they could see and probably hear someone. They began whispering to each other in the manner of the day before and once more they started looking back at me in what can only be described as a conspiratorial fashion. I said,

"Now then, children, I don't know what or who it is you think you can see, but there's no-one there and it's important that we start to head back to the Hall. Your mother will be home early today and she has especially asked if you can be back in time for her to take you out for a treat."

There was no response and they started whispering to each other again. I noticed the direction of their gaze changing, as if the invisible person on the bridge had come off it and was walking towards them. Their rapt attention suggested that they believed they were being spoken to, given instructions even. I decided the only thing to do was to stand directly in their line of sight to see if I could break the spell. They looked decidedly irritated at my intervention and tried to see round me. I said,

"No, no more fun and games with Mr. or Mrs. Invisible. You heard what I said, dears, it's time for us to be on our way, come on, shoo, shoo, I'm going to pretend you are sheep and I'm the shepherd. Come on, let's get moving so that you can be back in time for your treat."

The wrestling match inside their heads between continuing to listen, or pretend to listen, to the words and ill-wisdom of the invisible man, or going back home for something that promised to be highly enjoyable, was finally won by the promised treat. They about-turned, albeit reluctantly, and finally did as they were asked. What worried me, however, was what they had been told, or thought they had been told, by the real or imaginary invisible personage on the bridge before my intervention. Their refusal to let me in on what had been happening and their secretive whisperings to each other suggested that whatever was involved was something that I would not approve of. That in itself was worrying.

Matters continued in much the same vein for the rest of the week, with the two little ones appearing to be as ordinary in their behaviour as when I had first met them for part of the time and then becoming distracted by 'noises off' for intervals in which I seemed to become the enemy, or at best 'the untrusted'. The only occasion on which I'd actually seen, or thought I'd seen, someone they seemed to have been listening to during one of these sessions was in the church. The singular isolation of that incident made me increasingly doubt whether I had actually seen the woman in the photograph, or whether Engel was closer to the mark when he'd wondered if my overactive imagination had been as busy then as the children's. It could have been, as I had previously suspected, that I had seen her in a photograph before and forgotten about it until something in the general strangeness of that afternoon had 'auto-suggested' her into life within my imagination. Yet, try as I might to rationalise things in this way, it didn't work. If I had indeed had a conversation with someone who was a mere figment of my imagination, then I must be going bonkers and bonkers I most certainly didn't feel.

My mind, in short, was becoming ever more tangled in a web of confusion over the real or imaginary nature of the invisible people the children seemed so convinced inhabited the estate. I couldn't help noticing the echoes here and there of Henry James as opposed to M.R. and felt, as so often before over those last few days, that I had become part of someone else's story – that they might even be taking the proverbial mickey out of me.

All of this weighed heavily in the evenings when I was on my own, sitting at my writing desk, trying to put together a couple of new tales for the next storytelling event on Engel's schedule. The cottage's dark past, which at first hadn't bothered me in the slightest because at that time, ironically, I most certainly didn't believe in ghosts, now seemed to be closing in on me. I didn't see anything or hear any voices, but I began to feel that I was being watched and that there were presences within the building which wished me ill. For the first time, the stories which I was attempting to write began to feel as if the evil that they focussed on directly and indirectly was something more than fiction. It was almost as if it was seeping into my mind from malign sources that had become trapped within the four walls of the building. Like Henry James long before me, I began to be frightened by my own tales and afraid to turn out the light when I went to bed. In a bizarre way, this was good news because it enabled me to give my latest emerging stories an air of authenticity that had been much harder to generate before. But there was also a downside, and that was a subtle and gradual darkening of my mood. This was accompanied by the almost imperceptible descent of a cloud of depression that made each morning seem more a source of non-specific dread than the beginning of a new day in the life of someone who, theoretically, had everything to live for. I wasn't becoming the overwrought governess of Henry James's novella, but I was most certainly being affected by something poisonous in the atmosphere of the estate, the dark echoes from the more disturbing aspects of its past. This caused me to return to my earlier ponderings on whether the storytelling job was one that I really wanted to retain, despite the generous salary going with it. The psychological burden that it was now beginning to impose on me was becoming a little too heavy on top of the bizarre real or imaginary haunting of the children.

CHAPTER SEVEN

It's said in some cultures that snow winds are the carriers of angels; that deep within their ice-breath and the curtains of pure, freezing whiteness they unleash are the ethereal forms of beings who have seen the face of God. Sometimes they are the brothers of Gabriel and sometimes the servants of Satan. As I looked up at the flickering snowflakes that fell like confetti out of the dark, menacing, sky I wondered which spirits they would bring, the angelic to vanquish the Earl, or the demonic to reinforce him. It was now a full two weeks since the episode in the church and the children still seemed to be half under my authority and half under the malign control of unseen forces.

There was still an hour to go before I was due at the Hall for the children's morning classes, so I decided to use the time to take some photographs of the cottage and the surrounding trees as the snow softly shrouded them. Rather than the pretty Christmas-card snowscape which such a quaint and ancient setting might normally present, the scene around me contained a hint of menace, as if the icy blanket coating everywhere provided an extra layer of concealment for the dark forces that haunted and hunted all around the estate.

My thick woollen sweater was little protection against the biting wind that seemed to come from nowhere as I began to take photographs of the cottage garden and the swirling, ice-laden sky above it. As I did so, my eye caught sight of something else in the heavens. It was coming towards me in every sense, descending rapidly from the clouds and seemed to be heading towards the expansive Hall lawns that stretched right up to the edge of the walled cottage garden. The deafening throb of its engine and its enormous, overblown size confirmed that it was Engel's personal helicopter, presumably bringing him back from the airport. Normally, it landed in the large stone-paved courtyard at the rear of the Hall, but today, for some reason, things were clearly going to be different. The machine touched down thirty yards away from the cottage and the familiar figure of my employer climbed out.

As he walked towards me, wrapped in a cashmere overcoat that probably cost as much as a small car, there was a look of urgency on his face. He said,

"Fetch your coat, hat and gloves and get in the copter. We're taking the children on a little expedition that's very important. Mrs. Jackson is bringing them over in a couple of minutes."

Somewhat surprised by the suddenness of this announcement and concerned for the children's safety because of the weather, I asked,

"What about the snow, won't it be risky to fly in this kind of weather with the little ones on board?"

He said,

"No, the pilot's checked it out and the snow will stop in an hour. With all of the technology on board this thing, we're pretty well safe to fly in most weathers, so don't worry, just get your stuff and we'll be ready to go in a few minutes. I'm on a strict schedule because I need to be in London for a meeting tonight, so the window I have for this thing is narrow."

Quite what 'this thing' was I couldn't imagine, but there was clearly no changing his mind. As I rummaged about in my tiny wardrobe for my warmest hat and gloves, I worried about the fact that I'd never travelled in a wingless aircraft before and most particularly about the tendency for helicopters to plunge straight into the ground if their engines failed. My head for heights was limited at the best of times and I wasn't sure how well it would hold out in such a potentially vulnerable lump of flying metal.

When I went outside again, the children were just climbing on board and Engel was gesturing frantically to me to hurry up. I marched across the three-inch deep carpet of snow to join them, my every footstep making a satisfying crunching sound as I did so. As soon as I was on board and everyone was safely belted in, the co-pilot shut the door and we took off. I tried not to look as the cottage, the Hall and everything around became smaller and smaller below and then vanished from sight completely as we headed out on Engel's magical mystery tour. He was seated on the other side of the aisle across from me, animatedly haranguing some unfortunate underling over his smartphone. The children had been placed on the inner seats beside me and by the frightened look on their faces as we took off, I judged this to be their first trip on their daddy's giant flying machine. To my surprise, Emily wanted me to hug her, presumably more for protection than affection, and I did so to the extent that the seat belts allowed. The hostess, whose main job was to look after the needs of Engel, came over from her seat at the front to ask if they would like any sweets or anything else to help distract them from the fact that the safety of the ground was disappearing at a rate of knots. Her offer was accepted instantly and gratefully by both.

Having finished his call, Engel looked across at me and said,

"This will be good for the children, they have to get used to flying in one of these things and today will be useful experience."

I said,

"Where are we going and why is it so important for them to go there today?"

His reply was both fascinating and unexpectedly expansive. It turned out that his grandfather had been a highly decorated American pilot stationed in Britain during the second world war. His plane had crashed into hills in northern Lancashire when returning severely damaged from a bombing raid over Germany. It should never have been anywhere near the hills, but its navigation systems had been shot to pieces. Two of the crew had survived, but his grandfather had died of his wounds and it had been the family's wishes that he should be buried near to where he fell.

"He's buried in a big, hillside cemetery a couple of miles away and today is the anniversary of his death," he explained. "I only found out last night, totally by chance when I was on the phone to my uncle about something completely different. The man was one of the most-decorated war heroes in American history and I had a sudden feeling this morning that his great-grandchildren should be there to honour him on his anniversary. It'll be a great history lesson for them and the anniversary will bring it home to them more than on any other day, it'll make it special. I also thought seeing the memorial to this guy would give them a better role model than the Earl, if we're talking about the dead, that is."

While I'd been highly doubtful about both the wisdom and the ethics of taking the little ones somewhere by helicopter on a day of such bad weather, his last comment sold me on the idea. Anything that might divert their attention away from the diabolical atmosphere permeating the estate was a plus. He asked me to explain the purpose of the trip to them and I did so. He said he wanted me to see the grave, understand its historical importance and then use the next day's lessons to help the children develop a sense of connectedness to their great-grandfather and what he achieved. That was the reason for my going with them. Emily being Emily, she had a couple of questions she wanted answering about her heroic ancestor right at the outset. She shouted them across to Engel, forcing him to deal directly with his offspring rather than through a delegated underling in the form of myself. He gave me a reproving look afterwards, for being a failed gatekeeper, no doubt, and then returned to his iPad and his phone, cajoling or berating a series of faraway people whom he needed to sweet-talk or prod.

When he'd finally finished his 'conferencing', he said,

"Don't forget the storytelling schedule for this week, by the way, you're performing in the gatehouse of Kenilworth Castle on Friday night. It's a nicely spooky venue and they'll have a roaring log fire going. Everything you've done so far has gone down really well. Don't forget what I've said about your endings and you can't go wrong."

"Absolutely, I'll second that," a darkly seductive voice volunteered from somewhere behind. I hadn't noticed anyone else when we'd got on board and Engel also looked surprised. We both turned round to see a suave and impossibly handsome middle-aged man in a perfectly tailored, black Saville Row suit with a matching Hollywood hair perm. He smiled, so briefly it was almost as if the gesture had been unintended. Engel said,

"This is my closest business associate, Lucian Green. He's joining me at the London meeting and coming along to the Lancashire stop-off just for the ride."

His explanation had more than a whiff of being half true and half spur-of-the-moment invention. The good Mr. Green no doubt was a close associate of some kind, but I was certain from the look on Engel's face that his presence at the back of the aircraft had been as much a surprise to him as to me.

"Pleased to meet you, my dear," Mr. Green said. "I'll be going to your performance on Friday. I've been to several before and I've always most thoroughly enjoyed myself. A good ghost story is right up my street, isn't it, Sebastian?"

Engel raised his eyebrows and nodded, a curious combination of gestures. I said,

"I don't remember seeing you in the audience."

He smiled and looked across at Engel, knowingly. He then fixed his eyes on mine with a gaze that seemed to penetrate right through me. He said,

"I have a special talent for being able to blend in wherever I go, to sit always at the back and look like 'just one of the crowd'. You will have seen me, my dear, but my face will hardly have registered. Isn't that the case Sebastian?"

Engel nodded awkwardly.

His eyes still locked unblinkingly on mine, Green said,

"It must be wonderful to be blessed with an imagination like yours, my dear, to be able to summon voices, ghostly creatures, vile and terrifying aberrations, whole regiments of things possessed from deep in the earth's belly, or from the trees or clouds above – and all with a simple swish of your fingers across a keyboard. What most people would give for such a talent. It must never be lost."

He then bent over and whispered into my ear,

"I sense that you have been considering abandoning the storytelling job which Sebastian has so kindly given you, my dear. I've known you would reach this point right from the beginning so, all of the time, I've been thinking ahead, making provision here and there along the way. I must persuade you not to even think of stopping doing what you do so well, I really must. I will provide you with some excellent reasons for continuing – just leave it with me, my dear, I will provide them in so numerous a form that they will outnumber all of the birds in the sky."

I tried to reply, but no words came. I was transfixed by his gaze. It was as if he'd pinned me to the spot and I was unable to move a muscle until he released me. He then smiled again, a gesture that seemed somehow more imbued with menace than warmth, and it felt as if I was released from being suspended in mid-air, crashing down onto the floor with a bump. All this was impressionistic, of course, I had no evidence that he was in any way trying to impose his will or interfere with my normal thoughts and movements. But there was something about his presence that seemed to immobilise and disorientate me mentally whenever he engaged me eye to eye.

"Are you coming to see the grave with us or staying on board?" Engel asked him.

"Oh, I couldn't possibly intrude on such a special and private moment," Green replied. "I'll finish off my correspondence and then go for a short walk, just to stretch my legs."

He somehow managed to smile pleasantly and unpleasantly at the same time, another curious combination of gestures. Engel nodded and the conversation was clearly over for now. I had never seen him look less than in complete control of any situation, but he looked distinctly uncomfortable with the presence of the extra passenger. Emily, on the other hand, looked strangely alert and receptive, as if there was something in Green's voice that resonated with her. She had been watching him with the same attentive expression that I had noted when she had been listening to the real or imagined 'invisible man' on the packhorse bridge. I found that even more disconcerting than the effect he had had on me.

Twenty minutes or so later we were hovering over the graveyard in Lancashire. The pilot eased the huge machine down into a nearby field and we landed gently on grass that had been untouched by any depth of snow. As we got out it was bitterly cold and grey, but mostly dry. The co-pilot, a jolly and bewhiskered man, helped the children down onto the ground and then Engel led his little party across the couple of hundred yards to the main entrance to the cemetery. He found a map board showing the location of military burials going back to the nineteenth century. He took Emily's hand and said,

"Come on, you can give me some support. This is an emotional event for me. According to the map and the directions my uncle gave me, it's this way."

"Haven't you been before Father?" she asked.

"No, never. It's something I've kept meaning to do and today is the day for all of us."

They walked off under deep grey skies, with William holding onto Emily's other hand and me following behind like a bit of a spare part. We went down one of the long paths through the rich green grass, the cold wind blowing occasional sleet flurries into our faces, as Engel hunted for the airman's grave. We came to a large stone obelisk that had been erected in memory of the soldiers lost in the Crimean War of a century and a half ago. Engel stopped briefly, looked at it and said,

"Amazing how things resonate down the centuries historically. In the news now, in the news then."

I couldn't help thinking that the children were far too young to understand in any meaningful way the significance of his remark or, indeed, to appreciate adequately the nature and importance of his grandfather's sacrifice. But it wasn't my place to offer any thoughts on the matter.

William was in a bit of confusion due to one of his shoelaces having come undone and with a wisdom and a competence beyond her years, Emily bent down to sort things out for him. Finding that his foot was half out of his sock, which in turn was half out of his shoe, she decided wisely to manoeuvre him over to a little bench ten yards away from us. She sat him down on it so that she could get a proper handle on the situation. As we waited for them to sort matters out, Engel was unusually patient and avoided haranguing them. Looking around, he said,

"So many graves, so many dead and so many who are not even here but thrown away as ashes. None of it makes any sense beyond your own family line. I can't relate to any of these people, only to the flesh and blood that was the precursor to my own existence. That's the most that's understandable."

Looking up at the old stone chapel a little way off, I asked a question that would have come naturally in Ireland but not here, not with him and not at this moment. I felt I might have stepped well over the line as soon as I had asked it. I said,

"Do you believe in God, or any religion and things?"

103

To my surprise and relief he didn't take it as impertinence, although his reply ended on a characteristically gruff note. He said,

"God? The idea of someone or something that has existed forever without being created? It's an idea that's hard to get your head round. As I'm here and didn't create myself, as indeed was the case with all of my predecessors, then I have to assume that something extraordinary started the whole process off. But what it was and whether it was good or bad, well that's another matter. It's the kind of question Mr. Green is very preoccupied with – maybe you should discuss it with him some time."

Mr. Green, with his cold smiles and more than a hint of something sinister, was probably the last person I would want to ask about anything, but it was interesting that Engel should mention him in such a context. In any case, I had no need of such a discussion in relation to my own beliefs, which were as decided as they would ever be and were in many ways similar to Engel's – the main difference being that I didn't believe it possible for whatever had created existence to be evil. My thoughts on such matters had been deeply troubling for a period during my adolescence. But I'd resolved the issue as best I could by deciding that, while the *idea* of an uncreated creator who had always existed didn't make any sense and I and everything else were therefore impossible, such a conclusion was contradicted by the fact that I, the world and the universe *did* exist. Therefore, it was quite possible there was a God or whatever, but a total mystery as to how he, she or it could have pulled off such a stunning magical trick as to exist without ever having been brought into existence. That was as far as I'd got and that was the extent to which my belief in the Almighty was defined – a set of conclusions remarkably similar to Engel's. For the children, however, I played safe and drew upon what I assumed to be the overlaps between my Irish Catholic upbringing and their mother's High Anglicanism. I didn't feel it was my place to do anything else.

Emily and William came skipping back over and they all linked hands again. We walked on for another few minutes until the area where the map had shown the grave to be came into view. Engel told the little ones that the headstone was known to have had a plane carved into it. He asked them to run on ahead and see if they could find it for us and they skipped off happily with the innocence of children untouched by the heavy burden of death that hung all around us. I said,

"My grandfather was everything to me, but I was lucky enough to have him around for all of my childhood and beyond. It's a shame that so many children are deprived of their parents and grandparents by wars."

He nodded and said,

"My grandpa's as far back as I can trace my reason for being alive in any meaningful sense – he's still in the living memory of the surviving oldest members of my family. I'm alive because of him and my grandmother and I'd like to have met them. Coming here is the nearest I can ever get to that in his case. Outside of my business concerns, I owe nothing to anybody but my own parents, my grandparents – and their parents – and Emily and William, those are the only non-financial debts that I have to pay. I'm paying one off by coming here today – and by bringing the children to see him with me."

His musings were brought to a halt by three short words. The children had come running back and ironically, given their circuitous travels around the gravestones, had stopped a mere eight feet away from where they had started – and from us. Emily said,

"Here it is."

We looked down and there indeed was a simple gravestone in the military style of the cemetery bearing the name George Engel, pilot, US air force, 1914-1944. There was an aircraft carved into it as Engel had been told. It looked like the amateur work of a friend, possibly a fellow airman, and had most probably been added after the headstone had been erected. Engel said,

"How small it is, how very small. No wonder it was so hard to spot. I must do something about that."

I said,

"You three should be alone, this is a special moment, a family thing. I'll go and take a walk up to the chapel and wait there until you're ready to leave."

He nodded, and put a hand on the shoulder of each child, drawing them close to him. I smiled and started to walk off. My thoughts turned to the loss of my own grandparents and of how deeply that had affected me. I felt the need to sit down somewhere quiet for a few moments as all of the still raw emotions came back into my head. I walked up the slope to the simple stone porch of the chapel and found that the door was slightly ajar. I went in and was instantly grateful for the old building's shelter from the cold breeze and the feeling of quiet calm that seemed to envelop me as soon as the heavy wooden door creaked shut. The silence that the thick stone walls engendered made me feel I was in the presence of something benign and soothing. I sat down and remained in perfect stillness for a few minutes, my mind almost in a trance as I let the calm of the building seep into every corner of my thoughts. For a little while at least, it consoled me for past losses and quietened all of my anxieties about the malign influences at work on the children back at the estate.

I was startled suddenly by a cough from the shadows at the back of the chapel and turned round so quickly that I almost fell out of the pew. A figure rose and walked slowly into the shafted light from one of the larger windows. It said,

"I'm terribly sorry if I startled you. I come here once a week to pray for the souls of all of my parishioners who are buried here. You looked so deep in thought when you came in that I didn't want to disturb you. Unfortunately, coughs come when they please and often when we would least wish them."

He was a benign and gentle-looking priest, Catholic or High Anglican by the look of things, and he must have been in his mid-seventies, possibly even a little older.

I smiled and said,

"No problem. I didn't realise anyone else was here and was frit, that's all. The fact that the door was open should have told me that there might be other people inside."

He said,

"You are with the gentleman who arrived in the helicopter?"

"Yes," I replied.

He said,

"Sorry, I don't mean to sound like the Inquisition. I noticed the two of you together when I arrived – and the children."

"He's my employer," I replied. "He's come to find his grandfather's grave and to show his children where it is."

"It's the American airman's grave – I saw him looking at it through the window, so I assume that he too is an American. It's interesting how far some people travel to visit the last resting places of their forebears - and such a complicated business."

He smiled and sat down in the pew behind me.

"What do you mean by complicated?" I asked.

"Oh, so many different motives," he replied. "Some good, some not so good, more often than not a mix of all sorts of things. Some just want to give the family tree a visual dimension and old photographs and graves do the trick. Others have heard a lot about a grandparent who died before they were born and feel they almost know the person – they hope that where a grave exists visiting it will be at least a little bit equivalent to meeting them. Then there are those who have done well in life who come to see if the grandparent's grave is grand enough, or whether it needs a monument or two, a more impressive headstone, or whatever is thought to be a more adequate testimony to the high social standing of the visitor and the line from which he's descended. It is usually a he."

He smiled, but I had the distinct feeling that within the way he emphasised his words he had implied that my rich transatlantic employer was likely to be at the less commendable end of the spectrum of possible motivations. He got up and walked over to a window overlooking the spot where I had left Engel with the children. He said,

"Your employer appears to be measuring the plot. Yes, a very efficient man who knew what he was doing when he came here. He appears to have brought a tape measure. I assume a grander monument is being planned. Well, well, it will add to the existing architectural grandeur of the cemetery, no doubt."

He turned back towards me and smiled again. He said quietly and gently,

"I'm intruding too much on your memories and past grief. I've had my weekly time with the dead of the parish, so I'll leave you in peace."

He walked with a measured, rheumatic slowness to the door. As he stepped outside, he paused and looking at me both pointedly and caringly said,

"I know goodness when I see it in people and I see it in you. There are those who will try and make you their instrument, corrupt everything you stand for and use you for purposes that are intensely evil, and they will have a power that you will find almost impossible to resist. But you must resist them to save yourself and others. I know little of that probably makes sense now, but it will."

He smiled again and then was gone.

Momentarily stunned by what he'd said, I sat in motionless silence for a few minutes. Then I got up and hurried out into the grey light of the graveyard. From my position at the top of the mound I tried to spot the priest as he walked back to whatever church he'd come from. I wanted to question him further, to find out in more detail what he'd meant. There was no sign of anyone other than Engel and the children. A panic came over me as I wondered if I'd had been speaking to another ghost – or, even worse, imagining that I'd been in such a conversation. Then I calmed down with the thought that I'd been sitting in shock long enough for even a rheumatic to have walked back down into the cover of the leafy evergreens and disappeared from sight. I looked over to where I'd left Engel and saw him busy on his smartphone to somebody, in no rush to find me. He'd set the children busy, tidying up the grave. My mind was too much on edge to be able to go back into the chapel and return to the silent contemplation that the priest had accidentally destroyed. I felt I needed something to temporarily distract me from his strange and puzzling warning, which was a little too much to take on top of my existing worries about the children and the malign influences at work on them back at the estate. I decided to wander over to a large, curious-looking family tomb that dominated everything around it. I would see what I could discover about the lives of the people who lay beneath it from the inscriptions lining its sides. That would give me something to keep my mind off things until Engel was ready for us all to leave. I would wait until I had a glass of wine inside me back at the cottage before I tried to work out what on earth the priest could have meant.

As I meandered over to the ornate tomb, I had the uncomfortable feeling that I could hear whispering; at first on either side of me as I walked along the path, but then all around – in the branches above, in the bushes below and even among the birds that swooped high in the sky or perched haphazardly on the tops of gravestones. What initially was quite hushed and discreet became rapidly louder and louder, until what had been a whisper became a series of chattering, gossiping conversations that appeared to be conducting themselves without any human intervention. I had the distinct impression that I was the focus of all of them. As I got nearer to the monument, it felt as if the occupants of the graves beneath had joined in as well and my ears were filled with the sound of laughing and joking, only the jokes all seemed to have my name in them and the humour had a sour, cutting edge. I stopped dead in my tracks and decided that my imagination was either working overtime, perhaps inadvertently stimulated by the priest's comments, or that there was something indeed strange and unpleasant about the tomb and its occupants which made a visit inadvisable. I turned round and started to walk back towards the chapel, but, if anything, the voices became louder with each step. I felt more frightened than I had ever been in my life and began almost to run. The voices now were right in my face, speaking in languages that I had never heard, with words spat out rather than spoken. Then all of the different words became one and that was of real and frightening concern because the one word was my Christian name. I felt almost physically sick as that single, familiar set of consonants and vowels was spewed, spat, belched and roared into my ears. The cacophony of voices seemed to grow louder by the second and then to spin round and round the outside of my head as if I was in some Dantean circle of hell. I walked faster still, but that only provoked them more, with a deafening train of unseen pursuers shouting, hissing and sneering my name as if it was verbal excrement, which they wanted to hurl at me from every possible direction. Inevitably, I failed to keep an eye out for broken and uneven sections of path and tripped, falling heavily into the grass at the side of a grave, my head narrowly missing a broken and jagged headstone. The voices seemed to gather and rise up above my prone body and then hurtle down directly into my brain with a huge, thought-crushing roar. Soon the only thing I could think or feel or hear was their violent rage bouncing continuously and unbearably off the insides of my skull, to the point where it seemed as if the signal between my eyes and my brain had been turned off and I could see nothing of the world around, my only contact with anything being the maelstrom within my head.

But then things took another, even more frightening turn as my vision suddenly returned. Seven crows hurled themselves down from the branches of nearby trees and began pecking with knife-like precision into the skin of my arms and hands as I tried to protect my face. Simultaneously, the voices inside me egged them on. Try as I might, I couldn't fight off the birds' flailing claws and beaks. Unable to bear any more, I screamed so loudly and piercingly that anyone within a quarter of a mile must have been able to hear me. Engel's 'associate', Lucian Green, appeared as if from nowhere and as soon as he arrived, the birds stopped attacking. As one they fled back into the high branches from which they had swooped. Simultaneously, all of the voices in my head sighed and fell silent, as if whatever had been driving them had fled with the birds.

A woman's voice said,

"I've seen that once before."

I looked up through the haze that clouded my eyes as my vision tried to return to normal. Gradually the stern face of a middle-aged blonde woman became clear. Apparently, she and her husband had been thirty yards or so away, but on their knees and all but invisible while they tidied the grave of her father. Green so far had said little, other than to ask how I was. He was staring up at the birds which, in turn, had their eyes riveted on his.

"What do you mean?" I asked the woman.

"I saw someone attacked like that by crows when I was little. They were less lucky than you and quite badly cut in the face. My father chased the birds away. He said the crows had been taken over, that they were possessed – the devil's servants, he called them."

Green turned to her and said in a sharp, dismissive voice,

"Don't be so silly, woman, if there was a devil, he'd want to ride on the back of far grander birds or beasts than crows."

She said,

"Oh, really, I thought maybe I was looking at him, they seemed to know you when you appeared from nowhere and fled like they had a demon on their tails."

Her husband took her arm and said,

"Come on, Martha, this isn't the place to get into a fight with people, everybody who comes here has lost someone and that's enough of a cross to bear without having an argument as well."

She cursed under her breath and gave Green a look that would have withered Goliath as her husband guided her gently but firmly back to the grave they'd been tending. She shouted,

"You'd better be careful, young lady, my father said that when the devil sent carrion crows after someone, he was after their souls, not their bodies. That weirdo looks as if he's after both with you."

Green simply turned away, laughing contemptuously and bent down to help me get back on my feet.

He said,

"Come on, my dear, up you get, it could have been worse, you're not as badly cut as you think. The pilot will have a first-aid kit and will be able to patch you up. Come on, you're a little toughie, if I may use the common English slang – Sebastian doesn't take wimps on his books."

Almost simultaneously Engel came running down the path with the children. He said,

"Sorry, we were delayed, William had wandered off while we were tidying the grave and got himself lost. What on earth happened?"

The pilot and co-pilot had also come running over by this time, having heard the scream from as far away as the helicopter, and Engel told them to take the children back to the aircraft while he established what had been going on. Once the children were out of earshot, Green told him what he had seen and I filled in the rest. Green omitted the detail about the way the birds and the voices stopped attacking me as soon as he appeared, so I filled it in for him. Engel gave him a knowing look that also communicated serious displeasure. A flicker of a smile touched the edges of Green's mouth and he said,

"Pure coincidence I'm sure, Sebastian," and then turned away and started to follow the others.

"What does he mean?" I asked, sensing that an accusation had been made and denied.

Engel said,

"Lucian Green is a man of many mysteries in what he says and what he thinks. Perhaps we should just be thankful that he was on hand to scare the birds away before you got badly hurt. Are you together enough to walk back, or do you want a minute or two to rest?"

In Engel's frantic macho business world a minute or two probably seemed like a long time, even when the victim had been through a major psychological trauma, so I bit my tongue and resisted the temptation to tell him to have more consideration. I am, as Green had observed in his condescending way, a little toughie, so I simply nodded and said I would walk back to the helicopter with him. He said,

"Come on then, we'd better get back to the copter if I'm to make my London appointment tonight. I'll have my doctor take a look at you when you get back to your cottage in case you need any jabs."

As we hurried along, the 'little toughie' in me started to be pushed into the background as the terrifying nature of what I'd just experienced came back fully into focus. I said,

"This is all beginning to really frighten me, the thing with the children and the real or imagined Earl, and now this. It's as if I'm no longer in charge of my own ghost stories, as if I've been demoted to being a character in one being written by someone else."

"These ethereal things that worry you," he said, "the malign presences you think the children see and the voices of a few minutes ago, maybe they do really all exist and you're simply sensitive to them in a way you didn't realise before, I don't know. On the other hand, you have a fearsomely inventive imagination and it may simply be going into overdrive on occasion and causing you to see stories that are forming in your mind as if they were happening to you – and the birds may simply have been in a freak mood and out for a fight with anything that came in range. I've seen many weird things over the years and I don't have any explanations for them. Sometimes things resist all attempts at rational understanding and the only thing to do is to put them out of your mind and get on with life."

"It's going to be difficult to put today's nightmare out of my mind."

He said,

"Just be thankful that little episode is over and we're going away from this place, and leave it at that. I don't want you freaking out on me – you've got a whole schedule of storytelling events to get through over the next few weeks. Be strong, be smart, just regard today's little happening as something you can weave into another story. Use it as raw material – that way you can think of it as a gift instead of a nightmare."

I didn't react to his dismissive little homily, not least because it didn't ring true. I was sure I hadn't been imagining his implied accusation that Green had been responsible in some unknown way for what had just happened to me – and his mysterious 'associate's' response had been both strange and ambiguous, to say the least. I felt there was something that both men weren't telling me about the likely cause of my terrifying ordeal. Certainly Engel had a strong interest in me carrying on with the storytelling job he'd given me and I suspected that to be the main reason driving his desire to gloss over things. He was possibly worried that I might be put off writing ghost stories on the grounds that they would just keep reminding me of today's unwanted adventure. My tales' deeply puzzling, but apparently essential role as part of the pre-dinner party entertainment to help amuse and court those useful to his business would then be lost. Green also had made clear his own interest in my continuing storytelling, although I couldn't tell whether that was simply a penchant for ghostly tales or something of an undefined and more calculating nature. He was an enigma in every way. He had an almost sulphurous air of power and influence about him. It was in his eyes, as ruthless as those I'd once seen in a painting of Cecil, the Elizabethan spymaster – the last eyes a man might see before his death. He was the first person I'd come across whom my bullish employer clearly didn't feel he could boss around or sweet-talk. The very fact that he'd been able to board Engel's very personal helicopter, apparently without having been invited or bothering to announce himself, was a statement all on its own. But the source of his influence over Engel was as yet a mystery. Perhaps, I thought, more might be revealed on the return flight.

I kept an anxious eye on all of the birds high up in the trees as we headed back to the aircraft, but none showed the slightest sign of even noticing my presence. As I climbed back on board, I was startled by an unexpected voice behind me.

"The woman who is pursued by dark forces that ultimately become part of her art is a wonderful story waiting to be written, don't you think? I do hope you find a way of writing today's excitement into your next performance, my dear."

I turned round to see Lucian Green following me into the cabin. Again, he appeared to have come from nowhere. Before I could say anything, he had swept past me in his grand fashion and retreated to his personal space at the back. The fact that his head went down straight away as his attention disappeared into his computer told me that was the beginning and the end of the conversation. I had the unnerving feeling of somehow or other being a pawn in his hands. I wondered if maybe he had a role in the whole storytelling thing which I hadn't been told about and if now he was even trying to shape the tales that I told. My imagination began to run ahead of itself and I speculated whether the whole event in the cemetery had been some kind of theatrical exercise to impress on me the power of a story that for some reason he wanted telling – a spectacular and terrifying show he'd created via auto-suggestion, general playing around with my mind and that of the crows, who knows. The way he'd locked onto my eyes for so long when first speaking to me made me wonder whether he'd been engaged in some form of subtle hypnosis, one that had begun to do its highly potent work while I was visiting the grandiose old tomb. That might explain the voices, but the birds were a different cup of tea altogether. If he could hypnotise them as well, that really would make him a frightening man.

The pilot spent a few minutes temporarily patching the thankfully minor wounds that the crows had inflicted and then scuttled off back to the cockpit under the imperious gaze of Engel, who was leaving him in no doubt about his wish for us to get moving. I closed my eyes as the helicopter took off, not daring to look out of the window until we were once more high in the sky with some apparent certainty that we would stay there, instead of hurtling down at breakneck speed to death and destruction. When I next looked, we were heading over vast swathes of hilly moorland, all part of the Queen's great estates in her dual role as Duke of Lancaster, or so the hostess told me when she came round to see if I or the children would like anything to drink. Both of the little ones had fallen fast asleep, exhausted by their hyperactivity in the cemetery and the excitement of their helicopter flight with daddy. We decided that it would be best not to disturb them. I wondered what they had made of seeing me covered in cuts from the crows' attack, but Engel had ensured that they were ushered away quickly enough to avoid hearing any gory details. Presumably they thought that I'd simply fallen over and that was that.

When we arrived back at the Hall, Engel ordered the pilot to land in the same place as before, which meant that, in effect, I was dropped off at my own front door. He said he would be a few minutes while he collected some papers for his London engagement from his study and then they must leave straight away if he was to make it on time. Lucian Green had been all but invisible during the flight, communicating with no-one on board and very much engrossed in his laptop at the back. To my surprise he suddenly emerged from his purdah, joining Engel and me as we left the aircraft. Looking over at the cottage, he said,

"So, Sebastian, this is the site where the blighted Earl met his demons face to face and didn't live to tell the tale, how fascinating."

He said to me,

"Sebastian has told me remarkable things about the Hall and its past, my dear - and your little home and what happened there has been the most intriguing part of the story. I must admire your bravery for agreeing to live in a building that was host to such a strange event. What I'd like very much is if you'd just let me have a look at it for a minute or two while Sebastian gets his papers together."

"You do that, but we mustn't leave even a second after quarter to if we're to get there on time," Engel said brusquely. The two men exchanged glances which were even more mystifying than before. If I could turn looks into words, it would seem that Engel was saying that he knew very well what his 'associate' was up to and some or all of it did not meet with either his support or his approval, even if he lacked the power to do anything about it. He then turned on his heels and strode off across the snow towards the Hall, his patent leather shoes crunching fiercely through the frozen crystals. Green smiled at me, a strange, characteristically ambiguous gesture that was lacking in all warmth. It was reinforced by the snow-coldness of his eyes and seemed more like a command – "I'm being friendly, now you be friendly and show me this place." He had the look of a man who was capable of doing anything in order to enforce his will. He said,

"Lead the way, my dear."

Rationally or irrationally, my earlier speculations about the strange nature of his influence over me caused me to avoid his eyes in case he was indeed the hypnotist I feared. I said,

"There's really not very much to see, it's rather small and very old, a slightly strange atmosphere as you might expect given its history, but that hasn't bothered me until now."

As we walked into the little cottage garden, he said,

"Until now – does that mean that today's events have changed your feelings about your little home, or about writing any more ghost stories even?"

"It's shaken me up, as you'd expect. You saw what happened, Mr. Green, even if you say you didn't hear the voices. I think I'm in some kind of delayed shock. I can't say I feel very inclined to sit down in a chair and dream up any more scary stories right at this moment."

He said,

"If Sebastian was right, the Earl was found face down somewhere around here, is that not correct?"

Green's diction was itself somewhat correct and his accent difficult to place. It wasn't American, British, Irish, South African, Australasian or any of the other national variations of English with which I was familiar. I said,

"From what I've been told, he would have been discovered pretty much in this part of the garden, yes."

"How fascinating, a man who flew too close to his demons and fell to earth with his wings on fire. You really do live in the most fitting place for a writer of ghost stories, my dear – and a writer of ghost stories you must remain. Sebastian and I have too much resting on your delivering what you promised for it to be possible for you to stop. Besides, no rational person would want to give up the kind of money he's paying you. No, as I said in the cemetery, you must regard what happened today as raw material that you can remould and recycle into a new story. In fact, I explicitly want you to do that for this coming Friday. Change the characters around as you like and don't make any of them recognisable, be as creative as you wish with the plot, but keep the key events. I'm sure Sebastian will say exactly the same, if he hasn't already done so."

"I can't guarantee anything until I manage to at least begin to get my head round what happened earlier," I replied, still carefully avoiding looking into his steel-cold eyes, "and that's even before you start taking into account the children's belief that the Earl is alive and kicking and talking to them on a regular basis. That's enough for me to try and deal with in itself. I presume Mr. Engel has told you all about that?"

He didn't respond immediately, but stood looking at the cottage as if he were surveying its every stone. He turned around suddenly and transferred his laser-like gaze to the birds in the trees around the edge of the garden. To my astonishment, as one they began squawking and crowing as if in terror for their lives and shot up into the sky, leaving the branches bare and silent. He laughed and turned back round to me, saying,

"A classic case of mass hysteria – one short-sighted crow thinks it sees a cat at the foot of its tree and panics all of its companions into flight. Birds are the strangest of creatures, my dear, and one should never get overconcerned about their behaviour. It would have been something similar today that caused those crows to attack you – a case of mistaken identity or heavens knows what. No, you must start writing again and you will. You must write today's events into your next story, as I have advised you – you must. I know a thing or two about storytelling, I am in part a master storyteller and I consider you my apprentice. So let me give you some useful advice about how to deal with this fear that you seem to have, some basic psychology if you like. Stories have power, so imagine that each new story you write has the power to keep the Earl you worry so much about at bay – and believe me, they will. They really will have that power. The children will remain undisturbed by him as long as you write and it will be your writing that is buying the safety of their innocent souls. I guarantee it, as surely as if I had caused their haunting simply to bring us to this point – which, of course, I would never dream of doing. So yes, believe that your writing will protect them and it will be so, and you will be writing the best tales that you have ever produced. But that power can work the other way as well – give up on your writing and performing, leave poor Sebastian bereft, with no tales to be told and the Earl will reign supreme on the estate. The children will be his and you will have failed them totally. You will have given him a free hand to continue moulding the little ones for the dark and dangerous roles he has in mind for them. Think the same way about the voices you heard today – write as required and they will stay away, renege on your commitment to us and they will come back, fortyfold. It's all a fantasy, I know, another story that I am creating just for you, but believe it and everything will be well. Believe it and believe me."

He smiled vacuously and said,

"You see, I've kept my promise just like I said I would. I've given you several important reasons for not giving up your storytelling job. The one thing which can always be said about me, my dear, is that I'm a man of my word."

He smiled again and this time his smile was even more devoid of warmth than before, if such a thing were possible. If anything, it seemed more like a warning. Looking across towards the Hall and the helicopter, he said,

"Sebastian is coming back with his beloved papers, so I must now leave you. Think carefully on what I have said, my dear, and I look forward to your next performance on Friday. I will be there – and so will you."

With that he was off, his fierce strides across the snow resembling the march of a military man. I had never before encountered anyone with such a cold presence. He was ambiguous in his every act, from his smiles to his relationship with the birds, which might be either strangely controlling or as innocent and explicable in simple terms, as he had suggested. There was no way of proving things either way. That seemed to be the source of his power, his ability to create situations in which he could unleash fear, panic or threats behind a smokescreen of ambiguity. I couldn't work out what on earth he was, a masterly manipulator of human and animal psychology, some kind of a hypnotist, something supernatural, or simply a highly skilled bluffer or a conman. Certainly, he'd tried to mess with my mind regarding the Earl and the children and the writing of my tales – and if that failed, he'd planted very firmly in my brain the prospect of losing instantly the king's ransom which Engel was paying me if I suddenly gave up the whole business. With the children, it sounded as if he was implying one of two things: either that he'd in some way been responsible for their haunting, whether it be real or imagined, and could stop it immediately if I obeyed his wishes; or, even if he wasn't directly its cause, that he had the power to stop the Earl, or whoever else might be responsible for the children's strange state of mind, from continuing to persecute them. The manipulative, blackmailing aspect of all of that would at least give the children's disturbing experiences and behaviour some bizarre meaning, even if I found it difficult to regard it as a credible explanation for what had been going on.

But what was most disturbing was the realisation that, by one means or another, he was bringing me directly under his power. The words of the priest were now beginning to have meaning.

CHAPTER EIGHT

The morning after the airborne visit to the cemetery and its various dramas saw both of the children grounded. Emily had started with a flu-like virus and William also had a temperature, so it was decided to keep them in bed under the close eye of the head housekeeper. Having unexpected free time on my hands, I resolved to try and blow away the frightening chaos and confusion of the previous day's bizarre events by taking a walk. Looking down on the estate was a low, brooding hill with an unpromising name but a fascinating legend of doomed lovers attached to it. Such bleakness was in tune with my mood and the path to the summit looked walkable. An overnight thaw had reduced the already shallow snow by half. Coated and booted to the point where I was generating as much heat as a small power station, I set off on what proved to be a gentle and easy climb.

When I reached the top, the cold breeze bit into the still fresh but thankfully small scars resulting from my one-sided wrestling match with the bully-boy crows and I wrapped my scarf around my face to protect it. Beneath a tall, leafless, wind-bent tree I found a large stone plaque with a verse carved into it:

"They walked and talked these lovers, in a dream,

Up hills, through valleys and over flowing streams.
Their souls united nightly, on this cursed hill,
Until the lord of vengeance
Came swiftly for the kill."

Their story was in a little booklet which I bought from the post office in the nearby village when I first arrived. She was the wife of the lord of the manor and he was the blacksmith's son. They fell 'truly, madly, deeply' in love and used to meet under the tree at night during the spring of 1614. They'd go at it like rabbits for a couple of hours, then creep back home as if nothing had happened. This little performance went on for several weeks until the wily lord was tipped off by a local shepherd. He'd heard some pleasureful moans which were nothing like the sheep's "baas" that he was used to and had gone to investigate. So off went the lord with his sword in his hand, following his unsuspecting wife up the hill to the very spot on which I was now standing. He waited a little while, then heard their cries of illegal delight. Moving closer, he saw their antics in more detail than he'd wanted or dreamt. So, he stormed over in a fit of blind rage and pinned their naked bodies to the ground with his sword. They died in each other's arms. Being a man without morals or mercy, he dumped the blame on the shepherd who'd tipped him off. The poor man was arrested for murder and strung up on the same tree under which the lying lord had killed the couple.

And that's why the hill is called Killer's Hill. Locals say it's not a place where you linger at night and that the lord's ghost still haunts the spot, forever damned and forever doomed to relive the moment of his crime. For me, it was a possible source of inspiration for one of the two tales I'd promised to deliver on the Friday of that week and I carefully noted as many atmospheric details of the location as seemed relevant. The phantasmagoria in the cemetery had frightened the living daylights out of me and would have deterred forever a normal and sane individual from even half considering the writing, never mind telling, of any more ghost stories lest she terrify herself into an early grave. But, in the balancing of one thing against another, yesterday's nightmare was outweighed by my fear of tomorrow's unknown. What Green might do, should I renege on the storytelling schedule which he seemed so determined should proceed, was an unknown that was at best unsettling. I had no doubt that it was not advisable to seriously annoy him and that weighed heavily in my calculations. I had no idea precisely what he was, but I had become convinced that, somehow or other, he had got into my mind on the flight over to Lancashire and made me susceptible to auto-suggested illusions. In retrospect, the whole experience of the voices seemed as much artificial as it was terrifying and Engel's nods and winks appeared to make his 'associate' the prime suspect for its creation. His party trick with the birds outside my cottage had convinced me that he had also been responsible for the violence of the cemetery crows – through some strange ability to control the minds of small creatures as well as those of humans. Whether he had been responsible for, or was simply exploiting, the haunting of the children as a means of trying to manipulate me into doing his will was a matter on which the jury remained out. Hypnotist, sorcerer, psychotic fantasist or whatever, he was clearly both possessed of dangerous, exotic skills and determined that I should perform on Friday as planned. I had never encountered anything like yesterday's experience, or anyone as quietly sinister and menacing as him, and for the moment the wisest course of action seemed to be to keep him happy while I tried to work out a way to escape from his influence.

When I got back to the cottage I felt exhausted, probably more as a result of the previous day's unwanted excitement and my fraught deliberations over my continuing storytelling activities than the length of the walk. I slumped down into my little swivelling chair and fired up the internet. I interrogated Google for almost an hour, trying to find out as much as I could about the strange Mr. Green. There were a number of links and references to him, but, bizarrely, all turned out to be dead ends. It was almost as if every piece of information on him had been written in invisible ink. Frustrated, I went upstairs to rest for a while before lunch and promptly fell into a deep sleep.

I was awoken at midday by the repeated ringing of a hand-bell. At first, this seemed annoying rather than strange and I attempted to bury my head in a pillow. Then, as the ringing continued, it gradually registered on my exhausted semi-consciousness that it was not early morning. The sound I was hearing was not my cheap, old-style alarm clock, but the metallic ringing of a brass or copper bell. I dragged myself up into a sitting position to try and work out what was happening. As I did so, the ringing stopped. I wondered for a moment or two whether I'd been the unsuspecting host of a waking dream, but then heard a clattering noise from downstairs. That was odd. If I'd been of a forgetful disposition and had left a window open through which a cat could get in, then fine, a small furry creature would be the most likely suspect. But I was not normally forgetful. Whatever had caused the noise had got in by illegal means or, in the case of Engel, by another abuse of his rights of ownership of my little home.

Gingerly, in case I had a burglar, mad axe murderer or something three times worse at loose in the house, I slipped out of bed and crept barefooted out of the room and down the eighteenth-century staircase, being careful to avoid all of the creaky stairboards. I tiptoed over to the half-open kitchen door and peered through the gap between the hinges into the room beyond. The noises had definitely appeared to be coming from in there, but there was no sign of anyone, burglar or ghost. Unwisely, given my complete lack of armament or assistance, I pushed the door delicately open and entered, but again, there was nothing to be seen. There appeared to be something wrong with my vision in so far as the room kept slipping in and out of focus. As it did so, I became aware of something curious – the slightly out-of-focus room had none of the cluttered furnishings and technology of my kitchen. The only items of note were an old wooden dresser, a large storage trunk and a primitive stone sink. No sooner had I established what each item was than they disappeared and the modern-day kitchen came back into fully focussed view. I closed my eyes tightly for a good ten seconds and then opened them again. I hoped that this would magically ensure that I was fully awake and make the disorienting view from the past – presumably an imaginary one – disappear. I was disappointed. The first thing I saw when I opened them was the historical kitchen again, this time in even greater detail and now fully in focus, with the cold, stone flags glistening from having been freshly scrubbed. The door into the garden was open – not the present door, but a stout oak door with a heavy iron lock. I could hear the sound of someone singing outside – it was a woman's voice, calm, contented. The song sounded as old as the room looked and it felt very much as if somehow, I'd stepped back into the past, or the past had stepped forwards into my present. I crept cautiously across the wet and slippy flags and looked through the open door into the garden. It too seemed different, more of a textbook kitchen garden from a previous century than the inadequately tended remains of an ornamental garden that were the present reality. It was also bathed in brilliant, midsummer sunlight, which was more than a little puzzling. Part of one of the beds looked to have been just dug up. A single worm-eaten carrot lay abandoned at its side, but clearly a large batch of others had been removed, presumably for washing and cooking. There was no sign of the songstress, however, and indeed her voice had fallen silent.

I heard suddenly behind me the sound of a sharp knife rapidly and repeatedly impacting on wood and turned round to find that a table had appeared in the centre of the room. It was made out of solid, square planks of oak and bore the scars of a hundred chopping knives. Some of the carrots were laid out on it ready to be cut up and one had been chopped from top to tail. As I'd turned around, it seemed as if I'd caught a glimpse of a female figure disappearing out of the kitchen into the small downstairs passage and I hurried as fast as I could after it, my bare feet slapping against the flagstones. The passage also was now as it had been in the past and as soon as I ran into it, I hit hard an immovable object that turned out to be a smiling man in the finery of his times. The smile was not pleasant and reminded me more than anything of Lucian Green. He said nothing, but grabbed my arm and marched me out of the cottage to where his horse stood ready saddled and munching a carrot that the kitchen maid had just given it. He swung up onto it, then pulled me up behind him before I could even begin to run away. The horse set off at a gallop and I was forced to put my arms around my kidnapper and hang on for dear life. We shot off down the estate's drive, out of the main gates and off in the direction of Killer's Hill.

I saw little along the way, my eyes being shut in sheer terror at the thought of falling off and hitting my head on a stone, or breaking a limb. At last we drew to a halt and I saw that we were on the very top of the hill, at exactly the spot where I had been standing earlier. He jumped down onto the damp ground, then grabbed me round the waist and pulled me down beside him. As I looked out on the wild beauty of the moors below, he suddenly took me in his arms and gave me a long, lingering kiss. At first, it was a pure delight of the divine senses and I felt as if I wanted it to never end. But then something strange started to happen. It seemed as if the gentle hug of his warm arms around me began to tighten fiercely until it was so compacting of my ribs that I feared they'd break. Simultaneously, what had started out as a kiss turned into a bite that was so painful I started to cry. I managed to pull my face away from his, but his hands had now slid up to my neck and he was slowly and cruelly choking me. I was by then wandering in and out of consciousness. I tried to scream but couldn't. His face seemed weirdly blurred, as if I was seeing it through the bottom of a wine bottle. Then my head rolled back as my grip on consciousness began to fade rapidly and all I could see was the brilliant blue of the summer sky, with the sun half visible through a low-sitting cloud. Everything began to spin, as if I was undergoing anaesthesia. The half-sun became a whirling dot, and the vast sky and legions of thin cloud flew round in tandem with it at ever-increasing speed. Ultimately, everything flipped over from wildly spinning lines of light to complete darkness and silence. The silence was pregnant with something menacing and, apparently still in some strange state of consciousness, I waited in fear to find out what it was. It wasn't long in coming. I heard what sounded like a deep intake of breath and then a young man humming a tune. There was something cruel in his voice that spoke louder than words. After less than a minute he began to sing a doggerel verse to the same tune. The words were as cruel as the voice. He sang,

"If you kiss on Killer's Hill,
The Killer will,
He'll kill you.
He'll tear you
Limb from limb,
Very grim.
So if you've kissed
For foolish bliss
Then come what may
This very day
The Killer will,
He'll kill you."

I wanted to run, hide, anything, but I didn't seem to have any existence other than consciousness. I could feel no body, had no arms or legs to move and could see nothing other than total darkness. The voice laughed softly and said,

"Yes, that's right, you're dead, killed by my hands. Dead, alone with me, for me to deal with as I wish. You're descending to the ultimate hell, with a man who knows no mercy and was shown none. Now you're mine, for all time. Just think what that's going to be like."

He laughed softly again. Instead of fear, I felt outrage. What did he mean descending into hell? What had I done to deserve being in any 'hell' and who was he to lord it over me? As with my horrifying experience in the graveyard, I suspected that something had got into my mind and was trying to break my will and leave me as a terrified, malleable wreck open to the dictates of the likes of Green. It was trying to frighten me half to death with an imaginary murder and a hell that was entirely a fiction being written within my skull. I was determined to break free, to take charge of my own thoughts again and expel whatever it was that was doing this. I remembered my own ghost story about the woman being dragged towards a bonfire by unseen hands controlled by forces within her head. As I appeared to have become a character in someone else's story, I decided to do what my own character did and that was seize back control of my mind. I concentrated on the voice and willed it into silence. As I did so, it began to fade and to start fiercely cursing as it did so. As it grew weaker and weaker, my consciousness of the world around me began gradually to return. Suddenly my body felt connected and alive again, the darkness gave way to the daylight and my vision returned. I opened my eyes to find myself lying on the same bed on which I had gone to sleep an hour or two earlier.

Rubbing my eyes and pulling myself up into a sitting position, I couldn't decide at first whether I had simply had a nightmare, or whether I had indeed been in real danger of being killed by dark, psychological or spiritual forces that had somehow got into my head. The fact that the horseman's smile had been identical to Green's was particularly chilling and I remembered the suspicion that the whole experience had somehow been 'injected' into my head to leave me as a biddable, scared 'servant'. That would make it much easier for Green to get me to do exactly as he wanted with the old storytelling lark. But, as I came to more and more and went downstairs to make myself a cup of tea, it seemed that the only sensible conclusion which I could reach was that it had all been just a bad dream. It had riffed on Green and Killer's Hill as prompts taken from my most recent adventures. What it had done, however, was give me material for another ghost story and it also gave me the opportunity to avoid following Green's instructions slavishly. I would use the graveyard episode as part of the first tale I would be telling on Friday, but I would blend it in with the Killer's Hill material and make a single tale that would include what he required, but much more besides. If he objected to any of the additional material, I would simply point out that he had been a prompt for one of the characters in the second part of the unified story and keep my fingers crossed.

By the following day both of the little ones were under the doctor's care and confined to their bedrooms for the week while they wrestled with what seemed to be a particularly nasty dose of flu. I used the time to write up the first story as planned and to work up a set of notes I already had on file into a second tale ready for the trip down to Warwickshire on Friday. I half-hoped that I would go down with the flu also and escape having to perform, but my luck was out. When Friday morning arrived, there was the expected knock at my door and the car that Engel had sent to whisk me off to Kenilworth Castle was waiting outside, in exactly the same spot from which I had been dragged up onto the horseman's steed in my nightmare.

The first thing to strike me when we arrived was that, even as a ruin, the castle was a romantic dream. The warm, red sandstone of its walls and various buildings glowed gently in the slowly setting sun and its role in the courting of an English queen gave it an extra historical resonance. I was trying to avoid thinking about the assorted resident ghosts that my research had told me were supposed to haunt its various bits and to focus instead solely on those in my stories.

Engel's gathering of notables was being hosted in the completely intact gatehouse. My little performance was scheduled for the Oak Room, named unsurprisingly after its ancient panelling. When I'd finished, the esteemed company would retreat to the dining room for what I presumed for many would be the real event of the night. I never viewed myself as anything more than a sideshow to the food and networking, and remained permanently puzzled as to how I could be even that. The audience, so I'd been told, consisted of leading luminaries from the art and antiques auctioneering and valuation world, so I'd done my best to tune my second ghostly adventure to what I hoped might be something that would interest them.

Nobody other than the castle staff and the caterers were around when I arrived, so I ensconced myself in a comfortable, leather armchair in the Oak Room and began to work my way through some last-minute changes to the tales. The fading sunlight mixed atmospherically with the mute interior lighting and helped set my mood ready for the ordeal to come.

After an hour, the table at the back of the room was stocked with glasses and bottles of expensive wine ready for the arrival of the first guests and, shortly afterwards, Engel appeared in the doorway. He looked slightly harassed, and after checking that everything was in order in terms of wine, nodded at me to acknowledge my presence and strode over. He said,

"You need a bit of make-up on a couple of those scars from the episode in the cemetery. I'll get my PA to fix you up with some of hers when she arrives in a minute. You said you've got two stories ready to fly, so that's fine. Have you tuned them to the audience?"

"The second one, yes," I replied. "I couldn't do that with the first tale because your associate Mr. Green was so insistent that it should adopt and adapt the events from Monday and they had nothing to do with art and antiques auctioneering businesses. Perhaps you should just stress that the second tale will be directly relevant to them."

"OK, we'll make do with that, Lucian obviously has something in mind with the first tale. Give them everything you've got with the second story, so that it impresses them enough to talk about it over dinner. I want them to remember something from their evening with me that they couldn't get at any other business gathering and that's where you come in. You're part of my brand now. Which reminds me – have you made sure that your endings are within the scope of the templates I sent you after the Cambridge problem?"

I nodded, while consoling myself with the thought that

complying with them was more the result of the natural arc of the stories than any subservient doffing of my cap, and asked,

"Will your friend, Mr. Green, be here tonight?"

He said,

"I'm not sure that Lucian is anyone's 'friend'. He will most certainly be here, working his way so subtly around the room you'll hardly be aware of him. But he'll be watching you like a hawk. He's very much bought into the way I'm using your performances in our little roadshows."

His phone rang and he moved away a little to answer it out of earshot. When the call finished, he strode off without the courtesy of a 'see you later' and made it to the doorway just in time to meet and greet his first bow-tied guest of the evening.

By half past six, there were around thirty of the great and the good of the art and antiques world busily chatting and networking within the room. As Engel had predicted, the unsavoury Mr. Green was smiling and glad-handing his way from one to another of them. Quite what it was that he and Engel were up to in these little gatherings – beyond the very limited amount of information they had given me – was a mystery. At length, Engel appeared on the small stage that had been erected at the far end of the room and began his customary address. He then handed over to me.

The first of my tales had required some complex blending of the two sets of events that they were based on and I had been anxious as to whether the seams might show in too obvious a way. To my relief, there was no problem and enough of the audience enjoyed what they heard to allow hearty clapping at the end. It was considerably more than the genteel politeness that I would normally have expected at such a stuffed-shirt gathering. Two or three of the audience expressed their appreciation directly, as I weaved my way through the throng to grab a glass of Engel's expensive wine during the interval. While usually I would have been cautious about drinking any booze halfway through a performance, the events of the past week – and my anxieties over the intentions of Lucian Green – persuaded me that I needed a relaxant instead of the orange juice that would have been wiser under normal circumstances. I was so thirsty after my throat-scorching first tale that, foolishly, I knocked back the entire glass at one go. Having not had much to eat during the course of the day,

I soon noticed the effects and realised that my tipple must have been considerably stronger than the everyday wine which I was used to drinking. A familiar and unwelcome voice suddenly whispered into my ear,

"How very good you were, my dear, and I'm pleased to see that you worked a version of Monday's events into things as requested. The additional material was a surprising but most welcome addition – it sounded very much like a bad dream. Was it? It was so much what I wanted I might almost have put it into your head – but, of course, such a thing would be completely ridiculous."

Green smiled emptily and the combination of the knowing look in his eyes and his pointed choice of words again gave me the uneasy feeling that he had some kind of inexplicable access to my mind, either to read my thoughts or even plant thoughts of his own into my dreams. He seemed not so much to walk off but to swagger, as though he had the satisfaction of having made me do not one, but two things that were of his devising. The idea that the dream might have been somehow inserted into my mind by him was unnerving but, once I had thought about it in a more measured way, entirely ridiculous, as he had himself said. What he was so good at, perhaps, was not in exerting actual control over my mind, but in making me think that he could. My musings were interrupted by a sonorous male voice,

"May I just say how enjoyable your performance was, Miss O'Donnell – and I see you know my good friend, Lucian Green."

I turned round to find myself being addressed by a smooth-suited man in his early fifties. His vibrantly coloured silk tie probably cost more than my entire outfit. With an alcohol-induced loss of both judgment and restraint, I said,

"Oh, thank you. I've only recently met Mr. Green, to be honest – perhaps you could tell me a little bit about him as you know him so well? I've looked on the internet and all the links about him seem to be dead ends, but he's clearly such an interesting man."

His look darkened a little with obvious suspicion and he said,

"Oh, Lucian is the only man who can tell you precisely what he is and what he does. Perhaps you should ask him directly, my dear?"

Another expensively attired individual sauntered over to ask the man with the amazing tie if he could have a word about something.

The tie told him about my interest in Green and he gave me an even more suspicious look than his colleague. He said,

"Lucian will be flattered when I tell him that an attractive young woman is showing such a detailed interest in him."

He smiled at me with what seemed like a hint of menace and then headed towards the buffet table in deep conversation with his colleague. They both looked back at me briefly as they were talking and I had the distinct and highly uncomfortable feeling that I had just made a costly error in my choice of people to ask about Green. I began to suspect that they were here at his personal invitation and for his very specific purposes. It is never wise to let your enemy's friends know that you are checking up on him.

My anxieties were doubled when Engel suddenly called everyone back to their seats and began his introduction to the final tale ten minutes before he normally did. I'd no idea why this was and, after doing the best that I could to bring the alcohol-induced fuzziness inside my head into focus, hurried back to the little stage ready to begin the second and final part of my act.

The bow ties among the exceedingly well-heeled audience were beginning to look vaguely askew or adrift as the ultra-expensive vintage wine that Engel had provided began to do its job. I'd noticed that most had swallowed at least two glasses of the superstrong holy water. There was a generally relaxed air within the room, but my misadventure with the two associates of Mr. Green didn't allow me to share in it. I decided that the only way to distract myself from my worries was to launch straight into the tale and ride high on the adrenalin rush that would result. Hopefully, the rush would not be turned into successive verbal trips and stumbles by my overhastily consumed vino. I said,

"Ladies and gentlemen, my second tale of the evening, *An Artful Haunting,* is on familiar ground for a gathering such as this. It centres on an auction of a spectacular collection of eighteenth-century European art, one that is occasioned by the financial difficulties of the collection's owner. I should warn all who might be of a nervous disposition that it highlights one of the hidden dangers of the art and antiquities business, the displeasure of a malevolent ghost at the sale of his favourite paintings."

A little chuckle reverberated around the room and I took that as an encouraging sign. I continued,

"Christina Judge was a specialist expert on the art in question. She had been contracted to conduct the valuation on behalf of the auctioneers after their own valuer had been incapacitated by a heart attack. The story begins with her on the train from Euston to Edinburgh, where she was poring over the inventory of the house's art, making her initial calculations as to the value of each of the paintings of interest. She wouldn't be in a position to firm them up until she had had the opportunity to examine the present condition of each of the paintings and had completed some outstanding provenance checks.

The Pendolino train slid through the countryside like butter on metal, the world outside a mere movie and the window the screen. The only noise of note was the usual mixture of overloud, tedious monologues on mobile phones and the raucous laughter of a small group of salesmen that was heading to Edinburgh to inflict its golden wit and intellect on the unsuspecting populace. Christina slept on and off, in between her complex calculations, as a result of the ungodly hour that she'd had to get up to make it to the station on time.

The auction was being held in the huge and atmospheric Georgian stately pile in which the paintings had been housed, a country house some sixty or so miles away from the city. As her taxi rolled through the elegant grounds towards the imposing stone façade of the hall, Christina was busy completing her checking and double-checking of the inventory that the auction house had given her. She was determined to hit the proverbial ground running as soon as she arrived. She had other pressing work back in London and the sooner her Scottish assignment was completed the better.

The owner, an earl, had left his son, John McCrae, to handle all of the details of the sale. It was he who greeted her as she walked into the domed, Adamesque entrance foyer, decorated with fine plasterwork and gently gilded ornamentation in a delicate blending of soft pastel colours. McCrae sported a beard that was so luxurious it could safely have been laid out as a small rug. He was thirty something and there was a friendly glint in his eyes that she found instantly endearing. He'd put on a bogus 'ancestral' kilt for the occasion. Noting at once that she was far too canny to be fooled by such a prop, he openly admitted to its dubious status in an act of gentle self-mockery that increased her liking of him further still.

He explained that the hall's collection of paintings had been a passion of his all his adult life and if he had had any say in the matter, they would have stayed where they were. However, due to some ill-advised and disastrous business dealings of his father, he had been instructed to organise their sale to enable the family to hold onto the hall. He walked her through the rooms in which the pictures selected for auction hung, so that she could inspect the condition of each, an enterprise that lasted a considerable time given the variable degrees of care which had been taken with the different items. She then went through the various outstanding provenance issues, which he was able to resolve satisfactorily in each case.

Proceedings were interrupted in the early evening by a splendiferous dinner in the hall's state dining room at which his father joined them. Christina was struck by the difference between the two men, with the son seeming genuine, courteous and full of charm, while the father spoke to her as if she were a servant back in Victorian times. He startled her by saying that he'd rather chop off his left leg than lose the house and that he expected the highest valuation possible on all of the paintings. With a daring twinkle in his eye, John wondered aloud how the old man would fulfil his desire of giving McTavish, the banker to whom he owed a fortune, a kick up the backside with only one leg. His father literally snarled back, saying that McTavish could go to the devil for all he cared and his only concern was holding onto the house in the family name – and damn the paintings, they were just money hanging uselessly on the walls! He thumped the table hard to emphasise his determination. Her hands shaking a little with fear of this fury of a man, Christina pointed out that she could value the paintings as highly as he liked, but if the figures she suggested were out of tune with their market value, then they would be a very poor guide as to what everything might fetch at auction. Her comment sent him even further into the blackest of moods and he threw down his napkin and left the room without a word. John McCrae apologised for his father's behaviour. He said,

"It's all money down the drain, basically – he'll only spend whatever's left over from the sale proceeds on even more ill-advised investments, or use it to pay off future gambling debts. We'll be selling the legs off the Gillow chairs if he carries on the way he is doing. There's no reasoning with him and, frankly, he's almost as rude to me as he was to you."

Besides her unpleasant encounter with the old earl, an undercurrent of nervous concern ran continuously through Christina's mind, regardless of her every effort to suppress it. Its source was the memory of her recent visit to another country house rather like this one, Georgian in period, with a similar but slightly less opulent Adamesque interior. She'd been providing an independent valuation of several paintings for the owner prior to his putting them up for sale and had been left largely to her own devices in the dusty and cavernous rooms in which they hung. At the end of the afternoon, she'd been engrossed in her final calculations of the value of the most significant piece in the collection when she was distracted by a tap on her right shoulder. She turned round to find no-one behind her and concluded that she must have imagined it. She carried on working, seated at a beautifully carved, period writing desk in the centre of the owner's study, when she was tapped a second time. She turned round, but again, no-one was there. Puzzled, she got up and walked around the study trying to work out what was going on. Just at the point where she decided that maybe it would be a good idea to move to another room, a sudden burst of fiercely mocking laughter hit her like a punch in her left ear and she cried out in shock. The room was still echoing with its violence when she turned round to try and find its source and again saw nothing except for her own terrified face in the ornately gilded mirror over the fireplace. In a panic she hurried over to the Gillow desk to grab her papers, but they were scattered as if by a burst of strong wind just as she was about to pick them up. She kneeled down to desperately scrabble them together, but it seemed like an unseen foot was kicking each out of her reach as she attempted to grab it. Now utterly terrified, she hauled herself up and ran towards the nearest door, only to find that it slammed in her face as she approached. She wrestled with the handle but found it to be immovable. She ran across the study to the only other exit and this time she was let through into the drawing room next door. She paused for breath, wondering how she was going to explain this to the owner, when the laughter punched her for the second time, this time in her right ear. It was male and malevolent, mocking her fear and delighting in her misery. She ran out of the drawing room and all the way along the front of the house until she reached the entrance foyer, where she literally bumped into the owner who was coming in through the main doors as she attempted to go out. He said,

"What on earth's the matter, my dear, you look as though you're having an extraordinarily bad turn."

She said,

"It's haunted, the house is haunted and whatever it is that's on the loose in there is after me."

He raised his eyebrows and said,

"Ah, that'll be old William, the second earl. I wondered if he might pop up again after I decided to sell the Dutch paintings. They were bought by him you see, his absolute favourites. Apparently, he swore that if ever anyone tried to take them out of the house, he'd leap out of his tomb and seize them back with his own bare hands. He was a very colourful and quite diabolical character as far as his behaviour and beliefs went and there's been evidence before that he meant what he said. My grandfather tried to sell them and, according to his diaries, had so many unpleasant experiences that he was forced to change his mind and leave them where they were. From what you've told me it sounds like everything's starting again. I'm not a man to be put off a chosen course by anyone, so I'm afraid William's not going to get anywhere with me. I'm made of sterner stuff than my grandfather – I don't need to call on the help of an unlistening God to put the devil to flight like he did. I've got all the guts I need to do the job myself."

She was so disoriented and fearful as a result of her experience that she could hardly take in what he was saying and simply said,

"All my work from today is in that room, I can't go in there to get it. I need someone to get it back before I go."

He said,

"No problem, just leave it to me, I'll get it. I'll go into the study and tell the old curmudgeon to get back into his eternal bed."

Too afraid to remain inside the building, Christina waited on the steps outside. After a short while, she was startled by a terrible noise of an indescribable nature that came from deep within the house. She ran back a good ten yards from the entrance, shaking from head to foot and not knowing what on earth to do. She stood in that state for ten minutes or so before the owner finally appeared at the door with her papers and bag clutched in his hands. He looked ashen-faced and gaunt and a good ten years older than when he'd left her to go to his study. He shambled across the old stone flags and placed the papers into her hands, his whole body trembling. He said quietly,

"Send me the valuations as quickly as you can. I think I may need to sell the house as well as the paintings."

Two days later, after she'd posted him her final report with her bill attached, she was startled to see his face halfway down the BBC news online home page. She opened the story to read that he'd been found dead in his study, a look of terror frozen onto his face. The autopsy had failed to find any sign of a physical attack, but blood had flowed out from both of his ears and badly stained the priceless carpet on which he'd been found spreadeagled. She was so badly shaken that she'd taken to her bed for two days and now here she was in another Georgian pile, with an uncomfortably similar commission. She'd thought about refusing the job when it had been offered, but the auctioneers in question paid well and had frequently turned to her as their first reserve, or for a second opinion, in the past. It would be unwise to offend such a regular source of income and cause them to look to someone else to replace her.

After dinner, McCrae took her to see the remaining paintings. The memories of her recent nightmarish experience receded to the back of her mind as he continued to do what he had done so well earlier – to recreate the hall's rich and often surprising history as they went round the various rooms in which the art was displayed. His theatrical delivery stopped just short of self-parody, and gave vigorous life to the stories and characters that populated his entertaining recounting of the building's colourful past. His smiling eyes had cushioned even the most harrowing of tales and allowed him to weave a true storyteller's magic as he led her, quietly spellbound, around the state rooms, bedchambers and numerous nooks and crannies in the enormous building. It was only when he wandered off for a few minutes to take a confidential phone call that the fun started to go out of the proceedings. She was left alone in a huge, marble floored room.

She was standing contemplating the faults and virtues of a large, lifelike portrait of a past earl when she heard the sound of footsteps echoing loudly behind her. At first, she assumed that it was McCrae returning, but when she turned round there was only the sight of her own reflection in a mirror on the other side of the room. She felt a vague shiver run down her spine, but also a deep feeling of anger and frustration that she was being played with yet again by forces of an indeterminate, invisible and most probably malicious nature. Frightened she may be, but she decided that it was time she made a stand and she wouldn't be bullied or taunted by someone or something that couldn't even be bothered to show its form or its face. She walked determinedly into the centre of the room to take control of the space, trying as best she could to keep her interior fear to herself. She stopped, folded her arms and stood there, looking around defiantly in all the directions that she thought the unseen presence might be watching from. A blast of cold air suddenly hit her and made her shudder involuntarily. Something ruffled the back of her perfectly cut hair, as if fingers were being run through it. Then she had the extremely uncomfortable feeling of a face close up against hers, with cold, unloving eyes staring curiously into her own, as if trying to look into her soul and weigh up what she was made of and whether she could be terrified for fun, or even mastered. Again, beyond these unnerving touches and feelings, there was nothing to actually see. She reacted by simply walking over to the other side of the room and standing with her back to the wall. She was most definitely frightened, but determined not to show it. She heard a squeaking noise immediately behind her and turned to find a long squiggle drawn in grease or butter on the large mirror there. She looked at it more closely. It seemed to be part of a signature, although it was impossible to read due both to its careless execution and the fact that it started to fade almost as soon as it had appeared. This was just part of the game of her spectral persecutors, she thought, presenting and then withdrawing illusions and the indication of presences, causing her to doubt her own sanity and her grip on the realities of the world around her.

She decided that she would simply ignore what was happening and pulled her smartphone out of her shoulder bag. She would start hunting for train times for when she intended to return home. She had no sooner switched the device on than it failed, dying as surely as if the battery had been removed. She tried repeatedly to restart it, but there was no response. She felt again freezing cold air on her skin, this time on her hands and face. It felt suddenly as if someone was blowing a kiss onto the back of her neck and she physically jumped with shock.

Then all returned to normal, as if nothing had happened. The room warmed up again within seconds, her mobile came on and a bird started singing outside the window. At least she thought it was outside, until she spotted a large silver cage on a stand at the far end of the room. She walked cautiously over to have a look. As she approached, the bird inside was unmoving and she assumed that it was watching her intently. As she got closer, however, it became apparent that it was stuffed, a prop to help recreate some of the hobbies and foibles of past owners. She was about to turn away when she heard from somewhere above the swishing of large wings, as if an eagle or a hawk was soaring up and down the high-ceilinged room, from one end to the next. She heard suddenly the terrifyingly loud scream of a smaller bird being grabbed by the invisible predator. She felt a whoosh of air on her face, followed by a glancing blow from a muscular wing as something swooped dangerously close to her. Then, as suddenly as it had started, it all stopped. Simultaneously, John McCrae walked back into the room, his attention focussed on something that he was reading on his mobile. He said,

"I'm terribly sorry for abandoning you for a few minutes, that was a call I had to take."

Putting his phone back in his pocket and looking up, he saw that Christina was visibly shellshocked. He said,

"Good lord, are you all right? You look as if you've seen a ghost."

"No, not seen, heard," she said. "Is this room haunted?"

"Well," he replied, "there are places all over the house that are supposed to be haunted, but it's not something I can really help you on. It seems to depend on whether one is sensitive to such things and I clearly am not. I've never had the slightest feeling of unearthly creatures anywhere in the house or grounds, but by the look on your face, you have and my mother used to say that she had a couple of encounters she could have done without. Afterwards, she wouldn't go into the parts of the house where they happened. What exactly was it that you felt in here?"

"Oh, all sorts really," she replied, "predatory birds and cruel men, nothing that you wouldn't find in the real world, but it's all that little bit more disturbing when you can't actually see them."

"Indeed," McCrae replied, not knowing quite what else to say.

"You must think me a little mad," she said.

"No, on the contrary, as I said, my mother told me of a couple of frights she'd had and there are a great many people who have experienced strange things in different parts of the house. There was a past owner who used to let his pet hawk have the run of this room for sport from time to time. He was an extremely nasty piece of work and would trap a sparrow or some other unfortunate small bird in the same room and then take bets from his equally unsavoury friends as to precisely how quickly the predator could catch the prey."

"That's what I heard," she said, "a small bird screaming as it was caught and killed."

"Remarkable," McCrae replied, "that's not a story I've told for a long time and, as far as I know, it's not recorded anywhere else. It sounds as if you did indeed experience a little echo of the past."

"I hope that's the most it is," she replied, "echoes I can live with, it's the idea that nasty pieces of work like your gentleman bird fancier are actually still around that really spooks me."

"They used to say that he had sworn that nothing he had bought for the house could ever be taken away and that if it were, he would wreak a terrible vengeance on those who tried to remove it."

"Sounds rather like an unsavoury ghost at another house I've been to recently," she replied, "it was so annoyed when the owner tried to sell its favourite paintings that it chased me off the premises, in the way your resident spook seems determined to do here also, and then frightened him to death. He was sure of his power to take on a diabolical spirit without any help from the Almighty, but apparently he was wrong."

"Really?" he said. "Well, ghosts or no ghosts, my preference would be to give the whole blessed building to the National Trust and keep the paintings safe and sound where they've always been. It's too big a house for so small a family – and times have changed."

"Perhaps that's why the ghost appears to have left you alone," she replied.

He said,

"Well, as long as the old man's alive I've no say in the matter. You heard him say he'd rather chop off a leg than lose this house."

He'd no sooner spoken than the temperature in the room plummeted and a dark shadow passed over them and seemed to disappear through the ornately plastered ceiling high above. There was a sudden and piercing cry of horror that could be heard throughout the whole building, followed by a thunderous crash. Christina literally quaked with fear and McCrae held her in his arms until the voice went silent. He said,

"God knows what that was, but it sounded like it came from Father's room. Wait here, I'd better go and take a look."

"No," she replied, "I'm not staying here on my own, not after what happened before. I'll come with you."

McCrae wasn't happy with the idea but reluctantly agreed and they hurried up the grand staircase that led to the second floor. He ran down the echoing corridor to his father's room, with Christina following closely behind. He got as far as the doorway, then stopped in horror, saying only,

"My God."

Christina crept cautiously up to his side and then buried her face in her hands at what she saw. The loud crash that they had heard was a huge and very heavy oak bookcase that, for reasons unknown, had fallen forwards onto the floor. The glass from its doors was scattered everywhere. Underneath the bookcase, flattened, ashen-faced and completely lifeless, was the earl, McCrae's father. Only his head and one of his outstretched legs extended beyond it and a large shard of glass was embedded deep in the back of his neck. Somehow, in the general catastrophe of the event, the leg had been severed.

In the hands of the new owner, the house was transferred to Scotland's National Trust within months and the paintings guaranteed safe and continuing residence in the home they had inhabited for centuries. Several visitors reported having frightening experiences in the room where the earl had been summarily flattened and the hall's reputation as a haunted house grew and grew, much to the benefit of the Trust's bank account. After a period of counselling and medication, Christina recovered enough of her sanity to be able to return to work, but not in anything as dangerous as art valuation. She took up a post as an art lecturer at Trinity College in Dublin – and that, ladies and gentlemen, is the end of my terrifying and cautionary tale."

To my surprise, the audience seemed to appreciate having its leg pulled – but not severed – as part of the story and a chorus of chuckles filled the room, followed by polite but generous clapping. Engel did his usual polished routine of thanking the storyteller and whetting the little assembly's appetite for the excellent meal they were about to enjoy at his expense. As everyone rose and began to make their way to the gatehouse's dining room, he turned to me with a highly satisfied look on his face. He said,

"Excellent, Miss O'Donnell, an excellent job. If you can tune all of your stories to their audience as successfully as that, I will add an extra bonus to your fee. As soon as you are ready you must come through and join us. I think your tale will be quite the talk of the town."

The strong booze, unfortunately, had not finished with me and I was determined to air publicly the voices within my head that a more sober wisdom would have kept private. I said,

"To be honest, I think I may need a little break from our schedule. When I signed up for it, I thought I would simply be working for you, with freedom to tell the stories that I wanted to tell. But things seem to be going in a different direction. I don't feel entirely easy about my loss of control over the content and endings of some of my tales that has been growing as a problem since the Cambridge event. Now I seem to be more under Mr. Green's control than yours and that seems to be bringing even more interference. We maybe need to have a discussion about his role, do you think? I wondered if perhaps you could explain what is going on and provide some reassurance."

"I thought we'd sorted the problem with content and endings," Engel said, with obvious irritation. "Just stick with what I've advised and things will be fine – what we're asking is relatively minor and you're free to write whatever you want within those minimally restrictive guidelines. There's no discussion to be had about Lucian Green, I'm afraid, he and I are partners and it's vital that we stick to the schedule – absolutely vital. You must excuse me while I join our guests."

He stalked off and I was left feeling abandoned by the only

person who possibly might have been able to provide some kind of a buffer between Green and me. He had seemed to do precisely that immediately following the strange events in the cemetery, but clearly I had read too much into his behaviour then. If they were in cahoots, then I was in trouble. This had not been the best place or moment to raise the issue with him and I cursed my folly in gulping back the supercharged, judgment-blurring vino that commonsense should have made me avoid. With his usual uncanny ability to appear from nowhere, Green suddenly slithered over to my side. With an especially vacuous smile, he said,

"What an extremely talented author and performer you are, my dear, I'm so glad you decided to take my advice and keep to your contract for today's performance. However, I couldn't help overhearing your conversation with Sebastian and it would be most unfortunate if you decided to interrupt your commitment to us. I hear from two little birds also that you have been enquiring into who or what I am. It would be so much better if you put your questions to me directly, don't you think? I can't help but feel a little disappointed in your attitude. I think maybe you need to come and see me in London to talk more about the role that I – and Sebastian as well, of course – have in mind for you. I could explain a little more of what it is that the two of us hope to achieve from these convivial evenings of which we find you such an essential part. We'll speak again soon, but for now I have work to do with my colleague. We must use the good humour that you've promoted among our guests to our advantage. Do join us, please, for dinner – I'm sure there'll be no shortage of people wanting to speak to you."

As he marched away towards the dining room, the leather souls of his handmade shoes clat-clatting in military style against the floor as he went, I wondered, as so many times before, precisely what that 'advantage' was. For all their celebration of my skills as a storyteller, I was very clearly little more than a foot soldier laying the groundwork for the playing out of the generals' grand strategy. Green's involvement made the possibilities more sinister than simply entrepreneurial. The nature of the whole enterprise felt to have darkened since I first signed up, thinking I was working for Engel alone. Whatever I was to be told in London, it was clearly going to be the gospel according to the will of Green. It didn't sound as though Engel would be there. Even if wisdom counselled caution towards any idea of a complete and immediate pull-out from their curious joint enterprise, given Green's continuing implied threats, I was determined nevertheless to work on a longer-term exit plan. The tricky bit would be guaranteeing the safety of my passage away from him and his disturbing ability to get inside my head.

CHAPTER NINE

The fear as old as houses is the fear of the knock on the door. Every day after Green's promised summoning of me to his lair my blood ran cold each time the postman or a courier called until, finally, on my day off, what I had dreaded came to pass. I opened the door and a chauffeur was there, a man with an insistent smile who told me that he had been sent to drive me to London for a meeting with the individual I least desired to meet. I wanted to say no, that I should have been asked in advance if I could spare the time, but there seemed little point. Green retained at every point the advantage of surprise. I'd already decided that the only way I could resist the unknown power that he held over me was to play along, to pretend to bow to his will until I worked out a means of countering his manipulations and threats and escaping back into the life and liberty I'd enjoyed before ever I'd met first Engel and then him.

The drive to London was long and tedious, but the drop-off point was mind-boggling. Dublin has its own stick in the sky with the Stiffy on the Liffey, as the Spire is known, but London's Shard seemed to me to be architectural willy-waving of an altogether more ludicrous nature. I said,

"You're telling me his office is in here?"

The man with the insistent smile said,

"You'll find him on level twenty-nine point five. There's extra security on the door for a VIP visit today, so just look for our man waiting in the foyer and he'll see to all of the procedurals to get you in – you can't miss him, he's wearing a green suit."

He smiled in a self-satisfied way at the thought of the visual pun. Then he got back in the limo and whooshed away, leaving me to find my own way into the lion's den.

The hyperfast lift meant there was little more than the space of a heartbeat or two between the ground floor and the odd-sounding level twenty-nine point five, just the kind of weird office address that someone like Green would choose. I felt akin to an angel on rocket fuel, hurtling upwards into the sky, with the roar, diesel stink and hammering clamour of street-level London disappearing into the distance below. I seemed to rise into the silence of the clouds themselves before the lift stopped at the appointed floor and opened into the ante-chamber of Green's vast office suite. My stiletto heels made no sound as they sank into the blindingly white, deep pile of his omnipresent pure wool carpet. A soft but commanding automated voice spoke from nowhere,

"Welcome to the Green Corporation. Please take a seat until you are called."

I did as instructed, sinking into a leather armchair that was so large I felt like a small child between its giant arms. I had more than a faint suspicion that a sense of relative smallness was precisely what this welcoming procedure was supposed to induce in visitors.

I heard the click of a door opening somewhere nearby and was surprised to see a figure emerge from a corridor on the left. It was a small, regal, black cat. It sauntered over and leapt effortlessly onto the armchair opposite, where it sat, sphinx-like, staring at me, eyeball to eyeball. I tried a few soft words and imitation purrs to gain its trust and persuade it to present itself for stroking, but it seemed to be above all such minor vanities and desires for affection. It exuded an air of its own self-importance and surveyed me, unmoving, as if I were an exhibit in a cage. It remained there, motionless, for some time and I had the uncomfortable if irrational feeling that it had unnatural powers which were being exercised on behalf of someone else, in particular an ability to read my mind and transmit my thoughts to its master. I had no idea that Green possessed a cat, but it seemed somehow to have absorbed some of his controlling personality traits and to be doing his bidding.

I decided to take my mind off the cold, sterile nature of the ice-white surroundings and my unwanted furry friend, and pulled my smartphone out of my bag. I'd hardly started checking my sparse incoming mail when, without sound, ceremony or warning, Green's PA suddenly appeared in front of me. She smiled vacuously and said,

"He'll see you now. Walk this way, please."

As the sharply dressed marionette turned to lead the way, she snapped her fingers and the cat jumped instantly off the chair and followed her, its muscular legs taking strides that would not have looked out of place at the court of Cleopatra.

The ice-eyed functionary stopped in front of the large oak-panelled door that led into Green's office and knocked twice. She was invited to enter and she and the cat went in, the door sliding shut behind them. I was kept waiting a further five minutes before the marionette exited, beckoning to me to go in as she did so.

Green was engrossed in a document that was spread across his enormous desk and affected not to have noticed that I had arrived. I stood irritated and increasingly impatient with his lack of respect for the person he and Engel presented publicly as the star attraction in their little roadshows for the great and the good. I had a strong suspicion that, had I been a man, I would have been treated differently. Eventually, he looked up with a slow, cold appraisal of my appearance and said,

"You look very charming if a little overdone today, I must get my style people to do a little work on you before your next performance. Do sit down, my dear."

I knew better than to rise to the bait of his deliberately patronising half-hearted compliment and did as instructed, without betraying any emotions. I sat expressionless in the chair provided, which I noticed was set considerably lower than his so that I and other visitors automatically had to look up at him. Always mindful of my first encounter with his malign and mesmerising eyes, I was determined to avoid looking directly at him for anything more than a second at a time. My suspicion that he possessed powers of hypnotism had not in any way lessened. He went back to reading his documents as if I wasn't present. I was startled when the cat sprang from nowhere onto the desk and seated itself at his right hand. He looked at the animal and then at me and said,

"You've met Virgil, I presume?"

"We've shared a silent few minutes together," I replied.

"Wordless, soundless, but not without communication, I think," he replied. "Virgil is a very good communicator."

He returned to his reading. The cat sat watching me intently for five minutes, then stood up, arched its back and hissed. It jumped off the desk and circled my chair slowly several times, brushing my shins as it did so. It sat down beside me and I began to wonder whether it might actually be warming to me in its peculiar, undemonstrative way. Then, for no apparent reason, it lashed out with its claws, laddering my tights and drawing blood. The pain caused me to cry out. Green looked up from his reading and said,

"Bad boy, Virge, you're supposed to be nice to our guests. It's time maybe you went and kept Madeleine company. You wouldn't dare do that to her, would you?"

He pressed a button on his desk and the door slid open. The cat eyed the world outside briefly and then exited with the muscular stroll that clearly was its trademark: the king of feline cool. The door slid shut behind it.

"That cat is jealous of you," he said. "It thinks that you'll distract me from it and take up all of my time and attention."

"Will I?" I asked.

"That depends," he replied. "You can be of great interest to me or nothing at all, all in the space of a few seconds and depending on the extent that you do what I want. What I want needs to be much more echoed by what you want than has been the case so far. Do you understand what I'm saying?"

"I'm not sure that I do," I replied.

He looked beyond me towards the vast panoramic window that took up the whole of the wall opposite his desk. He rose and said,

"Come on, come over here and let me show you all the things that you're not seeing."

I followed him over to the window, two thin slivers of blood running down my sore right shin where the cat had struck. Minor first aid or other basic human concerns didn't seem to be on Green's agenda. He said,

"I'll let you into a secret, I'm going to tell you what my favourite movie scene of all time is. Have you seen The Third Man?"

"A little before my time, I think," I said irritably, his lack of concern at my obvious physical discomfort beginning to annoy me severely.

"Great art is never before anyone's time, my dear, it is forever present. You must see the movie. There is a scene in Vienna where Harry Lime, a ruthless gangster, goes up in a big wheel with an old friend. When the wheel reaches the top, Harry looks down at the people far below and compares them to dots – from that perspective, he wonders, who would notice if any of them were to be killed? From a great height it is possible to see that individual human lives are no more important than those of insects when set against the vastness of the planet – never mind the universe. The only people who have real importance are those who realise this fact and use it to their advantage in pursuing their ambitions. You look surprised, even horrified, that I should say such a thing, my dear."

"That's the kind of view that only someone without any morals or care for anyone but themselves could have," I replied. My leg was now as sore as a burn from the devil's breath and what he'd just said had deeply disgusted me.

He laughed and said,

"How very feisty, my dear, and how daring. With that one sentence you could have lost everything that I have to offer you and yet you took the risk when your high moral values were offended – however, before the year ends those same values will have had to make a compromise you could never have imagined if the things you most treasure are to be protected. You don't believe me, do you?"

"To be honest, I'm very tired, I have a sore leg and, as far as I remember, we're here to talk about what you want me to do next in terms of the direction of my storytelling," I replied, hobbling back to the undersized underling's chair opposite his desk and flopping down onto it.

"Indeed we are," he said with a smile which would have vaporised concrete, "let's just say that this is all about putting that new direction in a little bit of context."

He pulled a small remote control out of his pocket and stroked its screen. The door slid silently open and, to my alarm, the cat padded back in. Green smiled at me again and stooped down to pick it up. He said,

"Come here, my little tiger, come to daddy. You'll have to stay in my arms so you don't frighten my guest. You can listen to what I have to say to her and tell me what you think."

The cat looked across at me as if it understood every word, something that would be faintly cute with a normal animal and in other circumstances, but which on this occasion made me feel distinctly uneasy. He said,

"Remember always what I said about Mr. Lime and the dots, that you and nearly every human being mean less to me than this animal. When you realise that your worth is less than a pussy cat's you will keep a sense of proportion and give what I tell you the attention and respect that it deserves, something which was a little lacking in our conversation a few moments ago, don't you think?"

I sat frozen and expressionless, as afraid of what it was that he was going to be asking of me as I would be if told to step out of a space station with nothing but a short cable to stop me floating off into the infinity of the universe and towards certain death. He said,

"What I want from you is something that you will not like but which you will have to get used to. You will have no choice, it is as simple as that."

He smiled. The emptiness behind the gesture was so vast it could have swallowed an entire planet. He stroked the cat and whispered into its ear something I couldn't hear and the animal turned and stared at me. I found the creature spooky and unnerving. Green looked up at me and continued,

"I must say you don't look at all enthusiastic, my dear. Let me whet your appetite a little more and then you'll start to warm to the idea, mmm? You see I run a business, a very, very lucrative business, the nature of which you might define as psychological or magical, or supernatural even – any one of these terms might be used, although all or none might be correct. It amuses me to keep people guessing. Now, you've been using far too much of your considerable brainpower trying to work out who exactly I am and what I do, instead of devoting it to what you do best, which is writing new stories. So I'm going to save you a lot of effort and tell you what I do. That's what Virgil thinks is best, isn't it, my little tiger?"

The cat looked up at him and then at me. There was something very old and disturbing which seemed to be viewing me through the unpleasant little creature's eyes and I had the chilling feeling that it wished me nothing but harm. Green continued,

"I'm in the business of knowledge exchange. Clients make a substantial payment to me and in return I pass on insider knowledge and tips that are guaranteed to make them huge amounts of money. I give them information that is unavailable from any other source. Sebastian is one of my clients and you can see for yourself how rich he has become. When he came to me, he earned little more than the average Joe in the world of business management. Now, you're going to ask how much he paid me for access to my little service."

I wasn't, but decided it best to take the cue and humour him. I said,

"How much did he pay you?"

"The most that any man could," he replied.

"What do you mean?" I asked.

He looked at the curse of a cat and said,

"Shall we tell her, Virge, do you think she'd believe us? Yes, I think Virgil wants me to share with you – don't you think that's a good word, 'share'? From the look on your face, you don't seem to be impressed by it, my dear."

"I'm just interested to know what kind of a hold you have over the man I'm supposed to be working for," I said, with the momentary courage of a woman who had become seriously irritated by his constant patronising references to her as 'my dear' – and who had an increasingly sore shin. Most of the time, my responses to his general unpleasantness were kept in check by the thinly veiled threats he had made against both me and the children during his little visit to my cottage garden.

He said,

"How very direct you are, my dear, I do like that, how very Irish. Directness should always be rewarded. Very well, Sebastian has given me his all in the most literal of senses and by that I mean he has given me his soul."

The cat's head snapped round so that its eyes could glare deep into mine as if it was looking into my own soul to see how I would react. The ludicrous nature of what its master had just said made it impossible to hide my incredulity, irrespective of the underlying fear of him that tried desperately to seal my lips, and failed. I half laughed and said,

"You're joking, aren't you? Why do you keep playing these mind games with me?"

"Well, I may or may not be joking, I leave that for you to judge, my dear, but Sebastian certainly wasn't when he signed on the dotted line as surely as if he were the good Dr. Faustus himself. Whether something as ethereal and invisible as his immortal soul was his to give, or mine to take, is an interesting question, as I'm sure you will agree. What is not in doubt is the fact that he believed he was signing it over to me at the time and has hung on to that belief, sensible or ridiculous as it might seem according to your beliefs."

I said,

"You're not telling me that you gave him all of the insider information that he needed to hit the jackpot in exchange for something as intangible as 'his soul'? Why would you want it – whatever else you are, you're hardly going to tell me that you're the devil incarnate, are you?"

He laughed and said,

"I could claim to be many things, but hardly that. But I might be his broker, don't you think? Or there again I might not. It's all so uncertain, so difficult to unravel. You see, people like Sebastian also have to pay me a percentage of their earnings each year, so I could be using the diabolical theatricals, with all the 'selling of the soul' business, to simply give myself that special aura of mystery and power which persuades people to part with their money as well. I could be doing all sorts of things – and be all sorts of things – and you could waste a lifetime trying to work it all out. Or you could cut to the chase and just focus on what people believe and what that means for you. You see, Sebastian really believes he sold his soul in return for everything he has and in that respect, by your values, you may well judge him to be a fool. But if he is, then he is also a wise fool, because the deal he signed up for has an escape clause that lets him keep both his soul and the wealth he believes it has bought. That was very sensible of him, wasn't it, Virgil?"

The creepy cat looked at him, then back at me, as if following every word of the conversation. He continued,

"So, I hear your mind saying, how on earth could a slimeball like me persuade someone as canny as Sebastian to sign up to such superstitious nonsense? Well, my dear, you would be surprised what the most intelligent human beings can be persuaded of when approached in an appropriate manner. And when people come from the kind of strict religious background that Sebastian did, it can very easily leave them with little love of the hard-hearted God that it often preaches and a ready belief in the devil. And if that devilish being, real or fictional, can be presented in a convincingly urbane, civilized and even generous fashion, then he can seem quite an attractive fellow to deal with – and a lot more user-friendly than the constantly reproving and punishing version of God that was preached in the Engel household. So maybe Sebastian met a rather different version of me than you and found him and his introduction to all things diabolical surprisingly convivial. Particularly when I was able to point out to him how I could help him set up a dynasty, with his children being the first in a long line of rich and wise descendants to carry his name and reputation far into the future. Never underestimate a man's vanity, my dear – and his desire to see his children become little hims and reflect back his own new-found greatness. Now do you begin to understand?"

I said,

"What if I were to tell Mr. Engel what you've just told me – why are you taking the risk that I might?"

"I'm taking no risks, my dear. You know very well that the consequences of you so doing would be terrible beyond belief for both you and the children. Now, I told you how canny Sebastian is and how the escape clause was the clincher in persuading him to sign up, so what on earth is it? Rather a clever little thing is what I'd call it. In the business we refer to it as the Rule of Ten. All Sebastian has to do is help me persuade ten other individuals to sign up to the same deal as him and then he is released from his commitment to surrender his soul. With your cynical mind, you might well conclude that, surrendered or not, I had and have no power to take it from him. Well, let's just say that's a little matter of conjecture which I have neither the time nor the intention to discuss now. What I do most certainly have is the power to benefit from the money that he is paying me – and all of the extra money that the people he persuades to sign up will bring to me as well. It all helps pay the bills here and keep a high-rise roof over Virgil's head, isn't that right, Virge?"

The cat leapt off his desk and sat bolt upright on the deep pile carpet, staring up at me. Green continued,

"Now, if you were less sceptical about such matters, you might also note that the more people I could get to sign up to Rule of Ten deals, the more likelihood statistically there is of some of them failing to find ten new signatories – and thereby forfeiting their souls. So if I was, in fact, the devil's broker in disguise, I would be doing my master a considerable service by trying to sell as many of these deals as possible. But as I've said already, I also benefit financially from every deal, so you could just as plausibly believe that I'm simply in the business for the money and that the Faustian stuff is just a sham. What precisely it is that I am and what precisely it is that I am about is for me to know and you to simply guess – and guess – and guess. I will never tell you and you will never find any evidence that proves this theory or that. But what I have told you is, very precisely, the kinds of deals that I engage in with people like Sebastian and what he believed he had committed himself to when he signed up. I've done that for a purpose, haven't I, Virgil?"

The cat looked up at him again and he smiled at it as if expecting an answer. He continued,

"You see, that is where you come in. Sebastian and I use your little performances as conversation-starters at the various dinners and dinner parties that he organises. In amongst the various rather more mundane deals that he tries to conclude at such events, he is looking out for those people of a more psychically susceptible disposition, people who we might be able to lead gradually towards the same kind of Rule of Ten deal that he signed up for. We're suitably subtle in how we do this, first through hypotheticals and then, if we detect the necessary degree of receptiveness, we move, step by step, towards the real thing. Your little stories have proved to be a brilliant way of getting people into the right mindset to enable the conversations to get started. Their potency lies in the powerful and convincing nature of your performances and your kind agreement to permit the little insertions and tuning of endings that we insist on – and I do emphasise the word 'insist'. Their spooky storylines and the reactions they provoke make it easier for us to spot those amongst the moneyed many who are likely to be persuadable about the entire spiritual dimension and, in particular, that someone as ethereal and elusive as the devil actually exists. If our subtly unobtrusive questioning enables us to find that such a susceptibility is combined with the kind of unhappy religious upbringing that Sebastian experienced, one that extinguishes the love of God but leaves a belief in the devil, then, glory be to all things dark, we are ready to move in for the kill – figuratively speaking, of course. You may only be the monkey to our organ-grinder, but without you our little act is much more laboursome. That's why we're so insistent that you stick to the contract you signed. In fact, Virgil is even more insistent than we are, aren't you, Virgil?"

The cat startled me by opening its mouth impossibly wide and appearing to show tiger-like fangs. It turned away and looked back up at Green, who smiled at me. He said,

"You look as though you've had a bit of a shock – was it something Virgil said, or is that famous imagination of yours working overtime again and seeing things that aren't really there? Now where were we – oh, good heavens, my dear, I nearly forgot to explain the most important thing of all, isn't that strange? You see the thing that really makes you quite indispensable is the fact that you're an ancient prediction come true! Isn't that incredible? Here, let me show you."

He opened a heavy, leather-bound volume that had been sitting on his desk and turned to a page in the middle, which he pushed under my nose. He said,

"Recognise anybody?"

I was startled to see a hand-drawn portrait of me. Rather than being in any way contemporary, it was dated 1771. He said,

"You look puzzled, my dear, let me explain. This is a very rare eighteenth-century Austrian book, The Satanic Testament. This picture is of 'The Storyteller', an unwitting servant whose presence at gatherings, so the good, or should I say, bad book claims, would be a secret sign of the devil's guarantee of any diabolical bargain that was being struck there. In fact, it goes further, saying the Storyteller's presence would be almost equivalent to the devil's signature on any deal that was agreed. When I show this page to those who are wavering about signing up for the Rule of Ten – and point out how you and the woman in the picture are identical in appearance – it more often than not swings them in favour of adding their signature. And, when I show them all of the antiquarian booksellers' certifications of the genuine nature of this ancient volume, that really clinches things. So here you are, a perfect match for the woman in the picture. How remarkable is that?"

The likeness was indeed remarkable – and chilling. So this was why they really wanted me. I'd been lured into a venture that I'd believed was simply an eccentric foible of a wealthy man when, in fact, it was of a frighteningly dark nature, irrespective of whether or not the devil allegedly at the centre of it all actually existed. I was, for one of the few times in my relatively short life, completely lost for words. Green, however, wasn't. He said,

"Perhaps you are not so much the likeness of the Storyteller but her reincarnation, perhaps you and the devil have been playing out this strange relationship over centuries. Perhaps you've been just as difficult and defiant as you are now and these little reinventions of your character will continue from century to century until finally you are broken and agree to do precisely as you are told. Only then will you find peace maybe, what do you think? I've got such an overactive imagination my dear, I could continue forever with such fantasies and speculations."

"What I think is that you're trying to play with my mind, to manipulate me within a story that you're building around me. The only fantasies that interest me are the ones that I construct within my own stories. I'm not someone to be broken, to be treated like a robot at someone else's command," I said, recovering my powers of speech a little.

"Oh, but you are most definitely at our command my dear. You have signed a contract if you remember and I always hold people to contracts, as, indeed, does Sebastian. Now, while everything that I've told you registers more fully on your overtaxed brain, I need to explain our requirements of you over the next few months."

"Irrespective of whether he's supposedly sold his soul to you, the devil or the seven dwarves and the King of Killarney, my contract is with Mr. Engel. Shouldn't he be here if you're going to talk about my role?"

I wondered at my own courageous feistiness and suspected that it was now being generated by uncontrolled panic.

"Sebastian has said that he is quite happy for me to conduct today's business with you alone, my dear," he replied, "not least because he is in Hong Kong for the whole of this week."

The cat stood up and circled my chair several times as if winding an invisible rope round my ankles. Green smiled unpleasantly and said,

"Isn't he a cute little animal? As I said before, he has an extraordinary ability to communicate without saying a word. Now, my dear, this is what the situation is. Sebastian has signed up six new clients for a Rule of Ten deal. In his view that still leaves him four short if he is to avoid surrendering his soul should he be so unfortunate as to have a heart attack, or be run over by the proverbial bus. So he is not unnaturally anxious to find the final four. He wants you to hone your act a little more to the task in hand, so that he can sign up the remaining people as quickly as possible. I also have an interest in this, as I've pointed out already. Whether you believe I'm the devil's servant hunting souls or simply an avaricious conman out for as much money as he can get, I most certainly would like to see as many as possible signed up for the deal. As you will no doubt have calculated, each new signatory who sincerely believes they are gambling their soul in return for vast wealth is the potential source of another ten signatories – and so on and so on: a veritable escalator of financial gain for my company."

"Before we go any further," I said, "how have you managed to persuade people that the fate of their souls can be determined by a piece of paper, a legal agreement? Given that most major religions believe that the final destination of a soul is a matter for God alone to decide, how can you claim to usurp this through such a puny device as a legal contract?"

The cat bared its hidden fangs again and hissed threateningly. Green said,

"How indeed? It's a mystery, isn't it, in the same way that pain and suffering being tolerated by a supposedly loving God is a mystery. Why such things should be allowed to exist is as big a mystery as you could ever hope for. Mysteries are by definition the causes of effects that defy explanation – and as there is no explanation of why people should believe me in the way that they do, then that also is a puzzle devoid of an answer."

I said,

"I don't understand how Mr. Engel can believe any of this, with or without the aid of a coincidental likeness of me in a book with the unlikely name of The Satanic Testament. He doesn't seem to believe easily in ghosts or the diabolical presence of the mad Earl – he told me he didn't believe my cottage was haunted and he has found it very hard to accept that the children might be having conversations with the long dead on the estate. He seems perfectly rational and I respect him for it. So if he's that sceptical, how could he believe in all of this diabolical stuff?"

"It is strange, isn't it, my dear," Green replied, "but then, as I said before, you haven't heard my sales technique. Sebastian is indeed sceptical about the dead having any power over the living or ability to communicate with them. However, he does most certainly believe in the existence of the gentleman downstairs and his fearsome friends, given that they are not, nor have ever been, dead in the human sense – and he seems to think that I am able to call on their powers in all kinds of magical and most unlikely ways. I think it was because I appeared so able to deliver on my promises of vast wealth that he became convinced that the diabolical is very real. Initially, he persuaded himself that it might be as urbane and convivial as I have appeared to him, but now is beginning to revise his view a little and is very anxious to escape its grasp – while holding onto his spoils, of course."

The atmosphere in the room was truly 'diabolical', whether or not Green was 'the devil's servant'. The seriously weird and malicious cat, the sulphurously repellent character of the man himself and the mad, macabre and ethically repugnant nature of his bizarre business all combined to create the impression of a desolate moral sewer that I was desperate to claw my way out of. I might be frightened of what this unprincipled and quite possibly insane monster manipulator might do should I try to break my contract, but that didn't mean that fear would lead to inaction. The more I listened to him the less desire I had to continue writing and performing stories for either him or Engel – and the more my thoughts returned to the urgent need to find a way of escaping from their grasp. Should I even try to leave my seat, however, I was in no doubt that the vicious little feline would take that as a licence to attack my unprotected shins with all the sharp implements nature had put at its disposal, so for the moment I had little choice but to hear its master out.

As on previous occasions, he seemed to have a disturbing ability to read my mind. He said,

"I can sense that you are disgusted by what you feel to be the immoral nature of my business, my dear, so let me put it into perspective for you and then maybe your view of things will soften. You seem to me to be preoccupied with the notion of evil – that I'm evil, that what I do is evil, that Sebastian has allowed himself to be drawn into an enterprise that has contaminated everything he does, his family and now you. My dear, you are surrounded by evil. Every country in the world was built by it, through war and conquest, and is built on it – it is written into the laws that permit vast inequalities of wealth in this country and pretty well everywhere else, it is written into the ruthless machinations of the powerful in business, in government, even in what supposedly are the public services – and it has corrupted churches, charities and everything that people have put their trust in. It is as much, if not more, a part of life as anything you might define as good. Whatever you do in your time on this blighted planet, you will nearly always end up working for something that is at least in part evil. So if you think that Sebastian and I are in the business of evil, then it is quite possible that you are right, but switching employers would simply change the evil which, in part or in whole, you work for. It would be the proverbial case of out of the frying pan into the fire. And even if we are as evil as you think, we propose to do you no harm, not unless you renege on your obligations to us. In fact, should you do as we ask, we have guaranteed to pay you a very substantial income – and at the end of our agreement with you, when Sebastian has his ten signatories, you are free to do as much good as you wish with your ill-gotten gains. If you think of things from that point of view, then we are giving you the power to do good, if you so choose. Should you not take our money then, equally, you are choosing not to do the good which otherwise you could have done – and does that not then become a kind of evil, the withholding of kindness and charity which our money would have enabled you to deliver to the truly needy? You see, where good and evil are concerned, my dear, there are very few absolutes, they are nearly always woven in with each other and the job of the wise is to try and unpick more of one than the other and then to do the best that they can. All things considered, is it not more sensible to work for the devil you know than the one you don't?"

"If I were to ask the devil to make a case for evil being indistinguishable from good, then your little speech would do the job," I said, "but that wouldn't save the logic of that case from being wholly diabolical. There's nothing you can say that will persuade me that any work I do for you is anything but tainted by the nature of your business."

He said,

"My dear, I do so commend your feistiness and bravery, most particularly given that I know how very afraid of me you are underneath it all. That fear is, of course, well justified and greater wisdom might have framed your words in a gentler and more respectful way. For all you know, I could be mad, I'm most certainly bad and it would not be unreasonable to assume that I'm very, very dangerous. I've already hinted what will happen if ever you repeat what I've told you today. You need always to remember that and you need to remember also that your job is to do as you are told. I've explained why it is so important to Sebastian to complete his list of ten new recruits – and why it's important to me also. I've explained precisely why you are crucial to our success. You need now to play your part in bringing the new sheep to what you no doubt regard as their bad shepherds. Now you know everything, there is no reason for you to waste any more valuable time trying to find what it is that we are about. I have a little list of things I want you to weave into your next few stories, my dear, and I want you to pay very close attention to it when you write and perform them. There can be no deviation from, or dilution of, my requirements – you must deliver every one of them in full. Madeleine will give you an envelope, with everything that you need to know, on your way out. You will most probably find the various things that you need to insert in your little tales quite baffling – they will look innocent of any of the purposes I describe. That is not for you to worry about – they are designed to work subliminally on the minds of susceptible members of the audience in a way that you won't understand. All that I require of you is that you do what you are told. Do so and all will be well between us. Don't and – well, Virgil will be able to tell you about that better than me."

The cat hissed and stared at me in a manner that redefined the notion of the malign. Green said,

"Now, that concludes our business for today. I can't say I'm surprised at your unwelcoming reaction to all of the things that I've told you, but I know that when you reflect on them, you will doubly understand the need to do exactly as I have said. Consider yourself flattered that I have bothered to tell you so much – as I have said already, I have done so to stop that incredibly intelligent little mind of yours wasting time trying to find out what Sebastian and I are up to when we need you to concentrate all your efforts on your work for us. Goodbye, my dear, Madeleine will show you out."

I looked round to see that the functionary had appeared silently behind me, with the promised envelope in her hand.

As I limped out of the room, my shin for some reason feeling twice as painful as when it had first been clawed, the cat padded along behind me. I had the distinct impression that the devil was on my tail. The malignant little monster stood glaring as I headed back towards the lift, its shadow seeming to follow me all the way down to the ground floor as if it were seeing me off the premises.

When I walked outside, the man with the insistent smile swept up in the limo, appearing as if from nowhere. He leapt out of the vehicle and opened the door in a manner that was as much of a command for me to get in as an invitation. Clearly, he had instructions that I was to be whisked back to the estate as swiftly as possible, so that not a moment would be lost in my getting to work on the various stipulations within Green's worryingly thick envelope. I had other ideas, but not yet the courage, or an understanding of how, to implement them. A start would be a detailed internet search when I got back to find out if what I had in mind was going to be feasible. My most urgent priority was to discover someone with the necessary expertise and experience to advise me on things as strange as my relationship with the rancid Mr. Green and the various weird events that had undermined my authority over Engel's children. Find them and I would at least be on the first rung of the ladder up towards the escape hatch.

On my return to the cottage I decided to do a bit of background research on the Green Corporation, the outfit that my unsavoury friend ran from the great heights of the Shard. I was surprised to find no trace of it on the internet. When I rang the Shard reception the following morning and enquired after it, things became stranger still. I was told that there was no level twenty-nine point five, the floor on which I'd spent an unhappy hour or two. They'd never heard of Mr. Green and when I described him, nobody could recall ever having seen anyone like him.

It appeared that I'd had a meeting with the invisible man in an office that didn't exist.

CHAPTER TEN

The landscape had all the familiar ingredients of a 1960s' horror movie. Mist swirled across the moors and soon enveloped the centuries-old church tower that rose fifty feet or more above the damp, rich earth in which it was rooted. The low-hanging sky was so grim and dark that it seemed more like dusk than early afternoon. The still, quiet air was filled with the smell of decay, as if something dead was rotting nearby, and the night-black crow that clung to the telephone wire in the lane beyond the graveyard had the air of the devil waiting for the souls of the newly deceased. Had it not been so real, eerie and immediate, I would have dismissed it as vintage Hollywood.

I shuddered and asked myself why on earth I'd decided to come here. 'Needs must' was the reply within my head – desperate remedies fit desperate times. While I still wanted to try and cling onto my increasingly fragile scepticism about the strange and the supernatural, I had had to acknowledge that what had been happening around me had been continually pulling the rug from under my efforts. The cumulative burden of my various disturbing, ethereal experiences with the children, the terrifying events in the Lancashire graveyard and the unsettling threats, manipulations and magical manifestations in non-existent offices of Mr. Green had become too much. The exhaustive search for help on my return from London had led me to a book by a highly respected cleric that contained case studies similar in various ways to some of my own experiences, together with discussion of the explanations various authorities had offered for them. The merits or otherwise of a variety of means of dealing with such hauntings, or manipulations of the mind, were discussed in some depth. I'd emailed the author to see if he could tell me more about this aspect of his investigations and offer some advice on my own situation. He'd agreed to meet up to see if he could help. There were numerous online testimonies to his honesty and reputation as a provider of sound advice on such matters, but, like much on the internet, they could be fabricated of course, and there was always the possibility that, underneath the surface gloss, he was a god bothering fantasist, a persuasive charlatan, or something much darker. But I had to take that risk. As soon as I had a couple of days off from my duties, I took him up on his offer.

Given the remote location of his Northumberland parish and the eccentricity of the satnav in the car that I had hired to get there, it had taken me quite a while to find it. Having parked the vehicle I tramped wearily up the gravel path that led past the church to the rectory. A light was on downstairs and within the swirling mist it seemed like a beacon lit to guide the lost. Either that or a wrecker's lamp designed to lead the unwary onto the rocks, although I felt that I was already in serious danger of foundering, with or without such malicious help. The door opened suddenly as I approached and a large, rotund figure came out to greet me. It said,

"Miss O'Donnell, I presume, how nice to see you. Do come in."

The rector of St. Agnes the Blessed was a priest of the old school, a man of courtesy and genuine warmth, who shepherded me into a parlour that looked pretty much unchanged in many details from the eighteenth century. A welcoming fire greeted me and I sat down in an ancient, leather armchair that creaked unflatteringly as my slim figure settled into it.

"I've just made some tea, will you join me?" he asked pleasantly.

I nodded enthusiastically. An ornate Spode tea set nestled comfortably on the coffee table and he proceeded to pour us both a cup of aromatic Earl Grey. He sank back into the sofa opposite me, his considerable bulk depressing the fabric so much that I feared he would disappear into it and never be seen again. He smiled and said,

"Since my book came out, I have more visitors like your good self than parishioners. I think some of them make the mistake of assuming I'm some kind of medium or exorcist, but from our telephone conversation it's clear that you don't. That's good, a very good start. I'm simply someone who's done a lot of research into the kind of things you seem to have experienced. I'm not absolutely sure I can be of very much help, but I'll do whatever I can."

I said,

"It's good of you to find time for me. Your book offered me the first chinks of light in trying to understand what's been happening with all of this weird stuff."

"Well, chinks maybe," he replied, "just as long as you remember I don't guarantee any specific answers. I'm no wiser than the sum total of my research. I listen to what people tell me and if there's anything I can suggest that might be helpful, then I will suggest it, but that doesn't necessarily mean that it will work."

"That's fine," I said. "I just know that the book opened my mind to possibilities I hadn't considered before and helped convince me that I wasn't going insane."

"That's excellent," he replied, "I couldn't ask for more. If the book has done that as the very least of the things it has achieved, then it's served its purpose."

I said,

"What I need is your help in trying to distinguish the more credible possible explanations for the bizarre goings-on from the less likely ones. Then it might be possible to work out some means of stopping all the weirdness. While there are some striking similarities between my experiences and those in your book, there are also some crucial differences, which make the solutions tried in some of your case studies difficult to apply to my situation. If you want to use my case for your next book in return for helping me, I'm happy with that, providing that you conceal my identity."

"That's very kind of you," he replied. "I'll be delighted to be whatever help I can. Please, start at the beginning and tell me everything, then we'll see what we can do."

It took me nearly an hour to describe all of the things that had been happening to both the children and me. When I'd finished, the rector looked as though he'd seen a ghost himself. He said,

"What you've just told me is immensely disturbing, my dear, I'm amazed you're able to describe it all with such apparent equanimity."

"I've wondered for a while how I was managing to handle it," I said, "but then I realised I'd subconsciously developed a technique for coping with severe stress after losing my granddad. We'd been so close I'd half-believed he was eternal and the shock of suddenly not having him around was unbearable at first. The brain, as you know, is an incredibly clever little box of tricks, quite independent of its owner in lots of ways. Mine took a huge part of the agony of loss from out of my conscious mind and put it into a little virtual box in my subconscious – and that's where it sits to the present day. If it hadn't hidden it there, I wouldn't have been able to cope. Having done all of that once before, my brain has been doing the same thing again with all the ghostly stuff and the malign influence of the diabolical Mr. Green. I shouldn't be able to cope with it, but I can because the subconscious part of my brainbox knows how to cushion it all."

"Yes, the brain is indeed a remarkable thing," he replied. "I've often come across people who've said that's also how their grey matter works. My own mind has had to cope with so much awful stuff over the years and I've often wondered how I've managed to deal with it all, but I think the process has been just as you've described it."

I smiled, without quite knowing why. Then my smile faded as I saw even thicker fog blocking sight of everything outside the window. He followed my gaze and said,

"Ah, yes, it can turn bad like this quite quickly round here. It comes in from the sea on a still day and suddenly you're cut off from the world as surely as if somebody had wrapped a giant wodge of cotton wool round the house. You'd be safer staying the night – you're very welcome. I keep a bed permanently made up in the spare room in case people get stuck when they're visiting."

"That's very kind of you," I said. "No resident ghosties, I hope."

He smiled and said,

"None that have bothered me, but I sincerely hope that none

come looking for you my dear."

"Yes, so do I," I replied.

"I think it would be a waste of even the most determined ghost's time trying to terrify me at night," he replied, jovially, "when I go to sleep, it's as if someone has hit me over the head with a mallet. It takes two alarm clocks ringing at the same time to wake me and even then I've almost been late for a couple of early morning funerals. But let's get back to the main point of why you're here. You wanted me to help find a credible explanation for what's been happening to you."

"Yes, yes, please, if you could give me even the smallest bit of help in that respect it would be enormously valuable."

"Well," he said, "if I was to sum it all up in a nutshell, I'd say that the whole mind-bogglingly astounding nature of the universe and the planet on which we spin through it is of such a scale that anything is possible. If you think of the myriad of things that had to happen in an apparently quite random and unplanned way for life to sprout on earth – and then evolve into creatures like us – you realise that we should have been impossible. But we weren't and we aren't. That fact means that all kinds of other things which rationally we might regard as ridiculous or out of the question might be just as possible as ourselves. Things we call ghosts, evil spirits or whatever are all possible, although not necessarily understandable. We shouldn't be surprised at the existence of things we don't understand in a universe that seems always to find new ways to be puzzling. That's the first thing to say, although it might seem like a bit of a get-out."

"No, not at all," I replied.

"Good, but that's the easy bit," he said, "the broad-brush approach. What's much more difficult is to try and understand why some types of experiences, the hauntings at the estate and the graveyard voices that have been affecting you, for example, happen to specific people. Why should you be singled out for so much attention? Are these things the manipulative work of this Green character, or is there some other explanation? That's what you most want to know, isn't it?"

"Yes, absolutely," I replied. He said,

"After we've finished our tea I'll scour my archives and see if there's anything I can find in the handling of past cases, someone or something that might be helpful to resolving all of this so that you can get free of all these ethereal shenanigans and this dreadful Lucian Green chappie."

"That's really, really helpful," I said.

"Excellent," he replied. "In biblical times some of the none-too-cheery forces that have been harassing and manipulating you would have been referred to as evil spirits, but the complex nature of reality and beyond makes me think that is far too simplistic a term. As yet, we don't really have the beginnings of understanding such things."

"That's what's so frightening," I replied.

"Well, we're at least in the right place for finding ways of unfrightening ourselves when dealing with frightening things," he said, smiling. "Have you heard of Sir Roger Belvedere?"

"No, never," I replied.

"Well, he's one of the reasons why the church next door is mentioned in all the guidebooks," he said. "He was a tad eccentric as well as being a wealthy landowner and, when he died, he left instructions for a poem to be carved onto the side of his rather splendid stone tomb in the little Lady Chapel. It's all about being frightened by strange things and putting one's trust in the Lord in the hour of need. It's actually quite witty – come, I'll show you before it gets dark. You should see the inside of the church while you're here anyway, it's quite beautiful."

He hauled his considerable bulk upright with a surprising agility and beckoned me to follow him. I put on my jacket and my thick woollen scarf as barriers against the cold. He opened the heavy, eighteenth-century front door of the rectory and we stepped out into the fog. The top of the Norman tower was only faintly and intermittently visible as we crunched our way across the stone chip path to the front porch of the church and went in. As the centuries-old door creaked shut behind us and the rector switched on the lights, I was taken aback by the stunning, simple beauty of the interior. The mixture of Romanesque and Norman arches marching down the surprisingly long nave dated neatly the different parts of the building and formed a stone avenue of rare beauty. Somehow, the varying colour tones of the ancient stone, and the particular mix of architectural styles of which they formed a part, combined to create a sense of warmth and welcome that made the building feel as if it was filled by a benign gathering of invisible humanity. He said,

"I know what you're feeling and you're not the first. Someone once described it as the welcome of all the good souls that have ever worshipped here. I've felt it myself and it really is quite extraordinary."

"And what of the bad souls?" I asked.

"Oh, they're here as well," he replied, "and that's the other thing. The same person said they were so bad in some cases that the good were afraid to leave the building in case they took over. That's why you feel the presence of so much warmth – it's here to leave no room for the darkness."

"And do you believe all of that?" I asked.

He laughed. "Well, it could all be the product of overactive imaginations, but you have to admit the theory is interesting – and a little reassuring. Roger Belvedere certainly was aware of it even way back in the eighteenth century. That was what inspired him to write his witty little poem and leave instructions for it to be inscribed on his tomb. Come, it's over here, I'll show you."

Before he could do so, his mobile phone rang. He answered it but the call kept breaking up. He said,

"I'm terribly sorry, it's one of the parishioners whose wife has been seriously ill for some time and he thinks the end may be near. Mobile reception is terrible round here. I'll have to go back into the house and ring him on the landline, otherwise I'm only going to hear half of what he wants to ask. Will you be OK by yourself for five minutes while I sort this out?"

"Yes, absolutely," I replied, "it's a fascinating building. I'll have a look around while you talk to him."

Once I was alone I sank down into the nearest pew and closed my eyes, exhausted from the long drive earlier in the day and the emotional strain of the subject matter we'd spent over an hour discussing. I sat unmoving for a good ten minutes, my mind only half-awake and focussing on little other than the sound of my own breathing. Suddenly I was pitched back into full consciousness by a knock at the church door. I hurried across to open it and found a figure in a very traditional clerical outfit standing outside. I was puzzled as to why he hadn't simply come into the church. He said,

"Miss O'Donnell, I'm Hardy, the curate. The rector wants you to meet someone who may have answers to what you want to know. He lives very near to here and it's only safe to go while it's still light, so we should hurry. Would you like to follow me?"

"Oh, yes, of course, he didn't mention that he had a curate," I replied.

"No, I live in the village, not the rectory, with my mother. She's very old, you see, needs looking after. Mind that you wrap up well, it's getting very cold outside."

Having been unable to find my scarf anywhere, to the point where I almost wondered whether I'd imagined bringing it into the church with me, I zipped up my jacket and followed him through the graveyard and out onto a path beyond. The temperature had plummeted in the time that I'd been in the church and my teeth chattered with the cold. The curate was a solemn-looking man with thick, wavy hair and eyebrows that nearly met in the middle. He said,

"Follow me closely, the path can be quite treacherous in the fog."

I said,

"The rector was supposed to be coming back to show me the writing on the Belvedere tomb, isn't he coming with us?"

He said,

"He's gone on ahead to check that it's safe to go down to the cottage where the old man lives. Sometimes the rocks can be dangerously slippery when the rain or the fog moistens them."

I did as he said and followed as closely as I could in his footsteps. For five minutes or so we walked in silence, down across the moor that led to the cliffs above the sea's edge. I could hear a foghorn sounding atmospherically somewhere in the distance. Gulls squealed high above us and through the calm air I could hear the low throb of a fishing boat as it cut its way through the silken waters far below.

"How much further is it?" I asked.

"Nearly there," he replied.

We carried on for another couple of minutes, the ice-air cutting into my delicate cheeks like a knife. Then he said,

"There at last. It's only a short walk down from here."

The fog was so dense at this point that I could hardly see more than a foot in front of me. I said,

"Are you sure it's safe? I can't see a thing."

"It's no problem if you know the ground. I'll go first. It's only a few feet, so you're not going to come to any harm. What you see when you get there will explain everything. I'll shout as soon as it's safe to follow."

He went forwards and at the same moment I heard the rector calling my name in the distance. I stopped and shouted back,

"Over here!"

"For God's sake, don't move!" he replied. "I can't see you but down there is right by the cliff edge. Don't move a muscle until I get there."

I was puzzled why the rector was so far behind us when supposedly he had been going on ahead. I assumed the curate must have got lost and turned back round to ask him. As I did so, I froze utterly. The mist had cleared temporarily, just a little, in the way that it does in between one bank of sea fog moving on and another coming ashore. The ground onto which the curate had so confidently stepped did not exist. I was no more than six feet away from the cliff edge. Horrified, I realised he must have plummeted straight onto the beach below. I stepped a little back and dropped down onto my knees and then flat onto my stomach, inching my way towards the edge and trembling in anticipation of what I might see far below. I have no head for heights and this was the only way for me to look down without losing my balance and tumbling over into oblivion. I crawled right up to the edge, to the point where I was able to look over. The mist had cleared enough to see all the way down to the pebble beach a hundred feet below. Expecting to see the shattered body of my clerical guide, I was surprised to see nothing at all. I wondered at first if he had had some kind of miraculous soft landing and been able to walk or crawl away from the point of impact. I then noticed something which immediately scotched that idea. The area immediately below and stretching a few yards forwards to where the pebbles began was sand that was still wet from the tide having been recently right in. Had anyone fallen onto it, there would have been deep marks and the outline of the body. There was nothing. No sign of an impact and no footprints from anyone having got up and walked away. When he had stepped forwards over the edge, the curate had very literally vanished into thin air.

As I tried to grapple with this, I heard the heavy, rapidly advancing footsteps of the rector.

"Over here," I shouted, and within seconds he lumbered into view, desperately short of breath and the most worried man I had ever seen.

"Thank God," he said, "in the most literal sense. How on earth did you get down here – and why?"

I dragged myself up and he immediately pulled me several feet back from the edge.

"Come on," he said, "let's get back to the rectory while we can actually see a few feet in front of us. You can tell me what happened as we go."

After we were safely back in the warmth of the parlour and holding comforting mugs of coffee, the rector said,

"I didn't say anything while you were telling me what had happened on the way back because I wanted to check the church records. I keep them safely under lock and key here in the house, given the penchant of some thieves to steal such things for dishonest collectors nowadays."

"And?" I asked.

"I did a quick search through the historical listings of past rectors and curates while you were getting warm by the fire and there was indeed a curate who lived in the village with his mother. In that sense your guide was perfectly genuine. But he was a wrong 'un as they say round here and the cause of some scandal for the church. He used his ability to enter all of the houses hereabouts, on the pretext of priestly visits, to make a note of where the wealthier farmers and other folks appeared to keep their money – and the best ways of breaking in. Made quite a living for himself until the local magistrate put two and two together and he was caught red-handed. In attempting to escape, he knocked flying one of those trying to arrest him. The unfortunate man hit his head hard on a stone fireplace and couldn't be revived. Neither could the curate – he was hanged shortly afterwards, in 1793. The Reverend Jeremiah Hardy – the man who tried to lead you over the cliff's edge – died over two hundred years ago."

I sat ashen-faced and silent. He said,

"You told me he knocked on the door of the church, but didn't go in and that when you got outside where he was standing, the temperature plummeted."

"That's right," I said.

"Some of the people who take an interest in such occurrences would immediately say two things," he replied. "First, that he didn't go in because the forces for good inside the church were too strong, he knew he would have been repelled. Second, not going in also enabled him to fool you into thinking that the temperature outside was so freezing cold because of the weather and not a phenomenon that frequently accompanies manifestations like him."

"So you believe that what I encountered was an evil spirit of some kind?" I asked.

"Well," he replied, "as I said earlier, that's the traditional way of seeing such things, but from my own research into this kind of area, matters seem to be too complex for such neat and simple classifications. Let's just say that you encountered a force decidedly hostile to your interests, which may or may not be supernatural."

"Not very cheery, whichever way you look at it," I said, a desperate smile flickering across my lips. "If you hadn't shouted when you did, I could have been your first funeral for next week."

"Yes, I know, a somewhat sobering thought," he replied. "But the fact is that someone did warn you in time and that's the other side of the coin. It could have been coincidence that I spotted your scarf in the graveyard, at the start of the path down to the cliffs. As soon as I saw it, I realised where you'd gone. But then others would argue that God, good, whatever you want to call it, frequently intervenes through coincidence and that your life was saved by more than good luck."

"The fact that you saw my scarf on the path is a puzzle," I said. "When I was leaving the church, I couldn't find it anywhere and didn't take it with me."

"Well, that leads me neatly into the next set of possibilities," he said. "The whole episode with the curate could just as easily have been devised to put the frighteners on you, to make you realise what could happen if you try to disobey and escape from the good Mr. Green. I know that might sound fantastical, but let's consider what might at first sight seem ridiculous as well as the obvious, because where evil is concerned, the most unlikely things can sometimes turn out to be the solution to otherwise unfathomable puzzles. From what you've told me, this very strange man – if mortal man he is – is so wealthy he could have arranged for your phone and emails to be hacked, so that he knew of your intentions far enough in advance to be able to put a counter-strategy in place. I know that sounds like the ravings of my overactive imagination, but let's just remember how controlling and determined he is. Hacking would come as second nature to such a man if he wanted to monitor your whereabouts and your intentions. Knowing that you were coming to ask for my help, he could have paid a suitably biddable out-of-work actor to do the necessary for you to be scared off from trying to wriggle out of his grip. Again, it's not as unlikely as you might think, that kind of thing has been done before and it's been the stuff of countless film scripts and TV dramas. I suspect there's probably information about the murderous curate on one of the local history sites on the internet, so he could easily have found it if looking for a dramatic and frightening way of getting at you.

"So, let's just take all of this to its logical conclusion and see what we're left with. If Lucian Green was indeed behind it all, then the mysterious disappearance of your scarf and its laying down for me to find in the nick of time could have been carefully improvised as part of the plan to threaten you, without actually going to the next stage and bumping you off. I know it might sound at first a barmy suggestion, but just think about what actually happened. The curate's promised call for you to walk over what was, in fact, the cliff edge didn't materialise and might never have done so – and there was I, alerted by your scarf, to come to the rescue. There was no explicit linkage made between your near-death experience and the purpose of your visiting me, but there didn't need to be. If it was Lucian Green, he was being subtle, leaving you to draw your own conclusions.

"I have no evidence to offer you for any of these possibilities, but the point I want to make is that there's no reason for automatically jumping to the conclusion that Lucian Green is able to haunt and pursue you via supernatural means. He may well simply be a very wealthy conman who's determined not to lose a key asset from his complex scams – you, 'The Storyteller'. If necessary, he's prepared to half frighten you to death to retain his control over you. A mere mortal is rather less terrifying and

173

hopefully easier for us to deal with."

I said,

"I was half-asleep when the knock on the church door came. If there had been someone hiding in the church they could have taken the scarf without me noticing. That would fit with your theory."

As I was speaking, we both became aware of the sound of the church organ wafting across the still and silent space between the rectory and the church. The rector said,

"How curious, our organist is a very elderly gentleman in poor health and he's in hospital at the moment after an unfortunate fall. Maybe we have a visitor to the church who decided to have a go without the usual courtesy of asking me first. I think I'd better go and take a look."

I didn't want to be on my own after the episode at the cliff edge, so walked across with him. The church door was ajar and as we got near, it became very clear that what was being played bore little relation to traditional church music. It sounded both jaunty and more than a little Greek, as if it should have been played on a zither rather than a pipe organ. I said,

"What is that tune?"

He said,

"A very famous one, if I'm not mistaken – our surprise guest organist is playing the theme from The Third Man, one of the all-time greats of the movies, as they say."

Every hair on my head seemed to stand on end. I remembered Green's chilling use of precisely the same film to remind me of how little I or my life meant to him and the need for me to deliver what he commanded. As soon as we stepped inside the church, the music stopped, the echoes of the surprisingly powerful organ reverberating for a few seconds up and down the nave. The rector strode purposefully down the aisle and almost ran up the stairs to the organ loft. I followed him, my heart beating twice as fast as normal in anticipation of what we might find. When we got to the top, the sight that greeted us was baffling. The light over the keyboard was on, but nobody was there. The mystery organist would have had to have slipped over the rails at the opposite side of the loft and dropped down onto the baptismal font below in order not to be seen by us as we ran up the stairs. We heard the sound of the church door closing softly and hurried down to see if we could catch sight of our clearly very shy visitor. As we stepped outside, the mist had temporarily cleared and we could see for at least a hundred and fifty yards in all directions, but again, nobody was visible. The rector said,

"How very strange."

"It's more than strange," I said, as he locked the church door. I explained the episode with Green and his soliloquy on The Third Man as we walked back to the rectory. He said,

"This puts an entirely different complexion on things. Maybe your visit from the criminal curate was indeed simply designed to demonstrate what might happen should you try and escape your friend Mr. Green's clutches. The theatrical performance in the organ loft could have been thrown in for good measure to make sure that you got the message, as it were."

I said,

"Indeed. I'm in two minds as to whether Lucian Green is simply a highly accomplished illusionist or really has the kinds of diabolical power that he hints at. The stunt with the Harry Potter-esque half floor in the Shard suggests a dark sense of humour and that's apparent again in the choice of music just now."

"It could have gone badly wrong for him if you'd have slipped over the cliff edge," he replied, "you were dangerously near it."

"It could, but I didn't," I replied, "and as you said before, the invitation for me to actually walk over the edge may never have materialised."

"Indeed," he replied, "and again, let's consider the apparently ridiculous in case it hides within its unlikeliness the truth we would otherwise miss. For all we know, he could well have had some fail-safe in place to make sure that you didn't accidentally wander over the brink while you were waiting. If I was the first man and the curate the second, then perhaps, in line with the title of Green's favourite film, there was a third man also. If I hadn't come after you and shouted a warning so soon then perhaps the unseen third man, the magician who removed your scarf so skilfully that you didn't notice a thing, had been told to intervene, should your curiosity have taken you too near to the edge. Again such possibilities sound ridiculous and overimagined, but from what you've told me Lucian Green specialises in the ridiculous with all of the fantasies he weaves around the idea of the Rule of Ten. The scarf thief, hiding behind a nearby rock perhaps, could have been given instructions to shout and tell you to stop in a suitably ghostly voice, before vanishing, along with the actor-curate. Who knows? As I said before, with your strange friend the most ridiculously contrived theories may actually be the best match to the truth."

I said,

"Well, a third man would have been a suitably dark pun on Green's favourite film title – just the kind of thing that would amuse the type of person who punned on Harry Potter at the Shard. And thinking back on it, there was a long stretch of thick red ribbon nailed into the ground six feet from the cliff edge. I didn't think anything of it at the time, given my concern about the vanishing curate, but it could well have been placed there in advance to stop him going over the edge, while leaving just enough time for me to be stopped from going over as well. But whatever the truth of the matter, if I lose my nerve and go back to doing what Green wants, then putting on the frighteners will have worked and I'll be worth keeping alive. But should I succeed in escaping from him, things could become decidedly deadlier. He'd have nothing left to lose and, as in The Third Man, my life would be worth nothing more than an ant to him. That could well be the message in the music."

The rector said,

"If what you suspect is true, then this individual is using you almost as a plaything by writing you, an author of ghost stories, into his own rather hammy ghost story – something that he clearly finds amusing, but which equally is meant as a threat of violence to keep you under his control. If he is willing to go to such trouble to make his point – and able to do so on the occasion of our meeting which you presumably made every effort to keep secret from him – that is deeply worrying. Are you sure you want to take the risk of following whatever advice I may see fit to give you, instead of following his commands? I have to ask you this given the serious nature of the threat he appears to pose to your wellbeing."

"Yes," I said, without hesitation. "Even if I buy my safety now by doing everything he wants, who knows what he'll do when he no longer has a need for my services and maybe decides that I know a little too much to be left alone?"

"OK," the rector said, "I'll sleep on it and decide what best to advise you tomorrow morning. This is a most unusual case in so far as the darkness at the heart of it seems to have come right into the church grounds. But the very fact that no malign spirit has dared engage in mischief within the church itself during my incumbency leads me to the presumption that the phantom organist was, as you suggest, very much made of flesh and blood. As for the curate, who knows? As I said before, Lucian Green clearly has both the money and a sufficiently macabre mind to orchestrate today's bizarre happenings without a conscience or any other form of moral compass. All of that might lead me to conclude that we are dealing simply with a very devious, clearly very rich and powerful, but, in all probability, ordinary mortal using other mere mortals to do his dirty work. However, such things as the voices in the Lancashire graveyard and the vicious attacks by crows that Green appeared to be able to control throw a different light on things. They make it much more difficult to judge precisely what is going on in this case. We may well be looking at someone who operates through both malleable and biddable flesh and blood and spiritual forces of an unknown nature. If that is the case, it is a very dangerous and complex mix. I will need to think very carefully as to how we might best contain and then neutralise the attempts of this individual to control you for his own very obviously distasteful and evil purposes."

Our conversation continued far into the night and led me to the realisation that Green was so complex a being that I might never properly get to the bottom of who and what exactly he was.

On looking at the church through my bedroom window later, I saw that the lights in the nave appeared to have come on again of their own accord. I'd seen the rector turning them off before my own eyes. I thought of telling him but then, on reflection, decided that another investigatory visit to the church to see what was happening would just be playing into Green's hands and allowing him to manipulate our curiosities and fears as if we were marionettes. Accordingly, I simply pulled the flimsy curtains tightly shut. Difficult though it was given the fraught circumstances of the day, I determined to go to sleep as quickly as I could manage and exhaustion turned out to be a willing helper. Within minutes of slipping between the cold sheets, I drifted off into the dark galaxy of the night.

CHAPTER ELEVEN

Black crows circled the flagpole on top of the church tower as if it were a maypole for the dead. A feral cat watched and hissed from the bushes in the rectory garden. From the mist at the top of the drive a dark shadow emerged and moved slowly and determinedly towards the house. Within moments it was in the parlour where I was finishing the last of my breakfast. The rector pulled off the eccentricity that was his hat and flung it onto a chair. He said,

"Well, my dear, that was the dampest walk I've had into the village for a long time. It's a lot clearer than it was, that's one thing at least – visibility's about a hundred yards, I think – but you're welcome to stay for lunch and see if it lifts completely this afternoon."

"No, no, thank you, you've been far too kind already and I'll end up eating all of your food as well as drinking far too much of your tea," I replied. "I might as well go now in case the fog comes down as thick as it was yesterday and you end up stuck with me as a permanent lodger. The advice you gave me before breakfast regarding Lucian Green was just what I wanted. I need to get back and start doing what you suggest as soon as possible. But really, thank you for all your kindnesses."

I'm not the most confident of motorists and drove slowly and carefully down the narrow country lanes that led ultimately to the motorway, in the correct anticipation that not every vehicle I encountered would be driven wisely and well for the conditions. I had to brake hard on one bend as the headlights from a car large enough to give its owner the illusion of immortality veered into view, with the front onside wheel clearly straddling the centre of the road. It nearly forced me into the dry stone wall at the side. I let it pass before driving on, glancing resentfully in my rear-view mirror to see whether the perpetrator of my near-demise had managed to stay on the road. What I saw caused my heart to race. Just for a second another pair of eyes appeared to be looking back at me. They were those of the disappearing curate and they were cold and threatening. I braked heavily and pulled into the side of the road again. I turned round to check the back of the car, one hand on the door handle ready to escape in case the eyes and their owner were a terrifying reality. I was both puzzled and relieved to find nothing.

My heart still beating at twice its normal rate, I eased the car back onto the road and ploughed on through the mist. Visibility varied considerably. Sometimes I could see a hundred yards or more, sometimes barely fifty. The temperamental satnav on which I was relying was struggling to find its orbital guide due to the weather conditions and I found myself driving blind for a couple of miles at a time as contact was temporarily lost.

Finally I came to a crossroads where, unhelpfully, someone had collided with the signpost and knocked it into the bushes at the side of the road. The satnav remained mute and I waited frustratedly in the hope that it might resurrect itself. I looked in the rear-view mirror to check that nothing was coming up from behind while the car was stationary and saw the same cold eyes staring back at me again. I flung the door open and jumped out, running to the opposite side of the road before pausing to see if I was being followed. As before, there was nothing and I couldn't see anyone in the passenger seats. The only sound was that of unseen birds chattering in the trees and hedgerows, shrouded in the damp mist that filled the air all around. I crept back cautiously towards the car, my whole body shivering with the cold and peered inside. It was definitely empty. Reluctant to get back in, but struggling against the bone-freezing damp, I decided to risk it and slid gingerly back into the driver's seat. The warmth of the car heater was some reassurance – there was no sudden drop in temperature as had been the case when the curate had appeared outside the church. The satnav suddenly let rip with a series of discordant electronic beeps that only it understood and sprang back into life. The problem was that what came out of it was not its normal, confident, robot-controlled female voice, but something at once familiar and as equally disturbing as the phantom eyes in the mirror. It was unmistakeably the voice of the curate. It said,

"You can't run away. Go home to your cottage, stay home, do what you're told and serve the Master of the Rule of Ten. Every time you think of escaping from what's demanded of you, I'll come after you. I'm watching your every step. One step too many and you'll go over the cliff. Keep remembering that. One step too many and you're dead. Now, go straight across the junction and keep going, keep going home and keep to the deal, serve the Master of the Rule of Ten."

I sat rigid and ice-cold, my breath seeming to freeze in front of my face. The temperature in the car had plummeted to below zero and frost started to form on the side windows. I looked in the rear-view mirror and saw the manic eyes again, fixing me with a gaze that was so frightening and hypnotic I couldn't turn away. Then they faded and the voice in the satnav returned to its normal self, a demure, calm, robot-controlled woman who echoed the curate's instruction to go straight across at the junction.

I sat frozen and uncertain what to do for a couple of minutes, but was shaken out of my stupor by the fierce blaring of a horn behind me. I turned round and saw the high-rise bonnet of a Range Rover. It was being driven by a fierce looking man who probably believed that people like me in midget-mobiles should be made to travel across fields and never get in their way. I decided I'd better move before he got out and started abusing the peasant. I eased my way across the junction and followed the road the satnav's dual personality had recommended. I proceeded as gingerly as before in view of the thick shrouds of developing fog that kept obscuring my view and the narrowness of the carriageway. Such caution enraged my pursuer even more. After sitting so near to my rear bumper that the two cars almost mated and flashing his headlights so many times that I began to wonder if I was being tailgated by a Christmas tree, he suddenly sped past at a point where the road widened a little. Two fingers were waved at me from the passenger window and the oversized rear wheels sent a bucketful of mud hurtling onto my windscreen, making it even more difficult to see than before. I stopped and got out to try and clear the mess off with a cloth. As I did so, the car radio switched itself on. I was in the middle of nowhere, with only the fog for company and no chance of a knight in shining armour riding out of the fields to carry me away to safety. My brain was very close to pressing the panic button as I slid tentatively back into the driver's seat. The temperature at least had gone back to normal but, try as I might, I couldn't switch the radio off. There was nothing frightening in what was being said, it was just a gaggle of English middle-class voices babbling away about their favourite holiday destinations on Radio 4. Finally, giving up on my attempts to restore silence, I restarted the car and continued my slow progress down the wearily long and fog-bound narrow road.

I'd ploughed on for about five minutes when, suddenly, the competing voices on the radio were reduced to one – a familiar and disturbing, ice-wouldn't-melt-in-the-mouth, self-satisfied and commanding voice, one that resonated with the texture of ground glass. It said,

"Remember always that you are nothing, you came from mere atoms and you will return to atoms. Your sole moment of significance will be what you have done and what you will continue to do for me and that significance will exist only because it is a faint echo of my purposes and actions. The stupidity of this voyage to the land of belief in God, goodness and all such imaginary manifestations of the non-existent must never be repeated. Do as my servant has told you and go home - and stay away from fools like the rector. All they can offer you is a prescription for your own destruction. Do enjoy the rest of your journey, my dear."

Green's last word was followed seamlessly by the resumption of the middle-class holiday merriment, as if there had been no interruption. I began to wonder whether I'd imagined hearing his characteristically threatening warning, as well as the various preceding sightings of the curate's crazed eyes and the distinctive sound of his voice. As so many times before on this bizarre trip into foggy oblivion, I felt helpless, frightened and baffled. I had no idea how all of this could be happening and even of whether it was really happening, or whether my imagination had freaked out and gone into some kind of overdrive in which it was now writing me into its own ghost stories.

I somehow managed to pull myself together enough to drive on through the increasingly dense fog for what seemed like an hour or more. I slavishly followed the calm instructions of the female robot within the satnav, until finally I came across a sign saying that the motorway was only five miles away. My mind had been only half on the road for most of the time. The other half of its attention was focussed on the ways and means of as quick an escape as possible back to Ireland. I had the superstitious hope that the expanse of water between the two countries would act as some kind of moat which ghostly voices and other ethereal servants of the bullying Mr. Green would fear to cross. As I reached a point where aspiration changed into determination and I'd decided to make a dash back to Dublin as soon as I could, I was startled by the satnav woman going wildly off script and saying,

"That's not an option. Think of the children. What will happen to the little ones if you leave them and don't deliver on the deal? You know what will happen, you can't do that to them. You can't surrender their fates to the Earl. Do as you promised and all will be well, renege on the deal and their lives will be hell. Turn right in fifty yards and then right again at the cross roads."

I stopped the car again and contemplated with incredulity the device's seamless switch from the banality of map directions to dire threats and back again. This was turning into such a weird journey that I'd now almost passed the point of fear. I began to wonder whether, as in the Lancashire cemetery, Green had found his way inside my head and was playing virtual games with my reality. None of this stuff seemed believable, it was as if I was sitting watching myself playing a role in somebody else's movie. Either that or I was developing some of the symptoms of a psychosis, hearing voices in the radio and the satnav – and in dire need of psychiatric help. Whatever the truth of the matter, I needed to get moving and find my way home before the fog became any thicker and I ended up being hit by another speed merchant in an oversized four-by-four – *if* the cottage could be called home.

I determined to ignore any further voices I might think I was hearing and presume that they were either imaginary or malicious, implanted into my mind by 'Green the Sorcerer', if that was indeed how he might be best described. Psychology, psychology, psychology, I thought to myself. If that's what Green's using against me, I'll use it to blunt his impact. And, irrespective of whether the threats that had already been delivered via the satnav were real or imaginary, the children were Engel's responsibility and I'd done all that I could to try and ensure that they were safe and protected from malign influences. I pressed down gently on the accelerator and followed the remaining signs to the motorway. I hummed loudly an inane tune that was designed to blank out any other noises or voices in the car and enable me to get on with the challenge of battling my way through the fog. Mind over madness, psychology over superstition, call it what you like, it worked for the time being.

By the time I got back to the estate it was pitch-dark. I rolled the car gently up onto the hardstanding at the side of the kitchen garden and let out a heartfelt sigh of relief. The cottage felt almost welcoming – no strange presences or other uninvited guests appeared to be around. I poured myself a small glass of wine and flopped exhaustedly onto my favourite armchair. Within a few minutes I slipped easily into a light sleep.

I was awoken suddenly by a knock at the door. I hauled myself upright and went over to the front window to see if it was Engel. There was no-one visible. I decided I must have dreamt it. I turned and was about to go and sit down again when someone or something knocked for a second time. I pulled the curtain back immediately, fast enough to catch any pranksters before they had managed to run and hide, but again, there was no-one. My heart sank. I hurried round all of the downstairs windows and the back door to make sure that they were all securely locked, and then shut the living room door firmly behind me. I drink only occasionally and then only for relaxation purposes, but on this occasion I felt in need of a second glass to calm me and duly poured one. I sat down again, my nerves on edge and waited.

For a good five minutes nothing happened. I wondered whether to put the television on and see if there was anything worth watching. That at least might take my mind off things. I reached over to the coffee table for the TV guide, but before I was able to pick it up every bone in my body was shaken. BANG! BANG! BANG! BANG! BANG! BANG! BANG! BANG! The hammering on the front windows was so fierce it seemed they would shatter. Without thinking, my heart beating so fiercely it felt as if it would burst out of my ribcage, I ran to the curtains and flung them open. I stood panting, desperate and terrified. In the semi-illumination of the exterior security light I could see absolutely nothing and no-one that might have been responsible. I drew the curtains again, but left a small gap so that I could watch the front garden without being seen. I stood there, rigid, my nerves on a proverbial knife-edge, for a good ten minutes, but nothing moved other than the leaves of the evergreens in the gentle breeze. Finally, physically and emotionally exhausted, I returned to my chair and took a large gulp of wine. The instant that I did so, it happened again, if anything more loudly, but this time at the back window. The shock caused me to drop my glass, spilling wine all over my best trousers. I cursed and screamed.

Once again there was complete silence when the hammering stopped, this time for a good quarter of an hour. I began to think that whatever it was out there must finally have had enough and gone away, when it happened yet again. This time the pounding was on the living room door. It was so fierce that I could see the wood vibrating to the point where it looked as if it would be smashed from its hinges and I would be left confronting face to face the violent demon or whatever it was that was intent on persecuting me. Then again it stopped. I sat trembling and utterly terrified for a minute or two, gradually becoming conscious of something else odd that was happening in the room. Slowly but inexorably, despite the low-key lighting, it was beginning to get brighter. Simultaneously, my grip on what was going on around me loosened drastically and it seemed as if I was floating in and out of consciousness. The brighter the light became, the more it seemed to block out all of my other thoughts until I reached a point where I was conscious of nothing else but its blinding brilliance.

Then the knocking started again, only this time it sounded much less frenetic. It was accompanied by a voice. The words at first didn't make any sense, but gradually I began to pull myself together. The voice sounded familiar and the light too began to take on a less disturbing texture. My eyes had been squeezed tightly shut to reduce its burning impact, but now I felt able to open them again. I blinked for a few seconds, baffled by what I could see, but then gradually it all started to make sense. I was still at the rectory, in the very comfortable bed that I'd spent the night in. The brilliant light was the early morning sun that had come straight into my room through the paper-thin curtains. The voice was that of my host asking softly through the door if I was awake. Everything that had seemed so real and terrifying, the hammering on the windows and door, took a step back as the order of the daylight world gradually established itself. But they wouldn't give way entirely to the 'reality' of the new morning and the more conscious I became, the more they resisted all my attempts to dismiss them as simply a nightmare. They had the hard-edged feeling of a horror movie that had been somehow projected within my head, with myself as the lead character under duress, a means for Green to get into my mind through my dreams. Too much of what I'd experienced during my restless night seemed to be an echo of the Lancashire cemetery and other unsavoury moments in his company. The rector said,

"Miss O'Donnell, are you awake?"

"Yes, yes, I am," I replied.

He said,

"I'll leave your breakfast on a tray outside the door for you to collect when you're ready."

I said,

"Thank you, that's really kind of you."

"Did you sleep well?" he asked.

"Yes and no," I replied. "I'll tell you about it when I come downstairs."

"Righty-ho, as long as you're OK at the moment. You're sure you're alright?"

"Yes, yes, I'm fine," I replied, "it'll just be useful having a chat with you to try and make sense of a few things that went through my mind in the night."

He said,

"I'll be in the study when you're ready. I've left your tray on the floor. The cat's had its breakfast and is outside sunning itself, so your food should be safe enough there if you grab it fairly soon."

When I got downstairs later, I was confronted by the comical sight of the rector's substantial hindquarters as he knelt on all fours, sticking posters to large pieces of stiff card. He turned to greet me and said,

"Ah, good morning, my dear, you're just in time to see me sticking my fingers to these posters and making a general mess of things. It's all part of the business of trying to raise our parishioners' awareness of the plight of the poor around the world. As we only have a regular congregation of twenty or thirty, and many of them are elderly and rather poor themselves, I'm not optimistic about our likely receipts."

"Do you look after other churches as well as this one?" I asked.

"Four altogether," he said, "for as long as we have the money to keep them going. A couple are in need of very expensive repairs. They're all very old and beautiful, very spiritual places, it's such a shame."

"Then you must let me pay you for your hospitality," I replied, "you've been very kind and even saved my life, so I think that justifies a generous donation."

"No, good Lord, no, my dear," he replied, "I wasn't touting for funds, heaven forbid. Consider it the ancient hospitality of the monasteries, even though I'm very obviously not a monk, although I am beginning to look a little ancient. You were a guest who came to me in need and I don't charge for spiritual or advisory services. Now, the most important thing is that you tell me what was worrying you last night."

I recounted the unsettling narrative of my dreams. He listened intently and when I'd finished, he simply nodded his head and was silent for a few moments. Never comfortable with gaps in conversations, I added,

"On the one hand, there's the easy explanation that what I experienced was the normal stuff of dreams and nightmares. Accept that and there's nothing to worry about. On the other, there was the uneasy feeling, which I still have, that they were more than dreams – that Lucian Green had somehow got into my head again and was messing about with it in order to try and keep me under his control. I have no idea, no theories, as to how he does this, but he is an extraordinary and disturbing individual and I have this gut feeling that he knows how to get inside my skull."

He nodded again and frowned in deep concentration. He said,

"The person you have described to me in our conversations is undoubtedly unusual, to put things as politely as possible. He gives the impression almost of existing in some strange middle state between the physical and the spiritual. I would normally say that such a thing is nonsense and that what we are looking at here is an example of an outstanding conman – someone with the skill to make people believe all kinds of things about the powers he possesses and his ability to interfere directly in their lives. But the episode with the voices and the birds in the cemetery, and the strange hold he seems to have over such a powerful and strong-willed man as your employer, have vague echoes of a past case that comes to mind."

He paused for a moment, his brow furrowing deeply again while he reflected on the matter. He said,

"I realise this may be hard to swallow, but certain overlaps with that past case suggest that the diagnosis should consider the extraordinary as well as the ordinary. I know that when we were discussing your near-death experience with the dodgy curate, I took a different tack. I stressed that we shouldn't rule out explanations which placed Lucian Green very firmly in the realm of the mortal rather than the immortal. But the details of your latest dream and various other of your odder experiences have resonances that fit a little too close for comfort to the case that I'm thinking of. You see, unlikely as it may seem in this predominantly secular age, it is possible – and I stress the word 'possible' until we have evidence one way or the other – that Lucian Green may in reality be a diabolical presence, one that is manifesting itself as flesh and blood through its powers of illusion. That would explain his ability to enter your mind and no doubt that of Sebastian Engel. The theatricality of his summoning you to an office that doesn't exist in one of London's most spectacular and expensive buildings would suggest that he is playing with you as much for his own amusement as his darker purposes. With his wealth it is, of course, theoretically possible that he could have bought his way into the building through corrupt means – and even have set up a 'pop-up' office in such a way that the reception staff remained unaware of what was going on. If he did that, then he remains within the realm of the mortal world. But, equally, a diabolical entity would have powers of illusion that would make such time-consuming exertions entirely unnecessary and could have done it all by ethereal sleight of hand. The phantom curate may have been another manifestation of the same being, rather than the simple actor that I first postulated. If we are dealing with such an entity, then past experience suggests that we are faced with a very formidable opponent."

His serious and well-meant thoughts didn't exactly gel with my own. This was not quite the diagnosis that I'd been moving towards after thinking everything through after breakfast. I was careful not to sound too critical in my response. I said,

"While such a thing may in theory be possible, it now feels a little less likely than other explanations – and I don't say that to be rude or ungrateful for the suggestion. I've wondered something along the same lines from time to time and that was one of the reasons that drove me to get in touch with you. I thought I could see various echoes of Lucian Green-like figures in your book. But the more I've thought about it all since I've been here, the less I'm inclined to go for the diabolical-spirit angle. The whole business yesterday with the red silk warning line neatly set out, the supposed curate who probably just ran off under the cover of the fog and the organist playing The Third Man theme, reeks too much of a theatrical set-up, as you originally suggested. What I find much easier to accept is the idea that Green may be a supremely accomplished manipulator of the mind, highly skilled in the tricks of the trade of psychology, hypnosis, you name it – and a master of all the ways that subtle prompts can be devised and used for auto-suggestion. Put all of that together with his wealth and deviousness and you've got a man with the power to wreak havoc in whatever way he chooses. I wonder whether the apparent hauntings on the part of the Earl at Engel's estate are the consequence of something that is entirely different, over which Green has merely pretended he might have some control. Take those out of the present picture and Green, the mortal, becomes an eccentric but more credible suspect for all of the mischief that's been going on. The dream that haunted me last night might well have been the simple consequence of my having been psyched out by all of his theatricals, for example. But we do agree on one thing and that is the formidable challenge he poses as an opponent. And

I don't have any idea as yet of how he pulled off the masterly illusion in the Shard, nor any explanation of how he controlled the birds in the cemetery - and those at my cottage."

He said,

"I'm not in the slightest offended, my dear, what we have described between us are two sets of possibilities that we might test out and decide between. That would seem an eminently logical way of trying to solve the riddle of what exactly this very strange individual is and how to deal with him, wouldn't you agree?"

"Well, yes, I suppose," I said uncertainly, "but how exactly are we to carry out the testing that you propose?"

"The more I think about it the more I'm convinced there's something we have to do before anything else," he replied. "If it works out, then we'll have a much clearer picture of precisely what type of threat it is that you're facing – and once we've got that we'll be in a better position to consider possible strategies for dealing with it. Are you prepared to take a risk and accompany me on a journey which could be the most terrifying thing you've experienced in your life?"

A little baffled by such a proposition and what it might entail, I said,

"I don't normally make a habit of actively looking for trouble, but if you think whatever it is that you have in mind might provide some answers, then yes, although the natural coward in me would hope that the terror wouldn't be too great."

He said,

"I'd like to take you to meet a couple who live twenty miles away up in the hills. After yesterday's unpleasant little incident and everything you've told me this morning, I think that a conversation with them might be the quickest way to find out whether Lucian Green is a conman or a devil, if I can put things in such primitive terms without offending your sensibilities. I can take you to their house and see if they'll agree to a chat."

"OK, if you think it would be helpful," I replied uncertainly. "As long as the fog keeps away, I can stay around a little longer. Who are these people?"

"A farmer and his wife," he said. "She looks after the farm now and you'll see why when we get there. I'll warn you in advance, you might find what you see and hear upsetting and frightening.

But I think Bill may be able to tell you things I can't. I stressed when you arrived that I'm neither a medium nor an exorcist, but he is someone who, for reasons you'll discover, does have knowledge of things that go beyond our normal understanding of this world."

I nodded and said,

"OK, sounds intriguing. I'll play it by ear and see what happens."

The drive into the hills in the rector's ancient Volvo seemed to be at least ten miles longer than he'd estimated and the brilliant early morning sun had faded and hidden itself behind a bank of thick cloud by the time we arrived. The car squelched up the muddy track to the farmhouse and drew to a halt in the stone flagged yard. The buildings nestled within a natural alcove at the heart of the bleak and rocky hill on which they sat, providing shelter from the fierce wind that seemed to have come from nowhere as the sun made its retreat. The plaintive baa-ing of the sheep and the howling gusts that were battering a rusty, corrugated-iron shepherd's hut further up the hillside gave the scene a feeling of desolation that was so palpable it could almost be touched. The rector led me towards the dark-shadowed entrance porch of the large, eighteenth-century, weathered stone farmhouse, a building that seemed possessed of a watchful, brooding character all of its own. The farm guard dog started barking vigorously inside the building as we approached. The door opened and the farmer's wife came out to greet us. She quietened the dog and invited us in.

The parlour was as spartan as it might have been a couple of hundred years earlier when carpets on a working farm would have been impractical and probably unaffordable. The original small windows let in only a little light and that in turn illuminated only weakly the pristine stone floor, a couple of very traditional dressers with blue willow-pattern plates on display and the four clean but well-worn armchairs that formed a semi-circle around the fire. I was struck by what wasn't present and that was a television or any other form of electronic gadgetry. The woman, Elizabeth, excused herself while she disappeared briefly to take her overalls off and then reappeared with tea and biscuits. She was friendly and welcoming, but weary looking and haunted by an air of sadness and regret. When the rector told her of the purpose of our visit, she nodded solemnly and said she'd check if Bill was well enough to see us. She looked at me and said,

"It's only people with the kind of problems that Bill can throw light on that the reverend brings here, so I know that my husband will want to see you. It's just a matter of whether he's up to it, and how much of him is present at the time. That may seem a strange thing to say, but you'll see what I mean if you meet him."

"Oh, I don't want to put anyone to any trouble," I said, worriedly.

"That's very thoughtful but it's no problem," Elizabeth replied. "If Bill is feeling well enough to see you he will, if he's not he won't. You won't be causing anyone any problems. I'll go up and have a word with him in a minute. It's just that he's almost completely paralysed, you see, that's what makes things always so uncertain. He had a bad accident on the road into the village. It was his own fault. He drank too much and on that night he wasn't wearing his seatbelt. He went round a corner too fast, swerved to try and miss a car coming the other way and they collided head-on. Two people dead and Bill wishing he was as well."

"Oh, Lord, how terrible," I said, beginning to wonder whether I had been wise to agree to intrude into such a tragic house.

"There's nothing that can be done, so there's no point in any of us fretting over things," Elizabeth said. "Bill has paid for his stupidity every day and every night since. He did something without my knowledge, he got in contact with somebody who advertised herself as a medium, that's why there's no phone in his bedroom any more. I don't want him bringing any more disasters on himself or the house. He was desperate to get in touch with the people he'd killed, to see if they could forgive him and she promised to help him, God save us."

She stopped at that point, her voice shaking and her eyes staring into the fire.

"In a roundabout way that's how he may be able to help you," she said at length, "although God knows who can help him with what he knows – and who he knows."

She got up and said,

"I'll go and see if he's up to it."

We sat in silence for a few seconds, listening to the creaking of the old, wooden staircase as she made a weary progress up to her husband. Then I said,

"What is it that he knows that's so awful?"

The rector sighed and said,

"What he shouldn't is the answer Elizabeth would give you if pressed, but she knows there's little point trying to shut the stable door once the horse has bolted. Whether it was as a direct result of the self-styled medium or simply the result of Bill's own mind reaching out into things that normally should be left well alone, he found himself visited by all kinds of weird and often extremely nasty presences, forces, whatever you like to call them. His doctor tried to dismiss it all as some form of delusion, until something pushed her coming down the stairs after she'd done so and she broke her leg in two places."

"He went looking for trouble and was stupid enough to find it," Elizabeth said. They hadn't noticed her glide back into the room. "He wanted to make contact with the men who had been killed as a result of his drunken antics and ask them to forgive him. Forgiveness was a big thing with him for a while after the accident, as the rector knows. But everything that was known about the two men suggests they were anything but forgiving when they were alive, never mind dead, and if it was them that caused what followed, then I can only say that hell hath no fury ..."

"What did follow?" I asked.

"A seemingly endless stream of visitors, none of them nice, and all of them dead," Elizabeth replied.

"Dead at the time or since?" I asked.

"Dead for centuries in some cases, I'd think," Elizabeth replied. "But then I'm just a simple farm girl grown old and simpler still. More educated people might know better."

She smiled, a hopeless, lost kind of a smile. She said,

"He'll see you now, but if it's too taxing for him we'll have to call it off. We'll see how it goes. You may get some of what he wants to say, or it might be all them – they've so far taken him over that you never know and he seems content with that now, despite what it's doing to him."

We followed her up the dark, oak staircase, our combined footsteps composing a symphony of creaks. She led us along a narrow corridor to the end bedroom and opened a door that was old and worn enough to have been there since the building was constructed. I wasn't prepared for the sight or sounds that confronted me. Only the old man visibly occupied the room, yet it was full of whisperings and the sound of what can only be described as continuous clawing and scratching that seemed to be coming from underneath the floorboards.

"Christine O'Donnell," the voice rasped, as though it knew me from birth. "They've told me all about you."

Bill looked for all the world like a man already dead. His face was drawn, white and haunted and his lips hardly moved as he spoke above the ceaseless whispering that was interrupted every now again by subdued, hollow laughter.

"Who's told you about me?" I asked.

"All of them," he replied, "they all know about you. All of my visitors."

"He means the spirits," Elizabeth said, "they come any time and whenever they do, they give him a taste of hell. That's why he looks like he does, it's not the injury that's killing him, they're draining the life out of him and there's nothing that can be done to stop them. He won't let the reverend try and help him."

"They say you're a chosen one," he said.

"Chosen by who?" I asked.

"They say that's for them to know and you to guess," he replied.

"What have I been chosen for?" I asked.

His face suddenly contorted into a twisted grin and his skin turned momentarily from death-white to jaundice-yellow. He said,

"Holy works, you've been chosen by the almighty to do holy works!"

"It's them speaking through him," Elizabeth said, "and when they talk of the almighty they're always referring to Satan."

"The almighty is amongst us, he has visited you in his hidden glory and he will come to you again in human form," Bill continued.

"This is dreadful," the rector said, "we'd better leave before they get up to any more blasphemous mischief. Thank you, Elizabeth – if he changes his mind at any stage, let me know and I'll bring a colleague and pray all night with him to see if we can get his soul back from these parasites."

Bill laughed and shouted after us,

"They'll get yours before you get mine!"

As we left the house, I said, "Do you think he was referring to

Green?"

"The voices that he's hearing are by definition liars," the rector replied, "so they may well have simply made up everything that you were told in there. On the other hand, if they were right, the situation is, of course, extremely worrying. The seriousness of yesterday's event led me to conclude that we should at least find out what they would say. Whether we accept it or not depends on further evidence, but their claims do add an extra dimension to the picture of what might be going on."

I said,

"You don't think the voices may simply be the result of some kind of mental condition, dementia even? The scratching we heard could have simply been rats under the floorboards and the voices mere inventions of a disintegrating mind."

"I wondered that at first and voices most generally do turn out to be purely and simply a symptom of mental illness," he replied. "But I've seen and heard enough other phenomena in that room to make me think otherwise. I don't think there's any doubt that our unfortunate friend is in the grip of something that is decidedly not human – and it might be useful to bear in mind that I at no stage gave either the farmer or his wife your name and yet he knew you as soon as you entered the room. "

"So where does all of this get us?" I asked.

"What would you most immediately like to achieve in terms of finding out what's going on?" the rector asked.

"I'd like to be able to eliminate this demon stuff if at all possible – I believe in the existence of evil, but not in the idea of a 'devil' as such – and certainly not in the idea of him visiting me in hidden and human forms, whether they be Lucian Green, the curate or the Queen of Sheba. If we could show somehow that Bill or 'his voices' were simply lying in that respect, we would at least have narrowed down the field of possible explanations."

"OK," the rector said, "when you get back home you need to get hold of a copy of Prebender's 'History of Lancashire at the time of the witch trials'. You'll find in there his examination of the case of Mary Rowlands. I haven't had time to look into it myself properly yet, but my initial research suggests that it might be quite useful in helping determine what precisely is involved in the notion of the devil coming among us. Mary Rowlands was an interesting person who was ahead of her superstitious times in trying to be a little scientific and inventing rigorous tests to establish whether or not such a thing has happened. That will at least give you a starting point – let me know how you get on and if I can be of any further help."

The long drive back to the cottage was a monotonous task done with a heavy heart. Whether or not I believed what I'd heard in the old farmhouse, my encounter with Bill had left me notably depressed. It had seemed during my first talk with the rector that I might be getting nearer to the underlying causes of what had been happening to me, but the unsettling nastiness of the 'voices' allegedly speaking through Bill had thrown everything back into the mix again. If anything, they had left me even more unclear than before as to what was really going on. I desperately wanted to discount them as just the demented ramblings of a very sick old man – a hallucinating invalid who'd maybe picked up my name through something as simple as overhearing our conversations through the gaps between his bedroom floorboards before we went up to see him. But no matter how hard the rational part of my mind tried to do this, I couldn't escape the nagging thought that the very strange and disturbing atmosphere in Bill's sickroom was so strong and real that it might only be explainable in supernatural terms. That was not a possibility that sat easily with me.

CHAPTER TWELVE

The sky hung low, draped like a shroud over the rich green, sheep-filled fields and hills. The clouds were pregnant with melancholy rather than rain. As I drove into Bowland-in-Castledale's short main street, I was hit straight between the eyes by the imposing clock tower of its ancient church. It dominated the village from its position on top of a mound on which I could imagine grey-faced goblins sitting in a semi-circle, glowering at all who passed beneath. I drove on, past the pub and the church, until I came to a stretch of patchwork pavement, which ran parallel to a procession of tall trees, a village green, and an imposing line of history-filled stone houses. I parked and walked back to the church, ascending the mound on which it crouched by means of a worn stone stairway that still echoed with footsteps from centuries ago. The building seized my gaze as soon as I stood beneath it, a beautifully crafted mixture of accident and inspiration from different periods over its near-thousand years of existence and I was for a few moments mesmerised.

It was the weekend after my visit to Northumberland. I'd been so shattered by the aftershock of the weird experiences with the curate and the disappearing organist – and the mocking, acidic words and whispers in the farmhouse bedroom – that I'd sat on the fireplace rug for an hour after getting back to the cottage, staring into space. Then I'd had one of those 'snap out of it' moments that so often kept me afloat. I decided that while the rector's advice about checking out Prebender's book on witches and witch trials had at the time seemed to be verging a little on the eccentric, I nevertheless had no choice but to get hold of a copy. I needed to see if it did, in fact, have anything to reveal in the light of what we'd heard from the old farmer. The rector had stressed that what we'd been told in that shrivelled man's bedroom meant that, whether I liked it or not, I had to at least consider the possibility of Green being in some way a diabolical presence made flesh – or, only a little less dramatically, a normal individual who had become possessed by 'the devil', 'darkness' or equivalent malevolent force. The case of Mary Rowlands, the rector had implied, might help me determine if such a thing as the first of these possibilities could ever become a reality. If I didn't believe it could and wanted to eliminate it from my investigation of what was going on with Green, then Prebender would be a key means of helping me do that. Therefore, I had accessed and read rapidly a copy of the book, and from that had been able to draw up an initial plan of action for investigating the true nature of Lucian Green.

I found, as the rector had intimated, that Prebender's discussion of Rowlands' case and her original claims fleshed out in useful but very preliminary detail the question of what precisely was involved in the ancient notion of the devil 'coming among us' either directly or through his 'servants'. My trip to the churchyard in Bowland-in-Castledale, therefore, was spurred by what I'd read and was in pursuit of further information, most particularly from one of the gravestones. Two well-researched articles that I'd found on the internet had suggested that Mary's gravestone held vital clues to understanding key claims which she'd made. If, via Prebender and Rowlands and the additional vital clues that I believed one of the gravestones to hold, I could overturn and rule out the possibility of Green being some kind of 'demonic figure' made flesh and in any way genuinely possessed of 'supernatural powers', I could stop being quite so afraid of him. Finding ways of extricating myself from his grip would then seem considerably less daunting. 'Less daunting' would still not equate with anything that would be easy to achieve, however, and I was resigned to a significant struggle with such a wily and controlling individual, whatever the outcome of my investigations. Equally, establishing beyond all doubt that Lucian Green was a mere mortal would not provide any clues as to what had been going on in terms of the apparent haunting of the children back on the estate, and that formed another disturbing thread in my collection of worries. He could only be linked to all of that if he did indeed have dark spiritual powers of some kind.

So, in pursuit of the information that, with as much doubt as optimism, I hoped would help liberate me from his poisonous psychological control, I'd come to this remote and beguiling place in search of a very specific tomb. The graveyard that lay all around me was a mixture of grandeur and sadness, ranging from the splendour of an imitation Celtic cross that marked the last resting place of a long-deceased lady of the manor, to worn and weathered slabs which lay unevenly over the remains of those made nameless by the erosion of their details. I picked my way carefully across the lightly damp ground, respectfully trying not to step on the graves themselves, as I searched for a headstone with Mary Rowlands' name carved into it. As I did so, I became conscious of every sound around me, from the chatter of the birds in the trees of surrounding gardens to the persistent flap-flapping of the flag rope against the church tower's mast that pointed upwards towards the Almighty like a thin, bone-white finger. Apart from the occasional passing car and faint ripples of laughter that wafted on the wind as some revellers left the pub further down the street, there were no other sounds at all. As I wandered from grave to grave, musing about the contrast between those few of the long dead who had survived into old age and the many who had died in infancy or their early twenties, I became increasingly uneasy. I kept having the sensation of seeing someone or something out of the corner of my eye. Whenever I turned to look full on there was nothing visible, but the conviction that I had seen something, right at the extremes of the brain's ability to detect beings and motion, wouldn't go away. I had the impression that whatever was present was shadowlike and slender, watching my every move and letting me know that it was there, while melting instantly into invisibility as soon as I turned my full gaze towards it. I continued my search, looking for the grave while minding my back, until finally I found what I'd come for. I bent over to wipe some of the moss and dirt away from the inscription when I was startled by the sound of snapping twigs behind me. I turned to see a middle-aged rector approaching. He said,

"Good afternoon, are you looking for the grave of a relative?"

"Hello, no," I said, "I'm just here to see this grave. It's of interest in some research I'm doing."

"Ah, yes, Mary Rowlands," he said, "one of our most interesting residents, if some of the stories that have come to light about her are true. I take it that your interest relates to the stories?"

"Yes, if you mean Prebender's history of Lancashire at the time of the witch trials," I replied.

"Quite an important find," he replied. "To think that such a well-written and exhaustive analysis of all of the hysteria, its origins, exploiters and victims could have remained quietly hidden away and forgotten about in the rafters of an old house for so many centuries. If it hadn't been for the new occupants having a clear-out of their loft, the book might never have been discovered. Your interest in Mary is the devil, I presume, or rather her claims to have had regular conversations with him?"

"Yes, that's right," I replied.

He said,

"Prebender wrote his history fifty years after the trials, of course, and he wasn't sure how to classify the material that Mary gave him. He was interested particularly in the stuff that she claimed Old Nick had told her and didn't know quite what to make of it."

"Do you agree with the implication in his conclusions," I said, "that all Mary's supposed conversations with the devil were just her embroiderings as a talented storyteller?"

"I think I can distinguish between the devil's true words and works and the fancies of an imaginative young woman," he replied, squinting at me through spectacles that seemed too small for his remarkably large brown eyes.

"So does that ability to discriminate tell you that she was making everything up?" I asked, trying the same question from a different angle.

He smiled, a slightly condescending intellectual's smile and said,

"Prebender was very much the lawyer and in that respect a good historian, he took no-one at their word unless they had evidence to back up every claim they made. His way of thinking gave him no choice but to conclude that he couldn't endorse any of her claims that were not backed up by material evidence or witnesses."

"But what has your way of thinking led you to conclude?" I asked.

He smiled again and took off his glasses. He said,

"Prebender himself notes that everyone he asked about Mary's character said that whatever else may be thought about her and her unconventional ways, she'd never been known to tell a lie and that remained true until the end of her life. That was why, while choosing not to accept her oral evidence, he did not say it was wrong or made up, but rather simply lacking the factual back-up that would allow him to use it in the main body of his account. But he did, as you know, include some of it within his appendices as part of the detailed record of his investigations into the history of the continuing allegations of sorcery and the raising of the devil in the years after the witch trials."

"So what you're saying, between the lines, is that you see no reason to assume that Mary was lying," I said.

He smiled again. He said, while polishing his spectacles,

"Perhaps I could ask you a question. Would you think it normal for the devil to visit an honest clergyman's wife and chat with her about the history and mysteries of evil? Could you imagine the two of them dunking their ginger biscuits in their teacups while he kept the pot warm by breathing on it with his sulphurous breath?"

"I find it difficult to believe in the concept of the devil in the stereotypical terms in which you have somewhat satirically framed things," I replied, "but according to Mary, the man she claimed to have been the devil came to her in a very ordinary human form, with no cloven hooves or pitchfork in sight. Just as Christ came to His followers as a man and not in the shape of the all-powerful being that Christians claim Him to be."

He smiled again, a little less condescendingly than before, and said,

"I was perhaps being a little naughty in teasing out whether you'd read Prebender in the original, or just the factually inaccurate summary on Wikipedia, or, God forbid, one of the wacky ghost-hunter websites. Clearly you have read a transcript of the original."

He put his glasses back on and squinted down at the inscription on the headstone. He said,

"Let me put it this way, I think there are several different angles from which her story can be viewed. It is perfectly possible for her to have had conversations with a man who was so lost to evil that he might as well have been speaking for the devil himself. History is full of examples of individuals whose souls have been so completely taken over by darkness that they have become the children of hell even before they have died and gone there. I might easily have concluded I was in the devil's company when visited regularly by someone who had, in effect, become one of his foot soldiers. That is one way of viewing things."

"And the others?" I asked.

He picked up a discarded crisp packet from Mary's grave and scrumpled it in his hand, ready to drop in the nearest litter bin. He said,

"As you said yourself, Christ came among men as an ordinary human being, so why should the devil not attempt to do the same? Even if he could not hope to have Christ's power to be *born* as a man, he might adopt an adult *form* that so closely resembles you or me that everyone but God himself would be fooled. He might well do so regularly and the only reason we are unaware of his presence is because there are so many men in every period of history that become almost as evil as him that we think he's just another of his often unwitting servants, not the genuine article made flesh – or at least made to look like flesh."

"And another possibility is that she might simply have let her imagination run away with her, without having any actual intention to lie," I said, "it's amazing what people can make themselves believe."

"Indeed," he said, well aware that I was quite possibly thinking of some variations of religion as well as humanity in general. "Why is the inscription so important to your research?"

"Two of the sources I've used in my investigations suggest that the inscription is both her last words and a riddle that holds the key to the whole business of her supposed meetings with her demonic visitor."

"Oh, dear," the rector said, "I hope this isn't going to become the site of another Da Vinci-style treasure hunt."

"I'm a little more than a treasure hunter," I said, with a degree of acidity. "You could say I have some practical experience of the concerns that are raised by Prebender and by the alleged experiences of Mary Rowlands herself. I'd like to think I didn't register on the nutter or anorak scales."

"No, no, I'm sure you don't," the rector said, backtracking rapidly, "I wasn't referring to present company. I was merely worried that the tranquillity of the church grounds might be destroyed if Mary were suddenly to become a cause célèbre."

"I'll do my best to keep whatever I find to myself," I replied. "I've no interest that extends beyond what I need to know for my own purposes."

"Good, thank you," he replied. "For my part I'll be as helpful as I can to your enquiries, but there isn't a great deal more that I know than what I've already told you. This inscription – I've never been able to make out three of the words and that turns it into nonsense for me. It's the cheap stone that her husband chose, I'm afraid, it's eroding three times as quickly as the decent stuff."

I squatted down and ran the forefinger of my right hand around the faint outlines of the letters within each problematic word. I said,

"Touch is the only way of telling, there's just enough of the original carving left to feel. The first and second unreadable words are both 'proof', no, wait a minute, there's an s on the end of the second. It should be 'proofs'. The third is more difficult, there's hardly any indentation left in the stone at all. There are three letters and the last two seem to be 'a' and 'w'. The first letter must be 's', nothing else makes sense. So that gives us, "The one proof is the three proofs and all of those I saw.""

"How extraordinary," he said. "And you're the first to decipher the inscription, to my knowledge at least."

I said,

"It would seem that's the case in recent years. Neither of the sources revealed what precisely was carved onto the headstone and it's only the discovery of Prebender that's brought Mary back from obscurity. I wonder what on earth she meant by the three proofs? The only original copy of Prebender that's known to exist had several pages torn out, as you know – they might well have contained what she had to say on the matter."

"Maybe she was referring to the three proofs that her visitor was the devil," he replied. "That would make sense in the context of her earlier claims."

"So the three proofs would be enough to prove that he was who he said he was," I said. "Yes, that would fit, but we need more evidence to be certain that's the case – and then we need to know what the proofs themselves were. You've no idea where I might look for any of this, I suppose?"

He laughed.

"Well, not really, demonic riddles are a little beyond the normal experience of a country rector. I might have suggested a search in the loft of Mary's last dwelling place to see if you could be as lucky as the discoverer of Prebender's account. Unfortunately, however, I don't know where that is. The rectory across the road is now a private house and wasn't built until after her death anyway. She did have one child, a daughter, who in turn married and I presume had children. You could see if you could trace the family tree and find out if any of her diaries or whatever were passed down to her successors. There's always the chance that one of her volumes might contain a list of the proofs."

"Yes, that's a good idea," I replied. "That's one of the blessings of the internet, tracing the relatives shouldn't be too difficult. Thank you."

We said our goodbyes and the rector disappeared down the steps, leaving me alone with my thoughts. I decided to pay a visit to the pub before I left and see if anyone there knew where Mary might have lived.

The landlord said my luck might be in. The local amateur historian, the man who ran a respected website about a large chunk of the area and its past, was having a quiet pint at one of the tables near the roaring fire. I went over and introduced myself. He was an affable, warm-eyed man in his early sixties with a beard that looked as though it had been lifted wholesale from the back of a small furry animal. He was only too pleased to be asked for advice on a historical matter, being more commonly regarded as a useful provider of questions for pub quizzes than a scholarly resource for those who wanted to know about the past in a more rounded and detailed way. He said,

"Mary Rowlands lived in a small rectory on the site of the larger rectory that replaced it. You can actually see the foundations in the cellar of the present building, but that's all you'll see. You won't discover another forgotten loft with a find like Prebender hidden away in it."

"I thought that might be the case," I said. "I don't suppose you know anything about the inscription on her gravestone. I've managed to work out what it says but not what it means in any definite sense."

"You've read it with your fingers, I presume," he said, smiling, "I thought I was the only one who'd managed that and I've kept it to myself until now. You'd make a good amateur historian. You'll have done a bit of your own prior research or you wouldn't be interested in it – so what do *you* think it might be saying?"

"That she believed there are three proofs that can establish whether anyone who is suspected of being the devil in human form is, or is not. That seems the most likely meaning. That's what the rector suggested."

"Yes, indeed, she did believe that," he replied, "and you are going to ask me if I know what the three proofs were."

"Yes, that's right."

He said,

"You're aware of the psychological risks of looking too closely into this kind of stuff, whether it's all true or simply a load of superstitious hokum?"

"You could say my past experiences have made me alert to the dangers," I said. "I'm doing this research after careful consideration."

"OK," he said, "but be careful. The dangers are very real, perfectly sane people going bonkers and worse, that kind of thing. The three proofs that Mary referred to were outlined in a book thought to have been produced in a Spanish monastery in the 1500s. I'll write the title down for you before you go because I can never pronounce it properly. You'll find the book in the library at Durham Cathedral. She read it while her husband was attached to the cathedral for a short period before coming to this parish. I can tell you what it says, but you'll want to pay a visit and check it for yourself, I presume."

I nodded. He continued,

"Contrary to expectations, the proofs do not refer to the mark of the beast and all that stuff, although they are sometimes known as the three signs of the serpent."

"I'm coming to this whole business without any expectations," I said.

"Good," he said. "The first proof or sign is the demonstrated ability to grant and perform miracles, but not the kind that the gospels claim for Christ. These are miracles enabling someone to achieve a desire that simultaneously involves them in the commission of one of the seven deadly sins. The Dr. Faustus syndrome, if you like. The second is the proven ability to command all other evil spirits. This is an ability also claimed for Christ in the gospels, but whereas he commanded them to stop what they were doing, Lucifer instructs them to continue and to go forth and multiply their wickedness, so to speak. The third is the ability to take over the body and mind of another living being, human or animal, or to appear as someone who has recently died. If all three are present in the case of one man, then that is proof that he is indeed the big chief of the fallen angels."

"Rather a complicated and tough set of tests for a country rector's wife to apply to the fount of all evil, I would have thought," I said.

"Your words, not mine," he replied. "Mary was a very redoubtable, very bright and extremely tough woman."

"That she may have been," I said, "but, should he actually exist, I can't quite see fearsome Old Nick agreeing to submit himself to such tests as if he were sitting his GCSEs, can you?"

He laughed.

"From what we know, Mary didn't *set* him the tests. She was simply aware they existed and claimed to have seen hard evidence of him meeting the requirements of each – she had some means apparently of verifying what she saw."

"But that raises the question of why would he let himself be seen doing that," I said, "presuming that such a figment of the popular imagination ever existed. If you're the devil trying to tempt and manipulate people into committing one or more of the seven deadly sins, you'd surely be more effective if you portrayed yourself as some kind of friend, simply helping them do things that would bring them personal rewards which they *deserve*. If you were exposed instead as the devious, deeply evil ultimate conman who's dead set on nicking their souls and dragging them off to hell when they die, then you're going to frighten a lot of people away from you. You wouldn't want anyone knowing that their chum was the great Satan, so you'd make very sure that you weren't caught red-handed doing the things that would identify you."

He laughed again.

"You make an excellent devil's advocate in the most literal sense, doing everything you can to let our man off the hook and prove there was nothing truly diabolical about him. A fantasist perhaps or someone slightly deranged with considerable powers of persuasion, but definitely not in possession of a genuine set of cloven hooves."

I smiled and said,

"OK, so go on then, convince me of the other side of the case, what do you know about what Mary said that might give some weight to her claims? And why would Old Nick allow himself to be proved to exist when he could be much more influential and successful as an invisible tempter? One of my problems, you see, is that while the various tests might sound credible, in reality it would be gobsmackingly difficult to 'verify' the evidence needed for all three – I can't see any way that one ordinary person on her own would be able to do it. Unless there is a record of how Mary was actually able to use the tests to nail her chatty chum as the Mr. Big of the diabolical world, they're frankly not of much use or interest to me. Without any evidence they look more like a compelling fiction than a credible fact, as indeed does the devil himself."

He said,

"Well, I'm a historian not a theologian, but the questions you're asking are interesting in the way that any puzzle is to those who like a challenge," he said. "Let's look at what actually happened. Mary claimed to have *proved* that she had been speaking to the genuine item, Lucifer incarnate, but we have only her word for that. Even then, her original account has been lost."

"There you are then, the case for the prosecution is won," I said, flatly.

"Not yet," he replied. "There is no detail in Prebender of how she went about proving things due to its famous missing pages, but in the diary of a local lady of note that has survived, there is a record of a conversation with Mary in which she confided the details, but the diarist cannot actually remember them all. So what we have at the very best is a second-hand account that is also incomplete."

"As I said, the prosecution have it," I said.

"But do they?" he replied. "Think about it – it might not be unreasonable to assume that if Mary's conversational partner was indeed Lucifer, then he would know that such things as basic human forgetfulness would happen and that they would play very much to his advantage. On the one hand, such part-remembered recollections would provide just enough substance for those who might be attracted by the idea of a powerful alternative to God, if its existence could be established as more than legend or superstition – a being who they might believe offered them an allegedly pleasurable eternity under his protection in return for their self-satisfying breach of as many of the ten commandments as possible. He could nab their souls very successfully if they accepted Mary Rowlands' claims and ignored the uncertainty as to whether they could actually be supported by any credible evidence. There are plenty enough people who would fit into that category of the wilfully gullible and stupidly evil. On the other hand, that very same uncertainty would mean that most people wouldn't take any notice of the claims when they became known and Old Nick could continue his work of tempting most of the people most of the time, without their recognising the attractively presented evil in their heads as his handiwork. If they were not astute enough to recognise that they were being manipulated through a skilfully disguised appeal to their own worst instincts, then they would be much more likely to accept what was being suggested to them and go ahead and do it."

"So you'd argue that he gets the best of both worlds," I said.

"That's right," he replied. "He creates enough of a rumour that his existence has been proved to trap one lot of gullible fools, but leaves enough doubt about that same existence to create the perfect conditions for trapping another lot – a brilliant strategy, with an excellent chance of hauling in even the most intelligent idiots in his trawl for souls."

I laughed.

"So, on that basis we can confidently conclude that Mary may and may not have had the devil as a chum."

"Indeed," he said, "as is the case with so much of a historical nature. I'm sorry if that doesn't get you much further down the road than you were before."

I said,

"No, thank you for taking the time to talk to me, that's all been very useful. I'll do what I can to see if any of her diaries or other writings that might refer to the tests and how she verified them have been passed down within the family, or ended up gathering dust unrecognised in an archive somewhere, but I'm not greatly optimistic about my chances of success."

"History's a bit like being a detective really," he replied, "with the added complication that frequently all of the people involved are six foot under or cremated. You can at least get hold of the three proofs in Durham Cathedral library, as I said earlier. The person you need to speak to there is Canon Lafferty. If anyone knows where Mary's means of verifying her diabolical visitor's credentials might be recorded in any of the writings of the time, then he's your man – the archivist's archivist, as somebody once described him to me."

"I'll give him a ring," I replied.

As I walked back to the car, dusk was falling fast and the lights in the churchyard cut harshly through the gathering gloom. I suddenly had the sensation of someone or something following me, but as in my earlier experiences in the graveyard, there was no-one to be seen. I quickened my step, but then heard the definite patter of feet. They sounded at first like those of a child running to keep up, but the more I listened the more they sounded like something else - what I can only describe as the sound of claws scratching the pavement as whatever it was scurried along in my wake. I turned again, an icicle of fear sliding down my spine, but there was still nothing to be seen. Then I was startled to hear a voice high up in the trees above me. It sounded at first as if it was the wind itself speaking through the rustling of the leaves, but it became rapidly clear that it was the faint whisper of an old man. I quickly recognised the telltale aural signature of the owner. It was that of my grandfather, grand in the stories he told and his manner of telling, and kind in every bone of his body when he was alive – although whether it was actually him or some malicious spirit mimicking his voice, or simply my overactive imagination wishing him back into existence when there was only the wind to hear, was a question that I couldn't answer. The whisper, if whisper it was, was so low that I couldn't tell what was being said. The voice itself solved the problem of my difficulty in hearing it by soaring suddenly to a deafening, echoing exhortation,

"When the devil makes you dance, make him dance in turn!"

The cry filled the air around me, as if it was in every molecule of oxygen, before rising up into the dusk sky and fading rapidly to silence as it disappeared on the wind into the distance. It was just as I remembered from a masterly storytelling performance he gave the year before his death, standing on top of Hag's Head in Ireland, with the dramatic landscape of the cliffs of Moher in the background. The line I remembered well and it seemed obviously to have relevance to my current situation. But while I was trying to remember the rest of the tale from which it came, his voice was followed by that of someone else, one that chilled every bone in my body. It seemed to swirl around my feet like the hissing of an invisible snake. It said,

"Don't listen to the counsel of idiots, fools and fakes, your grandfather is dead and has no mouth to whisper, sing or scream. There is no devil, only your duty to honour your contract - and stay alive."

I couldn't believe what I was hearing and half-convinced myself that I was imagining both ethereal messages. The hissing was followed by a complete and eerie silence and I tried to tell myself that I'd heard nothing but two freak exhalations of air that had sounded like voices only because I was willing them to. Almost instantly, any faint belief I might have had in this possible explanation collapsed when the unwelcome sound of tiny, claw-like feet scuttling along behind me started up again and my unseen follower resumed the pursuit. Either something unnatural and terrifying was happening or my imagination had shifted so far into overdrive that I was in need of counselling, medication or both. The wisdom of fear persuaded me not to test out the two possible alternatives by waiting for the unseen creature to catch up and I turned back towards the car and started to run. I almost tore the door off in my desperate rush to get in and drove off at more speed than was wise or safe.

As the village disappeared from sight in my rear-view mirror, I had an intense, frightening vision of a shadow moving across the graveyard and pausing briefly at Mary Rowlands' gravestone before vanishing in an instant, as if into itself.

CHAPTER THIRTEEN

"Canon Lafferty at your service!"

I nearly dropped my coffee cup, visibly jumping as the booming voice of a man with a seducer's smile interrupted my deep contemplation of everything I'd unearthed so far about Mary Rowlands.

He thrust his hand forwards for me to shake. Putting the cup down, more than a little wrong-footed by such a direct, businesslike gesture from a man that I'd expected would be a repressed, stuffed shirt of a clerical academic, I duly obliged. His grip was firm and uncomfortable as a result of surprisingly calloused skin on his palms.

"May I?" he asked, pointing to the chair opposite. I nodded.

"Of course."

"You look a bit taken aback," he said. "Were you expecting a mild man in a dog collar?"

"Erm, I'd heard you were a very quiet man," I said, smiling.

"And now you find I'm really very loud?"

His smile was more that of a salesman than a priest.

"A little different to what I'd been led to expect," I said, diplomatically.

"Good, wouldn't life be boring if everyone and everything turned out precisely as we'd expected it? Would you like another cup of coffee? I'm having one," he said.

"No, no, thank you," I replied, "if I have any more I'll be hyper."

"Recommend it – hyper's where I'm at all of the time. Waitress, can I have a cappuccino over here, please?"

"Is that the book?" I asked in surprise.

"The one with the three proofs of the devil incarnate?" he said. "Why yes. Very old, all in Latin and very valuable. Shouldn't be taken out of the library according to the rules, but it's amazing what you can do when you're a canon with balls. Sorry about that. I was an army chaplain for several years – can't quite get out of the habit, as the monk said to the tart with a heart. You see, there I go again."

"Yes, so I've noticed," I said, with a frozen smile. "Do you have time to show me the relevant bits and translate them? I'll pay any reasonable fee."

"That's very kind of you," he replied, "but no need for payment. It's on the house. I've signposted the relevant sections with bookmarks, but if you can't read Latin, I'll give you a quick summary of what's in them."

"It's probably best if you tell me what the overall gist of them is," I said.

He did as requested and I noted that the proofs were identical to those outlined to me by the amateur historian.

"Do you know anything about the book, whether there's evidence of anyone who read it applying the proofs and claiming to have found the devil?" I asked.

"Yes, indeedy," he replied with his now tedious salesman's grin. He left a pause for effect and then said,

"Mary Rowlands made a meticulous record in her private diary of each occasion on which she'd seen Old Nick in human form. For many years the diary was presumed to have been lost."

"Presumed," I said, "does that mean that there's evidence of it having been found again?"

"Yes, indeedy," he said again, as if trying deliberately to be irritating.

"Do you know where I can find it?" I asked.

"Better than that, I can show it to you," he said, pulling an ancient and somewhat moth-eaten, slim, leather-bound volume out of his seemingly bottomless, inner jacket pocket. "This is volume six of the diary itself, lost for many years and rediscovered as a result of the patient detective work of yours truly. I'll show you the relevant bits. They're somewhat faded with time, but Mary had excellent handwriting and they're still perfectly legible."

He laid the diary on the table and opened it carefully at a bookmarked page. Turning it round so that I could read it, he pointed to a passage.

"You'll see here how she recalls seeing the evidence that she regards as the first proof, the working of a miracle that enabled someone to achieve a desire that simultaneously involved him in the commission of one of the seven deadly sins. Be careful not to touch the pages – they're very fragile."

I read how, apparently, Mary had watched as the 'demonic' acquaintance the rector had described had passed his hand lightly over the tops of vessels that she'd observed only minutes before to be full of the best wine. In doing so, he turned all of their contents into ditchwater. He'd been sitting opposite her and her husband at a lavish feast laid on by a wealthy wool merchant for a powerful nobleman. Increasingly annoyed by the cloying praise that their host was heaping upon his honoured guest, a rival merchant sitting on the other side of Mary had expressed the wish that the host, whose social climbing skills he clearly envied, might suffer some great embarrassment to pull him down to size. Her demonic acquaintance had smiled generously at the man and instantly got up on the pretext of needing to relieve himself, an intention that she noted had not been expressed in terms fully appropriate to the highest class of polite company. It was on his way out of the room that she'd observed his sleight of hand. Almost immediately afterwards the stewards had attempted to serve the wine to the guests, only to find that all of the pitchers contained ditchwater coloured with beetroot juice, making it look as though the host had been stupid enough to fall prey to a cheap con trick, or was too ignorant to tell the difference between foul water and wine. When she looked sideways and noted the gleeful and malicious quiet laughter of her neighbour, who was observing closely the host's mortified embarrassment, she realised two things. First, that not only had 'Lucifer' outrageously performed the miracle of turning water into wine in reverse, but, second, that he had enabled the person whose wish had come true to fall even further into the deadly sin of envy.

Canon Lafferty smiled and said,

"That's the first. Now for the second."

He turned several more pages of the diary very delicately, something that clearly did not come easily to a man with such large, calloused, labourer's hands (I wondered whether he was a keen gardener) and pointed to another passage. He said, "There."

The story of the second 'miracle' I found truly terrifying. Clearly Mary had the skills of a gothic storyteller long before Mary Shelley came on the scene and her concise but evocative prose literally sent a shiver down the back of my spine. The diary told of a large house in Bowland-in-Castledale, the village where she lived, that was presumed to have been cursed. It belonged to a rich farmer, but previously had been owned by one of the local lord's sons who had fallen out of favour as a result of his excesses and had been thrown out of the family mansion. He'd murdered his wife during a drunken fit one dark winter night and had been sentenced to hang at Lancaster Castle for his crime. On the night before his execution, one of the jailors reported hearing him making a deal with Old Nick, promising to do whatever the devil wanted in terms of corrupting his fellow humanity if his life was spared. This was more of a proposed change of character than might have been thought by those inclined to conclude that his dissolute behaviour had already been more than the devil could have wished for. His indolence and sloth previously had meant that he couldn't be bothered to make miserable the lives of anyone except those few unlucky enough to share the immediate space around him, his wife and servants. Now he was proposing to extend his malign activities to everyone in the village and beyond. Miraculously, on the same fateful evening, the judge who had condemned him was wakened by a midnight visit from a well-dressed man who said that he'd been staying in the village at the time of the murder. He backed up the dissolute son's story about one of the servants killing the wife and then intimidating the rest of the household into claiming their master had been responsible. He'd been passing at the time and had seen it all through a window. Spotting him, the servant had run out and hit him several times over the head with the butt of a pistol. Then, presuming him to be dead, he'd dragged him to a pit in a field behind the village and thrown him into it. He'd shovelled the contents of a nearby manure heap over him, but had failed to cover his nostrils properly. He'd lain there for over two weeks, undetected, in a coma, but had now woken up. Having been told that the wrong man had been sentenced to hang, he'd ridden to Lancaster straight away so that the truth might be told. Noting the strong, sulphurous smell of the manure about him, the obvious soiling of his expensive clothes and the presence of large bruises on his head, the judge immediately reprieved the son and ordered the arrest of the servant, who was hanged within the week, still protesting his innocence. Curiously, the witness who had been so crucial had never been seen before by anyone in the village and was never seen again.

The son thereafter had more than lived up to the oath that the jailor claimed to have heard him swearing to the devil, making a string of female farmhands and servants across the surrounding countryside pregnant, successfully tempting several previously God fearing young men within the village to gamble their limited wealth away, leaving their families destitute, luring others into heavy drinking, alcoholism and wife-beating and being suspected, but never proved, of being behind at least three murders. On his fiftieth birthday a visiting preacher, who it was rumoured had such strong powers of persuasion that he could have converted the very devil himself, had terrified him into such a fear of hell and an eternity of unbearable torment that he had recanted his vow to Lucifer. He promised to give generously to the poor and do penance for the rest of his life to make up for his sins. The same night that he did so the entire village was awakened by an ear-splitting screaming coming from his house. When people rushed out of their homes to see what was going on, they found his servants standing quaking in the street. A terrible, deafeningly loud babbling could be heard coming from within the house. It sounded like a hundred demons were all shouting and screaming at once in a variety of languages that no-one was familiar with. The son could be seen in the centre of one of the front rooms, with the preacher pulling desperately on one of his arms and invisible demonic forces pulling on the other, so that he stood in a cruciform fashion. He was screaming with pain as first he was pulled in one direction by those who'd come for both his body and soul as payment for the

215

breaking of the promise, and then the other by the preacher who was trying to save him from his fate. Clearly the force with which he had been yanked had pulled his arms out of their sockets and he was feeling the horrific, searing pain of a man on the rack. Suddenly, the voices rose to a terrifying, ear-splitting crescendo and a huge blast of wind came from nowhere. It flattened the trees at the front of the house and then blew out all of the downstairs windows. Simultaneously, his body was yanked so fiercely that the preacher, who had by now tied the wrist he'd been holding to a solid iron pillar to try and prevent the son from being hauled off, was left covered in blood. The arm that he had so firmly secured was simply ripped off and left behind as the son's body was dragged with demonic force through the back of the house and then outside, never to be seen again. The preacher was heard screaming that the demons may have won the battle for the body, but he'd won the soul, which would now go to heaven instead of hell.

Thereafter, it had been extremely difficult to sell the house because on every anniversary of the son's disappearance, the demons would go back into it and pummel and scream at whoever was inside, angrily trying to claim another soul to replace the one they'd lost to the preacher. All bar one such unfortunate had managed to flee outside before they'd succumbed to the blows and had immediately sold the house afterwards, taking care not to tell the new owner the real and terrifying reason for the sale.

On one such anniversary, Mary had been passing the house as night was falling, on her way back from visiting a friend, and had heard the annually repeated commotion coming from inside. Earlier, she had bumped into her devilish acquaintance, who regularly stayed at the local inn and he had offered to walk her home. She stood in shock, listening to the desperate farmer who lived there trying to haul open the door to escape and the repeated bangs as it was slammed shut again by his assailants before he could get out. She said,

"Oh, the poor man. My husband warned him when he moved in, but Mr. Brindle laughed off his kind words as superstitious nonsense. Now he has found out the truth to his cost."

"Your husband is a man of God, so why doesn't he cast out the demons?" her companion had asked. "Surely you should go and get him."

"He's tried in previous years," she replied, "but they don't listen to him. They don't attack him and they do quieten down a little bit, but otherwise they carry on as normal until the stroke of midnight, when everything goes quiet for another year."

"He's clearly not being commanding enough," her companion said. "Let me try."

With that he stood with his legs astride and his considerable chest puffed out and shouted,

"Demons of the night, desist! Your time here has gone and you should be up to your mischief elsewhere! Go, I command you!"

As soon as he'd spoken, the house fell into complete silence. The heavy, oak front door slowly creaked open, revealing the battered farmer slumped against the wall, and a breeze of freezing air floated out, icing Mary's cheeks as it passed. As it came by, she heard a host of whispers, all of which seemed to be saying 'sorry, master' and 'humble apologies, oh great one'.

At this point, the horror ceased to command my mind and it occurred to me that this last part of the story would have fitted very well into a Disneyesque 'Sorcerer's Apprentice' movie. I laughed quietly and looked up at the canon. I said,

"It almost had me, up until the end. Mary would have made a mint as a writer had she been born at the right time – she was way ahead of the pack on this kind of stuff."

"Really?" the canon said, nonchalantly, taking the book and carefully turning the pages until he came to the next section of relevance. He pointed to a passage at the top of a page and said, "And this is the third proof."

There was a smudge that made the first sentence difficult to make out, but I soon managed to decipher it and began reading the final section. On this occasion, Mary recounted the story of her travelling to York to see her sister, who was dangerously unwell after a difficult pregnancy. Her demonic companion happened to be going the same way and accompanied her. During the long journey he had, as usual, at no point admitted to being the devil, while engaging her in deep and fascinating discussion about the nature of good and evil, as he always did. As on every previous occasion, he argued very strongly that the virtuous life was that of a fool and that while he respected and indeed revered courteous behaviour towards beautiful women such as herself, he had no obligation to be so kind and thoughtful towards the rest of humanity. Had his arguments been presented by any other man, she would have been revolted and put as much distance between herself and him as possible. But her bewitching companion's irresistible charm won her over each time they met and she found herself locked in debates that challenged her intellect and her sense of morality equally. When they finally arrived at the inn in York that was their journey's end, her brother-in-law was waiting for her with the good news that her sister had suddenly and inexplicably shaken off her fever and was now sitting up in bed at their home, ready to greet her. Her charming companion said a quick farewell and disappeared into the crowds thronging the busy street. Waving after him, she turned to see that her brother-in-law was looking ashen-faced and shocked.

"What on earth's the matter, Stephen?" she asked. "You look like you've just seen a ghost."

"That's hardly surprising," he replied, faintly, "I think that's precisely what I have seen."

He was so shaken that they went into the inn, where he bought himself a flagon of strong ale and almost collapsed into a large corner chair. After several feverish gulps of the brew, he drew breath and explained the cause of his disquiet. The man she had been travelling with, it turned out, was his former employer, Josiah Richmond, a coachbuilder and repairer who had engaged him as his clerk.

"Oh, I see," Mary replied, "so that's what he does for a living. He never mentioned anything about that – but I don't understand why seeing him should cause such a great upset."

"Well, seven months ago it wouldn't have," Stephen replied, "but things have changed a little."

He took another long sup of his ale.

"In what way?" she asked.

"A very final kind of way," he replied. "We buried poor Josiah six months ago. I helped carry the coffin. He died of the fever, as until yesterday I feared Susan would as well. I helped put him in the coffin and saw it nailed down - and I saw him buried and watched the earth being thrown into the grave until it was level with the surrounding ground. And yet today I see him as plain as daylight talking to you. Where did he go?"

"I've no idea," she replied, astonished. "He didn't say. You must have made a mistake, surely. Six months is a long time and it's easy to forget precisely how a person looked and mistake someone else for them."

He took another long sup, draining the flagon and, still looking ashen-faced, said,

"No, there's no mistaking, Josiah had a unique birthmark, a red crescent on the side of his neck to which a small blood-red spot had permanently attached itself. That man had exactly the same mark. He walked with Josiah's slight limp, smiled as he did and dressed in the same clothes that he wore for his Sunday best. There is absolutely no doubt that the man you were with was Josiah risen from the grave and I have not the slightest idea how that could be when only the good Lord God and Lazarus have ever been resurrected."

"But, as I said, this man said nothing about coachbuilding," she replied. "In fact, I don't think he had the slightest idea about anything to do with it. He was a well-heeled gentleman, well-versed in all of the Scriptures and anything that has been written that you could care to name. He made no mention of having a business in York."

"When did you first come across him?" Stephen asked.

She thought for a few seconds and then said,

"About six months ago, I think. I met him in the graveyard. I was tidying up a grave after a recent burial, planting some flowers in memory of the little one who had passed away. He suddenly appeared behind me and said hello."

"That's it, six months ago," he replied, "the creature you met is not human. He stole the body of Josiah and used it to give himself a mortal shape. He jumped into a body in one graveyard and reappeared in another. Your friend is the devil, Mary, dear. Only he can pull off a trick like that."

I looked up at the canon and said,

"So those are they, Mary Rowlands' three proofs of having conversed with the devil? Where did you find the diary?"

"That, my dear, is for me to know and you to find out," he said, smiling. The coffee had by now sunk far within my system and was making urgent demands on my bladder. I said,

"I just need to make a quick visit to the loo. Perhaps when I come back we can talk about this some more?"

"Yes, of course, no problem, my dear," he said breezily, picking the diary off the table and returning it to the inner pocket of his jacket as I disappeared into the loo.

I wasn't gone more than three minutes, but when I got back to the table I found that a waitress had cleared it and the canon had disappeared. I went over to the till to enquire if he'd paid for his coffee and was told that he hadn't. He'd left without touching a drop and the waitress had poured it away. As I was paying the assistant and trying to work out why my informant had vanished without paying or saying goodbye, I noticed another clergyman come into the coffee shop. He was clearly looking around for someone he'd come to meet. Now he clearly was a churchman, I thought, with a face as white as his clerical collar from too much time spent reading the Scripture in the gloom of the cathedral library. His eyes suddenly met mine and rested there. He seemed to recognise me. I wondered if the canon had been called away urgently, to see a dying man perhaps, and had phoned an underling, given him my description and asked him to rush over to the coffee shop and apologise before I'd gone. He strode on over, an anxious-looking man in his early fifties. He said,

"I hope I'm not being rude, but are you by any chance Miss O'Donnell?"

"Yes, that's me. Has the canon asked you to give me a message?"

He smiled, a warm, slightly amused smile, not the seducer's smile of his master. He said,

"I am the canon. I'm terribly sorry for being so late, I had an urgent call to go and see an old lady in hospital who I was told was dying, but it all turned out to be a bizarre hoax. She was very much alive and kicking when I got there and in the process of trying surreptitiously to take a sip or two from a small whisky bottle that her sister had slipped to her when nobody was looking."

"But I've just been speaking to a man who said he was the canon, Canon Lafferty."

The churchman looked confused. He was about to reply when a woman who'd been staring through the window from the street outside came in, in a state of some agitation. She hurried over and said,

"Canon, I thought it was you, I don't know what to say, I've had the shock of my life."

"You're not the only one, Penny, dear," he replied. "Miss O'Donnell, this is Mrs. Norton, our Chief Visitors' Guide to the cathedral."

"It was Arthur Barratt," she said. "I saw him come out of here from across the street and then he came right past me. There wasn't a shadow of a doubt – the mole on his chin and everything. But he was dressed just like you."

"This man, was he in his late forties, square-faced, with grey sideburns?" I asked.

"Why, yes, did you see him too?" Penny asked.

"It sounds like the man who told me he was the canon," I replied.

The real Canon Lafferty was looking utterly baffled.

"But that's impossible," he said.

"I know," Penny replied.

"What's impossible?" I asked.

The canon and the guide looked at each other and then at me as if not quite sure what to say.

"Well," the canon said, "Arthur Barratt used to live next door to Mrs. Norton. He was an irascible former car salesman who died three months ago after losing his job on account of some financial irregularities. He departed this life in a drunken fit, I'm sorry to say. I should know, given that it fell to me to comfort the much-put-upon widow and conduct the funeral. So you see, both Mrs. Norton and you have seen someone who can't be seen, not least because he was cremated."

My face drained. I said,

"Considering what he showed me, and what the purpose of our meeting was, it's quite possible the man we saw wasn't him."

"I don't understand," he said. Penny said she had to dash off for the next tour, but begged the canon to let her know afterwards what I had to tell him.

"Can we sit down?" I said, "I think this might take some time."

I explained how the impersonator had shown me what appeared to be Mary Rowlands' private diary, with its record of her allegedly witnessing her diabolical visitor meeting the requirements of all three proofs of his being the devil incarnate. I said,

"You're going to tell me that there's no record of any such diary ever having been written or being found."

"To my knowledge, that's correct," he replied.

I said,

"And I'm going to tell you that by choosing to appear in the guise of someone recently deceased, thereby meeting one of Mary Rowlands' conditions for being the devil in human form, my bogus canon friend was having fun at both of our expenses. The fact that he took on the appearance of a dead man dressed as a cleric to impersonate a living one was a clever, bizarre touch that well demonstrates the rings that are being run around me."

I explained as briefly and concisely as I could some of the history of my very strange relationship with Lucian Green and why I thought he was the most likely suspect behind the bizarre impersonation. I said,

"I've no idea how Green did it – going through a list of your recent funerals, finding a photo, then getting an actor to dress and make up to be the spitting image of the unfortunate Mr. Barratt, who knows. Lucian Green has the wealth and the weird, dark sense of humour to arrange all of this. He's a self-confessed film noir fan – it's almost as if he's building some kind of scary movie world around me."

The canon said,

"How incredibly devious, showing that he has full knowledge of your investigations and then mocking you by providing apparent proof of the devil's existence that vanishes as quickly as the Barratt impersonator does – in effect, leaving you with nothing, after having seemingly hit the jackpot."

After ordering two fresh coffees, he sat down with me while I told him more about my various experiences with the very strange and menacing Lucian Green. It was impossible to disguise the quietly growing despair in my voice when I said,

"There's no escape for me, is there? This very peculiar man, entity – call him what you like – that's at the heart of all of this: somehow or other he knows everything that I'm up to and will simply block my efforts to get my life back. He's determined to keep me chained to the bizarre storytelling contract. He's making trebly sure I understand that he has the ability to reach me wherever I go to try and escape from his control. I came here today as part of my attempts to establish precisely what he is and isn't, and he brushed me off by simply making a fool of me. He's either a brilliant conman and illusionist who's had my phone hacked to spy on my every move, or, according to old Bill the farmer up in Northumberland, some diabolical entity that's writing his own tale of the macabre around me. What chance have I got against someone who can use the dead to impersonate the living? Or at least employ actors and make-up experts to do the same job. I'm no coward or bully's plaything, but I'm way out of my league trying to deal with a man who at the very least is some kind of super-magician and illusionist – a psychological terrorist, no less."

The canon sat back in his chair and thought for a moment. He said,

"I think there is someone who can help you, but you may be initially a little sceptical about my suggestion. That's because, on reflection, I have no doubt from what you've told me that you are dealing with a diabolical entity. I know such certainty isn't easy for you to accept and that you're desperately trying to keep an open mind on all of this. But no merely human illusionist could pull off all the things that you've seen since this 'Mr. Green' barged his way into your life. Even if he were Satan himself, he would not have the power to raise the dead, but, as a liar and deceiver with access to every living mind, I have no doubt whatsoever that his repertoire of trickery includes the ability to fool mere mortals into thinking that they have shared the company of the dead disguised as the living. This entity is a shapeshifter and can look like anything it chooses. You don't have to wholeheartedly accept my diagnosis of the situation, but I would urge you to give what I'm about to recommend a try before attempting to do anything else. I think your friend Lucian Green is far more dangerous than you realise."

"OK," I said uncertainly, "so who is this person you think might be able to help?"

He said,

"He's a Catholic monk at Trowminster Abbey. His name is Father Bernard Xavier. He specialises in an area of the clerical profession that is somewhat unfashionable – he protects those being persecuted by the forces of darkness from their would-be masters. There's no need to be alarmed, I'm not about to hurl you into a William Peter Blatty novel. Father Bernard has no interest in exorcism in the sense of all the dramatic stuff you see in horror movies. His preference and skill are much more for engaging the darkness on an intellectual plane and outmanoeuvring and blocking it. I use the word darkness because that is his own – he'll tell you that the simple notion of the devil is wholly inadequate to describe the forces of evil at work in the world. He keeps something that appears to be very powerful in the abbey, a relic that is said to have come from the one true cross. I know all of that stuff sounds like superstitious hokum from the Middle Ages, but the word on the clerical streets is that this is different, that genuine rarity, the real thing. If you can make it into his protection, then Green will immediately be in difficulty if he tries to follow you, whether he be the darkness itself or simply one of its principal servants."

"You're not suggesting that I should spend the rest of my life in an abbey?" I asked, my spirits sagging at the thought. "I had enough trouble with the nuns when I was knee-high to a grasshopper."

The canon smiled sympathetically. He said,

"Hopefully not. Once you've been there a few months, whatever dark power it is that's using the form of this man Green will most probably lose interest in you. The longer you're out of its reach the more likely it is to give up on your pursuit and find a replacement storyteller in order to get its strange little show back on the road. Once it has done that it'll no longer need you. I don't mean this in an uncomplimentary way, but the world is full of people who can tell good stories."

"It's not just about good stories as far as I can tell – it's *the right* stories that he's interested in and for some reason he sees me as the best person to create and tell them," I replied, "with a little help from his own insertions into my plots. And then there's the whole business of my likeness to a figure illustrated in a bizarre ancient book called The Satanic Testament and the way in which he can use that to help sell his mad Faustian deals. So he's not going to give up without a fight. If I'm very, and I mean *very,* lucky Father Bernard might succeed in ridding me of my malign stalker, whether he be diabolical or a supercharged conman, but then who's going to look out for Engel's children? Green made an implicit threat that if I reneged on my contract he would find a way to make them suffer."

"Well, I can't promise anything, but Father Bernard may well be able to help in that regard as well," the canon replied. "He is a quiet, brilliant, uniquely good man, much underappreciated in the small miracles he works, but absolutely fearless in standing up to everything that evil can throw at the innocent. If he can hold the darkness itself at bay, there's no reason why he shouldn't have a go at driving it away from the little ones."

I said,

"Well, OK, thank you. You're right, I have to be honest and say that I'm sceptical that this is a matter which can be solved in an abbey, but I'll at least have a chat with this monk and see what happens, then we can take it from there."

As I drove back to the estate in the early evening, the canon's advice ran through my mind on a continuous loop. The notion of the devil was something I continued to struggle with as a storyteller – it was too much of an ogre that could be created by the more fanciful side of the human mind to try and put a face on the inexplicable. The idea of the darkness was somehow a little more convincing in its vagueness and mystery. While I still held on determinedly to the possibility that other explanations might lie behind Green and his works, of a more theatrical and illusionist nature rather than something from the realms of the diabolical perhaps, the events of the afternoon had been several steps too far. I had now reached a point where I would try anything to get Green out of my life, no matter how left-of-field it might seem. I decided that it would at least be worth giving Father Bernard's good offices a try. If they didn't turn out to be successful, then I wouldn't have lost anything and would simply have to keep looking for something else that might work. I determined that I would get in touch with the monk as soon as I'd had a good night's sleep. The canon had kindly said that he would ring the abbey that same evening to provide an introduction to my situation, so that Father Bernard knew its full seriousness from a credible source.

The prospect of spending an unknown period of time in an abbey was not enticing – months spent living in relatively spartan conditions, having to mind my p's and q's and no doubt sitting through endless Masses and monkly chanting, would be a considerable challenge. But if – and it was a very big if - the priest could actually do something, and that was the price of freedom from the darkness that otherwise threatened to engulf me, it may be worth paying.

As I drove up to the cottage in the gathering dusk and parked the car, I had the feeling of being watched by hostile eyes. I hurried quickly inside and bolted the door firmly behind me, but now, in the shadows, the eyes seemed to be all around, unseen but all-seeing. I shuddered and ran straight up to my bedroom, bolting that door as well. That, I decided, was the final straw. I felt threatened within my own four walls. That was the very last night I would spend there.

I intended to be long gone before Engel or Green came visiting again – and breach of contract or no breach of contract, I would be leaving no clues as to where I'd gone. The children would need a new 'governess' and I wasn't easy in my mind at leaving them so abruptly, but in that respect at least I could be easily replaced. For now, I would have to place my trust in the canon's belief that Father Bernard may be able to protect them from the darkness that seemed to be behind both Lucian Green and the Earl. The main things concerning me most immediately were my own sanity and safety and without those I could do little to help anyone.

CHAPTER FOURTEEN

The peal of the great bronze bells pummelled the air, like the iron fists of angels, pounding the darkness into light. I could hear them through my half-open window as I drove relentlessly towards the bone-white mountain of an abbey. From the body of its church the tower rose like a sword, thrusting doubt and despair high into the clouds. This was a place that seemed like a counter-attack against evil and disbelief, its every stone a muscular statement of solid faith in the benign, silent power of its invisible master. This was in sharp contrast to what remained of my own faith in all things religious. A lifetime's doubts, occasioned by the less-than-rosy past of the Catholic Church in Ireland, made me as sceptical of the divine as I was of the devil. But given the malign pressures on my psyche generated by the machinations of Lucian Green, I was prepared to keep an open mind and see if the good Father Bernard really could do something to help. The recent bizarre episodes in Northumberland and Durham had badly unnerved me and I was feeling increasingly like a puppet on a string, being taunted and played with, before being firmly reeled back in under Green's malignant control. It was that final stage of his game which I was now desperate to avoid – I had a firm conviction that it would not end well for me or anyone other than him.

As I drove through the gatehouse arch and into the large courtyard, enclosed by a castle-like dry stone wall, the rich, booming sound of the bells was overwhelming in its power and beauty. They stopped as I got out of the car, their last notes still echoing all around. Then all was silence, apart from the sound of leaves swirling and scuttling across the gravel surface of the parking area. The air was filled with a sweet, citrus aroma and as I gulped it in, I felt almost as if I could drink it. The abbey church towered over everything, making me feel like a child standing in the presence of something much larger and more knowing than me. I unloaded my suitcases from the boot and headed off in search of the entrance.

As I wandered around the side of the cloisters, I heard the sound of plainsong chanting coming from deep within the building. It was as beautiful as the bells and haunting in a wholly benign way, evoking an ethereal otherworld of peace, innocence and tranquillity.

I decided that I'd better wait until the service was over before going inside the church to hunt for Father Bernard. Finding a cloister entrance, I crept in and parked my luggage at the side of a stone seat that was recessed into the wall. I sank into it, drinking in the calm, echoing voices that resonated gently within the long, shadowy corridors that intersected nearby. I fell swiftly into a deep, exhausted sleep.

It was a good half-hour before I was gently awakened by someone calling my name. I struggled back into consciousness and saw a smiling, rotund face looking down at me. Its owner said,

"Miss O'Donnell?"

"That's me," I replied, with some difficulty, "are you Father Bernard?"

"The very same," he said. "You look a poor exhausted little soul and I feel guilty for having woken you up."

His voice had a soft Kerry lilt to it and he looked to all intents and purposes like a heavily built cuddly bear in a habit. I felt instantly relieved at the sight of him and smiled gratefully at his presence. I said,

"Not at all, it's kind of you to take me in on the basis of such a strange story."

"As Benedictines we're obliged to be hospitable and in your case we are especially obliged. The power of evil is such that sometimes only a place like this can cushion the innocent against it."

He sat down next to me and said,

"You know that the darkness masquerading as Lucian Green will come after you and in several different forms and ways, as it has done already. You will need to be strong and you mustn't be afraid. Put your trust in us and we will look after you in every possible way. There is no stronger protection against the forces of evil than the walls of this church."

"I'm keeping my fingers crossed that I'll be safe here," I replied.

"Good, good, that's the spirit," he said. "If you're ready, I'll take you over to where you're staying."

"I hope that I haven't brought too much stuff," I said.

"Too much for what?" he asked.

"Well, I assume I'll be staying in a spare cell," I replied, "that's what bedrooms in abbeys are called, isn't it?"

He laughed and said,

"No, no, we don't put visitors in cells. We have a guest cottage in the grounds, that's where I'm taking you. You're our only guest tonight, so you'll have it to yourself."

He took one of the enormous suitcases and helped me carry it out of the cloister and into the grounds. I could just see the chimneys of what I presumed to be the cottage sticking out from a clump of trees about two hundred yards from the church. We passed another monk, who suddenly appeared from a path through the bushes at the side, deeply immersed in a prayer book, from which he was reciting. He looked somewhat startled to see us and while Father Bernard smiled and wished him a good afternoon, there was no reply, only a look of deep puzzlement. As we drew closer to the cottage, I became worried about the distance from the church and asked my host if it was safe to be so far away. He smiled and said,

"Ordinarily, I would say no, but this little house has something very special in it that will surprise you – wait and see and you will be amazed at what you find."

His somewhat enigmatic answer left me puzzled but was enough to make me take him at his word and follow him into the cottage. When he led me through into the little drawing room, the surprise was devastating. There, sitting on the rustic grey settee in the middle of the room, were Engel's offspring. I said,

"What are the children doing here, who brought them?"

There was no reply and when I looked round, the monk had vanished. I went over to the little ones and crouched down in front of them, smiling a hello, but there was no response, other than the occasional blinking of their eyes. They seemed to be in some deep, trance-like state. A familiar voice said,

"What a surprise, whoever thought we'd find you here."

I turned round to see Green standing in the doorway, a faintly sarcastic smile etched into his face.

"What have you done to them, why have you brought them here?" I shouted.

"Done to whom, my dear?" he replied. "These little angels are merely following the example set by the holy monks in the abbey and engaging in deep spiritual contemplation of the eternal mysteries."

I said,

"You've hypnotised them, drugged them, who knows. You've sunk below the lowest of the low and brought them here to try and bully me into working out the rest of my contract with you. If I don't do what you want, they stay like this or worse, right?"

"Really, my dear, what a preposterous suggestion," he replied. "I am indeed here to remind you that you are due to start delivering the next batch of stories soon and to perform them as was contractually agreed. You will remember also the crucial symbolic importance of your presence as 'The Storyteller' when I'm discussing the Rule of Ten with potential new clients. But what you decide to do is entirely your affair and I wouldn't dream of trying to pressure you into doing anything you didn't want to. As for the children, I'm sure they will be absolutely fine. Your apparent preparedness to flee from both them and me did, indeed, occasion them some great distress and caused them to descend into the spiritual trance that you see now. I would simply point out that one word from you and like the birds of the air, they will instantly be free."

"You have no right!" I yelled. "They're infants – if you have an issue, you take it out on me and leave them out of it. Bringing them here amounts to child kidnapping."

"My dear, calm yourself," he replied, in his familiar patronising manner, "you forget that the children are on holiday from their lessons at the moment and they are here with the full permission of their father. I said I was going on an adventure or two on which they might care to come, just to inject a little bit of excitement into their lives, and Sebastian was more than happy to agree. Any discomfiture within their present state is entirely down to you and, as such, within your powers alone to remedy. But, as I said, whether you choose to do so is entirely your decision. I'm not here to pressure you in any way."

"Who or what exactly are you?" I asked. "You seem little more to me than evil on two legs."

"Well, that's at least more charitable a diagnosis than evil on one leg, in which case I would be in imminent danger of toppling over," Green said, superciliously. "But why should you presume that 'evil' is something that can be embodied simply in single individuals, myself or anyone else? Humanity in general is so full of evil it is almost its default setting. All the little venal acts, the petty squabbles and acts of childish retribution that mark our daily lives, they all gradually and cumulatively drain and disempower even the most innocent of souls. That's the bread and butter of the earthly work of that which is so loosely called the devil or the darkness – and nothing you or anyone else might do will stop it. So there is nothing to be lost or gained from continuing your work for Sebastian and me, other than the sanity of these little dears. Evil will continue whatever you do, it is just that what you do is an effective way of helping me in my work and I require you to continue doing it until I say otherwise."

"The world is full of storytellers," I replied. "You could replace me with someone who actually believes in what you do. I'm little more than a light bulb – if I go out, you simply buy another one off the shelf."

"Unfortunately, my dear, that is not the case and I am not in a position to let you go out, as you put it. You see, you are a very useful little cog in my exceedingly big wheel – you have no idea how powerful your resemblance to the devil's favourite Storyteller is. There you are, way back in the eighteenth century, as seen in the pages of The Satanic Testament – and here you are now, one and the same! How incredible! It is crucial beyond words that such a respected book of the black arts declares that the presence of Satan's personal teller of tales at the closure of deals is a secret sign that he will guarantee them. He would not lend your services to anyone he didn't regard as his most loyal and special servants and here he is, lending you to me. So you have a unique role as a symbol, a secret sign of his direct interest in matters where he allows you to be in attendance. When you appear as the Storyteller, your face identical in every way to the figure in the dark bible, telling your little tales with their dark, ethereal plots and my subtle little inserts, something special happens. Those who are most susceptible to the temptations of my wealth-multiplying deals see you as a prophecy come true and that all-important guarantee. The darkness of your tales must mean that behind your so very endearing smiles and courtesies you are most certainly the dark lady of legend. As I pointed out when you visited me in London, your presence is often the clincher in getting them to sign on the dotted line. I show them the book and its provenance and they understand your significance. So, you see, I cannot let you go. You're a key part of my operation. Honour your contract and the infants will be fine, you have my absolute guarantee."

I said,

"But any resemblance between me and this ancient Storyteller figure is simply chance, pure coincidence. It's mad to think that my presence in a room is a guarantee of anything."

"Perception is everything, my dear," he replied, "what you think is irrelevant. What my clients believe is crucial. Enough of them see you and the Storyteller as one and the same to make me another fortune on top of my fortune, if you see what I mean. You may think them mad, I may even think them mad, but the only thing that is important is what they believe. As I have said, keep to your contract, keep playing the Storyteller role and I guarantee that the little ones will come to no harm."

"A man who uses infants as a bargaining tool has no credible guarantees to give. As long as Engel remains under your influence, these children are at risk and there's nothing I can do to affect that situation. This whole business with the Storyteller and some fanciful book of the black arts is ludicrous and I want out – now! That's why I'm here, as you well know, although how you know is a different and worrying question."

"Worrying indeed, you have a lot to be worried about, my dear. Oh, look, we appear to have visitors," Green said, "perhaps they're looking for you, d'you think? How very secure they've kept you so far – I'd never be able to find you in a million years."

I followed his gaze through the window and was startled to see a small posse of monks heading towards the cottage. I heard a bang as the back door closed and when I turned round, Green and the children had vanished. Almost simultaneously, the front door burst open and the monks hurried in. Their leader was a quietly commanding middle-aged man whose eyes darted all around the room before settling on me in a concerned but not unfriendly gaze. He said,

"Miss O'Donnell, I presume?"

I nodded. He continued,

"Father Lawrence here spotted you being led away from the church by an imposter. The man who brought you into the cottage is not a monk in our community. I'm Father Bernard – may I ask who he said he was?"

"He said he was you," I replied. "He led me right into the clutches of the man I'd come here to escape from – and he'd brought the two infants I've been teaching with him as a means of pressuring me to fall in line."

"And now he's vanished, I presume," Father Bernard said.

"As you came in through the front, he left through the back," I said.

"Or appeared to," the monk replied, "depending on whether your pursuer is flesh and blood or of a rather more exotic nature." He signalled to a couple of the little party of monks that had come in with him to investigate the gardens to the rear of the cottage. He asked,

"Did the children seem real or could they just have been an image, an illusion perhaps?"

"I don't know," I replied. "They seemed to be in some kind of trance. I wanted to give them a hug and take them away from him, but they'd gone before I could try anything."

The monks came back in and one of them shook his head when Father Bernard asked if they'd found or seen anything. He said,

"How very clever, now you see him, now you don't. Your friend seems to be very difficult to pin down from everything I've heard about him so far, Miss O'Donnell."

"He's the master of manipulation," I replied, "he's got inside my head and I don't know how to get him out again."

"Well, we can start by taking you back to the church," he said. "He was very anxious to divert you away from it, so we'll do exactly the opposite of what he wants."

"You think the relic will keep him away from the church?" I asked.

"The relic? Maybe, maybe not," he replied. "If he is the diabolical creature that Canon Lafferty believes him to be, it might deter him – but remember that the New Testament tells us that such a creature was unafraid of trying to tempt Christ himself, so it may well not be enough on its own. It may also be that Lucian Green is merely an accomplished conman, hypnotist or mind-manipulator, as you suggest, who's simply afraid of meeting me. I'm as much known for exposing fraudulent bullies as I am for confronting the ultimate darkness. If he is such a man, that fear may keep him away from the church and explain why he fled when I arrived just now."

He gestured for me to go before him and as we walked out of the cottage into the calm beauty of the grounds, I said,

"So how do you propose to find out just who or what it really is that we're dealing with?"

"By putting you in a safe place and then watching how he next tries to get to you," he replied. "He's clearly convinced he badly needs you to continue playing your part in the strange little game he's got underway, so if he's a diabolical presence and as unafraid as the darkness that tried to tempt Christ, he's going to make more attempts to break down your resistance, relic or no relic. If he does, I'll be watching him and the methods he uses will determine how I deal with him. If he's simply a very human, quite brilliant illusionist and conman, then he won't have as extensive a repertoire of means of getting access to your mind as the darkness. That would make things a lot easier from my point of view. The one thing you need to hang onto is that whether it comes in a human or an ethereal form, evil can always be blocked, providing it's caught early enough. It's never an incurable disease."

As we entered the cavernous abbey church, our ears were assailed by a thunderous rendering of Vivaldi's Gloria, which the organist and choir were rehearsing for a fundraising concert later in the week. Father Bernard remarked jovially that if that couldn't keep the darkness out, nothing would. The rehearsal ended very shortly afterwards, with the last rich, rumbling echoes of the organ reverberating through the ancient stones of the building for several seconds afterwards, before slowly fading to silence. He said,

"I'm afraid your quarters aren't very wonderful. There is a small room and anteroom through a door leading off from the side of the reliquary chapel. They used to be the Mass celebrant's robing room and a small storage room for hymnbooks, candles, that kind of thing. With the abbot's permission, I've had them converted into a small bedsit and bathroom solely for the use of people in your unenviable position. You are so near to the relic that, in our experience, if your pursuer is indeed a diabolical presence, he will not dare try and physically harm you, or take you from there. If Lucian Green is merely a very human illusionist, on the other hand, we will have that covered as well. Monks will take it in turns to sit in the chapel at night, so that the alarm can be raised if anyone breaks into the church."

"You said 'physically'," I observed. "Your reputation for precise wording, as with 'the darkness', suggests that you're not as confident that a 'diabolical' Lucian Green would be deterred from coming after me in other forms, should that be possible."

"Indeed," he replied. "All else having failed, I suspect that if he is a manifestation of the darkness, as Canon Lafferty believes, he may now try and come to you in the most terrifying form that you can imagine. He will use all of his powers on your mind, not your body. If he does, you must be strong and I will be with you. Whether he be a man or a proverbial serpent, we will together defeat him."

My accommodation was considerably less monastic than I'd feared, with a small television in the corner and a range of classic novels on one of the shelves, should I need something to read if unable to sleep. I was invited to take my meals with the lay staff of the abbey and I had more time than I could wish for to work on the stories that I really wanted to write, not those that Green wanted.

My first night in the church passed peacefully and without incident.

On the second night things changed.

I drifted off into a deep sleep at somewhere after ten-thirty, having finished watching the news and starting to read a 'suitably Catholic' copy of Brideshead Revisited that I'd found on the bookshelf. My unconscious mind suddenly kicked into life in the way that brains do when switching into their most vivid and real-feeling dream states. I found myself walking through the darkest and oldest part of the monastic cloisters, alone and alert, expecting the unexpected. Looking forwards into the gloom of the long, cold stone corridor down which I was walking, I became aware of a shadow floating far in the distance. It seemed to be moving towards me and yet stationary at the same time. The closer I got the more it acquired substance, yet simultaneously seemed empty of all living form, like a black hole, sucking in and destroying all hope. It emitted a strange and repulsive smell which seemed to penetrate my skin, lungs and skull, sitting deep within my entire being, provoking a constant wish to retch. I wanted to turn away and go back, but seemed to be pulled irresistibly towards it, as if seized by some kind of gravitational force. The nearer I got the more my stomach filled with a deep sense of gut-stabbing terror. I could see no face or other visible identifier of the creator of the utter, life-draining horror that my senses were picking up. It's difficult to describe the sheer power of the darkness that this unknown thing was emitting because it was so searingly intense and so many things at once – oppressive, overwhelming, spirit-crushing, hope-destroying, despair-inducing, unimaginably terrifying and productive of the deepest form of every known type of physical pain. My sleeping body and mind were being engaged on every sensory level and were in agony on each. I felt like I was being physically torn in half, outstretched arms being ripped from my torso by unseen forces while, simultaneously, a crucifier's nails were being hammered into my brain as well as my hands and feet. I felt in the presence of something dark, towering, powerful and unimaginably, pitilessly evil – the whole history of sadism, terrorism and wickedness embodied in one moment and in the one, faceless figure that loomed in the middle distance in front of me. I screamed uncontrollably in terror and agony combined until my vocal chords were incapable of anything more – and then it all stopped. The lights came on and Father Bernard was standing at the side of my bed.

Almost immediately, another of the monks hurried in with a hot drink, which I was instructed to treat as my immediate priority. Once I had calmed down, Father Bernard said,

"So, he came by the anticipated route, into your dreams. Tell me what happened."

I felt so completely drained of everything, most particularly the basic will to live, that at first I was barely able to speak. Seeming to understand my predicament from past experience, he said,

"Don't worry, what you are feeling is all an illusion created within your mind by a master of terror. The strategy is to hit you with the same thing every time you go to sleep until you're on the point of suicide and then to offer you a way out – which will be to agree to what your friend has been demanding. I've seen the same ruse several times before. Use that knowledge of what is being done to your mind as the rungs of the ladder which you climb up out of despair and back into normality."

His words somehow penetrated through the wall that the dream had built between my mind and the real world and grabbed my attention. They were enough to help me deal with the bafflement that often follows a waking dream, but which in this case seemed magnified by a factor of a hundred. Pulling myself up into a sitting position, I drank the coffee that had been brought and then slowly, painfully, described everything that I'd experienced in the nightmare. When I'd finished, he said,

"I guessed right, what you describe is what I suspected. The fact that you now know that this is a much-used tactic won't lessen the horror and the pain which you will feel every time you are subjected to it and you will come to dread the very thought even of trying to get some sleep. But it will help you draw away from the monumental despair that you'll wake up with after every recurrence of the nightmare because you'll know that nothing you've experienced is real. If you can hold out against it, that part of the persecution will soon end. But then, I'm afraid, you must be prepared for the fact that other means will be used."

"Such as?" I asked, despondently.

"To know what will be tried, you have to understand the nature of the darkness, because I think there is little doubt now that it is that you are dealing with."

"And what is that nature?" I asked.

He sat down in the small armchair next to the bed and said,

"Nobody, including me, knows for sure, but I do understand bits and pieces based on what I've observed over the years. I do know that it always prefers to have an agent through which it can act and that agent is always the human mind, whether it be yours, mine or someone else's. It persuades or tempts – whatever word you like to choose – and the mind that succumbs becomes its agent for whatever has been proposed. It can work through the imagination of that mind to devise, magnify or distort all kinds of ideas that can be translated into plans of action, all kinds of things that we interpret as evil. With your mind, it has at its disposal a storytelling machine whose power and nature fit its plans and purposes perfectly. It sees your mind as having some irreplaceable role in affecting the mind of a crucial someone, I've no idea who, whom it wishes to influence. Of that I'm certain from everything you've told me – it gave you part of the picture in the abbey cottage and from that I'm able to work out the rest. That irreplaceable role, combined with your resemblance to the Storyteller from the book of the black arts, is why it's so relentless in its pursuit of you. I think that knowing the power of that storytelling mind, it will try in some way to get it to work against you, its owner, in your dreams, to lure you to a place that is beyond any awareness of the illusion that is being created – and there to finally break you down and get what it wants from you. That is where mentally you will need to be at your strongest, because you will be wrestling directly with the darkness itself. I can warn you in advance of what is likely to happen, but the illusion that will be created will be so strong that it will be difficult to break, even when you wake up. I will give you all of the help and support that I can, but ultimately it will be up to your own strength and determination of mind if you are to beat this. If it wins – and you tell me that you intend to leave the abbey and go back to the estate to finish off your work – there will be nothing in law that I can do to stop you. It will be the victor and we two the losers. The stakes are that high."

The monk's warning turned out to be an impressively accurate prediction. Everything that he'd said would come to pass did. The repeated recurrence of seemingly endless variations on the first soul-destroying dream during the next ten days turned me into a nervous wreck. I was constantly tired and desperately trying to avoid falling asleep and re-entering the mental black hole that was becoming so deep it was threatening to swallow my sanity. Then, when it was clear that I was managing to hang on without actually breaking into pieces, there was a short interlude, a couple of days in which I was left alone. Just at the point where I began unwisely to hope that Green, the darkness, whatever it was that was attacking me had given up, the second onslaught began and that was, as Father Bernard had predicted, ten times more difficult to deal with. It did, as he had warned, turn the considerable storytelling power of my mind against me.

It all began as I was drifting in and out of sleep watching a late-night film in my compact little quarters. I seemed to enter a strange state between being fully alert and completely unconscious and within that a narrative started to unfold in which it was virtually impossible to distinguish the real from the imaginary.

As I sat in this limbo state, I became aware of a child's voice calling. Initially, I was puzzled as to what it was saying. Gradually it became louder and appeared to be coming from within the church. I hauled myself upright, feeling dizzy in the process after sitting motionless and half-asleep for so long. I opened the door to see what was going on. The two monks who had been posted to keep a night vigil outside my room were both fast asleep in the pews. I couldn't immediately see anyone else apart from them, but then the voice called again. It appeared to be coming from the far end of the nave, echoing from behind one of the large Romanesque pillars. It sounded very much like Engel's little boy, William, but I still couldn't make out what he was saying. While aware that this could be another of Green's tricks or illusions, I decided that I must investigate further and walked slowly down the aisle, trying to spot the child. As I got near to the pillar, the voice called my name and said, "Follow me, you must follow me or I'm lost."

I then saw the child's shadow highlighted against one of the church walls as he hurried over to the exit at the far end of the nave and slipped out into the gardens. My initial instincts were not to follow, but something deeper and primeval drew me onwards, an anxiety for the child as if it were my own and the fear that if I didn't follow and something terrible happened to it I would feel forever to blame. I couldn't be in the slightest degree sure that it really was William, but equally I couldn't forget that I'd seen him – or a likeness of him – on the day of my arrival at the abbey. I was naturally worried that the children were still here with Green and that he was intent on using them to lever me into helping him. Wisely or unwisely, I followed the child into the garden.

The grounds were half-lit by a harvest moon. I could just see the shadow that I assumed to be the little boy hurrying towards a clump of trees some forty or fifty yards ahead of me. I ran after him, his voice beckoning me on with little cries of "this way". The voice was now definitely William's. When I got to the trees I couldn't see anyone, but could hear both him and his sister, Emily. They were chattering excitedly somewhere within the gloom beneath the dense canopy of branches. I battled on through the thicket until I suddenly found myself in a clearing, in the middle of which was a large pond reflecting the brilliant moon high above. I could see both of the children kneeling at the edge of the water and staring into it as if they could see the entire contents of their souls in its depths. The little boy appeared to be talking to someone or something that he could see beneath the surface. Concerned, I crept up behind him to see who it was and was baffled to see his face looking back up at me from within the water. It was not a reflection and had an entirely different expression to the one that I could see on his innocent young face. It smirked at me with a knowing mockery far beyond its apparent years and, as it did so, the little one slid forwards into the water before I could grab him. He disappeared from view into what was obviously a very deep pool. My heart racing with panic, I waited a few seconds, desperately hoping that he would reappear, but there was so sign of him. I tore off my jeans and blouse and jumped in, plunging what seemed to be fifteen or twenty feet below the surface. Unable to see anything in the pitch-black water, I flailed around with my arms, but couldn't find any trace of him. With my lungs at bursting point, I swam back up, resurfaced for air and then plunged back down again. I repeated the same procedure more times than I could remember, trying to cover as much of the pond as I could.

Finally, I realised that there was no longer any chance of finding him alive. I swam back to the bank and hauled myself out, every muscle in my body hurting from the frantic vigour of my fruitless exertions. There was now no sign of the little girl either and my heart sank into the core of the earth with the thought that she might have followed her brother into the depths while I was looking for him. I lay flat on my back, gasping for air and distraught, feeling as though the centre of my being had been ripped out and my carcase left for the birds.

Suddenly I heard a sound from the other side of the pond. Pulling myself up into a sitting position, I was startled to see William climbing slowly out of the water. I watched, stunned, as he stopped and stared directly at me for several seconds. Then he turned and headed off into the woods. I couldn't believe that anybody could have survived so long underwater and wondered whether what I was seeing was some kind of illusion. My remorse at not having stopped him from falling into the pond in the first place was so strong that I was unable to resist the temptation to follow this little resurrected being, who may or may not be Engel's child. I felt both frightened and desperate for some kind of miracle, a confirmation that he was in fact still alive and OK, despite all the odds. I jumped back into the water and swam across to the other side.

From having initially moved so slowly and so strangely, the child was now marching forwards at a rate that I found difficult to keep up with. I ran after him, deep into the woods, hearing the crackling of twigs under his feet, but always twenty yards or more ahead of me. I kept bumping into low-hanging branches and nearly losing my footing, and each collision or slip gave him a few more seconds of a lead over me. Just at the point where I was beginning to believe that I would never catch up, I realised that I could no longer hear any twigs cracking or any other sound of him hurrying forwards. I discovered the explanation for this sudden silence when I burst through into a moonlit clearing and found him standing, waiting for me.

I stopped dead in my tracks when I saw him. He was watching me with a knowing look far beyond his years. When he spoke, the effect was instantly chilling. The voice was William's but the words were all Green's. He said,

"Well, my dear, the chickens have finally come home to roost, haven't they? I warned you what would happen if you defied me and here it is, right in front of your eyes. The child has drowned and I have taken temporary command of his form – one of the three signs of the serpent, if you recall."

"All I know is that you're the master of illusion, whether you're the serpent or a simple rat of a conman," I said. "For all I know, William may well be perfectly safe, tucked up in his bed back home on the estate. This could simply be a fantasy you've somehow managed to conjure up and drag me into."

"Oh, William is as drowned as if he'd fallen into the deepest ocean," Green replied, "of that you can be absolutely sure. One gone, one still to go – unless you stop being so wilfully obstinate and deliver what you'd promised you would."

"What do you mean, one still to go?" I asked.

"Exactly what I say," he replied. "I have Emily still. She is once more in a trance and should you fail to deliver, she will follow her brother into the deep. That will be two little innocents who you have on your conscience."

I said,

"I don't know whether I'm fully awake, half-asleep or lost in the middle of a nightmare. All I do know is that my inability to tell is the direct result of the convincing 'reality' that you've created all around me. I was warned that you'd use my mind's own storytelling power against me and I think that's what you're doing. I think this is all in my head and that you're somehow or other in the driving seat of my imagination. So I'm going to try something that may destroy all of your threats in one go – I'm going to throw you out of my dreams and out of my head. Then you are nothing – I believe it's just as the monk said, you can only tempt, you have no power to command if the mind that you're working on refuses to submit to your demands. Then we'll see things as they really are – William's death is a fake, you don't have Emily hidden away somewhere and you have nothing whatsoever to bargain with."

He stared at me with a look of terrifying malevolence for what seemed like an eternity, then smiled. He said,

"What a very, very clever young woman you are. However, I do assure you that William is dead and there is nothing that you can do to bring him back into the land of the living. This is your final chance to save the little girl and it really does look as if you're about to squander it."

I sensed that he was bluffing and that my words had hit home like well-targeted knives. For the first time, I began to lose my fear of him. I said,

"This is the showdown between you and me. If you don't stop exploiting both me and the children, I'll turn the tables. Instead of you trying to use a story created within my own mind to control me, I'll make you the centre of my tales. I have enough of a reputation now to get them published in their own right and who knows, they might even be strong enough to be turned into a film or two. I'll expose everything that you've been up to with your Rule of Ten con and all the other diabolical psychobabble you've been using to mess with people's heads. Then you'll be out in the open and your cover will have been blown so far into the clouds that your little double act with Engel will be playing to empty houses."

He smiled patronisingly and said,

"And what will you do when I come after you, when I make you the focus of all my malign attention? How do you think you'll feel when you have to spend every second of every day looking over your shoulder, not knowing when I'm coming for you and how truly terrifying my revenge will be? You were a gibbering wreck in the cemetery when the birds attacked you. How will you cope when something far more vicious than those little creatures makes you its prey?"

I said,

"Nothing will come after me. If you're some kind of diabolical entity incarnate, then you won't want to change the habits of a lifetime and provide solid proof of your existence. Coming after me as some act of revenge would get too near to doing that, especially when I make your threats public. The truth is that you've run out of options. You've lost your hold over me and that's an end of it. You've even lost control of this little horror story that you've been so busily constructing in my head. It's my mind you've been using, so I've taken it back from you and I'm telling you to get out of it and to leave the children alone."

"How very brave and very clever of you, my dear, I must commend you on the way that you've thought all of this through so thoroughly. I'm afraid, nevertheless, that you're a little too late with William – as I have explained already, he is no longer amongst the living shall we say. Your wilfulness has already cost the little man his life. As for your breaking your contract, you'll lose all of the money that you would have earned and will have achieved nothing – you are an inconvenience to me, that is for sure, but I will simply find other ways to achieve my purposes. That which you think of as evil, and which I think rather to be the most logical way of doing things in a world full of the corrupt and self-interested, simply works around people like you. If you get in the way, you are simply something to be jumped over, a mere fence on a racecourse. As I've told you several times, you are no more than a dot or an ant to me and if I choose to leave you alone, it is simply because you are not worth wasting any more time on now that you are no more use to me."

I said,

"I don't believe you, I'm sure William is still alive. You're just trying to make me suffer."

The shadow boy's face filled suddenly with a huge and grotesque smile and he laughed loud and hard, not this time with a child's voice but that of Green. He said,

"How amusing you are, my dear, and how very, very sad a little thing you will be when you discover that, unlikely as it may seem, I'm telling the absolute truth. I suggested to you once before that you, the Storyteller, have been born and reborn throughout the centuries and will continue being so until you submit to the power I represent. Even as I let you go for now, who knows, perhaps we will meet again in the next century – and the one after that and on and on and on. How terrifying for you, a struggle that will never end and which you can never win."

"Utter rubbish!" I replied. "Nobody is born a second time as the same person, never mind a third, or more. You're making it up as you go along – the only thing that is born repeatedly is your ability to think up new lies and fantasies to try and shore up the devious drivel you spew into the minds of those you wish to tempt or bully. Your power over me has gone, evaporated – and you're just going to have to accept that."

"Oh really my dear? You can waste as much time as you like on such wishful thinking, but the fact remains that, for as long as you are alive, you can never completely escape my power. And as a little demonstration of that power that you think is so broken, I'm going to make you scream, wake you up and bring all of the overfed monks scuttling into your room like obedient poodles on the end of my lead. Wouldn't that be a fitting way to say goodbye – for now?"

With that, he caused the child's body that he had hijacked to collapse onto the cold, damp ground. In its place another figure emerged from the very earth on which it lay, that of an adult woman. Its head turned slowly and I realised with horror that the face was mine. It smiled briefly and then jolted as if struck by lightning. The skin singed, burnt and smoked and then progressed through all the stages of death and decay in a matter of seconds, until nothing was left but a pile of bones. The rancid, brutal smell of rotting human flesh burnt into my nostrils. A sudden blast of wind came from nowhere and the skull was hurled into my face like a macabre football. As he had predicted, I screamed in horror and woke, still screaming, from the strange state between consciousness and sleep that I'd been locked in for the past hour or so. The monks burst into the room, followed rapidly by Father Bernard. It took several seconds for me to grasp that the skull which had just come flying into my face had been created only within my mind and was nowhere to be found. Sweating and still trembling a little from the shock, I explained to the priest what had happened. He wanted to know the full story, so I told him everything, including the threats about reincarnation and a never-ending struggle against Green's power. When I told him about the several declarations that William was dead, the expression on his face turned instantly from one of concern to deep sorrow. He looked for a moment as if he couldn't find the words that he needed, but then seemed to recover himself and said quietly,

"There was an item on the television news this evening – about your employer, Sebastian Engel. His youngest child drowned this afternoon, in the river that runs through his estate. The circumstances described were nothing like those in your dream and I do not believe for a moment that either this Green character or you had anything to do with it. I think rather that Green was aware of what had happened and used it to fashion within your mind a narrative in which he created the illusion of agency – of both his and yours. He was just exploiting the unfortunate little one's death as new and compelling material for the psychological theatre macabre that he has been using to try and pressure you into doing as he wants."

The horrified look on my face clearly shocked him and he said,

"I'm sorry to break this to you so abruptly. I thought it best to let you know the full details in case you picked up part of the news by accident and believed you were in some way to blame, as Lucian Green would have liked."

"So the children have never been here – their appearance in the guest cottage on the day of my arrival was simply another illusion created by him?"

"It said on the news that Mrs. Engel and the children had just got back from visiting her parents when the tragedy happened. They had gone away on the same day that you came to the abbey, so there was indeed no possibility of the children ever having been here. Whether it be through traditional hypnosis or some kind of supernatural means, Green had simply conjured up an illusion in your brain. He's a master manipulator of minds."

"So what of the showdown in my dream, did that have any degree of reality, was I really doing battle with him directly and have I finally succeeded in getting him off my back?" I asked desperately.

He sat down in the faded old armchair opposite my bed and looked around the room as if sniffing the air. He seemed visibly to relax as he did so. He smiled at me and said,

"With entities like Green, it's as if I can smell their presence. That's an inadequate description of the way that I sense them, but it's the best I can do. When you first arrived, it seemed as if he was all around, although I decided it best not to tell you in case it only added to your already considerable state of worry and concern. Now when I sit in this room, I feel nothing other than the peace of the abbey and the presence of my brothers and you. If I could have advised you directly what to do should you have encountered Green in the way that you did in your dream, then I would have told you to act exactly as you did. I think that you have called his bluff and there is no reason for him to continue his pursuit of you – you were important enough for him to throw everything in his power at you, but that has failed. He can't break you, despite all of his best efforts and no matter what he threatened about continuing his struggle with you into the future, he isn't one to carry on flogging a dead horse. Besides, and most importantly, as you yourself pointed out, he doesn't have the power to continuously reincarnate you. That would be a matter for God alone. He was just trying to salvage some pride in the face of a defeat. He has a much bigger agenda that he needs to deliver on than his efforts in this very small part of the world, this little England of ours – and having failed in this regard, he will simply double his efforts elsewhere, probably with renewed vigour and a proverbial firestorm of anger. That's good news for you and bad news for others. There is always an upside and a downside to situations like this."

Father Bernard's judgment seemed to be correct in so far as my nightmares ceased and I was soon able to start taking walks around the abbey grounds and beyond without any sign or hint of Green's presence. After a couple of months and just at the point where I was itching to go back home to Ireland, the priest told me that, as far as he could reasonably judge, the threat had ceased and it was safe for me to leave. I'd got as far as packing half of my stuff when my phone rang. The conversation that followed changed everything.

The voice on the other end of the phone was that of Mrs. Engel. I'd sent flowers and my condolences after the sad loss of the little one and she'd managed to trace where I was through a no doubt fearsome badgering of the flower-delivery firm. She told me that her husband had blamed himself after William's drowning and had gone back to America following the funeral and never returned. He seemed to have been descending into some kind of paranoia and had rejected all solace in his grief. She no longer heard from him and had been unable to contact him. Since the day of William's death, the little girl, Emily, had been free of the strange episodes that had blighted my last few weeks with the family. All of her 'ghostly experiences' had ceased. She was repeatedly begging for me to return, news that left me more than a little surprised given some of our more fraught moments together. It seemed that she'd bonded with me much more closely than I'd realised and with the sudden and appalling loss of her brother, followed by her daddy abandoning the family home, she was desperately in need of some of the stability and comfort which my presence had apparently provided. All of the grand confidence of the middle-class academic had gone out of her mother's voice and what I heard over the phone was deep grief and a heartfelt plea for me to come back to the estate. I would only need to stay there for a week before she and Emily moved to a large apartment near the university, within which there would be rooms for me. She was desperate for me to help look after the little one until she was able to adjust to all that had happened. She wanted me to help Emily chart out a new life, one that was minus two of the people to whom previously she'd been closest in her short childhood. She promised that I wouldn't need to stay in the little cottage with its strange and very dark history for the week that I would be with them on the estate. She would give me the use of a small suite of rooms next to her own bedroom in the great Hall itself, quite a step up for a humble storyteller. She was so distraught that I felt morally obliged to agree to her request. Given that Engel would no longer be around to badger me and that the haunting of Emily appeared to have stopped, the estate seemed a much more welcoming prospect. In any case, I would only need to stay there for a very short time. I consulted Father Bernard. He had both fears and reservations about my going back to the location of so many past troubles, but in his priestly conscience felt that I was making the right decision for the child's sake.

That was how I ended up back on the estate, in the splendour of the great Hall, acting once more as 'governess' for little Emily. As had been promised, at the end of the first week we all moved into a grand apartment near the university.

Things went well for two months. When I arrived back, Emily was waiting for me and ran straight into my arms, a whole little lifetime of grief and relief being released into my deep care at once. All of the strange influences that had for a while so distorted her attitude towards me had vanished and she was as when I had first met her, a bright and highly emotionally intelligent child. For the first week or two, I was more counsellor than tutor or governess and spent most of the time helping her reclaim from her grief a life that she felt was worthwhile and safe. Her mother not unnaturally was still so consumed with the loss of her youngest and the double blow of her husband's abandonment of the family home that she could only half respond to the child's needs. I had only my own experience of loss and that of my family to go on, so had largely to make things up as I went along, but what I did thankfully seemed to work and by the third week of my return Emily began to smile again. By the fourth week, I managed to ease her back into short lessons mixed with lots of play and storytelling. For one who had been hit so hard so young, she started to make a remarkable recovery. It was at the end of the second month that things went dreadfully wrong and I'm writing this final piece of the story at the moment it all happened.

I came back to the estate today to pick up an old album full of photos of my darling of a granddaddy. I'd stored it safely in a cupboard at the cottage – so safely that I'd forgotten to take it with me when I'd moved out. Mrs. Engel had taken Emily to see her grandmother for a couple of days, so I was free of all other obligations. The cottage itself felt surprisingly welcoming when I arrived. All the real or imagined darkness that I'd sensed at the end of my residency in it had now vanished and the place felt deceptively peaceful. I was sitting alone in what for so long had been my study, remembering how I'd begun this account of all the strange things that had happened, at this very desk. I flicked through the various chapters on my iPad and realised I'd more or less come to the final instalment. I was trying to think how to end it when the front door burst open. Expecting that the strong wind was the cause, I looked round more with interest than concern. What I saw changed my mood instantly. Engel clearly was not in America as his wife had believed. He was standing behind me, unshaven, bedraggled and filthy, with a look of acid-hot anger on his face. He said,

"I've finally realised. You're responsible for all that's happened. Had you kept to your bargain with Lucian and me, my boy would still be alive and I'd still have everything. I've spent the last God knows how many weeks hiding away from the world in the chapel and trying to pray, begging for forgiveness from a God I've never previously cared about, begging for everything to go back in time, for William to still be alive. But it doesn't work, nothing works and I'm going mad with grief and rage. And the more I think about it, the more I know where it all started. From the moment you arrived you were my nemesis, the end point of everything I'd hoped for. I placed half my hopes for escaping Lucian's contract in you – and the care of my children in your hands – and now I'm one child less and abandoned by Green, all because of you. I've just been back into the Hall to look at the accounts – without Lucian's help my business is starting to fall apart and from what I've heard from New York I might have to sell the estate to pay off some of the debts. I can't contact Lucian at all, he's completely vanished off the face of the earth – and my son's death has killed my will to try and get the extra Faustian contracts that would have freed me from my own damnation anyway. I find it hard to believe in a merciful God but I do believe in hell and you've made me a hell-bound soul. You've sent me there, you more than anyone else, so it's only right that you pay a price for everything you've done – and there's only one price that's high enough."

He moved towards me, a strange, slow lurching, the walk of a man who has spent weeks living off scraps from heavens knows where and descending gradually into paranoia. For the first time I noticed that he had a kitchen knife in his hand. I said,

"You're wrong about William. Green had nothing to do with his death and nothing that I've done affected it either, in any way. There's someone you need to speak to, a priest who's been advising me, he can confirm everything I'm telling you. Please, put the knife down and let's talk about all of this."

I could see from the vacant look in his eyes that he wasn't listening. He was moving almost as if he were an automaton, preset to execute a dreadful act with no second thought or hint of human mercy. I tried to get up and to make a bolt for the door, but he was already too close. As I rose, he thrust the knife deep into me, the searing pain burning into my chest like a red-hot poker and then repeated twofold as he pulled the weapon out. I'd managed to turn a little as he struck me, just enough for him to miss my heart, an error that thankfully he didn't spot. All the time he stared directly into my eyes like a man possessed, whether by insanity brought on by grief, or something deadly and diabolical, there was no means of telling. Then as I sank back into my chair, bleeding heavily, he turned away and shuffled slowly out of the house, like a dead man walking. Through the open doorway I saw him cut his own throat and drop like a felled oak, face first onto the ground. The uncanny echoes of the Earl's lifeless body being found in the same position were not lost on me. In a time so short that the enormity of everything that had happened was incomprehensible, a moment of evil, madness or perhaps both had taken his life on top of William's.

Life, as always, hangs on threads that are random and fragile. The ambulance I called has now been delayed and diverted because of flash flooding following a storm. The wound that he inflicted may kill me before it's able to get here, I don't know. I've done all I can to stop the bleeding. I can feel the life slowly draining out of me as I write, but writing is my only way of keeping myself conscious. Each word now is carved onto the screen with pain, but I'm as determined to finish the story as Engel was to finish my life. Ironically, if there is a hell, then perhaps he has done Green's job for him and consigned himself into its depths by this final, insanely evil act. Perhaps he's served Green's purposes also by stabbing me, an act of terrible revenge for my defiance. At least Green had no power to do it on his own. Without an accomplice, he would have been nothing.

But that's assuming he actually is the diabolical entity Father Bernard believes him to be and the natural sceptic in me still harbours doubts. The conundrum as to who or what exactly this strange reptile of a man is will now never be solved – he's vanished without leaving any conclusive clues. He could be any of the things he appeared – conjurer, supreme illusionist, brilliant conman, or even the devil incarnate. Who knows, only him, the now invisible man. My final memory of him is literally a dream – a suitably ambiguous encounter in the abbey grounds, the very nature of which precludes any attempt at proving that our parting battle was in any way real. Equally, he could have simply manipulated Engel's mind into believing all of his diabolical gibberish when, in reality, the only concrete power he had was based on insider access to business information – the intelligence that enabled those whose enterprises he shared it with to prosper. If that was the case then, as so often in the bizarre context of human existence, Engel has been killed by nothing more concrete than ideas based on a compelling but ultimately deranged mixture of fantasy and logic.

And what of Engel himself? The only 'point' of his pointless act has been to demonstrate the constant and inevitable futility of evil – that ultimately it is as lethal for the guilty as for the innocent. There are never any winners, only fools who think it has benefited them because of their own blindness or stupidity. If I'm a victim, then so is he and I at least have completed what I set out to do, to tell the whole bizarre tale of all of this as a warning. Let nobody who is tempted by a Faustian bargain believe that it can end in anything other than tears. Everything that has happened in the course of these strange events shows the dangers of doing deals with the forces of darkness, whatever their real nature may be.

As for me, I've finished with ghost stories. This last shattering event has been one too many. I'm gripped now by the fear that if I resume my telling of ethereal tales, Lucian Green will come back into my life and try to use and control me again. I haven't the strength to go through the struggles I had with him at the abbey a second time. Engel's death has killed with it any chance of returning to help with Emily's recovery – how could I even begin to explain why she will see her daddy no more? So, if I live then, like Lucian Green, I will simply vanish – in my case back to Ireland, to the family farm and the memory of my granddad, ever present still, a little bit of heaven set on earth every day he lived. I will return to the telling of less frightening tales, in the rural calm of the night, from the depths of my shattered soul.

This story I will leave on the table for whoever finds it.

If I die, then I will be among the ghosts in my own past tales. My only remaining existence on this earth will be through these words.

Whatever happens, dear reader, remember me.

Remember me – and if I live, as live I want to, then I will remember you.

Other mysteries by P.J. Anderson available from Nine Lives Original Books

The Spy with an Angel's Eyes: an Augustus Benedict Cold War spy novel

Something is going seriously wrong in mid-1950s London. An assassin is on the loose, targeting British and Russian spies, with no discernible logic behind his actions. It's time to call in a master of the unconventional, former MI5 and MI6 man, Augustus Benedict. What he uncovers is a conspiracy that seems to lead to the heart of London's criminal underworld, with the strings being pulled by a foreign power intent on wreaking havoc. Somewhere or other, the CIA fits into the picture. With several of their best agents dead, the KGB want answers as much as the British and the pressure is on Benedict to unmask the mastermind behind the carnage.

A Man Twice Dead: an almost perfect crime

As in all the best country house whodunnits, the family sit down to tea with the murderer, without, of course, having a clue as to who their nemesis is. And the family are such *charming* people. The brainiest daughter, Danielle, for example, in the words of her least favourite brother, "… boils and bristles with bile like a conjured witch rising out of a cauldron. … Every conversation is hand-to-hand combat, every third word a knife driven deep into a back. She is sympathy and empathy free, charging forwards forever like an engine of unquenchable ambition." And then we have another 'interesting' sibling, "… the man with no name, the Right Dishonourable Philip Andrews, Minister for Hot Air and Waffle in Her Majesty's Mis-government." And there are so many more of these cheerful folk – a bad time is sure to be had by all, except of course, for the murderer. A quite possibly deranged fan of whodunnits, he or she seems to be having the time of their life. Only one person can stop them and time is running out … **For A.B., a former book editor,** 'A Man Twice Dead', "… fizzes with inventiveness and ingenuity." **For Delwyn Swingewood,** it is, "… a country house murder mystery with a difference."

Printed in Great Britain
by Amazon

42535539R00148